For Jim with all my love

PRAISE FOR KOLYA PETROV SERIES

"Compelling! S. Lee Manning masterfully weaves traditional cloak and dagger plotting with a fresh new operative, Kolya Petrov, who will have you rooting till the very end."

LISA GARDNER, #1 Best Selling New York Times author of suspense.

"S. Lee Manning is a rising new star in the world of spy thrillers."

STEVEN J. ROSS author of Pulitzer Prize finalist, *Hitler in Los Angeles: How Jews Foiled Nazi Plots Against Hollywood and America.*

"Manning writes with such authority about the shady world and shifting loyalties of the intelligence community, it's a wonder her novels aren't riddled with redactions. At once terrifying, unpredictable, and all too believable..."

CHRIS HOLM, Anthony award-winning author.

IMMINENT RISK

A Kolya Petrov/ Alex Feinstien Thriller

S. Lee Manning

Library of Congress Cataloguing in Publication Data has been applied for. LCCN: 2025926302

Paperback ISBN 978-1-970286-00-7

Ebook ISBN 978-1-970286-01-4

Published by Misbehavin' Press in Elmore, Vermont 2026. https://misbehavinpress.com/

Imminent Risk

S. LEE MANNING

Chapter One

The tones of an incoming call at 1:00 a.m. on a Saturday morning startled Alexandria Feinstein from a sound sleep. *Who could possibly be calling?* Instinctively, she took a quick glance over her shoulder to check for the only person she'd expect to be calling at such an hour, but he was still lying next to her, breathing deeply and regularly. Grateful that he hadn't woken and was safe in her bed, she reached for the phone, checked the incoming number—not one she recognized—but pressed the green button to answer as she slid out of bed and headed for the hall.

It could be a client. Or a potential client. Or a spam call. Just in case it was important, she had to answer the damn phone.

"Hello." She spoke softly as she closed the bedroom door behind her.

"Alex?"

The voice was female and familiar, but she couldn't place it, either because it had been a long time since she'd spoken to the person on the other end or because distress was distorting the tones. "Who's calling?"

The response was only sobbing. Then after a minute, words came, in almost a scream. "Alex, it's Yael. You have to help me." The sobbing rose again.

"Yael?" She hadn't spoken to her high school best friend in years. "What's wrong?"

More sobbing. Alex waited. In the kind of law she practiced, she'd needed to learn patience. Phone to her ear, she descended the stairs so she'd be less likely to make any noise. In the kitchen she set the phone on speaker and flipped on the electric kettle, still waiting for a coherent response.

The sobbing eased. "They took my baby. My Lyra."

It was not what Alex was expecting. She hadn't known that Yael even had a baby. But then, why should she? They hadn't spoken since Alex had accepted a job in an intelligence agency, a job she'd kept briefly. She'd only told Yael that she was working for the government, but that had been enough to drive them apart. It was a sellout, as far as Yael had been concerned. "What happened?"

More sobbing and incoherent words.

Steam poured out of the electric kettle, and the automatic switch clicked off. Alex poured hot water into a mug with a white tiger and "Cincinnati Zoo" on the side and inserted a ginger lemon teabag. Not her favorite, but it would give her a momentary warmth and lift while allowing her to go back to sleep after she hung up. "Yael?"

"I told you what happened. They took my baby."

Who were they? But the details could be dealt with later. If Yael's baby was missing, she needed to act immediately. "Call the police."

Alex could barely make out the words.

"It was the police that took her."

Chapter Two

"Where are you, Yael?" Alex had a lot of other questions, but the first thing to establish was location. It mattered because to even give advice, she had to be admitted to the bar of the state where the case was taking place. It mattered because her advice could differ depending on the state and the city.

"New York. Manhattan. Near Columbia. 106 Street."

New York City had become even more expensive since Alex had graduated from law school at Columbia. The last time that Alex had heard from Yael Meyer, she'd been studying for a PhD in political science and was not likely to earn the kind of money required to rent or buy in Manhattan. Yael had also scorned people whose only goal in life was the accumulation of wealth. So how did she wind up living in one of the most expensive cities in the country?

To be explored later. First, get the essential facts.

Alex sipped her tea, trying to stay focused. "Did the police and child protective services take her?"

"Well, yeah, there was someone from child protective service. The police called her to my apartment." The narrative was interrupted again by weeping. "Lyra's only four months. She's never been away from me. And I'm breastfeeding her. I've never given her a bottle. I don't know whether she'll even take a bottle. She was crying when they took her. And they don't care if she starves. I tried to explain, and the woman didn't care."

Yael howled in her grief and despair.

"Stay calm, Yael. You're not going to help her by making yourself sick. Deep breaths." Alex drank more tea and waited. The hysterical crying subsided to sniffles and silence. "You okay?"

"No, I'm not okay. I'm worried sick."

"I understand. And you have every right to be worried. But you have to keep it together while we try to work out a plan." Alex then asked the next logical question. "Why were the police there in the first place?"

"What does it matter?"

"If you want my help, I need to know what happened. Why were the police at your apartment?"

There was a pause. "I called them."

"And you did that...why?"

"Because...it wasn't my fault. I didn't do anything wrong. I took Lyra to visit some friends, and when I got home, Ray was lying on the couch, not moving. So, I called 911. To get an ambulance, but the police showed up as well."

"Ray? Is Ray your partner?"

"He's a friend of my husband. Ray was staying on the couch for a few days after his wife tossed him out. He needed help, so I called. It turned out that he'd overdosed. And then...and then...they took Lyra. They said there was an imminent risk of harm. But there wasn't." Yael was weeping again. "I'm not using drugs. It's not my fault that Ray...I didn't even know he was using."

The removal at least made sense. Alex knew that one of the

main reasons that child protective services would be called in was related to drug use—or suspected drug use. "Did you take a drug test?"

"I offered. They said I could take one later. Meanwhile, Lyra's gone."

"And your husband?"

"He's away. Business."

Alex took a deep breath. "This isn't really my area of law, but I do know that if child protective services in New York take a child without a court order, they have to go before a judge the next business day. Since it's Saturday morning, you'll be in court on Monday. You'd be better off with an attorney who specializes in these kind of matters. I can make some calls for you and get someone good."

"You're the best lawyer I know. Please, Alex. Please. I really need someone I trust with me in court. I'm barely holding it together. Having some lawyer I don't know is just going to make me feel more alone."

"What about your husband? Won't he be there?"

"I already told you. He's out of town on business."

"His child was taken by CPS, and he's not coming back?"

"He can't."

What was Yael not telling her?

Alex knew what it was like to be in a relationship with someone who traveled on business and couldn't always be reached. But in an emergency involving his baby, a loving father would drop everything and return.

Unless he wasn't a loving father. Or unless he couldn't. For legitimate or illegitimate reasons.

"He can't come back—or he can't appear in court?"

"It's complicated."

"Complicated" was often code for not wanting to disclose information.

"Who is your husband, by the way? I didn't even know you were married."

"Brody and I got married two years ago. No big wedding. We went down to City Hall. Just us and a couple friends."

"What's he do?"

"Business. He's in business."

"What kind of business?"

"Why? What's it matter?"

"It matters because child protective services look at both parents to decide if a home is safe. Is he involved with selling drugs?" That would explain everything—from the overdosed friend to the quick action to remove the baby to Yael's reluctance to state her husband's business. "And anything you say to me is confidential under attorney-client privilege."

"No, nothing like that. I'll tell you everything when I see you."

Alex had just wound up her latest case, and she hadn't accepted another. She had planned on keeping her schedule light for the next few weeks, both at her practice and at the nonprofit she'd founded. But this wasn't exactly what she'd planned to do with the time. "It's a little hard for me to get away right now. And anyway, as I said, you'd be better off with someone who knows this area of law."

"We were best friends. Remember when we skipped class senior year, and we drove your Dad's car to meet up with some boys. You dented the fender, and I covered for you—told your Dad that it happened when the car was parked. Do you remember sneaking out of *shul* on Yom Kippur to go to the mall?"

Alex had a lot of memories of their friendship. "And I remember punching Becky Masters for making fun of your clothes."

"She was such a bitch, wasn't she?"

"She was. And now she's running some sort of nonprofit to help sick children. But she's still a bitch. I ran into her a couple years ago at a fundraiser. Still obsessed with money and status. She was very proud of her Hermès Birkin bag and told me that my Coach purse was cute for something so cheap."

"Did you punch her?"

"It was tempting, but I don't do that anymore. I'm a respectable member of the bar. Although I did consider shooting her."

They both laughed, although Alex had only been half joking.

"I'm sorry we lost touch for so many years," Yael said.

"Me too."

"You'll come? Please, please. I need you."

Alex sighed and surrendered. She could afford to take one or two days to help an old friend. "I can make it for the hearing on Monday, but then I'll have to bring in someone else to take over. That's as much as I can do right now. Okay?"

"More than okay. You're wonderful. I love you."

"Love you too. I'll call you when I get to New York."

What had she just agreed to do? Alex clicked off her phone and drained the rest of her tea. She knew she should go back to bed, but the conversation and the memories had woken her. She knew that Yael was hiding something important. And yet, Yael did need her help.

Even if Yael hadn't been a friend, the situation called to Alex's sense of justice. Tearing a breastfeeding infant from her mother was such an extreme act that it should only be done as a last resort. If Yael's description of what had happened was true, taking the baby had been an abuse of government power.

She didn't like people who abused their power. She especially didn't like people who hurt children in the process. But she was also aware that there could be more to the situation than Yael was sharing.

She glanced at the clock—2:00 a.m., and she could feel the tiredness. She'd have a lot to do before leaving town and being tired wouldn't help. But she was wide awake. If she went back to bed right away, she'd just toss and turn. *Maybe lavender tea?* It sometimes helped when she couldn't sleep. She flipped the electric kettle on again.

"You need something stronger than tea. And there's no way you're getting out of this with just one court appearance." The voice came from behind her. Her fiancé, Kolya Petrov, his blond hair disheveled from sleep, eyes tired, but wide awake. How did he manage to be good-looking even when just getting out of bed?

Kolya crossed the room to swing open the freezer door and pull out a bottle of vodka. He filled two glasses with two shots each and handed her one. He downed his glass in one gulp.

"How much did you hear?" She drank the vodka in two swallows and felt the warmth spread through her. He was right. It was better than lavender tea.

"Enough to know that I'm going to be stuck talking to the caterer, the band, and the hotel. And your family."

"Do you mind?"

"Not really. Even if you're the one who wanted a big wedding. I'm just concerned that you could be putting yourself into a difficult if not dangerous situation. Something doesn't sound kosher about the husband. About the whole situation."

"But I'll know more after you run a background check on him. And her. Which I assume you were planning to do."

"If you don't have a problem with me violating the privacy of your friend and her husband? Which I assume you don't since you seem to be asking me to do it." He poured himself another shot of vodka and held out the bottle invitingly. She offered her glass, and he poured for her. "I'll need more than a first name."

"His full name and address will be in the court papers." She downed the second shot. "And I'll be back by the end of the week to handle the caterer et al. The wedding's not for three weeks."

"Having to deal with wedding details is not my biggest concern. Just don't take any unnecessary risks."

She laughed. Kolya's whole job involved putting himself at risk.

He acknowledged the irony of his comment with a smile of his own. "Yes, I know. Still, try not to."

"I'll try. And you? You going to try too?"

"I'm in the office for the next few weeks. Nothing dangerous."

She studied him. He hadn't bothered to put on a shirt, and the burn scars on his chest were faded but still visible. "I've heard that before."

"The only risk to me in the near future is from your brother freaking out when he realizes the wedding menu isn't completely kosher."

She didn't believe him, but she had to let it go. "Fine. Just don't shoot Aaron, even if he's annoying. My parents would be upset."

Chapter Three

Brody McMillan clicked off the phone and threw it across the room, where it shattered against a wall, leaving a mark on the paint much as if he'd splatted an insect. But then it wasn't the kind of hotel that would either care or notice a mark on the wall. It was the kind of hotel that needed to be checked carefully for bed bugs. Which was one of the reasons Victor Forest could observe this display with the indulgence of a fond father. "Stay calm, Brody."

"I should be there."

"You know you can't." Victor, with twenty years on Brody, could understand the anger and frustration. Brody's desire to strike back was one of the things that had impressed Victor. One of the reasons Brody had become Victor's second-in-command. "And your being there won't help."

"It's my baby. I'm leaving my wife to deal with it alone."

"Your wife is a very tough, smart woman. She's got a good lawyer, from what I overheard." Victor liked Yael, even if he'd had some concerns about her background. But she was a good wife to Brody and a good mother. "She'll get Lyra back."

Brody's ruddy complexion, which matched his red hair, had

turned an even deeper red with anger. Now it was starting to return to its normal shade. "Yeah. I guess. But I should still go home. For moral support and all that. Yael is devastated."

Victor shifted his position. His back hurt constantly, one of the souvenirs of his previous profession, and the lumpy bed didn't help. But the lodging offerings in this rural area were slim, and not too many places anywhere accepted cash without questions. He had more than enough funds that he'd accumulated through donations and a bit of larceny against the overlords, but using a check or a credit card in his name could be dangerous. His last stolen credit card was no longer functioning, so cash had to do. Or Brody's credit card. "Understand that you want to support her, but not right now. We have a schedule."

"You can do without me for a few days."

"No, I can't. You know that. You're doing the introduction, you're helping screen everyone who comes in, and we have three towns to visit in three days."

Brody was one of the few people who knew why Victor couldn't appear in public. Victor shouldn't need to repeat the importance of his flying under the radar. But Brody, now pacing on the thin carpet, wasn't thinking straight.

Victor caught a glimpse of himself in the mirror. Bald. A short gray beard. Glasses. He'd also lost forty pounds after leaving the Company. All in all, while the changes wouldn't fool the trained agent, a casual observer would not connect his appearance to that of the man he'd once been.

The man who'd been betrayed.

"I can run down before Rochester and get back in time for the meeting."

"We have scouting to do in every town. You have to know where everything is. In case something happens to me."

"Nothing's going to happen to you."

Victor smiled thinly. "Never underestimate the cunning of

our enemy. Which might be why they took your baby. To lure you into a trap."

Brody paused in his pacing. Victor could tell that his last remark had struck home. It should have. Victor knew a thing or two about traps.

"You think?"

"Of course."

"And Ray...he's the reason Yael called 911. I've known him since high school. You think...he..."

"Was he in on it? Probably not. He was hospitalized, wasn't he? But once your wife called for help for him, they saw their chance."

Victor didn't need to explain who *they* were.

"Any way you look at it, this is all Ray's fault." Brody's face reddened again. "My friend. Who I let stay in my home. He's the reason they came into my home. He gave *them* the chance to take my baby."

"True." Victor's tone was gentle. "And you'll deal with him. But right now—we have to think about the greater threat. We need to deal with *them*."

There was a bottle of Glenfiddich Scotch on the dresser. Brody poured himself a drink and sipped. Victor didn't drink; it clogged the mind, and he couldn't afford to operate on anything less than full capacity. But he was indulgent with Brody.

He'd wanted children, but he had never married. Maybe because he had never found a woman who conformed to his ideals—beautiful and smart, but who knew her place. And maybe because he always had a larger purpose. Not that he'd been celibate. He'd fucked plenty of women in his time. But no children—at least as far as he knew. Now, at this time of life, he regretted it. Maybe that was why he'd been drawn to Brody, who regarded him with a mixture of respect and love, and whose thoughts and opinions he'd formed from unchanneled anger into a weapon.

Brody had absorbed Victor's teaching and become the son he'd never had.

That was why he could understand Brody's anger over his baby. Once you marked another human being as the inheritor of your essence, be it your biological child or not, the impulse to defend ran strong and deep.

But he also hoped that Brody could understand the importance of timing. A lesson that Victor had learned the hard way.

In a few days they'd be done with the planned meetings. Then, they'd return to New York. For Brody's baby girl. For a reckoning.

Chapter Four

Kolya drove Alex to Ronald Reagan Washington National Airport from their townhouse in Georgetown, a quick drive on a Saturday morning, in her car, a Highlander hybrid, instead of his own ten-year-old Subaru. He drove the Highlander because Alex preferred to ride in it, not because it mattered to him. Maybe because he hadn't learned to drive until his early twenties, he didn't subscribe to the usual American male love of vehicles. He viewed cars as a means of transportation, not as recreation.

Usually, it was Alex who drove him to a flight, and usually the drive was fraught with emotion. When he left for a job, both Kolya and Alex knew that he would be going into danger, and she'd seen what could happen to him—up close and personal. That knowledge made his departures difficult on both of them. But Alex's expedition to New York to help her friend, while less than optimal given their wedding in three weeks, didn't raise the same kind of concerns for Kolya.

Not yet anyway.

Kolya did want to know what was going on with Yael's husband—whether Brody was dealing drugs—whether he had a history of violence—either of which would put Alex's mission of mercy into a whole different category.

But until he knew more, he'd stay cool.

After parking in front of the departure doorway, he retrieved her suitcase from the back of the Highlander and set it on the sidewalk. "I can carry it inside and wait with you."

"I can manage. There are wheels on the suitcase." She wore sunglasses that concealed just how tired she was, her dark curly hair even more unruly than ever. As always, she looked beautiful to him. "And you have errands."

"Okay, then. What I said last night, about risks."

"And as I said last night, back at you. You doing okay?"

He knew she wasn't just asking about his feelings over her departure or the wedding preparations, but about the physical and psychological symptoms he'd suffered since he'd been held prisoner and tortured. There was only one answer. "I'm fine. But I'll miss you."

She smiled and then moved close, stepping into his arms for a long kiss.

A nearby security guard made gestures that Kolya interpreted as indicating he needed to move the car. "I should go. Before I get a ticket." But he lingered another minute, not wanting to let go.

"You're stopping to hear the band on the way home?" The band she'd previously hired had bowed out at the last minute, due to the vocalist running off with the bass player, who'd been married to the keyboard player. "Remember, no taking over on the keyboard. You're the groom, not the entertainment. Also, they have to be good at klezmer music, not just jazz. It's a Jewish wedding." She smiled. "Although a little jazz is okay."

"The development of jazz had a lot of input from Jews."

"Kolya." Her tone was both amused and irritated.

"Fine. Already agreed." He liked klezmer music, but he was

damn well going to have some jazz, which was his favorite music, both listening and playing. It was his wedding as well.

"The venue wants to go over some details as well."

"I told you. I'll deal with it. And you're going to text me Brody's last name and their address."

"Also, as we agreed."

He kissed her again, ignoring the scowl from the security guard.

* * *

The band was decent. Kolya listened to their renditions of two traditional Jewish songs, and then a jazz standard, "Moonlight in Vermont." With regret, he declined the invitation to jam with them. He had the appointment with the venue and couldn't let himself get swept up playing piano. His next stop was the venue, a nineteenth-century mansion with extensive gardens on ten acres, where the manager wanted his approval for various rain alternatives, on some last-minute menu changes, and on the desired seating for two hundred people. He liked the gardens, the multiple beds of red, pink, and white roses, liked the idea of the ceremony outside, rain or no rain, and didn't really care about the seating. However, he also knew that Alex would have definite opinions, so he tried to make the choices that he thought she'd prefer.

By midafternoon, with the wedding chores finished, he headed to the office. Not because he was particularly busy but because he had a few things he wanted to check out.

Including Alex's friend Yael—and her husband.

There was no sign over the door. The building could have been an apartment complex or business offices on F Street near Twentieth. Just a black façade and a larger-than-usual satellite dish on the roof. Nothing indicated that it was the office of the

ECA, an elite intelligence agency that reported directly to the president and was charged with covert antiterrorism missions, both domestic and international.

Even on a Saturday, a receptionist guarded the door. And even though she recognized Kolya, she checked his identification badge and had him undergo an optical screening before waving him on.

On Saturdays, the cafeteria had a skeletal crew, providing coffee and some cold options. He picked up coffee and a tuna sandwich before heading to the elevators. The halls were largely empty. The ECA was an intelligence organization that operated around the clock, but weekend assignments rotated, and agents not out on assignment did get time off.

At his desk, he tapped a text to Alex. *Everything okay?*

His text didn't get an immediate response. While waiting, he tapped the keyboard of his computer to play Miles Davis, *Kind of Blue*. With the door to his small office closed, he could play music without annoying anyone who hated jazz. The office was also decorated to reflect his passion: Vintage posters advertised performances by John Coltrane, Thelonious Monk, and Duke Ellington.

With the music playing, he turned to his job. His current work assignment was little more than writing up reports based on data gathered from agents in the field. He preferred being in the field, but out of respect for his upcoming nuptials and the two weeks he'd be taking off afterward, he'd been assigned to desk duty.

He checked on operations in Asia and Europe and found nothing that required immediate attention. However, a report from his friend and usual partner, Jonathan Egan, about a domestic terror threat from something called American Gold Posse did catch his interest.

Domestic terrorism was tricky. There were the issues of the

First Amendment and privacy. People in America had the right to be idiots, as long as they didn't threaten violence. In addition, the failure of Congress to pass any laws banning domestic terror groups required that surveillance be done carefully and with discretion. Then there was the politics of navigating around the FBI, which regarded the activities of his agency with something between jealousy and hostility. Not quite the level of hostility he had sometimes encountered with the CIA—but something that had to be taken into consideration.

Still, the current intelligence assessment was that the biggest threat to the nation's security was internal.

He checked the date, time, and location of the email. Jonathan was also in the office. Kolya picked up his coffee and wandered down the hall.

Jonathan, on his phone, dressed as usual in designer slacks and a polo shirt, raised his eyebrows in surprise at Kolya's presence. Kolya shrugged. Jonathan waved Kolya to the empty chair next to his desk and turned his attention back to the call.

Kolya's own phone pinged, and he retrieved it from his pocket.

All okay. Brody McMillan. 207 W. 106 Street, New York, NY.

He texted back. *Have a date of birth?*

Nope. Can't think of a politic way to ask for one either. How was the band?

Good. They'll play mainly klezmer, with a little jazz. As we agreed. But no being carried on chairs.

At some Jewish weddings, especially orthodox ones, the newly married couple would be swirled around the wedding hall on chairs held aloft by their friends and family. Although not religious, Kolya was respectful of his Jewish heritage—but he had his limits.

Also agreed. Talk tonight. Love you.

He sent his love back and clicked off as Jonathan hung up his own call. Kolya'd check out Brody and Yael when he returned to his office.

"What are you doing here today? Shouldn't you be out tasting appetizers or something? And how am I going to arrange your bachelor party if you keep hanging out in my office?" Jonathan grinned at him. Kolya had been best man at Jonathan's wedding years earlier. Even though his marriage had ended in divorce, Jonathan was returning the favor.

Kolya rolled his eyes at the mention of the bachelor party. Another reason he would have preferred a small private ceremony. "Appetizers were selected months ago. Alex is out of town, and I had a few things to do."

"In other words, you didn't want to hang out at home without her. That or you're a glutton for punishment."

Both were possibly true, but Kolya wasn't about to admit it to Jonathan. "Or I had work to do. Speaking of—what's up with American Gold Posse?"

"It's a sovereign citizen organization, and you know the sovereign citizen types. They're all nuts. I mean, they believe in insane conspiracy theories. We need to keep an eye on all of them, but right now, the focus is on this one. American Gold Posse thinks that going off the gold standard in 1933 signaled a hidden takeover of the US government by a global organization dedicated to bringing the entire world under its rule."

"Global organization? You mean Jews?"

"Among others. But yeah. Jews are always the target of conspiracy nuts. Along with aliens."

"From what country?"

"You mean—from what planet?"

"Oh fuck. They're that crazy?"

"Yup. That crazy. Anyway, there are some concerns right

now about American Gold Posse going full 9-11, and that's what I'm looking into."

"Some concerns?"

Jonathan waved a hand. "Nothing you need to worry about, not right now. I'm working with the usual team. And you're not getting involved. You're on hors d'oeuvres and other wedding shit."

Chapter Five

Alex picked up a framed picture of Yael and her baby. It was sweet, showing a baby and mother smiling at each other. "She's adorable."

"Isn't she?" Yael had tears flowing down her cheeks.

It was a large apartment for the Upper West Side, two bedrooms, the front door opening directly into the living room. Dark wood floors that needed either scrubbing or sanding. Modest furniture, a simple blue couch and two off-white armchairs that looked like they came from Ikea. Simple and practical. The couch still had the blanket where Yael's husband's friend had been sleeping and had overdosed. A seventy-five-inch television on a glass stand with a game console underneath stood against the wall opposite the couch. The photograph that Alex was holding had been placed on top of a white three-shelf bookcase that also looked like it came from Ikea.

It was also clearly the home of a new parent. A stroller with a basinet was parked next to the dining table. A woven basket held soft plush toys, appropriate for a baby. Boxes of baby wipes filled the table.

Alex replaced the framed photograph on top of the bookshelf. There were another five framed photographs—of the baby, of Yael and the baby. In the pictures, Yael looked radiant, a portrait of motherly love, her dark hair, even longer than Alex's, woven into a French braid.

No photograph of Brody, either with Yael or alone.

Yael still wore her hair in a braid, but it was disheveled, hairs escaping from restraint. And she looked emotionally drained, the opposite of the happy mother in the photographs. The carefree friend that Alex had known in high school had disappeared.

"Did CPS give you court papers?" Alex asked.

"I'll get them." Yael headed for her bedroom.

While she was gone, Alex surveyed the books on the bookcase. There were the books she'd expect of a new mother. Books on breastfeeding. Books on childcare. Some children's books. A few thrillers and mysteries. Some titles Alex didn't recognize. *What Really Happened. Gold Standard. Defending America.*

But Yael returned before she could examine the books more closely. Alex skimmed the legal document. It was pretty straightforward, giving the time and place for the hearing. And it gave the name of Yael's husband.

"So...what do you think? Can you get her back?"

"I'll do my best. But I can't guarantee anything. Going to court is always something of a crapshoot. We need to talk."

"Do you want to see her room? Her toys?" Yael grabbed Alex's hand. "Her clothes. Everything is clean and new. Safe."

"I'm sure you're a wonderful mother. But we still need to talk. About Brody and why he's not here."

Yael frowned. "I'm here. Why does he have to be here?"

"I already told you that. Last night you said it was complicated, but you'd explain in person. I'm here."

Yael sighed. "Okay. Sit down on the couch and I'll go make us some tea."

While Yael made the tea, Alex checked her texts. She tapped Brody's name and address to Kolya along with responding to his comments on the band and the venue, smiling down at her phone.

Yael reappeared, carrying a tray laden with a teapot, two cups, and a plate of what appeared to be homemade raisin-oatmeal cookies. She set the tray on the coffee table in front of the couch. "Who are you texting?" Her tone wasn't just curious. It was suspicious, almost hostile.

"My fiancé." Alex tapped her love and a promise to call later.

"You're engaged? I didn't know. Why didn't you say something?" Yael poured tea, her body radiating resentment.

Alex took a cookie. What was Yael upset about? Why would she be resentful that Alex—with whom she hadn't had contact for years—hadn't informed her about her upcoming wedding? Whatever. Alex felt her own resentment rising. She'd left Kolya —left her wedding preparations behind—to help Yael, and this was how Yael was treating her? But she pushed her anger down. Yael's baby had been taken away, and she was under incredible stress. "Last night was about you. It wasn't the time to say anything about my life. I'm telling you now."

"So, tell. Who is he? How'd you meet?" Yael's tone changed from suspicion to warmth. It was the tone of a close friend, wanting news.

"We met in law school. We were friends for years, and then one night, we talked and things just...progressed." Alex pulled up a picture of the two of them together and handed her phone to Yael. "This is me with Kolya in Paris last fall."

Yael studied the picture and handed the phone back. "He's hot."

Alex suppressed a smile. She knew how Kolya would react to that description of himself. "He's not bad."

"Jewish?"

"Yes. Not religious though."

"Still, your mother must be *kvelling*. Marrying a Jewish lawyer."

"The hard thing's been keeping my mother from planning the wedding. But she likes Kolya at least." It was all true, and she had avoided the question of Kolya's employment. Yes, Kolya had a law degree, and he'd even tried practicing law, for a brief time, before returning to the world of espionage.

"And the wedding?"

"In three weeks. He was texting me about the band and the venue."

"Oh, Alex. So soon? And you came here to help me? I'm sorry."

"You're my friend, and you needed me. I'm here, but I can't stay indefinitely. Your turn. Any pictures of you and Brody?"

Yael shook her head. "He doesn't like to have his picture taken."

Another red flag. "You were married at City Hall. Your parents didn't come?" Alex remembered Yael's parents as typical Jewish parents—overprotective but warm and loving.

Yael sighed. "He's not Jewish—and my family—well, we're no longer speaking. For a number of reasons. So, we just did it."

"Do your parents know about your baby?"

"No idea. Still haven't spoken to them."

"Call them now."

Yael wrinkled her brow. "I told you. We're not speaking."

"If the court doesn't return your baby Monday, would you rather have her with your parents or with a stranger?"

"Neither. I want her back with me and Brody."

"I understand. Still, we need to consider all the possibilities. The court might not return her immediately, regardless of whatever case we present. If that happens, what would you prefer? Strangers or family?"

"My parents are jerks."

"Still..." Alex knew Yael's parents, and she'd always liked them. Sweet. Funny. A little overprotective. But Alex was on the outside. "Does Brody have parents? Siblings?"

"Not that I know."

"You could call him and ask. Also ask him what he'd prefer."

"I'd rather not."

"Why?" A thought occurred to Alex. "You're not afraid of him, are you?"

"Don't be ridiculous." Yael picked up her cup and sipped her tea. "He's a wonderful man. Loving. Kind. A great dad."

"But...?"

"But his business means he has to be out of town. A lot. And I can't disturb him unless it's an emergency."

They were back to square one. "What's his business?"

Yael hesitated.

"I'm giving up a lot to be here. If you want me to get Lyra home, you have to tell me the truth. What's his business?"

"Organizer. He's a political organizer."

It was an unexpectedly banal answer. But why would Yael be acting so cagey if her husband was a political organizer? It was hardly illegal or dangerous. "What party?"

"He works for individuals, not parties. And the guy he's representing now—Victor Forest—well, he's very demanding, which is why Brody can't leave, but Victor's also not very popular."

Alex narrowed her eyes. "Popular? What does that mean?"

"It means that some people don't like him. And they don't like anyone who works for him either. And that's why Brody can't come. He's worried the court might hold it against him."

Yael looked down at her shirt. "Oh God, I'm dripping." Her breast milk had oozed through. She teared up again. "I have to go pump. I want to take my milk to the court. For Lyra."

She ran from the room, leaving behind more questions than answers.

Chapter Six

The baby wasn't eating. She'd refused the bottle, and she had been crying nonstop for hours. Barbara O'Brien, on the phone with the foster mother, could feel the frustration vibrating through the line. Officially Barbara was off on the weekends, and Saturday was her day to catch up on laundry, cleaning, and shopping. But a four-month-old baby who wasn't eating couldn't wait.

"Just keep offering the bottle." Barbara stuffed sheets in the dryer as she spoke. She was in the basement of the house in Queens that she'd lived in all her life, a house that had belonged to her parents before her.

"I've been offering it. Since last night. She's just keeps refusing. And I'm using donated milk. Not formula." Kristin Temple, the foster mother, had successfully fostered another baby for a year, hoping to adopt, but the mother had managed to get back on track, and her child was returned. Kristin had deserved that baby, and Barbara had been very put out by the court's decision. Barbara hoped that this new baby might be the one. After all, using drugs was a good reason to terminate parental rights and give a baby a new life.

Barbara set the heat at high and hit the start button. "Did you warm the milk?"

"Yes."

"Different nipples?"

"I already tried three different kinds."

"Did you walk the baby while you fed her?"

"YES!!" Kristin's voice rose. The wailing of the baby rose as well, as if in response. Kristin lowered her voice. "I'm walking her now. It's the only thing that keeps her from screaming at the top of her lungs."

Barbara sighed. She didn't really like babies all that much, even though her job required that she ensure their well-being. She preferred older children, whom she could talk to and who could talk back. It made life a lot easier, even if they didn't like being separated from their parents. But Barbara knew enough about babies to be concerned about this one's health if she continued to refuse to eat. Babies could get dehydrated quickly —and that could be disastrous. The last thing she needed was to have to explain to her supervisor, let alone the court, that a baby had become seriously ill under her watch. "I'm going to call a pediatric nurse to come to your house and help. Just hang in there."

* * *

Kolya, back in his office, switched the music to a Bill Evans album while he finished up a report providing background information on various people of interest that had been requested by an agent in Thailand. Then he began the background check on Yael and her husband that he'd promised Alex.

Nothing on either of them raised any alarms. At least not initially. No criminal records. No association with anyone known to be involved with drugs or drug trafficking. Yael had a

PhD in political science from NYU and then had worked for a nonprofit that helped women in third-world countries. All very innocent and even admirable. Her social media posts were limited to praise for movies and television shows. He skimmed the titles: *JFK. Red Dawn. Alien. The Brave. Yellowstone.* From the list, it was an easy guess about Yael's political leanings.

No posting of baby pictures—probably wise in this day and age.

Brody's history was equally innocuous. Graduated from SUNY with an engineering degree fifteen years earlier. He'd had various jobs as an engineer but hadn't risen very far. Then he worked for a few years as a salesman. In the last year, he described himself as self-employed.

On Facebook, but not X, posts were limited to friends, which didn't stop Kolya. Brody's posts, though, were as bland and uncontroversial as Yael's.

Everything was so bland that Kolya was suspicious. Spooks sanitized their backgrounds like this. Ordinary people made mistakes, said the wrong thing, posted the wrong message, had speeding tickets or fights with neighbors.

Spies or assassins—spooks—hid their foibles.

Kolya didn't have any social media presence. Searching his history would turn up as little as he was finding on either Brody or Yael. It would show his degrees and that he worked for a division of the IRS—a division that didn't exist but was the cover employment for agents in the ECA.

On the other hand, weren't there normal people who didn't do anything much? Had his profession and his history led him to see sinister shadows where perhaps there was only the mundane and the boring?

Still, it was worth looking a little deeper.

He shifted in his seat, stretching out his bad leg. Physical therapy and time had done what it could but staying too long in the same position—or the converse, pushing too hard—were still...problematic.

Leg pain alleviated, he checked the Way Back Machine, an internet archive that captured web pages from the past, even if the page had been deleted. But using it required knowing where to look. And when to look. He tried some random dates and looked for posts on Facebook from Brody. Still nothing. Which meant nothing—except that on those specific dates, he hadn't posted anything revealing.

His phone buzzed, and he scanned the text. More information from Alex. Yael had claimed that Brody McMillan was working as a political organizer for a guy named Victor Forest.

Political organizer? That explained the self-employment. Still moving from engineering to political organizer seemed a bit of a stretch. Although maybe Brody had volunteered for candidates and gotten into politics that way. But Kolya'd seen nothing to indicate advocacy of any cause or anyone. Just the opposite.

Who was Brody working for?

Kolya plugged Victor Forest's name into his search engine.

Victor Forest, unfortunately, was a common name. There were a dozen in the state of New York alone. A quick scan of the twelve names turned up nothing in particular. Most were just ordinary people doing ordinary jobs. For one Victor Forest, Kolya could only find a date of birth and a social security number. Interesting, but not enough to go on.

Kolya searched for Victor Forest, candidate for office in New York. The same names came up. He tried other states. Other names came up.

He texted Alex.

Have a date of birth or address for Forest?

No. And can't do this now.

Understood.

He clicked off his phone and tried again, this time coupling Forest's name with Brody's name. This time he got a hit.

It was a tweet by someone in Pennsylvania. *Saw Victor Forest and Brody McMillan today. Inspiring.*

Inspiring? In what way. He searched the other tweets posted by the same person, who seemed to have a strong predilection for conspiracy theories. The person was using an alias, but it took Kolya only fifteen minutes to pierce it.

He spent ten minutes researching the poster, only to conclude that the idiot was a conspiracy nut who'd posted shit on X but was not apparently dangerous. Kolya did find an email from the idiot to a friend in Albany, New York, urging him to attend a meeting with Brody and Forest two days ago.

What kind of meeting?

Kolya looked for credit card usage by Victor Forest in the small town in Pennsylvania where the conspiracy nut lived and in Albany on the date mentioned.

Nothing. Brody McMillan had used his credit cards at hotels and at restaurants. Nothing for Victor Forest.

Kolya returned to the Victor Forest for whom he'd only found a birthdate and social security number. He searched for a work history. For any kind of history. And found nothing.

This was beyond bland.

This was spook territory.

Five minutes later, Jonathan barged into his office. "Why are you researching Victor Forest without checking with me?"

Kolya's search for Victor Forest must have triggered an alarm on Jonathan's computer, which confirmed what Kolya already suspected.

Kolya swiveled his chair to face Jonathan. "I didn't know that I needed to. He's your assignment? You could have said something earlier when we were talking."

"No reason to tell you. You're not on this." Jonathan raised hands and shoulders in a shrug. "And you're not going to be. It's hot—and you're about to get married and go on your honeymoon. Why are you looking into him?"

"I'll tell you after you tell me who the fuck he is. And it's three weeks to the wedding, by the way. Until then, I can still do my job."

"Yeah, but if you get involved, and it fucks up the wedding plans, Alex may shoot me."

"If I get drawn into a case that fucks up the wedding, Alex will know exactly who to blame. And it won't be you."

"Okay. Fine. Whatever. Your funeral." Jonathan plopped into the chair that sat next to Kolya's desk. "Okay, then, Victor Forest. He's one scary motherfucker. Remember what I told you about a dangerous sovereign citizen group that thinks America was taken over when it went off the gold standard? Forest's American Gold Posse—or at least, he's the founder and the organizer. His real name is Craig Rand, and he ran covert operations in Eastern Europe for the CIA—until a mission went south, and he cracked."

"Went south? What happened?"

"Don't know. Above my pay grade. I do know that he was injured and assigned to desk duty—and then he went nuts."

In other words, Jonathan hadn't been briefed on what Forest/Rand had been doing that had caused the injury. Given that Kolya had been injured because of the decisions of his own agency's director, he found this interesting. "What *do* you know?"

"He downloaded some files, killed a couple CIA agents on his way out of the building and disappeared. He's using Victor Forest as an alias, and he's convincing people that the US is run by a global cabal."

"Not aliens?"

"Aliens infiltrated the global cabal, according to Forest.

Anyway, he's going to take back the country for the 'real' citizens —and for real humans."

"Take back the country? Violently?"

"Yup. As far as we know."

"Any details on his plans?"

"Not yet. He's smart, tough...and crazy. Good tradecraft, too. Haven't managed to get anyone inside yet—he's good at spotting spooks."

"Why are you on this? The CIA usually handles their own."

"The CIA just wants to take him out. Which doesn't mean the plans won't go forward—if he's got people in place—but the CIA is more worried about his embarrassing them than about preventing the attack. President Lewis thought that the CIA was too close, and the matter needed fresh eyes. Which is why we got it."

Kolya leaned back in his chair, listening to Bill Evans improvise on "Someday My Prince will Come." A year and a half earlier he'd played the tune in his mind to survive captivity and torture.

He thought of the upcoming wedding and his promise to Alex not to take any risks. But she was in New York helping a friend who could be involved in whatever Forest was planning. Alex could be in danger. And whether Alex was in danger or not, other people could be. This was what he did. "I might be able to help."

Chapter Seven

Victor had a map of every location in the United States that he wanted to check out, but right now he was checking out the place in Whitehall, New York—a little town about an hour north of Albany and half an hour east of the New York Thruway. It looked like a lot of the older towns upstate—Victorian homes in various states of disrepair. A few newer homes. A lot of homes from the early twentieth century, also needing paint and roof repairs. A couple restaurants. A bar or two. Everything a small town needed.

He smiled, knowing what was hidden from the town residents.

Brody drove, following Victor's directions, despite his anger over the confiscation of his child, but at least, the anger was controlled. Victor preferred to be the passenger—it was easier on his bad back.

"Are you sure it's still there?"

"They're all still there. Most everyone's forgotten." But Victor, who had had a lot of time sitting at his desk researching dark secrets after his last assignment had blown up, hadn't.

Brody pointed out a sign commemorating Whitehall as the

birthplace of the American Navy. Victor found it a little funny that this town, two hundred miles from the ocean, would have been so designated by Congress in 1965. "There's five or so towns that claim to be the birthplace of the US Navy."

"So why this town?" Brody asked.

"The ships built here won some battles on Lake Champlain, I think. Back when we still had ideals and followed them," Victor said. "Before everything went to shit."

"The men who fought in the Revolutionary War—they'd be fighting with us, wouldn't they?" Brody kept his eyes on the road. He hadn't mentioned the court case or the baby for at least an hour.

The man who'd commanded the ships that had earned Whitehall its Navy title had been Benedict Arnold. America's first traitor. If the history books were correct, which Victor knew they often weren't. "Probably. They fought for freedom. We're fighting for freedom. That's what's important."

"Freedom. And family."

Victor let the allusion to Brody's personal issues pass. They'd check this out, and then go to the meeting. They'd repeat in another town, close to Syracuse. Then one more town, one more location to check out before they could head back to New York City.

They crossed a bridge, passed a store that sold gas and root beer. Then Victor saw it. An impressive red brick building, built in the nineteenth century. One sign proclaimed it to be a Quaker meeting house. Another sign invited the public to the Starlight Athletic Club.

"A Quaker meeting house?" Brody's voice showed some confusion.

"What it was originally. Now it's a gym."

Brody parked in the lot behind the building. They sat in the car as a young couple drove up and swung into the spot next to them. Victor assessed the pair as they exited their Tesla. They didn't look like they belonged in this run-down working-class town. The young woman, blonde hair up in a ponytail, displayed her slim figure in purple stretch pants, a tight performance tank, a gold chain necklace, and diamond earrings. The man wore black athletic pants, a black T-shirt, and an Oris watch—which cost in the thousands.

They wouldn't be at the meeting. They were part of the problem. If they were even human. Which maybe they were—and maybe they weren't. *They* could be tricky.

He contemplated stepping out from the car and shooting them. That would be one way to determine whether they were human or not. But this was still too public. He'd be exposing himself and jeopardizing the greater plan.

Unconscious of Victor's gaze, the two headed for a back door, which was unlocked. Victor caught a glimpse of a hallway through the open door.

Victor looked for cameras. A camera would make things a little more complicated but not too complicated. He could deal with cameras.

He just had to know whether he needed to or not.

He didn't see any outdoor cameras. There could be some inside—but it was a small town, in the middle of nowhere.

"We could go in and ask about membership," Brody said.

"No. I don't want anyone to remember us. Just in case."

"Okay."

They sat in silence for another few minutes.

"So how do we get in?" Brody asked.

"Late at night and through the basement." Victor took one last look and then gave Brody a thumbs up. "Let's go."

He'd seen enough. Door in the back. No cameras. No security personnel. But why should there be? It was just an athletic club in a rural area. Nothing that needed extra precautions.

Chapter Eight

Noah Valentine, in Alex's year in law school, had graduated in the top twenty percent of the class and after some time working in the corporate litigation world, had wandered into family law, making a pretty decent living with high income divorce and custody cases. He sometimes represented parents whose kids had been taken away by CPS—which was one of the reasons Alex was at his apartment for Sunday brunch. He was also a friend.

It was a sunny three-bedroom one block from Riverside Park. Noah had bought the condo from his parents—who'd bought it in the early 1990s when the building had been converted from rent-controlled apartments to condos. The living/dining room was large by New York standards and tastefully decorated by Noah and his wife Iris with leather and wood furniture, photographs of early New York, bookshelves, and a cat tower in front of the window, where two Siamese cats were currently perched.

Iris, also in Alex's class at law school, was at her office, working on a deal. Unlike Noah, she practiced corporate law and had decided to stay on the partnership track at her midsize firm—finally making junior partner the previous year.

The four of them, Alex, Kolya, Noah, and Iris had hung out together at Columbia, sometimes frequenting bars where Kolya would jam with the musicians.

"Appreciate your offer to let me squat at your office downtown this week." Alex could work on her laptop in her hotel room, but it was small. She didn't have a printer. Or a secretary. Or a desk where she could spread out papers. Noah shared office space and a receptionist/paralegal with five other solo practitioners in midtown. He had offered Alex the use of an empty office for as long as she was in town.

"Hey, what're friends for? It's been too long anyway. So, tell me about the case."

Noah listened to Alex's recitation of her conversations with Yael as he spread cream cheese on a bagel. Then he gave advice. "Run."

Alex put down her coffee. "I've considered it."

"Do more than consider it. Go back to Washington. Next flight. I've had clients like your friend, and they're hell to work with. She's not even paying you, is she? Tell her to find another lawyer."

Noah had articulated what Alex was thinking. What Alex really wanted to do. *Go home and get ready for her wedding.* But as much as she did want to, she couldn't just run. Yael, like every other individual, no matter who, deserved representation. It was what kept the law as fair as possible and forced the other side to be honest. "Would you represent her?"

He put a slice of smoked salmon on top of the cream cheese and bit into it. "Good lox," he mumbled. "Maybe. If she pays. I've put up with a lot of shit from clients when they pay me for it. But not for the next two weeks. I've got a couple trials starting tomorrow."

Which meant that Yael would need representation at the Monday hearing. She would have trouble finding anyone competent at the last minute. Alex had to appear. And she had to stay until Yael could hire another lawyer, unless the case were dismissed and the baby sent home at the first court hearing, which Alex doubted. She didn't do these kind of cases as a general rule, but she knew that it was hard to get a baby back home immediately. Even a four-month-old, breastfed baby.

Despite the real possibility that Yael was engaged in something shady, despite Alex's conviction that Yael was hiding what she and her husband and had been up to, Alex and Yael had been close friends as kids. They'd grown up together, and Alex had a lot of good memories of their friendship.

Anyway, shady or not, everyone deserved a defense. It was a truth that Alex lived by. "Any chance you could step in after your trials? Assuming I don't get the case dismissed tomorrow."

"Not saying yes, but not saying no. I'll have to meet with her."

"I really need to be back in DC in two weeks at the absolute latest. And even that's pushing it." She and Kolya had delayed the wedding several times due to circumstances beyond their control. Now it was three weeks away, and she wasn't there to deal with whatever last-minute snags might come up. Kolya was there, but he wouldn't enjoy the wedding preparations. She would. Moreover, it wasn't fair to ask him to deal with her family members, who could be difficult.

"I know. I'm surprised you're here at all with the big day approaching." Noah winked at her. "By the way, Iris and I are expecting a good spread. And dancing."

Alex smiled. "That's the plan. I'm glad the two of you are coming."

"Been looking forward to it. How's Kolya by the way?"

"He's doing well. Still playing jazz. Still with the IRS." Alex regretted having to lie to a friend, but it was an unfortunate necessity of Kolya's profession. "Back to Yael's case: Do you have any suggestions for tomorrow?"

"I'd contact her parents, since you know them, even if your client doesn't want you to. Family is always better than strangers. Otherwise, you know the drill—assuming she's clean. Good mother. Young baby needs her mother. Yada yada. If she flunks her drug test, nothing you can do but get her into treatment. The social worker's Barbara O'Brien?"

"Yep."

"Word to the wise—don't trust her."

"Got it." Alex's phone buzzed, and she picked it up. A text from Kolya.

Coming to New York this afternoon. Where are you staying?

She glanced up at Noah. "I need to go. Something's come up."

"Nothing's wrong I hope."

"No, nothing's wrong." Or at least so she hoped. Although—she also knew Kolya.

Chapter Nine

It was a small boutique hotel in the West Fifties, not far from Lincoln Center. Kolya had seen bathrooms larger than the small lobby where he picked up the room key that Alex had left for him. The hotel bar and grill consisted of two round tables, with three wrought iron chairs each, all occupied, and five stools at a dark wood bar where patrons were crammed, legs touching, and in between the tables and the bar, expensively dressed young people holding twenty-dollar drinks and pressed together chatting, mouths to ears, breathing in each other's air.

No room for a piano, unfortunately.

But that didn't really matter. He was in New York for business.

Kolya squeezed into the elevator, two steps from the tiny bar, with six other people, the duffle bag that held his clothes placed strategically over his shoulder to conceal and protect the gun that he always wore. Not that he thought he really needed to do so, not with this crowd of European tourists. But still, one never knew.

He eavesdropped on conversations in French and German

about things to see and do in New York until the elevator door opened, and he stepped out on the fourth floor.

After tapping the key card against the room lock, he swung the door open. The entryway was just wide enough for one person, and in the main room, the bed took up all but two feet on either side and about three feet in front, where a half-foot metal ledge under the television mounted on the wall seemed to be intended as a desk.

Kolya dropped his bag on the bed.

"It's a little small." Alex, reclining on the other side of the bed, her laptop open, smiled at him. She was beautiful as always.

"A little?" He climbed on the bed and leaned over to kiss her. "And you're paying how much for this?"

"It's $350 a night."

"You're kidding—$350 a night? *Yob tvoyu mat.*" His favorite Russian curse involving mothers and sex. He knew that Alex could afford it, but the price felt like theft to him. He unzipped his bag and removed a MacBook, which he placed on his side of the bed.

Her expression was amused. "You've spent weeks in New York for the ECA. You didn't notice how expensive it's become?"

"No. When I'm here for work, I stay at the apartment the agency owns in the Village—and everything else is paid for with an agency card."

"I think the hotel's supposed to appeal to Gen Z. They like a minimalist aesthetic. At least there're no bedbugs. That I've found."

"Is there a closet?"

"Sort of. And there're hooks on the wall for stuff you don't want to leave in the bag but can't fit in the closet. Which will be most of your stuff, given that I've already used the entire space for my things."

He repeated the curse. "You couldn't get a hotel room where we didn't have to walk sideways?"

"I would have booked a more expensive place if I'd known you were coming. Which I didn't." She fixed him with her gaze. "Until two hours ago."

And now they were getting to it. The rules of the spy game required that any and all details of an operation were to be disclosed only on a need-to-know basis—within the intelligence community. Alex had worked briefly as counsel for the ECA, but she was not in the world, and her security clearance had lapsed.

She knew the drill and accepted it when he went out on assignment. But this was different. He was there because of her. Because of information she'd uncovered. Didn't she deserve to know that Kolya, along with Jonathan and the usual team, were in New York because her client had a connection to a man who was suspected of planning a terror attack?

Jonathan's admonition had been clear. "You can't tell Alex anything. Not unless it's absolutely necessary."

Easy for Jonathan to say. He wouldn't have to deal with Alex's anger if—no, when—she realized what Kolya was doing.

The job mattered to him. His relationship with Alex mattered more.

Still, after a momentary hesitation over lying to her, Kolya played it by the book. "It was a last-minute decision."

"Was it?" Her intelligent eyes never left his face. "Prompted by what?"

"Wanting to be with you isn't reason enough?"

"It is. Under normal circumstances. Still, our wedding's in three weeks. When I left yesterday, you said that you would take care of last-minute details until I got back. Because you had nothing much to do at work but write reports, which left you free to deal with music, caterers, and my annoying family. But suddenly you're here."

"Maybe I don't particularly want to listen to your brother kvetch."

"You didn't particularly want to listen to him before I left town. But you were okay with it when you dropped me at the airport yesterday. Now you're not? You don't do things casually, Kolya. What's really going on? Does it have anything to do with the background checks you ran on Yael or her husband?"

"No. They were both clean." That was a true statement. "Not as much as a parking ticket."

"Really?"

"Really, really."

Alex kept her gaze on his. "What about Victor Forest?"

"What about him?"

"Don't play games."

Fuck Jonathan. He had to tell her, not just out of respect for her providing the information that had led to the operation that was now ongoing to track down Forest, but because she needed to know what she had walked into. "Victor Forest doesn't exist. The man who's pretending to be Victor Forest is the reason I'm here." But he could only go so far. "And you know that I can't tell you much more."

"So you're here on assignment. Where's the rest of the team?" Her tone was calm, but he knew that was deceptive.

"Not here."

"I can see that. Kind of a small space, as you've noted. I assume that Jonathan and the usual suspects are downtown at the usual location."

He shrugged.

"What happened to your not taking any risks in the weeks leading up to our finally, finally getting married?"

"What happened was I followed up on names you gave me." He stretched his long legs out on the bed. At least it was a decent mattress. "As you knew I would. You practically asked me to run checks on Yael, her husband, and his employer."

"I did. But I thought that was to help me. So I wouldn't be going blind into a possibly dangerous situation."

"That's true. But what did you think I'd do if I found out that Victor Forest, and by implication Yael and her husband, were involved in something that could kill a lot of people?"

"I know what you'd do. I know you'd send the information on to people who would take appropriate action—and that's fine. I just didn't expect *you* to be one of those people. And I *did* expect that you would tell me just what the fuck was going on before you called in the ECA—not just show up here with some bullshit about missing me."

"That wasn't bullshit. I did miss you."

"I know. Nevertheless. Not the reason you're here."

"True." He hesitated again, Jonathan's words and his years in intelligence work competing with his obligations to Alex. He repeated his earlier thought. *Fuck the rules.* "So, okay, this is what the fuck is going on. Victor Forest is head of a sovereign citizens group. You know what they are?"

Alex nodded slowly. "I know a little. Crazy conspiracy types, aren't they?"

"Pretty much. Forest is believed to be planning some sort of violent action, but we don't know what exactly."

"In other words, you lied about Yael and her husband's background checks being clean."

"It wasn't a lie. Their checks came back clean—too clean. Their connection to Forest didn't show up until you gave me his name. Brody McMillian appears to be working with him. Your friend Yael may or may not be involved, but she is a way to get to Forest."

"Now you're here, not only putting yourself in harm's way, but planning to use my relationship with a client to get to a target?" Alex didn't raise her voice.

He recognized the danger in the calm tones. "I wasn't planning anything that would require you to violate attorney ethics. Or even involve you."

"Other than what you've already done." Her voice was still quiet.

He wasn't fooled. She was angry, and she had a right to be. "Other than that. And again, I'm sorry. But you know what I do."

"Yeah, I do. And I know what it's done to you. If you have the usual nightmares tonight, try not to wake me up." She turned back to her computer screen. "We'll talk tomorrow. After court."

Chapter Ten

The baby didn't look too bad, considering that she had been on a hunger strike for almost two days and that it was seven in the morning. For now, she was sleeping peacefully in the basinet that Kristen kept for the foster babies. Which was a relief. Barbara hated crying, hated the smell of dirty diapers, and the unceasing needs of an awake infant.

Barbara had stopped by the foster mother's home before court to check on the baby's health, because Barbara knew she'd be asked about it by the judge, and she had to have something to say. It was always good to present that a child was doing well in foster care, even better when it was true. Barbara wasn't above lying, but it had to be a lie that couldn't be easily exposed. That a child was unhappy or missed her mother was hard to document. A baby whose health declined—or worse died—because she wasn't eating was not. But with the baby now accepting a bottle, Barbara could tell the court exactly what was necessary in order to keep custody.

Still, the baby had lost weight. So better not to take the baby to court where the mother could see her and tell that to the judge. Not that she would anyway. Children didn't belong in court.

Barbara complimented Kristen on doing a fine job.

"It's not easy." Kristen's voice quavered. "I've been up most of the past three nights."

"You're great with her, though. She seems to be bonding."

"She's a sweetie. When she's not screaming." Kristen gazed wistfully at the sleeping baby. "Do you think there's any chance?"

Barbara again felt the unfairness of the system. The law favored the biological parents, so many of whom weren't deserving and hadn't proven themselves. Someone like Kristen, who *had* proven herself, deserved a baby, and she'd been denied the chance. Biology shouldn't outweigh competence.

And Barbara was a better judge of competence than most judges. But she had to play the game.

"Too early to know. I do have concerns about the mother and the situation." Barbara didn't want to get Kristen's hopes up, but there was a chance. She just needed to get the court to do the right thing. "You'll be a great mom."

Kristen smiled.

* * *

Victor felt that Sunday's meeting had gone well. Fifteen members, all of them vetted, had shown up and enthusiastically applauded every point.

The numbers hadn't been huge, but that was okay. They'd have the advantage of moral superiority. Anyway, he knew that he had to be careful about the people he recruited. He knew just how devious his former employers could be. He also knew who his former employers were in league with—and how dangerous *they* were.

And so did the recruits—now—who'd sworn the oath and were ready to fight when called upon.

Big numbers weren't important.

The American Revolution hadn't been won by numerical superiority.

The members knew in theory about the sites, but not specifics. He told them that they'd have weapons and more, but they'd get the details later.

Brody knew. But Brody had to know. Just in case the government caught up to him, which Victor knew they were trying to do, Victor had to have someone ready to step in. Even if Brody had an anger management problem. And family problems.

Monday morning, and they were in a small town in western New York, close to Syracuse, checking out the next site, inside the Whitney Library, which was an impressive gray limestone building from the nineteenth century. But it fit in with the rest of the town, a town filled with buildings over a hundred years old.

Victor liked older American towns. They evoked what the country had once been, and what he hoped the country would be again. But that required that his revolution succeed, which in turn required accessing secret bunkers, one hundred of them, hidden across America. The one in this town was deep below the library.

The library was open to the public with a steady stream of visitors, so Victor wasn't worried about not fitting in or about someone spotting him and suspecting what he was doing. Tourists came here to see the historic building. Locals came here for the library.

He and Brody were just curious guys, looking at the architecture while browsing for a good read.

He wanted to check more closely for the entrance to the

room. Maybe even go inside. He hadn't personally checked out any of the sites. And this was a good day to do it, after a successful meeting. His back wasn't hurting too badly either, which he took as a signal to go forward.

From his research, he knew what was there, what the government had planted close to seventy years ago. He thought everything would still be there in crates that hadn't been touched for decades—but it was possible that someone besides him had found out about the sites—and gotten there first.

It would be good to know that he could get in. That the crates hadn't been moved—or opened.

"I thought you didn't want anyone to see us." Brody was close behind as Victor opened the door.

Victor hadn't bothered to explain his thoughts to Brody. After all, Brody was the second-in-command, not the command. He needed to know a lot. Just not everything.

"I don't want anyone to remember us. If we'd tried to go inside the gym at Whitehall, we'd have stood out. Here—there are lots of people coming and going. No one will notice us particularly."

"I guess."

"Trust me. I know all about being inconspicuous."

Once inside, the building just looked like a library. An old and attractive one, but a library. Shelves with books. Tables with people reading.

Victor browsed through the mystery section. Mysteries, thrillers always amused him. Whoever wrote them had no idea what the real world was like—what real evil lurked in unlikely places. Things in mysteries were tame by comparison. A dead body, always, but the bad guys usually lost, and the good guys usually won.

Sometimes not—but usually.

Still, he took a book off the shelf. Something titled *Richter the Mighty* by an author he didn't recognize but that looked amusing. Victor liked to read, and he had read extensively, which was how he'd uncovered the truth. He couldn't check anything out, not being a member of the library, but carrying a book made him look like he belonged, and that was key to not being noticed.

Brody didn't even pretend interest in a book.

Still carrying the novel, Victor followed signs that pointed to restrooms. He descended the stairs to a basement, passed the men's room, and headed towards the far end of the hall. There were several meeting rooms in the basement, one very large, but the one that interested him was at the far end of the hall.

Followed by Brody, he entered a room labeled "Languages." The floor, wooden planks from another century, looked as he had expected. The room had more bookshelves, but with books in French, German, Spanish, Russian, and Chinese. In the center of the room, a table with six chairs, and a whiteboard in front of the table.

Written in black magic marker on the whiteboard: "Chinese for Beginners, 5 p.m. Mondays. Russian, 5 p.m. Tuesdays. French, 5 p.m. Wednesdays and Fridays."

"The global takeover in progress," Brody said. "Classes so we learn to speak with our overlords, I suppose."

"Don't be ridiculous. No one will have to learn a new language. It would be too obvious if the overlords didn't speak English. That's how they keep the masses calm—by not appearing threatening." Victor tapped his foot on the floor. Solid. He moved to a new spot. Tap. Nothing.

Now Brody was doing it too. Tap. Tap.

"Are you sure it's a trapdoor?" Brody asked.

"All I know is that it's below this room."

"You're looking in the wrong place." An old man emerged from behind a bookcase. He wore a wrinkled blue suit, a white shirt and red tie, and his face, lined and withered, looked like he was in his nineties if not older.

Victor cursed himself for not checking the entire room. He would never have assumed the room empty when he was in his old job. Was he losing his touch?

And did the old man actually know something? Victor decided to play ignorant. "What room?"

The old man chuckled. "The room you're looking for. I'm ninety years old, and I remember when they put it in. Back in the 1940s. Or was it the 1950s? Hard to remember the exact year, it was so long ago. But I think it was the '50s because they were scared that the Soviets would take over. My father was one of the people who built it. Anyway, they put it in, and then they forgot. But I didn't."

Victor tried not to look too interested. "You know where the entrance is, then?"

"Course I do. Been down there too." If he really was ninety, the old man was remarkably spry. And sharp. "Always wondered if someone or other might come looking for it."

"No one else has looked?"

"No. I've been waiting too. I've spent a lot of time here since I retired and the wife died. Figured someone would come sooner or later, and I wanted to be here. You from the government, finally? I've kept this secret for so long."

Victor considered the various lies he could tell and decided to tell a version of the truth. "I used to be. That's how I know about it. Now I'm writing a book." It was a good excuse. "A history of those times. All about things that have been forgotten."

"That's even better. You can put me in your book. The guy who knew all about it."

"Of course. Now can you show me the entrance?"

The old man grinned. "Sure can."

It was like one of those mystery movies. The old man pulled three books out, one in German, one in French, and one in Russian. After he pulled out the third book, the bookcase swung out, and a door in the wall was outlined. Victor touched the door tentatively.

"The last one's a little tricky. Three of them as well." The old man felt along the wall, pressed three almost invisible areas, and the door opened. "Come on."

He flipped on a light switch and something that sounded like a fan, before stepping through the door. "It's got its own exhaust system going straight to the outside. I think it's hidden somewhere in the woods," he explained. "Without the fan, there's no exchange of air."

Victor and Brody followed through the door, which opened to a circular metal staircase that wound down fifteen feet. Then at the bottom, a large cement space, maybe fifty feet by twenty feet, lit by a series of light bulbs that hung down on creaky chains. It was surprisingly clean—the cement floor looked swept, and the concrete walls were lined with wooden crates neatly stacked five feet high.

Victor knew what was in some of the crates. At least he hoped he knew.

So did the old man. "Don't touch any of that stuff over there." He waved an arm in the direction of crates marked with red paint. "It's deadly. So my Dad said, anyway. This stuff over here, though," he waved his arm again, "is just food. Canned peaches, apples, cherries, tomatoes. Some of them burst, but most of them are still good. Every now and then, I help myself to one of them. Hasn't killed me yet." He walked over to one of the crates and started rummaging through it. He held up a can. Most of the label was gone. "I think this is pumpkin. They thought, you know, that the Russkies might take over America. And the resistance would need food as well as the weapons over there." He jerked his head towards the far side of the room. "But, it hasn't happened. I figured no point in letting the food all go to waste."

"Surprising that the lights still work," Brody said. "And that it's so clean."

The old man chuckled again. "I've been changing the light bulbs. Every now and then, I sweep. But it doesn't get too dirty. Not with being airtight except when the fan is on."

"Who else knows about this?" Victor asked.

"My wife did, but she's dead twenty years now. Some of my friends knew. We used to hang out down here and drink. Do other stuff, too. They're gone too. Don't have any kids. Never really wanted them. Now I'm kind of sorry. No one to care when I'm gone. I figured I was the guardian, you know. Waiting to hand it over to the right person."

"I know what you mean. I never had kids either. Wish I had." Victor liked the old man, and he regretted what had to be done. He caught Brody's eye. Brody made a gesture, and Victor nodded. A bit sad, but they were fighting a war. Innocents sometimes suffered in war.

They left the old man's body in a corner and climbed back up, leaving the fan on so the smell would disperse into the woods.

Chapter Eleven

The judge had on a no-nonsense face while she listened to the CPS caseworker's direct testimony. Barbara O'Brien, a heavyset woman dressed in a blue pants suit, somewhere in her forties or fifties, or so Alex judged, oozed concern for the welfare of the baby as she testified. She explained that the decision to take the baby was based on the presence of a drug user and heroin in the home, describing the overdosed Ray stretched out on the couch, heroin found in his backpack. She went on to describe the baby as adjusting well to the foster home.

They were seated at the respondent's table. Yael had followed Alex's instructions and dressed in a conservative blue skirt and gray top.

Alex risked a sideways glance. Yael wasn't talking, but she was seething. Alex imagined a cartoon, with stream rising from Yael's ears.

"Bitch." Yael hissed the word in Alex's ear.

Alex scribbled a note. *Stay calm and don't talk.* For whatever good it would do. Given that Alex knew Yael was consorting

with conspiracy nuts who believed that the courts had no juris-
diction over them, Alex had prepared herself for bad behavior.

Always better to be prepared.

She knew what she knew about Yael and her husband only
because of Kolya. That slightly mitigated but didn't eliminate
her anger. He not only planned to use her connection to a client
to locate a target, but he was putting himself in harm's way. As
usual.

She had a sudden vision of Kolya, chained to a wall, half
dead after days of torture. Of the months of recovery that both
of them had struggled through. He'd never completely healed,
physically or psychologically, and yet he'd gone back to a profession that required him to risk his life. And here they were again.
Just days after he promised he'd stay safe at least until the
wedding.

Three weeks. That was all she'd asked of him. Stay safe for
three fucking weeks.

Yet this was the life he'd chosen. And she'd chosen him. If
she couldn't stand that life, maybe this was the time to back out.

But it was the thought of life without Kolya, if he got
himself killed, not the stress of living with his frequent absences
and his adrenaline addiction, that she found unbearable.

Not now. Focus.

She banished her concern and anger and rose for her cross-
examination. From the stand, Barbara O'Brien viewed her with
mild condescension.

"I understand that you were concerned about the baby's
well-being because a visiting friend of the family overdosed in
the house. When you arrived at the house, did you examine Ms.
McMillan for any signs of drug use?"

"Yes. Of course."

"Did you see any needle marks?"

"No."

"Enlarged pupils?"

"No."

"How about the baby? Was she alert—or was she sluggish?"

"She was very sleepy. That was concerning."

"You arrived at eleven o'clock at night, didn't you?"

The woman hesitated. "I think that's about right."

"And is it unusual for a baby to be very sleepy at that hour?"

"Babies this age often don't sleep through the night."

"That wasn't the question. It's not unusual that a baby would be sleepy late at night, is it?"

Barbara shrugged. "Maybe not. But where there are drugs, it's concerning."

"You and the police both searched the rest of the apartment, with my client's consent, didn't you?"

"The police did. I didn't."

"Were any other drugs or drug paraphernalia found?"

"You'd have to ask the police."

"I'm asking you—because you made the decision to remove a four-month-old baby from her home. In other words, you're unaware of the police finding any other evidence of drugs or drug use, isn't that correct?"

A brief hesitation. "Yes."

"It would be standard practice for the police to alert you if they had found any such evidence, given that you'd taken custody of the baby, isn't that correct?"

"I don't know what standard police practice would be."

"You don't know? Don't you work with the police?"

Barbara tried a smile. It wasn't a convincing smile. "I am called by the police when they have concerns. I'm not a police officer."

"And you didn't think that finding out whether the police had located additional drugs might be important to this hearing?"

"It would be a factor, but not definitive. Just because drugs aren't found on the premises doesn't mean that the parents aren't addicts."

"Was the baby tested for drugs in her bloodstream?"

"Over the weekend. Yes."

"If you had found the baby to have been exposed to drugs, you would have mentioned it in your direct testimony, wouldn't you?"

"If I was asked."

"That you didn't mention it—means that drugs were not found in her system, isn't that correct?" Alex glanced at the judge. It was always difficult to know exactly how an examination was going over, but Alex felt comfortable that she had the judge's attention.

"I haven't received word that they were."

"In other words, no. My client was tested too, on arrival today, and that was negative, isn't that correct?"

"We haven't done a hair analysis to see whether she's used drugs in the last few months."

"Your answer to my question is yes, she was tested here at the courthouse, and yes, she was negative, isn't that correct?"

"To the best of my understanding. But she could still be a past drug user. And we haven't tested her husband. Who didn't bother to come here today."

"Were you informed that the husband is traveling for his job? And that at this time, Ms. McMillan is a full-time mother, completely dependent on her husband's income?"

"Yes, but the fact that he's not here is a matter of concern."

"And if he should lose his job and be unable to support his wife and child, wouldn't that be a matter of greater concern?"

"Most people can take time off in family emergencies."

"But some can't without risking their employment. Isn't that true?"

"Sometimes."

It was said grudgingly, and Alex decided to move on. Given what she knew of Brody McMillan's "employment"—all from Kolya's intel—she decided it was best not to dwell on his job or his absence. "Was the home equipped with a crib and with age-appropriate baby books and toys?"

"I suppose."

"Any fire hazards? Any debris?"

"Other than the unconscious man on the couch—there were unwashed dishes in the sink."

Alex raised her eyebrows. "Do you think that the standard for removing a child from her parents should be that there are unwashed dishes in the sink? Does it matter how long the dishes were there—or how many dishes—or just the fact that a busy parent hasn't had time to wash up yet?"

"Objection." The attorney for CPS, a young man in a light blue suit, rose. Alex glanced over at him. He looked like he was still in high school.

"Objection overruled." The judge turned to Barbara. "I'm interested in the answer."

Good sign.

"No, no, of course that's not the standard. It's the totality of the circumstances." Barbara was almost stammering. She also had noted the sign from the judge. "It was the presence of an overdosed drug user along with the unwashed dishes. The combination raised my concern." She gained confidence as she spoke. "In my years of experience working with troubled families, parents who use drugs often neglect basic household chores."

"Isn't that also true that parents who are busy with jobs and taking care of their child don't always do the dishes immediately?"

"Sometimes." The caseworker glanced at the judge. "I'm aware that there are a lot of pressures on parents these days."

"Are you aware of articles from the NIH and the American Academy of Pediatrics on the importance of an infant bonding with her parents, especially her mother?"

"I read the literature." The tone was almost petulant.

"Have you also read the AAP on the importance of breast-feeding for the immune system in the first year of life?"

"Like I said. I read the literature."

The tone was more than sullen. It was downright hostile.

"So," Alex kept her tone almost conversational, "having read the literature on the importance of mother-baby bonding and breastfeeding, you believe that a visiting friend overdosing and a sink full of dirty dishes without any other evidence of drug use or of abuse or neglect by the parents outweigh the AAP recommendations on the importance of bonding and breastfeeding sufficiently for CPS to take and keep custody of a four-month-old breastfed baby?"

The attorney for CPS rose to object. The judge, with a stern look, overruled the objection— despite the fact that she probably should have sustained it—and that told Alex everything.

Alex had devastated the witness.

She had the judge on her side.

She was on the verge of getting Yael's baby returned. Immediately. No waiting.

It was the kind of moment that every attorney savors. But joy is short-lived in the legal world.

Despite everything Alex had told her, despite the stakes, Yael stood up, her face flushed with anger. "That's right you bitch. You had NO right to take my baby. You're a thug for an illegal and oppressive government."

Chapter Twelve

It was the usual team: Kolya, Jonathan, Teo, and Elizabeth. Jonathan, as usual, filled the role of team leader. Teo Lorenzo, the kid of the team, a twenty-two-year-old language prodigy, had gained confidence and some skills in the two years since Kolya had first worked with him. Elizabeth Owen, a seasoned veteran of the agency, had not modified her caustic attitude towards everyone on the team, including Jonathan, with whom she had an on-again, off-again relationship —currently on—all of which could sometimes make for interesting interactions. Still, they all knew each other's capabilities, and Kolya trusted all of them to have his back. As he would theirs.

They staggered their arrival at Yael's Upper West Side apartment building. One at a time, they trailed into the lobby wearing casual clothes and backpacks. The entrance security was electronic, no doorman, and the technical division had provided each with a device to bypass the system and open the door. Across the street, a retired agent who did the occasional gig for the ECA kept watch on the building's front door, in case

Brody McMillan, Victor Forest, or Yael McMillan made an unexpected appearance.

They took the stairs to the third floor. Kolya, the first to arrive, carefully picked the locks and opened the door. The rest filed in after him.

Inside the apartment, they fanned out. Two jobs: to hide audio and video equipment in every room and to search for any useful information on Victor Forest, Brody McMillan, or the organization. With four of them, they'd be relatively quick.

Teo headed for the bathroom; Elizabeth for the baby's bedroom; Jonathan remained in the living room.

Kolya, in the master bedroom, secured a mic under the bed, and then turned his attention to a black metal desk between two tall chests of drawers. Kolya pulled out the wrought iron desk chair, seated himself, and replaced the lamp lightbulb on the desk with one that contained a miniature camera.

Then, with a gloved hand, he opened the laptop and tapped the keyboard to bring up the screen.

Password locked.

As expected.

He inserted a flash drive into the USB port and waited. Five minutes later he was in.

Leaving the flash drive in long enough to install the malware, designed by the ECA technical crew, he checked his phone. No word from Alex. He'd asked her to text when her case finished, and she'd agreed, even though he suspected she knew what he'd be doing while Yael was out of the apartment.

Still, she hadn't asked. And he hadn't volunteered.

After removing the flash drive, he closed the laptop and opened the first of two desk drawers. He rifled through old bills, scraps of paper, some printed photographs, and scrutinized the photos—nature, cats, the baby, but no shots of Yael with her husband, no shots of her husband at all. Which showed Yael's consciousness of something being not quite kosher about the hubby.

The bottom drawer held a stapler, pens, empty pads of paper, and two tissue boxes.

"Anything of interest?" Jonathan called.

Kolya joined the others in the living room, where Jonathan had just replaced a book on the bookshelf. "Nothing. Malware installed on the computer. Mic and camera in place."

"Also in the baby's bedroom." Elizabeth joined them. "Although I suppose they won't be whispering secrets while changing the diapers of their little darling." She spoke with such disdain that Jonathan, who was a devoted father even if his marriage had failed, gave her a look. She didn't back down. "I don't much like babies."

"I like babies." Teo joined from the kitchen. "I used to babysit for my cousins. Babies are sweet."

"They scream, they smell, and they're a lot of work." Elizabeth read something in Jonathan's face. "But your son is okay, Jonathan, because he's ten. I can actually talk to him."

Kolya, whose opinion of babies was somewhere between that of Teo and Elizabeth, chose not to respond.

"My son wasn't born talking. He was a lot of work as a baby, but then, he was worth it. Enough." Jonathan gave a quick look around the living room. "Has everyone checked that we're not leaving any trace of our presence?"

Affirmative nods.

They moved towards the door.

But before they could reach it, the lock turned, and the door swung open. An unkempt young man in jeans and a sweatshirt stood gaping at them.

Chapter Thirteen

Yael, curled in a chair across from Alex's temporary desk in Noah's office, wept uncontrollably. Alex closed the door, supplied her with tissues, and waited for the torrent to subside.

After Yael's outburst, despite Alex's attempt to explain it as stress, the CPS attorney had persuaded the judge to delay returning Lyra to her mother until a full psychiatric evaluation could be conducted on both Yael and her husband. The judge looked almost apologetic when she issued the order, but she still issued it.

She did order the caseworker to arrange for Yael to have two supervised visits a week and to supply the foster mother with her expressed breast milk, the first visit to occur the next day.

Yael had wept from the moment the judge issued the order, through the ride to Noah's office on Tenth Avenue in the West Thirties, and to where she collapsed in the chair across from Alex.

Alex had conflicting emotions: anger, both at the decision and at Yael fucking up her own case. However, her anger towards Yael was tempered by sympathy. Alex couldn't imagine how hard it must be to have your baby removed.

Even if Yael was involved in a crazy conspiracy cult.

Hearing the sobs diminish, Alex decided it was time to try calming words. "The judge ordered the examination to be expedited, and then you're back in court in two weeks."

"That's very fast for one of these cases." Noah, fresh from court himself, opened the office door while Alex was speaking. "The judge must have liked you."

Yael looked suspiciously at him. "And you're...?"

"This is my friend, Noah. He's generously allowed me to use this office while I'm in town—which isn't for very long. I need to get back to Washington, and I wanted you to meet him. He has a lot of experience with representing parents against CPS."

"You're not leaving me! You can't leave me! You have to get my baby back."

"My wedding is three weeks from yesterday."

"Just two weeks. Just stay until the next hearing. You did such a great job."

Until Yael fucked it up. Alex exchanged glances with Noah, remembering him urging her to run. "I can possibly stay until the next court date, but then I'm out. Just in case Lyra doesn't come home then, I wanted you to meet Noah."

"Just in case?" The words were spoken in horror. "She'll have been away from me for two weeks. They could keep her?"

"It's possible. These cases can drag out," Noah said.

Alex cleared her throat. "Your parents are an option, Yael. Wouldn't it be better to have Lyra with them than with a foster parent?"

"No. I already told you that. I don't want to talk to them, and I don't want them to have my baby." Yael paused, taking a deep breath.

"You'd rather have her with strangers?"

"I'd rather have her nearby. They'd take her to Maryland. And they'd fight me getting her back."

Alex sighed and gave up. "It's your decision."

"Yes, it is." Yael sounded more together. "And I want you for my lawyer. You, Alex. I saw you in court. You're great."

Another exchange of glances with Noah.

"Thank you, and I know that you want me to stay. But I told you when I agreed to come to New York that I couldn't stay long."

"Your wedding." Yael spoke in a flat tone.

"Yes, my wedding." Although the groom was currently in New York working on counterterrorism. Would Kolya make it? Kolya being in New York and at risk was in large part why she was willing to stay another two weeks. "There are two hundred guests who're coming in from around the country." Mostly her family. Kolya had no family. He expected maybe a dozen people —coworkers and one or two friends—including Lisette from Germany, who was now living in Texas.

"I know. I know. I'm being selfish. I can't ask you to give up your wedding. You've done a lot for me already."

That Yael was willing to accept Alex leaving was a first step.

"And Noah really does have more experience than I do. For example, he can talk to you about what to say and what not to say during the psych exam."

Yael did need a lot of talking to. Probably her husband did too. Although how he'd react to being talked to was another question.

Yael turned to Noah. "How often do you get children back?"

"Most of the time. Especially if you're white, not on drugs, and living in a child-appropriate home. But it also depends on the client doing what needs to be done—and not doing what shouldn't be done. Do you understand?"

"Yes." Yael looked even more subdued.

"For example, yelling at the caseworker doesn't get you anything. Talking about government conspiracies doesn't either. Especially when you go for the psych eval."

Yael shifted her gaze from Noah to Alex. "You told him what happened?"

"I dropped in the courtroom for a few minutes and caught the end of Alex's cross," Noah said. "What was that all about?"

Leave it to Noah to ask what Alex wanted to know.

Yael shifted uncomfortably. "Nothing."

Alex took it up next. "It wasn't nothing. It meant something to you."

"It meant I was angry. That's all."

"Do you really think the government is illegitimate?"

Yael stared at the wall. "I'm not crazy."

"Neither of us thinks you are." Alex was pushing it in speaking for Noah, but what the fuck. "Still, we need to know if that's really a belief of yours. To do a good job as your attorney, I have to know the truth. And I'm bound by attorney-client privilege—so I can't disclose anything you tell me in private."

"He's here." Yael nodded at Noah. "Is he bound as well?"

"Since I'm here to discuss your case and for you to determine whether to hire me, yes, I'm bound as well," Noah said. "I'm willing to represent you when Alex leaves if your baby's not returned by then—but two things. You have to listen to me. And I'm not doing this for free. I get $300 an hour, and I'll need a $3,000 retainer to start."

"If it comes to it, we can pay—my husband and me." Yael's next words were directed at Alex. "To answer your question, yeah, I think the government's fucked-up. I've thought that for years. It's why I was upset when you went to work for the IRS."

Alex had worked for the ECA, not the IRS, a detail that Yael didn't need to know, especially not now. But Noah didn't know even the cover story. He raised eyebrows at her. Alex waved a hand.

"I was only there for a few months. Not the point. More important, those kind of beliefs raise a red flag with courts...and CPS."

"I screwed things up, didn't I? You told me not to talk, and I didn't listen. I'm sorry."

Alex didn't want Yael to feel worse than she already did—but truthfully, Yael had fucked up the case. But being too blunt would just raise hackles and lower the odds that Yael would do what she needed to do. Alex decided to soft-pedal it. A little. "It didn't help, but the judge might not have returned Lyra anyway. Still, what matters is how to go forward. That includes what to do on your visit. How to handle the evaluation. And how to act in future court appearances. No talking about government conspiracies. No statements about the social worker not having authority—or being an evil bitch."

"She is one."

"Even if. You will play nice and obey any stupid rules she sets out. When's Brody coming back?"

Yael shook her head. "Not sure. I texted him after the hearing to tell him what happened."

When? Yael had spent the last hour crying. But then, she had used the bathroom. Was that when she'd texted Brody?

"And?"

"And what?"

"How did he take it?"

"How do you think he took it? How would your fiancé take it if someone took your baby? He'll be here. I just don't know exactly when. Hopefully in time to see Lyra tomorrow."

Uh oh. While expected, the arrival of Yael's husband,

second-in-command of a dangerous sovereign citizen organization, was a concern—especially if he couldn't control himself any better than Yael could.

Was he violent as well? With Yael or the baby?

She remembered Kolya's words—that Brody and his boss were involved in something that could kill a lot of people.

Good that she knew, but there would be the awkwardness of meeting with him and pretending she didn't know.

More than that—Brody back in New York gave Kolya and company the opportunity to find out what American Gold Posse was up to. It also meant that the stakes had just increased.

She needed to tell Kolya that Brody would be returning. That would still be a violation of attorney-client privilege, but it was a minor one, and she could go that far. And she would as soon as she had a chance—in other words, when Yael wasn't around. Especially since she suspected that Brody's return would mean Victor Forest's return—and Kolya putting himself in harm's way.

Chapter Fourteen

Brody clicked off the phone. "I'm heading for New York. Now. You can keep the car and I'll rent something."

Victor weighed the pros and cons of arguing. But there really wasn't much to weigh. Brody wasn't going to listen. Few things stirred passion as much as a threat to a man's family, and Brody was pretty damn passionate about his baby being taken.

Victor mentally ticked off the list of things that they'd planned to do over the next few days: another two meetings, and one more site visitation. All of which could be postponed. "I'll come with you."

"You don't have to. It's my baby that they took. My wife who's devastated. She says we can see Lyra tomorrow. I have to be there."

"And you're my second-in-command. I'm not letting you face this alone." Especially since Victor feared it was all a trap, to lure them back to where they could be killed or captured. "Besides, there's Brooklyn. I want to go inside. And also meet with some of our people."

He'd viewed the Brooklyn site from the outside, much as

he'd viewed all the sites before the library in upstate New York. But seeing the secret room under the library had inflamed his curiosity. Brooklyn, close to the financial center that *they* had created, was one of the most important locations. He needed to get inside to personally check out what the boxes painted in red contained.

Wearing appropriate safety gear, of course.

Maybe even run a test.

Then he remembered reading that the vice president of the United States would be attending a fundraiser in lower Manhattan in a few days. Maybe it was a sign. Maybe this was the time to begin the revolution.

He liked the idea.

He'd have preferred the president to the vice president, but this was an opportunity to grab the attention of the American people.

Victor watched Brody check his Glock and then tuck it into his waistband. He shook his head. "You planning on using that to get Lyra back tomorrow?"

"Damn right."

"Not a good idea."

"You expect me to just walk in there and out again without my baby?"

"Yes."

"Not happening."

This was the other reason Victor had to go back. To keep Brody under control. "You'll be walking into a government building. There will be security. Metal detectors."

Brody frowned. "I can take care of some middle-aged security guard."

But a middle-aged security guard would only be the start. "Even if you can manage to kill everyone inside, the hunt will be on for you and Yael. They'll know who came to see the baby.

There'll be cameras, and even if you shoot those out, the images will be in the cloud."

"I don't care."

"You don't care about the cause?"

"Of course, I do. But my child comes first."

"What do you think will happen to her if they catch you? Do you think they'll care if they kill her and Yael to get you?"

"They'll come after me anyway. After American Gold Posse goes into action."

"After—they'll be in so much panic and confusion that they won't be able to stop us."

"Maybe..." But Brody's tone had changed. He was thinking about it. That's what Victor wanted—to get Brody to think before acting.

"You'll get Lyra back. Soon. Just not tomorrow. Not like this. Play the game for a little. Pretend you think that they have authority. For now. You can do this, Brody."

Brody didn't answer immediately. Victor could see that his rational mind was struggling with the anger he justly felt at the government's taking his little girl. Victor liked Brody's anger even if he didn't much care about the baby—but it had to be directed.

"Fine. But everyone involved in this...everyone responsible for what's happening to Lyra...is going to pay. Starting with fucking Ray. I gave him shelter, and he paid me back by over-dosing on my couch."

"Understood." Victor laid a hand on Brody's shoulder. "I'm with you on this. But we're going to be smart. We have to be."

* * *

Having a watcher inside the building lobby or outside the apartment entrance would have been too conspicuous and the watcher across the street wouldn't alert them to every individual entering the building. A large apartment building had a lot of people coming and going. All of which explained how the man in the doorway had managed to surprise them—since he wasn't Victor Forest. Or Brody McMillan. Who then?

Kolya remembered Yael's tale of woe—that her husband's friend had overdosed on the couch—thus prompting the call to the police that resulted in the loss of her baby. Could this be the "friend?"

Jonathan took the lead. "Who are you and what are you doing in this apartment?"

The unknown man managed to look both confused and scared. "I'm Ray. Ray Conover. I'm a friend of the family."

As Kolya had suspected.

"You have identification?" Elizabeth demanded.

Ray pulled off the backpack and started to tug on the zipper.

"Stop!" Kolya moved his hand to his hip, where his gun was concealed under a loose shirt and sweater.

Ray froze. "You told me to get identification."

"Yeah, but still. Drop it and step away," Jonathan said.

Ray followed the instruction, and Kolya searched the bag. No weapons, nothing that resembled drugs. He pulled out Ray's wallet, flipped it open, checked that the picture on the driver's license matched the face in front of him, and then handed it to Jonathan.

"Who are you and what are you doing here?" Ray's voice trembled.

"We're asking the questions." Jonathan closed the wallet and handed it back to Ray. "Checking out reports of drugs in this apartment."

"The police took them when they took me to the hospital. I'm clean. You're police?"

"We're from social services." Elizabeth didn't look anything like a social worker. None of them did, but then Ray didn't look likely to raise a challenge. "We do our own investigation."

"And you don't belong here," Kolya said.

"I just got out of the hospital. I'm supposed to go into in-house treatment when a bed opens, but there's nothing now. I have to wait. I can text Brody. He'll let me stay."

"It's not up to Brody." Kolya's phone buzzed, and he skimmed Alex's text. *Done for the day. Yael taking an Uber home. Brody coming back.*

Ray walking in on them was not good. Yael or Brody walking in would be a disaster. Kolya glanced at Jonathan, who read his expression.

"We'll find a room for you," Jonathan said. "For a couple nights, and then we'll see about finding you a bed in a program."

"You'd do that?" Ray's eyes swelled with tears.

"Yeah, we would." Elizabeth's voice oozed fake empathy. Kolya wouldn't have believed her for a second, but Ray appeared to be more gullible. "We're social services, aren't we?"

They couldn't let him go off and call or text Brody or Yael. Holding Ray in an agency safehouse with a babysitter for a few days might be a violation of his civil rights, but he'd be safe, and the mission wouldn't be compromised. No one would be looking for him.

Also...while Ray appeared to be nothing more sinister than a drug addict—it was quite possible he knew something about American Gold Posse and also possible that he'd blurt out everything he knew for a pizza and a cold beer.

Jonathan and Kolya took his arms and hustled him out the door. Behind them, Elizabeth and Teo locked up and turned off the lights.

Chapter Fifteen

The short-term rental on Eighty-Sixth and Riverside was small compared to her place in Georgetown, and the furniture was a little worse for the wear, but it beat the hell out of the hotel where Alex and Kolya had spent the previous night. A bedroom, a kitchen, and a living room—with a piano keyboard, which Kolya would appreciate. Except that he wouldn't be there enough to play. He'd be out playing spy versus spy.

Still, Alex would enjoy the extra space. She had qualms about short-term rentals increasing the scarcity and price of housing for the average person. But since this apartment belonged to a professor at Columbia who was spending the summer abroad, her conscience was clear.

She'd texted Kolya the address after sending the information about Yael and her husband. Now, at eight o'clock and with no sign of him, she considered whether to call. But she knew better. Texts were okay when he was on assignment because if he was in the middle of something (which he always was), he just wouldn't respond. Calls were not okay.

He'd get in touch sooner or later.

If he could. If he wasn't dead or kidnapped.

She banished the thought and contemplated dinner. She'd purchased a few staples, cheese, milk, eggs, olive oil, fruit, and coffee, but she didn't have the makings of a full dinner. Even if she did, she hated to cook. Kolya usually cooked. If he was in town.

If he wasn't too badly injured.

Her phone buzzed, and she glanced at it. *Running late. Sorry.*

How late?

Not sure. Order something for both of us, but don't wait. Thai?

Thai is good.

A thumbs up in response.

No further explanation. She hadn't expected one.

She found a nearby Thai restaurant and ordered drunken noodles, grilled chicken with peanut sauce, and vegetable spring rolls.

The food arrived half an hour later. Kolya did not. She ate a spring roll and half the drunken noodles while watching the news about the upcoming election. She wasn't a fan of President Lewis, but she'd vote for him since the alternative was an idiot. Worse than an idiot—Lenny Rhodes was a demagogue who promoted conspiracy theories. She didn't believe he'd get elected—although Kolya, more cynical about the American electorate, worried that he could win. Rhodes had been an action movie star, and people seemed to believe he was the evil-fighting character he'd portrayed.

She hoped Kolya was wrong.

She clicked to a British comedy about a doctor, finished it and the drunken noodles, and was thinking of putting the rest of the food in the fridge when she heard a soft tap on the door.

Then a text on her phone.

It's me.

She swung the door open to let him in. He looked tired, but he was alive, and he wasn't hurt.

"I was going to put your dinner up." She handed him the container of grilled chicken with peanut sauce. He opened it.

"Did you get drunken noodles?"

"I did. And I ate them."

"I like drunken noodles."

"I know."

He followed her into the kitchen for water and silverware, and then they both headed to the living room. He took a seat on a Queen Anne chair with a faded white-and-green flower pattern on the upholstery, opened the container, and started on the chicken. She sat on a green couch that a cat had used as a scratching post at some point in the past.

"Sorry you lost in court today." He ate hungrily, as if it had been many hours since a meal —which it probably had been. "Don't go with Yael tomorrow, though."

"How do you know what happened in court? Or what's on for tomorrow?" She then realized how he knew—and where he'd been while she was arguing the case. "Never mind. She's still my client—and my friend—Kolya, even if she is involved in some crazy conspiracy cult. She needs support. It's why I came to New York."

He finished the chicken and placed the empty container on a glass coffee table. "I'm aware. I'm further aware that you're angry."

"Moi? Angry?"

"I can read the noodles." He smiled at her, that damn appealing smile, and she felt herself melting. Why the fuck did he have to be so good-looking? "I'm sorry about your friend's situation and that we're using her to try to find Forest. But it's important. And necessary."

"I understand all that."

She stood then, picked up the empty chicken container, and headed to the kitchen. He trailed her.

"I know that this puts you in a difficult position, and I don't want you to violate the rules of attorney ethnics or privilege."

"I kinda already have." She set the coffeepot timer for the morning.

"Not really. The only thing that you've disclosed is her husband's name and the name of his employer. And when she headed for home today."

"So you could finish bugging her apartment before she got there?"

"Neither confirming nor denying. But if I were doing that, anything I learned wouldn't be a violation of her confidential disclosures to you. There's also the crime-fraud exception to attorney-client privilege, and if she's involved with American Gold Posse, which it looks like she might be, you're operating within the rules."

"I know." Alex searched for the coffee she'd just bought and filters. "I just don't like lying to a client—a friend. I don't like being in the middle. Even so, I understand what you're doing and why you're doing it. That's not really what's bothering me."

She poured water into the coffeepot and began scooping the coffee into the filter.

"Too much coffee." He leaned against a wall to watch her.

"You could do it." But she removed a scoop of coffee and returned it to the bag.

"I usually do."

"Unless you're on assignment. Or in a hospital. Or too badly injured to get out of bed." She swung around to face him.

"That's why I didn't get any drunken noodles? You're worried about me getting hurt? I thought we had this talk, Alex, and you were okay with my job. I wouldn't have gone back if you hadn't agreed."

"Yes, I agreed. Even knowing what can happen. And you told me that at least you'd be in one piece for our wedding. Three fucking weeks, Kolya. That's all I'm asking."

"Is it?" He raised eyebrows.

"Yes, that's it." She knew she was lying too. She wanted him safe for much more than three weeks. That was something to discuss in depth. Later. She was focused on the immediate. "We're finally getting married. Everything is set up. My family is coming. I know you have a risky profession, but this was supposed to be a special time, to affirm our love."

"I affirm my love for you every day."

"Yes, I know. And I love you too. Still, marriage means something. Your being in one piece for the ceremony is important to me. You said that you weren't doing anything dangerous for the next three weeks. And yet here you are."

"The greatest danger I was in today—was of being bored to death by a totally useless interrogation of a talkative drug addict. Which was why I was late."

She had a good guess as to who the talkative drug addict might be, but she let that go. "I was worried."

"I know. I'm sorry. But as you can see, I'm fine. I did text so you wouldn't worry."

But being with Kolya meant nonstop worry. Always hanging over them both—the memory of the assignment almost two years earlier, which he had assured her was a milk run—a nothing—that had resulted in his being kidnapped, tortured, and almost killed. He'd quit the spy game for eight months following that experience, but then, despite the injuries and PTSD he still lived with, he'd gone back to it. And she'd agreed.

She thought about the eight months that he'd spent practicing law—his unhappiness at the work—his restlessness—all the reasons she'd accepted his returning to the intelligence world. Their relationship wasn't going to work if he was miserable at his job.

Was it going to work if she was miserable at him doing his job?

And what if they had children? She wanted children.

She'd have to hide from her children the fact that their father might not come home every time he left for an assignment—hide all her own fear and pain.

And then, if he didn't come home one day...

Later. She'd deal with it later.

"I appreciate that you texted and that you're here safe. But tomorrow? When Brody shows up—with his boss? Will you be fine then?"

He shrugged. "I can't say for sure. I can just promise that I will do my best to be careful. You need to be careful, too. Because Brody is planning to go to the visitation tomorrow. And he's pissed as hell."

"I'll do my best as well. But I'm also doing a job."

"I know that, but I worry, too."

She reached out to touch his cheek. He kissed her hand. She pushed the questions out of her mind. They loved each other, and they were good together. They'd figure it out.

Chapter Sixteen

Ray ate french fries drenched in ketchup one by one and regarded the middle-aged man who sat on the opposite side of the table. One of the guys he'd found in Brody's apartment—the youngest one—had dropped off a burger, fries, and a Coke after Ray had complained of being hungry. Apparently, they didn't trust Grubhub or other delivery services. He wasn't sure just what was going on, but he knew that he wasn't free to leave. And he didn't like it. "You don't have to watch me eat."

"Trust me, I'd prefer not to."

But the man didn't leave the table. What was his name? He'd said it once, but Ray had forgotten.

"I was thinking of going out after I finished." Ray knew that he wasn't, but he was interested in what the man had to say.

The man smiled. "Hit a few bars? Maybe chat up some women?"

Ray nodded. "Sounds like fun."

The man shook his head. "Sorry, buddy. Not tonight."

Which was the response Ray thought he'd get. "Are you police? Am I under arrest?"

"I'm from social services. As we've already told you. We're feeding you and giving you a place to stay. Isn't that what you wanted?"

It was. But not somewhere he couldn't leave. Not with a guy sitting there watching him.

And the man had his phone. It was locked in the drawer of a desk in the living room. Ray had asked for his phone earlier and that request had been refused. Just as the request to go out was being refused now.

The man seemed to know what was on Ray's mind. "We're saving you from yourself. So you don't wind up overdosing again, which means, no you can't go out to bars where you can find drugs and no, you can't have your phone to call up your dealer friends."

"Don't have any dealer friends." But the mention of friends brought the thought of the other people to Ray's mind—the people he'd found in Brody's apartment. "Who were those guys? The guys asking me questions."

They had all been a little scary. Especially the blond guy, although the woman had been almost as frightening. Maybe more.

"Also from social services. We have to collect information for our files."

That reminded Ray of an old song. And it didn't sound benign. He felt a rising panic, a terror at being held by unknown people. What did they really want from him? Were they going to kill him?

Anything was possible.

One thing was for sure: They weren't social workers.

"You have a gun?"

"Me?" The man widened his eyes in mock shock. "No. Why?"

"I think those other guys did."

"Maybe. New York is a dangerous city."

Also not something that Ray could disagree with. He was more and more afraid. What had he gotten himself into? Whatever it was, he had to get out. And he had to get hold of Brody. His friend should know that these people—whoever they were—had been in his apartment. But how?

"Hey. What's your name again? I need to use the bathroom."

"Bob. The name's Bob."

Bob walked Ray to the door of the bathroom. Ray closed the door and tried to secure it but found that there was no lock.

"Sorry about that," Bob said. "You can close the door, and I won't come in. But no lock."

"OK." What else could he say?

After closing the door, Ray crossed the bathroom and looked out the window. The ground looked very far down, which it was, five stories below. But he would have tried it if he could have gotten the window open. Which he couldn't. It was sealed on all sides, and he suspected that he wouldn't be able to break the glass. The pane looked thick, like what he'd seen in some of those skyscrapers. And if he tried, Bob, standing outside the door with no lock, would hear.

Then he turned his attention to the rest of the bathroom.

A tiled shower with a sliding glass door. Nothing he could use. A toilet. A sink. A cabinet under the sink where there were extra rolls of toilet paper, some Ajax, and extra soap. In the corner, a toilet brush. No plunger.

The toilet had a plain white seat and white cover, secured to the base with large bolts and wing nuts. He fiddled with the seat and found that one of the wing nuts was loose. He rocked the cover and loosened it more.

"You okay in there, Ray?" Bob. But he didn't come in.

"Stomachache," Ray called back. "I'll be a few minutes. Privacy please."

He used his fingers and managed to work the wing nut loose on the left side. Then he did the same on the right.

He pulled the cover and seat free and quietly set it on the floor near the sink. Then he braced himself and shoved a roll of toilet paper into the drainpipe, the cold water up his arm to his elbow, while imagining germs from pee and shit clinging to his skin. It was a nasty thing to do, but he didn't have a choice. He had to get out.

He'd wash afterwards.

He pushed until the toilet roll was firmly lodged. Then he stood up, the water dripping from his arm, and he flushed.

The water began to fill the bowl. He flushed again. The water rose higher and then poured onto the floor.

He watched the bathroom flood, feeling almost giddy at his cleverness.

Then he picked up the seat and cover to the toilet, stepped behind the door, and yelled. "Bob. Help. Toilet's overflowing."

When Bob rushed into the bathroom, Ray stepped out and hit him in the back of the head. Bob went face down into the water. Ray knelt next to him to check that he was breathing. He was.

Ray turned Bob onto his side so he wouldn't drown. Then he fished Bob's wallet and keys out of his pocket. He flipped through the wallet quickly. A driver's license from Virginia, an employee card from the IRS—the IRS, not social services, what a laugh—and about a hundred dollars in cash. He pocketed the cash and dropped the wallet next to Bob's inert form.

He washed his hands and his arms up as far as the water had reached. His shirt was damp from the toilet water, but he couldn't worry about that.

Fumbling with the keys, he found the one that unlocked the

desk. He retrieved his phone, checked that it had power, and then unlocked the front door. Stepping outside, he listened for footsteps, then descended the stairs two at a time, wanting to get out of the building and far away before Bob woke up or any of the others came back.

He slowed his pace when he hit the street, not wanting to attract attention. Running could do that, especially at midnight.

He checked the corner street signs. He was somewhere in the East Twenties. He didn't know the area all that well, but he knew there had to be a subway nearby. He just had to head east and south, and he'd find an entrance to one of the many lines that ran through Manhattan in the Fourteenth Street range.

The subway would be a safe bet. Maybe go to the Bronx. No Brooklyn. Bigger than the Bronx—which was better. And anyway, he knew a place where he could hang out. They wouldn't find him in Brooklyn.

In the morning, when he was sure that no one had tracked him down, he'd call Brody. Until then, he'd keep his phone off.

Chapter Seventeen

The call came in at five o'clock. Kolya, his arms around Alex, had been dreaming peacefully of skiing down a snowy mountainside in Vermont, escaping the nightmares that too often plagued his sleep. The trilling of an Ellis Marsalis tune on his phone woke him.

He clicked it on, listened for a minute, and then cursed and rolled out of bed, phone still to his ear. He left the bedroom so as not to wake Alex. In the hall, he spoke quietly.

"We shouldn't have left Bob alone to babysit."

Bob, a retired ECA agent who lived in Hoboken and did the occasional gig for the agency, had been thought adequate to manage the situation and Ray. After hours of interrogation in an apartment kept for safeguarding informants, the team had concluded that Ray had nothing more sinister about him than a propensity for bad food and illegal drugs. No indication that he knew anything about American Gold Posse, Victor Forest, or Brody McMillan's conspiracy theories.

A background check had turned up no concerns about Ray. Other than his being a high school friend of Brody McMillan.

The interrogation was why Kolya had been late for dinner with Alex—and why he'd missed out on drunken noodles.

But the team had assumed that only one babysitter was necessary—and had called in Bob to keep Ray under wraps—after which Kolya'd headed out to stay with Alex. Jonathan, Elizabeth, and Teo had retreated to a different apartment in the West Village that the agency used as its New York headquarters so they could take turns sleeping and monitoring the electronic feed in Brody's apartment.

They'd all miscalculated.

Fuckups happened. But in Kolya's world, the consequences could be dire.

"Agreed. After your interrogation, we were all convinced that Ray was a harmless idiot." Jonathan sounded as annoyed as Kolya felt. "Obviously not harmless."

"Not a complete idiot, either, as the stunt with the toilet proves. Bob okay?"

"Sore head and humiliated but otherwise fine."

"The apartment's compromised."

"I know. Bob's cleared out. The question is how much harm could Ray do? Other than alerting Brody and Forest to the possibility of electronic surveillance?"

"Other than identifying all of us you mean. Other than pushing Forest's plans to a new level of urgency, if he realizes a dreaded government agency is closing in on him? And maybe putting Alex in jeopardy—if Brody connects her to me."

"Well, fuck."

"Something of an understatement, Jonathan."

"I know."

"So—what now?"

"We're watching for Ray's phone. He took it, but it's powered off, and he hasn't turned it on yet. Once he does, we'll be able to locate him. And we're keeping tabs on Brody's apartment. Brody and Forest are there."

It would be easy to move in and take the two of them in—but that wouldn't necessarily stop whatever Forest had planned. People in his organization could still act. The team needed to know what was happening and, if possible, who else was involved, and neither Forest nor Brody was likely to cooperate.

"Anything interesting?"

"No. Not yet. Not much discussion last night. Yael cried a lot. Brody cursed and threw a few things. Forest just went to sleep. Elizabeth and I are doing surveillance on the street, and Teo's watching the electronics."

Kolya cursed again, this time in Russian. Then he calmed himself. "Okay then. I'm going to stick with Alex. She's going to Yael's visitation with her baby. Brody should be there as well."

"Okay. Be careful."

"I try to be. You too."

He turned to see Alex standing in the doorway. He waited for her to speak. She didn't. Instead, she walked back into the bedroom, closing the door behind her.

* * *

Victor was up making coffee when Brody walked into the kitchen. Victor flipped the switch on the coffee maker. "What we talked about yesterday."

"Yeah, yeah. I know. Not going to do anything that could hurt Yael or Lyra." Brody's tone was sullen. "You? What're you going to do?"

"Also what we talked about. Checking things out." And making the decision about the revolution going forward. But Brody didn't need to know that. Not yet.

Brody's phone rang. He pulled it from his pants pocket,

glanced at the number, and his expression hardened. "It's that son of a bitch Ray." He tapped the green button and then put the call on speaker. "I let you crash at my home, and you fuck my family over. What the fuck are you calling me for?"

"I'm sorry about what happened. I didn't mean for the police to come." The answer was a whisper. "I need to talk to you. It's important."

"Okay, talk."

"Not over the phone. They could be listening."

"Who's they?"

Brody had let Ray, an old friend, crash on the couch. But he hadn't been included in American Gold Posse. Ray's drug addiction could lead him to say the wrong thing to the wrong people.

"I don't know. But they're watching me. Come meet me. This morning."

Brody exchanged looks with Victor, whose interest was piqued.

"I can't. Going to see my baby that the government took because of you." Victor tapped Brody on the shoulder and pointed to himself. Brody nodded. "But I'll send someone."

"Who?"

"Someone I'm close to. I'm not saying his name, seeing as you're worried about being overheard. He'll know the name of the girl I dated in high school. Like you do."

"You trust him?"

"Absolutely."

"Then okay. Where we met up for drinks after my wife kicked me out. Don't say it out loud. Eleven o'clock."

Brody clicked off his phone and turned to Victor. "It's in Brooklyn. I'll text you the address."

"Where I was headed anyway. I'll find out what he knows and then take care of everything."

"What are you taking care of?" Yael had emerged from the

bedroom, wearing a white bathrobe, hair damp from her shower, her eyes dark and shadowed from lack of sleep. Victor liked her and appreciated that she was one of the good ones, someone whose support he could count on. And yet, there was only so far he was willing to trust a woman and a Jew.

"Nothing important. You go see your baby and don't worry about anything else." Victor smiled at her.

Chapter Eighteen

The visitation was set for ten o'clock at an older brick building in lower Manhattan that looked like it might have been a school a hundred years earlier but that had somehow escaped gentrification—except for the windows and doors on the ground floor, which had modern glass and security. Alex strode through a revolving glass door, not looking to see if Kolya was behind her, which of course he was.

She wondered whether he was armed, since he passed through the metal detector as easily as she did, but she didn't ask.

She did, however, turn to him at the elevator. "You can't come up." Visitation was in a room on the third floor.

He gave her a slight smile. "Of course, I can. I *do* have the ability to get on the elevator. If what you mean is that you'd prefer I not do so, you should say so."

"I was an English major too. Don't play games."

"I'm not playing games. I'm completely serious. I'm coming up. I won't come into the visitation, but I'd like to be close. Just in case."

"Just in case Yael's husband turns violent."

"Among other things."

"He'll see you."

"Since I can't make myself invisible, it's a distinct possibility. But so what? You should introduce me to Yael, by the way."

"Introduce you?"

"You don't think your friend is curious about me? We're getting married in three—no, two and a half weeks. Just tell her that I took a few days off work to be with you."

"You don't think there's a risk her husband will connect the dots—realize who you're working for?"

"Yes, that's a risk. But not a large one since I'm not wearing my intelligence officer sweatshirt today. Still, I'll risk him figuring it out over risking your life."

Alex couldn't argue with that choice. However, protecting her was only part of Kolya's motivation. He was on a job, and she was providing him an opportunity to get close to a target.

The elevator doors closed, and it was just the two of them. Like the rest of the building, the elevator appeared to be a relic from another century as it lurched upward. As they slowly ascended, Kolya removed a pen from his jacket pocket, unscrewed one end, and shook small metal pellets into the palm of his hand. From another pocket, he retrieved a small plastic object that resembled a toy. Only it wasn't a toy.

Which answered her earlier question. Of course, he was armed.

"Kind of small, isn't it?"

He nodded as he loaded the plastic gun. "Not what I prefer to carry, but there's a metal detector. It's hard to conceal larger rounds. And it's better than nothing."

Agents were never to identify that they worked for the ECA. Not to law enforcement. Not to security personnel. Their standard cover story was that they worked for a branch of the IRS—which meant that they'd have no reason to bring a gun into a public building. Which meant that carrying inside a government building was a little tricky.

"Maybe you need a better cover story so you can carry in these kind of situations. Maybe your cover should be that you're working for a branch of the Secret Service?"

"Sounds good. I'll propose it at the next ECA board meeting."

"What board meeting?"

"Exactly."

The elevator shuddered past the second floor. "Remember that there are children here, Kolya."

"Which is one of the reasons I have a gun. Brody McMillan could be dangerous." He tucked the plastic gun into a small holster on his waistband and pulled down his shirt, concealing it. The elevator reached the third floor, the door squealed open, and they stepped out.

* * *

Kristen had brought Lyra to Barbara's office in a new blue stroller, with a basinet that doubled as a car seat, which Barbara estimated as costing a couple hundred dollars. It was a small office, consisting of a desk, a chair behind the desk, two chairs in front, and a filing cabinet. The stroller barely fit inside.

Barbara stood and moved around her desk sideways and looked down into the stroller. The baby was dressed in a brand-new outfit, a one-piece sleeper decorated with images of bunnies and kittens. A soft toy giraffe lay next to her.

Kristen took the baby from the stroller and held her tenderly. She had tears in her eyes. "I shouldn't come in?"

Barbara shook her head. "No. I'm sorry."

"You'll make sure they don't do anything to hurt her?"

"Of course. I'll be there for the whole visit. Is she taking the bottle?"

"Better. But still fussy."

"It takes time. It's just two hours, Kristen. Maybe you should take a walk until it's over."

"No, I'll stay here. In case you need me. In case, she needs me."

The baby opened blue eyes and smiled. *Why did all babies have blue eyes?* The thought occurred to Barbara more as an intellectual question than anything emotional. She wasn't moved by the smiles of an infant. On the other hand, Kristen melted.

"She smiled. That's the first time I've seen it. She knows who I am. She loves me."

It was probably gas. Barbara didn't believe that babies this age actually loved anyone. They loved to be held, and they loved to be fed. They just smiled at whoever was feeding or holding them. In a few months, by nine months or so, the baby would actually have something of a personality, and Barbara, though she still preferred children over three years old, could relate a little better. Not now.

But Kristen didn't need to hear that.

Kristen gave the baby a kiss on the forehead and then allowed Barbara to take her.

Barbara cradled the baby in her arms. She knew how to hold a young baby, even if she didn't care for them that much. She did care, though, that Kristen was suffering. She had been a dependable foster mother.

"I know this is difficult for you. But it's a long process, even if eventually you are able to adopt Lyra."

"I know." Kristen was trembling. "I'm trying not to get my hopes up. But she is such a beautiful baby, and I love her already."

Kristen would be a good mother. Kristen deserved to finally be a mother.

Barbara would do everything in her power to make it happen. She replaced the baby in the stroller for the trip downstairs to the visitation room. "I need to be there before the parents to see that everything is in order. Don't worry about anything. I'm taking care of Lyra."

Chapter Nineteen

Victor had visited New York as a college student, and Brooklyn had been very different back then. Now it was like the rest of New York: an overpriced playground for the rich parasites who had taken over the country. The park surrounding the Brooklyn Bridge was filled with them, not with the kind of people who had built the bridge and the skyscrapers, but with the new inhabitants. Victor strolled through the park. Despite his disdain for the gentrification, he was enjoying the May sunshine and the greenery. *Just like Prague that spring.* The spring when he was shot.

His back ached at just the thought of it, and with that, his enjoyment of the spring day evaporated.

He turned his mind to business.

The Brooklyn Bridge spanned the East River, connecting lower Manhattan and Brooklyn. It was an old-style suspension bridge, built sometime in the nineteenth century, and now it was a tourist attraction. People from around the world walked its length.

Victor hated international tourists almost as much as he

hated the hipsters. He suspected that many of them weren't even human.

At the far end of the park in Brooklyn, a set of stone stairs, the entrance partly blocked by an ice cream truck, led up to the bridge promenade. A locked iron door at the back of the stairs was marked "Electrical Equipment, Employees Only," and "Do Not Enter." Victor, who was wearing a sweatshirt embroidered with the words "City of New York" and carrying a duffle bag labeled "Property of New York City" waited until the staircase was empty before removing a tool from the bag. He picked the lock and entered.

A small room held electric boxes and various equipment, but Victor wasn't interested in any of it. Instead, he looked for the door that would not look like a door.

The walls were stone and ancient. Nothing had been disturbed for decades. Still, he knew the door had existed in 1951 so it had to still exist. In some form or the other.

He examined the floor, crawling across it, feeling for cracks, but he found nothing, just the dirt accumulating for more than half a century over stone tiles.

He probed the walls, checking for cracks that weren't just from the passage of time. Again nothing.

He felt anger rising in him, but he controlled it. Anger was a liability, and he couldn't allow any liabilities.

He knew that a bunker existed. And that the entrance was somewhere in this room.

He walked around the room again, and then he stopped and looked at the electrical panels set on a three-by-ten-foot panel of hard wood screwed into the wall. He pulled a screwdriver from his pocket, loosened the wood panel, and pulled it forward.

The door was behind it.

It was also locked, and the lock was rusted. But there was no one watching, and after he left, he'd screw the panel back in case someone came in.

He broke the lock with a crowbar from his bag, opened the door inwards, and using the flashlight from his phone, entered.

Another set of stairs, this one winding down beneath the bridge. The stone steps were cracked and dusty; cobwebs thickly hung from the ceiling. His hand came away red from the rust on the iron handrail.

The stairs were narrow and steep. Halfway down, there was a ninety-degree turn. If there were anyone in the room below, he'd have been concealed up to that point.

The bunker, when he reached it, was not unlike the one he'd seen under the library. Dirt and dust so thick his footsteps were muted. A musty smell that might have been mold. But in this room, unlike the room under the library, no one had been visiting or raiding boxes for canned goods. It was huge, maybe one hundred feet by fifty feet, wooden boxes with faded lettering piled neatly.

The lettering on the boxes was at least readable. Some had English labels for canned food. Other crates had only a series of letters and numbers, and to know what was inside, one had to know what the letters and numbers meant. The documents that he'd found deep inside CIA files revealing the existence of the storage sites had also provided a guide to the symbols, which was helpful.

He pulled the printed list from a pocket. *Never trust anything important on a computer.* He kept the list on his body. Always. It listed the locations of the bunkers and what was contained therein. The aliens would have to kill him to get it, but first, they'd have to find him.

As he suspected, the crates were stacked in similar order to those in the library. Food at the front. Explosives next. And at the back—the nerve poison and biologicals.

He pulled rotten boards from one of the crates marked as explosives and stared down at the wrapped bricks of something that was either C-3 or C-4. Harmless without a detonator. But was it still effective after all these years?

If still viable, the explosives could blow up the entire bridge, and several surrounding blocks in Brooklyn and lower Manhattan. Would the blast reach the location of the vice president's fundraiser? Maybe it would and maybe it wouldn't. But the biologicals and the nerve poison would—and very little of either would be required to kill.

This was the opportunity he'd been waiting for. This would trigger the uprising against the aliens.

He looked at the room and envisioned what he'd have to do to set off the explosives. It wouldn't be hard. And he could stream the image of the room with the clock ticking down to the blast. That would get millions of views, wouldn't it?

Although he needed something a little more visually exciting than just an empty room. Maybe a person waiting to be blown up as well. Maybe.

He thought about grabbing Ray, letting him die in the first strike. But he was meeting Ray in a public place—and Victor was alone. It would be too complicated to grab and hold him. Maybe they could just take someone off the street when they were setting everything up.

Anyway, Ray was a liability to be taken care of sooner rather than later.

And he needed to be sure that the plastic explosives still worked.

He placed three bricks in his duffle bag. Then he checked out the other crates. He recognized the symbol on the side of one crate from the list he carried on his person, and he knew it was bad shit. He carefully opened the lid. Packed in faded newspaper from the 1950s were tightly sealed small bottles of death. He started to close the lid again but then reconsidered, picking up one of the bottles and placing it in a pocket. The glass was thick enough, the lid tight enough that he should be safe from the nerve poison it contained. Unless he needed to use it. If they caught up with him, he could at least take some of them with him.

Finally, he located a crate with detonators and loaded half into the duffle bag next to the C-4.

Next: Meet with Brody's old friend Ray and find out what Ray wanted to tell Brody.

And test the explosives.

* * *

"Ray turned the phone off again," Teo said.

Teo had a talent for the obvious. Jonathan had found it almost endearing, even though he knew how much it could irritate other agents. Specifically, Kolya.

The three of them, Teo, Elizabeth, and Jonathan, were in a van headed for Brooklyn. Elizabeth was on the phone with the technical division. Teo was on a computer.

Jonathan drove because that was what he usually did. And anyway, he could mediate any arguments that broke out between Teo and Elizabeth.

Ray had turned the phone on briefly, and from the listening devices inside Brody McMillan's house, they knew that he would be meeting with Victor Forest in a few hours at a bar where Ray had met up with Brody at some point.

No clue as to what bar.

They also knew from the cell tower that had picked up his call approximately where Ray had been when talking to Brody.

Unfortunately, that was all they had.

Ray had undoubtedly moved on after calling Brody.

"I think that Ray's going to be dead when Forest catches up to him." Elizabeth was on hold with the guy on duty at the technical section who was checking the cell towers.

"Not if we get there first," Teo said.

"Fat chance of that."

"You're such an optimist, Elizabeth," Teo said.

Jonathan knew that Teo was right—that Elizabeth could find the cloud behind any silver lining. But he was also in agreement with her on this point.

If they didn't reach Ray first, he didn't have much of a future.

"Text Kolya," Jonathan said. "He's with Alex, and he'll be seeing Brody and his wife. Maybe he can find out the bar that Ray mentioned."

Chapter Twenty

Yael, her eyes shadowed, wore her dark hair in her customary French braid. A muscular six-foot man with red hair, wearing a sports coat and a polo shirt, who Alex assumed was Brody McMillan, the husband and father, was waiting with her in front of a closed door to room 301. Yael had her arms wrapped around herself. Brody stood still and stiff.

Yael spoke first. "The door's locked. When are they going to let us in?"

Alex checked her watch. From what Noah had said, Barbara O'Brien would time the visit precisely. "In five minutes would be my guess."

"We got here early. Just in case." Yael looked on the verge of tears.

"I know. But stay calm. It's important that you see Lyra, but also that you not do anything that could be held against you."

"*They* took our baby for no good reason, and *we* have to behave." Brody spoke for the first time, barely controlled anger resonating in his voice. "How fucked up is that?"

"Very fucked up." Kolya weighed in, his voice gentle.

Yael looked at Kolya questioningly.

Introducing them had not been on Alex's playlist—but she didn't have much choice. "Yael, this is my fiancé, Kolya. Kolya, my friend Yael. He's briefly in town for business. We had some things to discuss about the wedding, so he decided to shadow me today. He's not coming into the visitation."

Yael nodded an acknowledgement of Kolya's presence, but she was clearly less than interested. Her focus was on the upcoming visit with her baby.

But Brody's reaction was different. He glowered at Alex. "You brought your fiancé? I thought lawyers were supposed to keep their clients' private shit private."

Generally speaking, that was true. But not always. Alex had some qualms about lying to a client—and a friend—but feeling the violent aura emanating from Brody, she appreciated Kolya staying close. Even if she was torn about the fact that he'd put her in this position.

Even if she found lying about who he was and what he was doing to be uncomfortable.

But Kolya stepped in to save her from additional lies. "All she told me was that she had to meet a client here—and her client was her high school best friend. I don't know anything about the case. Other than what *you* just said."

"Good," Brody said. "Because it's none of your business. Now fuck off." Brody, filled with anger and too much testosterone, was taking it out on Kolya. He was about the same height as Kolya, although broader and more muscular, but Alex would bet on Kolya winning. If it came to a fight. Which she hoped it didn't.

Although Brody seemed to want to fight someone.

However, Kolya didn't rise to the challenge. "Of course, it's not my business. Nice to meet you, Yael. I'd love to hear about Alex's high school days on a more appropriate occasion." He turned to Alex. "I'm going to find the men's room, and then I'll be down the hall. If you need me."

She hoped she wouldn't.

He walked off, removing his phone from his pocket as he walked, and Alex focused on Yael. "Are you okay?"

But Brody answered. "She's fucking not okay. Neither am I."

"I know," Alex spoke softly. Whatever Brody was up to in Kolya's world, he was a father whose child had been taken away. "I'm sorry."

The door to room 301 swung open, and Barbara O'Brien, dressed in a tweed skirt and jacket, motioned for them to enter.

Chapter Twenty-One

The room should have been cheerful. There was a brightly colored area rug, decorated with flowers and a rocking chair next to the white crib. From a cardboard box on the edge of the rug, stuffed animals peered over the side as if begging to be hugged. An airplane mobile spun in musical circles, suspended over a changing table complete with diapers and wipes; a small refrigerator next to the table probably held formula or snacks. Three more wooden chairs, painted blue, green, and red, formed a circle around the carpet. Images of kittens and puppies pranced in the folds of the floor-length curtains hanging in front of the two small windows. The room should have been cheerful. It wasn't. At least not to Alex. She found the room to be oppressive, like fresh pastel paints over rotting wood. The windows behind the curtains were dirty and let in little light. The room was garishly lit by fluorescent bulbs in the ceiling that cast harsh shadows. The yellow paint on the walls was peeling and stained. There was an odor of something sour. A feel of something...wrong. A feeling of all the sadness from the parents who were forced to visit with their small children in this room.

But she kept silent. Her impression was irrelevant.

Neither Yael or Brody seemed to notice or care about the atmospherics. They were both focused on the crib and on the small child sleeping inside it.

Barbara O'Brien stepped in to block their rush to their baby.

"We need to go over the rules."

Yael sidestepped to the left to go around her. Brody fixed the social worker with a glare. "Rules?"

Barbara again stepped between Yael and the baby. "I'm here to see to the safety of the baby. You're here to prove that you're capable of responsible parenting."

This wasn't what was in the court order, and Alex wanted to forestall any explosions. "No, actually, not what the court said. They're here to bond with their child. Not to prove anything."

Barbara shot her an angry glance. "Every visitation is part of the record. Every visitation is part of proving the ability to parent. Why are you here anyway?"

"At my client's request. And to see that the court's orders are followed."

"What the lawyer said, bitch. Now get out of the way." Brody had been more restrained than Alex would have anticipated. He too seemed transfixed at the sight of the baby.

Barbara O'Brien pursed her lips, thought better of it, and moved. Yael made soft cooing sounds as she scooped Lyra up into her arms. The baby opened bright blue eyes and smiled. Lyra was a lovely child with a round face that could have graced a baby food jar, the beginnings of dark hair peeking out from under a pink hat, dressed in a pink-and-white onesy.

Brody placed a kiss on the top of the baby's head. He put his arm around Yael as she cradled the baby.

It was a touching and sweet scene. Even with all that Alex knew about both Yael and Brody, even with the threat of violence that she could still feel emanating from Brody, she was moved by their love for their child.

But the sweetness only lasted a minute. Barbara had to insert herself into the family scene.

"The rules." Barbara cleared her throat. "You are to do nothing that could disturb the child's adjustment to her foster home. She's on a bottle now, and we don't want her to be refusing it."

Yael ignored Barbara and settled herself into the rocking chair. She began to unbutton her shirt in preparation for nursing.

"Did you hear me?" Barbara said. "You can't nurse her."

"She needs to nurse," Yael said. "Doctors recommend breastfeeding for the first year. And she's hungry."

"You've supplied pumped milk. It's just as good as nursing. I can give you a bottle from the fridge."

"Our baby doesn't need a fucking bottle. She needs her mother." Brody's voice held a clear threat.

"It was hard to get her to take a bottle in her new home. Nursing her will just make that more difficult." Barbara had either not understood the threat or chose to ignore it.

Alex did not.

Conflicted that she was over Kolya's using her and her relationship with a client for intelligence gathering, she still knew the importance of his job. She also knew that he would protect not just her but Yael and the baby, and she realized that Brody was about to lose control. Stepping back so none of them could observe her, she dialed Kolya's phone and then slipped her phone into a pocket.

"New home?? She's not in a fucking new home. Her home is with us." The anger in Brody's voice continued to rise.

"That's yet to be decided." Barbara had a smug smile—as if

she knew she would win this battle. "It depends on whether I find you fit."

"You find US fit? Who the fuck do you think you are? I don't find YOU fit."

"I'm not the issue."

"You are, bitch. Our daughter was kidnapped by you, and you're holding her prisoner, you fucking piece of shit."

"That's enough," Barbara said. "You're threatening violence and that's not acceptable. We're cutting this short. Give me the baby. You have to leave. We'll take this up with the court."

Yael clutched the baby against her. "You're not taking my baby. I get two hours. The judge said so."

"Not if the baby's at risk."

Alex raised her voice. "The court order was for two hours. There's no risk to the baby, Ms. O'Brien. You've provoked a confrontation, and I have to wonder why."

"I'm not provoking anything." Barbara was shouting. "My job is to protect children. This child needs protection against a violent father."

The loud voices startled Lyra, and she began to wail. Yael didn't move from the rocking chair.

And Barbara's last comment destroyed any shred of remaining self-control that Brody might have had. "You're the one who needs protection. We're taking our baby and leaving, and if you try to stop us, I'll break your neck."

"I'm calling security."

"You do that. You just try to stop us." Brody took Yael by the arm and pulled her out of the chair. "But you'll be dead before they get here."

"Yael," Alex spoke softly. "Don't go with him. I know how much this hurts, and how angry you are, but the police will come after you and it will be so much worse once they find you."

"You shut up." Brody turned his anger on Alex. "Your job

was to get our baby back, and you didn't do it. You're fucking useless. And now you're siding with *them*. I'll kill you too, if you get in my way."

Alex took a step back.

* * *

As he walked down the hall, away from the room where Alex, Yael, and Brody McMillan would be spending time with the baby, Kolya read the text from Jonathan. *Need the name of the bar where Brody met his friend Ray. Can you get it from him?*

He rounded a corner and called Jonathan, who then explained what they needed and why. "Without the name of the bar where Brody met up with Ray, we have no shot of getting there before Forest does." Jonathan's voice was tense. "And apart from Forest learning that we're trying to track him through Brody—there's the question of whether Forest might see Ray as a liability."

"Brody is in the visitation with his baby. I have no reason to go in."

"Find a reason."

"But keep my cover."

"That would be ideal."

"And I'm supposed to do this...how?"

"You'll come up with something. And you need to do it now."

"Understood. I just need to come up with an excuse to stroll into a room where I'm not supposed to be and then worm the name of a bar out of Brody where his boss is meeting his friend and not raise any suspicions about who I am or what I'm doing. I'm open to suggestions since I don't see Brody buying any of this. Especially given that he was flexing his testosterone before I even said hello."

"No ideas. But you'll think of something. I have faith in you."

"Oh, fucking please." What did Jonathan think he could do on the spur of the moment? Kolya was good at improvising, but in this case, he didn't even know where to start. But as if in response to his thought, his phone buzzed with an incoming call from Alex. "Hanging up now," he told Jonathan and then hit the green button switching to her call. He raised the phone to his ear and listened.

Then he sprinted back towards the visitation room, ignoring the protest from his leg.

The door was locked. Kolya didn't have time or patience for picking the lock. He took a step backward and kicked hard. The door flung open.

Inside the room, everyone froze, startled faces turning towards him. Kolya saw Brody, one hand grasping his wife's arm, the other raised threateningly towards Alex. He glanced at Alex. She was okay—which was more important than the information he had been tasked with gathering.

"How's everything going? Sorry about the door." His voice was casual, a little apologetic, as if he'd just walked into a family gathering a few minutes late.

It took another second. The first reaction came from the woman that Kolya assumed was the social worker—Barbara O'Brien.

"Who the hell are you?"

"Nobody in particular. I just heard a lot of yelling and thought I should check it out."

Brody did not let go of his wife's arm, which was turning red from the pressure. She, in turn, clutched a crying baby. The hostility he'd shown towards Kolya earlier had now escalated tenfold. "Get the fuck out of our way, buddy, if you don't want your butt kicked."

"I don't think Yael wants to go with you, Brody," Alex said softly.

Kolya raised eyebrows at Yael. "Do you?"

She was shaking her head. "I don't know."

"Then maybe you shouldn't go with him."

"You have to be strong, Yael," Brody said. "Stand up to the bastards. We're what matters. You. Me. Lyra." He turned to Kolya and Alex. "You have no say in this."

"But Yael does." Alex wasn't backing down. "And she's worried about what will happen to Lyra. As you should be."

"Shut up, bitch. Yael, let's go!"

But Yael wasn't moving, frozen in indecisiveness, the baby's head resting on her shoulder.

Barbara O'Brien took out her phone—presumably to call for help. Brody let go of his wife's arm and punched Barbara before Kolya could react. She shrieked, dropped the phone, her hand covering her bleeding nose. Brody stomped on the phone.

Yael now began to cry, even as Brody turned savagely on her. "You're coming."

But she shook her head. "No."

"You need to leave, Brody. Now." Alex issued the command as she moved towards Yael, placing an arm around her waist. "You're not helping your wife or your child. In fact, you're doing the opposite."

Brody grabbed at Yael, but as she and Alex backed up, Kolya stepped in, and with a sweep of his leg behind Brody's, sent him crashing to the floor.

"Don't get up." Kolya had the concealed gun under his shirt. But he would only pull it if he perceived a lethal threat —in which case, he'd shoot to kill. He didn't want to kill Brody. Killing Brody would complicate things both for Alex and for the investigation he was helping. He also didn't want anyone hurt, not Alex, not Yael, not the loathsome social worker...and not himself. Best for everyone if Brody just stayed down.

But he didn't.

Brody rose up on his knees and then managed with one motion to push onto his feet and charge. Kolya waited until Brody was within a few feet and then, balanced on his good left leg, used the weaker right leg to do a snap kick to Brody's groin, following with the flat of his palm to Brody's chin. The impact hurt his bad leg, but not nearly as much as it hurt Brody, who went down again.

Suddenly the room was quiet except for some moans from Brody.

"Kolya, get him out." Alex still had her arm around Yael. Barbara recovered sufficiently to rush from the room.

Kolya helped Brody to his feet. Brody first tried to fight him off and then accepted the help, staggering and calling his wife's name.

"Go. I'm not coming, Brody." Yael's voice showed no hesitation.

"You heard your wife, buddy. Let's go." Kolya kept a grip on Brody's arm.

"I'm going to rip your heart out, you son of a bitch." Brody's words were barely audible.

"Of course. But not right now. Right now, you need to leave before the cops arrive."

"Fuck the cops." Brody was undiminished in hostility. "Fuck you too. A man takes care of his family."

"You won't be taking care of your family if you're in jail."

"Okay, yeah, I'm leaving, asshole." Brody's words were mumbled, but the anger still shone through. "But not because you tell me to. I got better things to do than be here with losers. This isn't finished."

"Yeah, sure." Kolya didn't care why he left. He steered

Brody out of the room, to the elevator, and punched the call button. He stayed with Brody until the elevator arrived and then propped him against the wall inside the elevator.

Brody glared at him with unrestrained hostility even though he could barely stand. "Tell my wife I'll call. Not going home."

"Good decision."

Kolya hit the first-floor button, stepped out, and waited until the elevator began its rickety journey downwards. He watched it descend, hoping that Brody would recover enough to get out of the building before law enforcement arrived. Brody being arrested for assault on a social worker would not be helpful to the team's finding out what American Gold Posse was planning.

He then returned to the visitation room where Yael, in the rocking chair, sang to her baby while tears ran down her face.

Alex gave him a hug and spoke in his ear. "Thanks for handling Brody. And for not shooting him. Must have been tempting."

"Only a little. Too much paperwork." Then he turned to Yael and spoke so she could hear. "Your husband dropped his phone in the hall." He pulled it out of his pocket. It had been an even exchange. Kolya had removed Brody's phone and left something very small in return. "He said something about going to a bar to meet with Ray in Brooklyn. If you know which bar, I can take him his phone."

Kolya felt Alex's gaze on him, and he knew that she knew what he was doing. He didn't imagine that she was ecstatic about his taking advantage of the situation to get information from her client. On the other hand, Brody had just demonstrated that he was out of control. And Kolya had just kept both Alex and Yael from getting hurt.

She might not have been ecstatic, but she wasn't objecting either. He could live with that.

"Thank you, that's kind of you. But I'll just give it to him when he gets home." Yael shifted the baby in her arms, lowering her to her breast. It was a sweet picture, and Kolya felt a pang of guilt at deceiving Yael. But only a slight pang.

"After what he just did—he's going to have to stay away from your home if you want any shot of getting Lyra back. At least until he gets a psychiatric evaluation," Alex said. "When Barbara O'Brien shows up again, she'll be out for blood. It'll help a lot if you tell her that he's out of the apartment. I think having Kolya drop off Brody's phone is a good idea."

Alex was telling the truth, but she was also supporting what she must have realized Kolya needed to know. It was Kolya's turn to be grateful.

He'd thank her later.

"There's this place near the Brooklyn library where they've gone drinking a couple times. I went there once with Brody, but it was a guy thing, so I didn't go again. I think it's called Reilly's. It used to be a neighborhood dive, but it's gone upscale. Like every fucking thing else. You find him—tell him to call me."

Chapter Twenty-Two

From the secret bunker under the Brooklyn Bridge to Reilly's bar was a fifteen-minute walk. Victor liked walking; generally, it helped his bad back, and it was good to get a little exercise. He also didn't mind the crowded streets of Brooklyn. As much as he disliked the newest residents of what used to be a comfortable middle-class neighborhood, he could blend more easily on a crowded New York street, where no one made eye contact or noticed anything. But carrying the duffle bag that was now loaded with bricks of explosives put him off balance, and he could feel the strain in his shoulder and the small of his back.

Ten years. It had been ten years since his betrayal by the CIA, and he still suffered from it. Well, it was his fault for not realizing the real nature of the so-called American government and for working to prop it up.

He took satisfaction, despite the ache in his back, that the fake American government would soon suffer in turn.

The vice president would be there in two days. In two days, the American government's reign of terror would begin to unravel.

He shifted the duffle bag from his right hand to his left hand, which caused him to bump the bag into a man in a suit, texting on his cell phone as he walked. The man issued a curse. Victor ignored it and kept going.

That had been a mistake. The man might remember him. But probably not. It was New York after all.

At least the contents of the duffle bag wouldn't be triggered by a casual bump against a passerby.

He reached Reilly's, a bar occupying the first floor of a historic red brick building. An awning proclaimed the name of the bar and the year of its opening—1913. He liked the look of the outside; it reminded him of what America used to be, back in the early twentieth century before everything went to shit. And he had a moment's hesitation. Maybe this wasn't the place to test whether the explosives were still active. Maybe he should let the building stand for future generations.

Then he pushed the door open and went inside.

The interior had been completely redone, or so Victor assumed. Everything looked modern, except for the bar itself. The tables were white plastic, the plastic chairs were red, purple, blue, and orange, and swirled paintings that looked like cheap Georgia O'Keefe imitations hung on the walls. The bar was crowded with the very young and the very fashionably— and expensively—dressed. Except for Brody's old friend. Ray, whom Victor recognized from a photo, sat on a blue chair at a white table in the far corner, dressed in unfashionable Dad jeans and a loose, stained sweatshirt. He nursed a large beer and an expression that Victor interpreted as nervous or angry or possibly both.

Victor slid onto a purple chair opposite Ray, setting the duffle bag on the floor and against the wall. "I'm the guy Brody sent. His girlfriend in high school was Dana."

Ray nodded acceptance of the password.

A server appeared, and Victor ordered a draft beer.

"They've gotten a little pricy," Ray said. "Used to be a beer would cost about three dollars. Now it's ten dollars."

"Like everything in New York." Victor had reconsidered his momentary hesitation about his choice of the bar for a test. "Why would you meet Brody here?"

The server reappeared and placed a tall, frosted glass in front of Victor. He then disappeared into the crowd.

"Old times sake," Ray said. "I knew that Brody would know where to come without me saying it. Also," he gestured at the very loud crowd, "no one's going to overhear anything."

"Good reasons." Victor had assumed that Ray was stupid as well as a drug addict and a liability. Ray was smarter than he appeared, which didn't negate the last two facts. "Now what's so important that you couldn't tell Brody over the phone?"

"It's about these people who were in Brody's apartment." Ray leaned forward, speaking so quietly that Victor had to strain to hear. "They said they were from social services, but they weren't. And they took me prisoner."

He launched into the story, describing how he'd been taken to some apartment and how he'd escaped, with a show of pride at his cleverness for getting away. Victor wasn't interested in the escape.

"Describe the people in the apartment." Victor knew what they were. Spooks. Spies from one of the government intelligence agencies that were hunting him. He just didn't know which one. Or who the spooks were. Both were important bits of knowledge. The descriptions might help.

"Three men. One woman. The woman was maybe black or maybe Hispanic. Or mixed race. Dark hair around chin length. Dark eyes. Pretty. Really pretty."

Victor restrained the impulse to roll his eyes. How attractive a woman spy might be wasn't the point. "And the men?"

The men—two were maybe in their thirties—and a young guy. The young guy and the guy who seemed to be the leader had dark hair. One guy was blond."

"Anything else?"

"They were mostly polite. One of guys—this blond guy—was scary. He asked me a bunch of questions, and he had kind of a mean look in his eyes."

"Mean look?"

"Yeah, like he'd be okay with killing me."

"He hurt you?"

"No. Still, he looked like he could. And would. But I didn't tell him anything." Ray was obviously very proud of himself. "Nothing."

Not that Ray had anything to tell them. Victor took a sip of his beer. "Anything else about the blond guy?"

"He had a slight limp." Ray thought for a minute. "He might have had an accent. But it was very slight, too, and I only noticed it once or twice."

The descriptions didn't fit anyone that Victor knew from the CIA. That wasn't definitive, of course, because the descriptions were pretty vague. Anyway, Victor had been out for years, and they could all be new agents. Or they could be from another agency.

"And they took you where?"

"Apartment in the Village. You want the address?"

"No. They won't be there now." Whatever safe house they'd taken Ray to had been blown. *They* would have long ago cleared out. He also didn't know of any CIA safe houses in New York.

"There was a guy babysitting me after the others left. Named Bob."

"Probably not his name."

"Yeah, probably not. That's the name he told me, though."

"Figures. What'd he look like?"

"Older. Maybe fifties or sixties. Kind of out of shape. Glasses. Otherwise, nothing really stood out."

"Probably some retired guy—brought back for this job."

"I felt a little bad about hitting him."

"You didn't kill him, did you?"

Ray was indignant. "Of course not. What do you think I am?"

A fool, but that wasn't an answer that Victor would give. "Then no reason to feel guilty."

Victor drank more of his beer. He'd received useful information that he wouldn't otherwise have, although he should have suspected that something like this would have happened. But his own failure wasn't the point. Brody's apartment was compromised, undoubtedly bugged, and the internationals were closing in. This reaffirmed his thought of the timing of the first attack. Do it quickly before they got too close. Although he wanted to know who they were, and what they knew. He had the description of the team, and although nothing was specific enough for him to draw any conclusions as to their identity, he'd be on the alert for that specific group of people—one black woman, two men in their thirties, one of them with a limp, and one young guy—traveling together.

But none of this would have happened if Ray hadn't overdosed on Brody's couch. The cops wouldn't have been called; the baby wouldn't have been taken, and *they* wouldn't have been alerted to Brody's association with him. But for Ray, Brody's apartment would still be safe. Whatever *they* might have gleaned from eavesdropping or a search of the premises wouldn't have been disclosed if Ray had kept his appetite for drugs under control.

The information wasn't enough to make up for what Ray had done. Just as the old facade of the bar wasn't enough to save it from being everything he detested in modern America.

"So, what do I do?" Ray's question brought Victor back to the moment. "I told Brody that I was sorry for all the trouble I caused. And I'm clean now."

"How long you been clean?"

Ray closed his eyes to think. "Couple days. They gave me drugs to counter the cravings in the hospital. I'm supposed to start rehab, but there won't be a space for a few weeks. You know how it goes."

"I know." Victor did know. He'd known a lot of addicts in his time. He'd used addicts from time to time—back when he was with the CIA. The physical cravings could be managed. The psychological cravings were harder. That's what made addicts unreliable. Useful at times, but ultimately not desirable soldiers. Not that it mattered—but Victor was playing a role now, the kindly big brother. "We're going to find someplace safe for you to stay. I gotta go use the can and then make a couple phone calls. Wait here."

He walked towards the men's room, leaving the duffle bag.

Chapter Twenty-Three

"Reilly's. Across from the Brooklyn Library in Brooklyn Heights." Kolya's voice was matter of fact. "It'll take me about twenty minutes on the subway."

"Not necessary," Jonathan said. "We'll be there in ten. The three of us can handle Ray."

"Forest could have beat you there."

"There's still three of us, and we have the advantage of surprise. We're not looking for a confrontation with Forest, just to get Ray safely under wraps again. Besides, if Forest is watching, you could blow your cover. Stay on top of Brody. Good job planting the device on him."

"Unless he finds it."

"Unless he does. But meanwhile, you can keep track of where he is and any communications. If he talks to Forest, let me know."

"Will do." Kolya clicked off without further ceremony.

Jonathan, driving the van, estimated that they were less than ten minutes from Reilly's without traffic, but it was New York. There was always, always traffic. Jonathan didn't need to be pulled over by one of New York's finest. While he was willing to bend some laws, he wasn't going to exercise the high-speed driving skills that he'd developed over the years.

"If Forest is there, what do we do?" Teo was worried. "The whole point of taking Ray into custody is that we don't want Forest to know we've connected him to Brody."

"I'm all for killing Forest. Solves a lot of problems," Elizabeth said.

"Can't do that." Jonathan was team leader, and he wasn't about to let Elizabeth go rogue.

"Why not?"

"Whatever he's planned could still go forward. We don't know what he's planned or who's involved."

"Brody would know whatever we need to know."

"Maybe." Jonathan swung into the left lane to get around a truck driver who'd suddenly decided to triple park. "And maybe not."

"Still." Elizabeth checked her gun. "It would simplify matters."

"It's not what we do," Teo said. "The ECA. We don't assassinate people. It's one of the rules."

"There's exceptions to every rule, boy wonder."

"Stop fucking calling me that."

"What the kid said," Jonathan weighed in. "On both counts. Stop with the boy wonder shit. It's been two years. And besides, the fact that Teo's right—we don't do wet work—it's orders from on high. Forest has critical information. We need the information."

"Yeah, I know." Elizabeth slumped down. "Didn't think we'd actually do it, but it was worth a mention."

* * *

The wonders of technology. Using a device and an app created by and installed on his phone by the technical department, Kolya could not only track Brody McMillan's journey, but he could eavesdrop on any conversations Brody might have with other people. Both in person and on a cell phone.

Somewhat illegal, but Kolya wasn't the police.

He left Alex to stay with Yael for the rest of the visitation. She'd have to deal with the aftereffects of Brody's meltdown, and anyway, he felt uncomfortable intruding on Yael's time with her baby.

Nor did he want to witness her pain when the baby was taken away to be returned to the foster home.

Whatever her faults, Yael was a devoted and loving mother. He could sympathize with Brody's anger at the government removing Lyra from their home, but only with the anger. Not with the behavior. And not with the anti-governmental activities that Brody, Forest, and possibly Yael were plotting.

Brody's cell phone would also be an interesting tool, if Kolya could access it. Unfortunately, getting into it without the password would require technology that Kolya didn't carry on his person.

He'd come prepared with the small tracker he'd planted on Brody but hadn't anticipated needing to break into a phone.

He traced Brody's steps after leaving the building—first to a pharmacy and then to a Starbucks—and back out on the street somewhere near Chambers. He heard sounds of crowds, of people passing, and then Brody tapping numbers into his phone.

Calling someone.

The phone rang twice and then a male voice answered. "Identification."

"It's me. Brody."

"Not how it works. Identify."

"Brody McMillan. 587954."

"Okay. You ditched your phone?"

"Lost it after a fight. Bought a burner. I know. I know. Not what I was supposed to do. But it happened."

"The burner is probably just as well. You're being watched."

"What?"

"What your friend told me. Your apartment isn't safe. Your old phone was probably tapped."

"Fuck."

Kolya debated texting Jonathan that Forest had met with Ray, but he didn't want to miss anything that Forest might have to say. He decided to wait.

"So—meet at backup location?" Brody's voice sounded even more strained.

"Affirmative. And your friend will be taken care of. He thinks I'm in the bathroom, and I'm going to take him somewhere safe. He'll be surprised. Along with about a hundred of the new ruling class currently enjoying the very tasteless redo of a traditional bar."

"You sure the stuff works? It's been sitting a long time."

"We'll know in five minutes. That's how long until it goes off. It should be big. You might even hear it from across the river."

Kolya didn't need to hear more. He searched for Reilly's number on his phone and dialed. The bar's phone rang four times before someone picked it. Kolya lowered his voice, making it deeper and hoarser. "There's a bomb in your bar. Going off in four minutes. Get out."

He ended the call without waiting for a reaction and dialed Jonathan.

Chapter Twenty-Four

Yael's parting with her baby was every bit as painful as Alex had anticipated. Afterward, barely able to speak, Yael let Alex drag her into an Uber and then accompany her upstairs to her apartment—the apartment where Alex hoped Brody would not be waiting.

To her relief, he wasn't.

Yael wept on the living room couch while Alex hunted through the kitchen for mugs and tea bags. She fixed two cups of Earl Grey and returned to Yael, setting her cup on the coffee table.

Yael ignored the tea, rocking back and forth on the couch, hugging herself. Alex sipped her tea, checked her phone—no message from Kolya—and waited for Yael to calm herself.

It took another twenty minutes for Yael to pick up the now lukewarm tea. "Kind of you to stay with me." Her voice was barely audible. "But you can leave. I know you've got your fiancé in town and things to do."

"I'll stay for a while. Unless you'd prefer to be alone."

"No, I'm happy to have you here. Given that Brody...that Brody..."

"Can't come home."

Yael nodded.

That Brody McMillan needed to be banned from the apartment for the foreseeable future had been made quite clear by Barbara O'Brien when she returned with a washed face and three security officers.

"If I get any information that he's home—I don't care for how long—even five minutes—that's it." Barbara had been filled with self-righteous indignation. "That baby's never coming home."

"That'll be up to the court, not you." Alex had made the statement almost reflexively. Yes, it would be up to the court, but Brody's violence and threats would be pretty persuasive evidence against the judge returning the baby.

Still, it meant that Yael would be alone. No husband. No baby.

And Alex would be there for only a few more hours at best.

"Do you have any friends who could stay with you?"

Yael shook her head. "Not necessary. I'll be fine. You think your fiancé can find Brody? What was his name again?"

"Kolya. And I don't know if he can, but he'll try. He's very resourceful." Alex felt a small pang of guilt at the deception. Of course, Kolya was very resourceful. It was in his job description.

"Yes. I noticed." Yael picked up her teacup again. "He's pretty good at fighting, too—for a lawyer."

"He takes martial arts classes. Keeps him in shape—and he has fun. Besides, sometimes lawyers need to know self-defense. I've had death threats over the years."

Alex had almost forgotten that she'd let Yael believe that Kolya was a lawyer. Not a complete lie—Kolya had a law degree and had kept his membership in the bar even though he had only practiced briefly. But with the mention of Kolya's fighting abilities, something in Yael's tone had shifted. Was there a note of suspicion? Yael was married to a high-up in a sovereign citizen group—by definition, a group of conspiracy nuts—and Yael was possibly a true believer. Alex couldn't let her sympathy for Yael and her baby blind her to the fact that Brody—and possibly Yael—were plotting some terrible act. Yael suspecting Kolya's real profession could be dangerous for Kolya and his mission—which was the last thing Alex wanted.

"Sure. Everyone should know self-defense." Whatever the tone meant, it was still in Yael's voice. "He's very good at it. Interesting that he just happened to be there when Brody went nuts."

"I explained why he was there. He had some business in town, and we have things to discuss for the wedding. Besides, he wanted to be with me."

"Yes, I remember. Still, kind of weird coincidence. He's such a very capable fighter and he just happened to be on hand."

Alex took a deep breath. "What are you really trying to say, Yael?"

The directness of the question threw her off. "I'm not trying to say anything. I'm just noting it's weird."

"It's weird that my fiancé wanted to be with me? You know what I find weird—is that I dropped everything to come and help you, even though I should be in DC, finalizing preparations and enjoying the run-up to my wedding—and YOUR husband threatened to kill me AND my fiancé."

"Yeah, I know. Brody lost it, and he shouldn't have. But he was upset. He loves Lyra."

"That's not an excuse for violence. And if Kolya hadn't been there, Brody might have hurt you. Or me."

"I know that."

"Further, if you'd left with Brody and the baby, the police would be hunting for you. Sooner or later, they'd find you, and then you'd have a very hard time getting Lyra back."

"I know that too." Yael's voice faded back from suspicious to subdued. "I appreciate that you were there to help. Kolya too. I'm sorry. I sometimes get carried away and imagine bad things."

"Bad things?"

"You know—that there's something else going on than what seems to be happening. Like I said, I'm sorry."

Alex knew what Yael was saying and decided not to pursue it. Especially since Yael was right. "Don't worry about it."

Chapter Twenty-Five

As the team approached Reilly's after parking the van illegally, Jonathan was startled by the people pouring out of the bar and onto the street. Some running. He managed to grab the arm of a young man and ask what was going on.

"Someone called in a bomb threat." The young man yanked his arm away. "Run." He took his own advice and dashed down the street.

Jonathan felt the vibration of his phone. He also heard the distant wailing of sirens as more people struggled to get out the door.

If Ray had been in the bar, would he still be there, waiting to meet with Forest?

His phone continued to vibrate. Probably Kolya calling to warn them. He clicked it on. "Forest planted a bomb?"

"Yes," Kolya said. "I called in the threat to the bar."

"Figured it was you. Any details on the device?"

"He carried something into the bar and left it. Don't know what. It's going to blow in approximately four minutes. Get out of there." Kolya clicked off.

"Shit," Teo said. "We still need to get hold of Ray. We go in?"

"Not enough time." Jonathan scanned the faces of the people rushing into the street.

"Victor Forest." Elizabeth pronounced the name with anger. "The bastard. I told you we should kill him. You think Ray's already dead?"

"Nope." Teo pointed. "There he is."

Ray, still in the sweatshirt he'd been wearing when he'd arrived at Brody's apartment but looking even more disheveled than he had the previous day, emerged from the bar, lugging a duffle bag. The young and well-dressed patrons of the bar on either side of Ray were shoving each other in their desperation to get out.

"Where'd he get the duffle bag?" Elizabeth asked. "He didn't have it when we took him to the safehouse, did he?"

No, Ray hadn't had a duffle bag. Just a backpack—which they'd relieved him of and sent to a lab to check for anything interesting. But there he was, with a duffle bag—just the right size, too.

"Fuck," Jonathan said. "It's probably the bomb. What the hell does he think he's doing?"

"The idiot probably thinks he's doing Forest a favor, bringing him the bag that he forgot," Elizabeth said.

"Or he knows it's a bomb and he's trying to get it away out of the building in some sort of heroic gesture to save lives," Teo said.

"Not the smartest move given that everyone's leaving the bar," Elizabeth said.

Ray turned a startled face as he recognized them, and then he began to run down the street, towards the subway. Still carrying the bag. Still surrounded by about a dozen people close to him, with another dozen ahead of him, and even more behind him.

"Oh God. He's going to blow himself up. And everyone nearby." Teo dashed after Ray before Jonathan could stop him, shouting. "Ray. Drop the bag. Drop the goddamn bag!"

Jonathan started to sprint after Teo, but Elizabeth caught his arm.

"Don't. It won't help if you get blown up too." Then she shouted. "Teo, stop! Get back here."

She had a commandingly loud voice, but Teo either didn't hear or chose to ignore her. He increased his speed, still shouting at Ray to drop the bag.

Ray gave a quick glance over his shoulder, and then he also sped up, although the weight of the duffle bag made his progress awkward. He dodged among the other patrons of the bar, all still running, bumping various people with the bag. Teo was half a block behind him and closing in. Jonathan and Elizabeth were almost a full block behind Teo.

Then Ray disappeared into a cloud of smoke, fire, and dust, along with the people nearest him as the ground shook under their feet. Windows shattered, and glass scattered. As he fell to the cement, Jonathan threw his arms up to protect his face. The impact with the ground left him breathless, and he lay stunned, in shock. After a few minutes he caught his breath, remembered where he was and what had just happened.

Elizabeth had fallen on the sidewalk next to him. Shifting his head to look at her, he was relieved that she met his gaze and that he could see no blood or obvious injuries. He reached out to touch her shoulder.

"You okay?" he asked her.

"Hell no. But nothing serious, I think. You?"

"Not sure yet, but I think I'm okay." He could feel some small cuts on his hands; he'd banged his left knee in the fall to the ground. But it didn't seem to be too bad. "It'll take a minute or two to know for sure. But looks like I lucked out."

"We're breathing in this shit. Can't be good." She coughed. "Where's Teo?"

He raised his head higher but could see little through the dust and debris that swirled in the air. He could hear screaming from the injured, and the sirens, which had been distant, were almost on top of them. "I don't know."

He pushed himself up on his elbows, then tentatively stood and offered her a hand. She accepted the help, which indicated how shook-up she was. He noted that she too had small cuts on her arms, her hands, and her face.

"How's it now?" he asked.

"The same. Nothing serious. We need to find the kid."

The dust was beginning to settle, and Jonathan could see figures lying on the sidewalk. In the street, a car had crashed into a lamp post. Two other cars had slammed into the wrecked car. The front of the building that Ray had been closest to when the bomb exploded was caved in, a pile of bricks lying on the ground, and there was a six-foot crater where Ray and about five people had been a few minutes earlier.

The cries and screams were louder, and the first police cars were pulling up.

"There's a lot of people hurt. We need to help if we can. And look for Teo." Jonathan feared the worst, but he wasn't going to say it. He could see that Elizabeth was thinking it, too.

Chapter Twenty-Six

Victor was back at the Brooklyn Bridge, on the walkway to Manhattan. Only he wasn't walking—he was waiting for Brody to arrive, and then they would take a subway deeper into Brooklyn to meet with supporters who lived in one of the few areas that still had some white middle-class residents. Meanwhile he was watching. From where he stood, leaning on the rail of the pedestrian walk, he had a view of Brooklyn Heights and Reilly's bar. At this distance, humans on the street in front of the bar were small ant-size figures.

He wanted to see personally just how well the seventy-year-old explosives worked.

And he was both pleased and dismayed with the results.

The dismay came as he realized that something had gone wrong. He could see the ants streaming out of the bar, too many to be anything other than an evacuation, and he could see that they were running.

Which meant that the bar wasn't going to be filled with the rich and annoying residents of Brooklyn Heights when the bomb went off. Which also meant that Ray might escape as well.

Then the explosion happened. It was as big as he'd hoped it would be, but it didn't destroy the bar, because the bomb wasn't in the bar. It was somewhere on the street. How or why it had gotten there, Victor didn't know. And that was what really bothered him. Along with the question of what had happened to Ray.

Had Ray looked into the bag after Victor had left the bar and realized what was in it?

But then, why had the bag been removed from the bar?

It would be worrisome enough if he didn't have the information that Ray had supplied: An agency of the government had been in Brody's apartment. Brody's place was compromised, and anything they had discussed there was compromised as well.

Someone must have alerted the bar that there was a bomb. Someone had removed the bomb from the bar.

He'd spoken to Brody. Told him that the apartment was bugged at the same time he told Brody about the bomb.

Had one of *them* gotten to Brody?

He'd taken Brody under his wing, nurtured him, instructed him, even though Victor knew that Brody's temper could be a problem. More importantly, he'd trusted Brody. Made him second-in-command.

Could Brody have turned? If so, it meant that Victor had to eliminate the risk. Brody could be the one to be blown up on camera. If he was a traitor, that would be appropriate.

He hated that thought. Brody had become like the son Victor had never had. He'd tapped Brody to carry on if anything happened before American Gold achieved its goals. Equally disturbing—it made him wonder whether he'd completely misjudged Brody. One thing he always trusted was his own judgment. Had he made such a serious mistake?

Or was he jumping to conclusions? Maybe there was another explanation. If *they* knew enough to bug Brody's apartment, maybe they had figured out some way to listen in on his conversations.

He saw Brody approaching from the Manhattan side of the bridge. *Don't show any suspicion. Just talk to him.*

Brody stopped next to Victor, and leaning on the rail, looked down on Brooklyn Heights. "I saw the explosion as I was crossing. It was big. But it didn't take out Reilly's."

"A little disappointing. Reilly's deserved to be taken out," Victor said. Brody's chin appeared bruised, and he was holding himself stiffly. Victor remembered that he'd mentioned being in a fight. "Rough time at the visitation?"

"Yeah." Brody's tone was almost embarrassed. "And I know what you told me. I lost it. I fucking lost it. My baby was there, my wife was so upset, and this social worker was such a bitch."

"You fought the social worker?"

"Not exactly. I did punch her, but I wouldn't really call it a fight. So, what happened? Why didn't Reilly's blow up?"

Victor noted that Brody had avoided stating who he did fight. Victor would get back to that later. He explained that someone must have alerted the bar to the presence of a bomb, which had gone off in the street, and he watched Brody for any sign of self-consciousness. He saw none.

"And Ray?"

"Don't know if he's alive or not."

"Hope not. He's the fucking reason my little girl was taken away."

"He did provide some interesting information." Victor continued to evaluate Brody's tone and reactions.

"That my apartment is bugged. He say how he knows?"

"He walked in on four people in your apartment who claimed to be social services but clearly weren't because they held him in an apartment until he escaped. Three men. One woman." Then Victor narrowed his eyes at Brody. "So, who did you fight?"

"The fiancé of my wife's attorney. He was outside the room waiting when that bitch of a social worker made me so angry, I punched her. This guy stepped in, and we duked it out. I gave as good as I got. That bastard won't mess with me again. Then I got out of there before the police showed up."

"The fiancé of your wife's attorney? What the hell?"

"Yeah, I thought it was kinda weird that he was there. And that he was so quick to fight me."

And apparently good at fighting as well, despite Brody's bravado.

"When did you realize you lost your phone?"

"After I left the building. I checked, and it wasn't there. Figured I dropped it during the fight."

"Where was your phone?"

"Jacket pocket."

Brody was wearing a sports coat, which was appropriate for a respectable member of society and a responsible father. He'd dressed for the role. Too bad he couldn't keep his temper under control.

"Take it off," Victor ordered. Brody looked surprised, but he obeyed. Victor grabbed the jacket. "Which pocket?"

"The phone? Inside pocket. I'm not stupid."

No, he wasn't, generally speaking. But Brody had been acting stupid since his baby had been taken. And he'd never trained as a spy. Victor had. He knew to be suspicious of anything "weird." He also knew that a fight could be good cover for something else, and not just to take Brody's phone.

To plant something.

Victor first checked the outside pockets of the jacket, just to be sure. They were empty. That was as expected. He then felt every corner of the inside pocket. Nothing. No listening or tracking device.

But then he realized that there was a small tear in the lining of the right outside pocket. Very small, but large enough for a tiny electronic bug to fit through. *Clever.* He should always remember not to underestimate them.

He patted the lining of the jacket all the way down to the seam at the bottom—where he found a lump, small enough that he wouldn't have noticed it if he hadn't been looking. He produced a pocketknife and cut into the lining. A small device, about the size of a large postal stamp, fell into his hand.

He showed it to Brody and then flung it into the river.

"Tell me about the attorney's fiancé."

Chapter Twenty-Seven

Barbara O'Brien tried to ignore her throbbing nose. It was not just physically painful; it was a symbol of the humiliation that she felt—for letting the situation get out of hand and for needing to be rescued by the boyfriend— fiancé—whatever he was—of the mother's attorney.

And they'd all seen it. The baby's mother, the attorney, the whoever he was. They'd seen her struck, and they'd seen her run out of the room.

She'd always been in control. This time she wasn't. And she hated not being in control. Even more, she hated other people seeing that she wasn't in control.

Barbara wheeled the blue stroller back to her office, where Kristen had been anxiously awaiting the return of the baby. Even though she'd washed her face and applied wet towels, Barbara's injury was clearly visible, and although Kristen didn't ask questions, Barbara knew that she saw the swollen nose. But she wasn't about to explain.

She was embarrassed enough. She didn't want Kristen to know how badly things had gone. She liked that Kristen thought of her as competent, strong, able to take on even the worst kind of parent.

In the stroller, the baby was crying again, maybe because of the separation from her mother. Barbara pushed down her dislike of infants and reached into the stroller. The baby wasn't placated, continuing to wail.

Barbara ignored it and placed the baby in Kristen's arms.

"It's okay baby. You're okay," Kristen cooed. The crying continued. "The visit must have been so traumatic for the poor thing. Being with those people."

"It was." Barbara hadn't seen the baby crying while her mother held her, but even a four-month-old infant must have felt the vibrations from her father's violent temper. "I'm afraid they're not fit parents."

And it was no longer simply a question of wanting Kristen to finally have the baby she deserved. Barbara had been assaulted, and she'd been insulted. She was going to do everything in her power to ensure that neither Yael McMillan nor Brody McMillan ever got their baby back.

Whatever she had to do to persuade the court.

She wouldn't have to work hard, not to get rid of the father at least. He'd demonstrated his unfitness with the violence he'd unleashed at the visitation.

The mother, though, was more problematic. Outside of making a few crazy statements about government control at the court hearing, the mother had no strikes against her. No display of violence. No drug use. No instances of unsafe conduct around the child.

But Barbara could find something. She knew psychologists who depended on her recommendations for business. She knew police who owed her favors.

All she'd have to establish was that the mother was continuing to have a relationship with her unstable husband.

The attorney might be a problem, but Barbara wasn't worried. She'd handled difficult attorneys before.

* * *

After leaving Yael's apartment, Alex took an Uber back to the office space that she was temporarily inhabiting. She'd considered returning to the apartment to banish the difficulties of the day through a relaxing meal, a drink, and maybe something more intimate, on the assumption that Kolya would be available. That was before she received a text. *Work emergency. Don't wait dinner.*

Another evening alone watching television didn't appeal. Not after the scene at the visitation. The violence had been upsetting, but it was the vision of Yael clutching her baby that haunted her. Alex wanted children, even though now, in her mid-thirties, she knew it might not happen. Kolya was ambivalent, wanting to make her happy, but not completely sold on the sacrifices that a child would require. Going into parenthood with anything less than full commitment would be a mistake, so she wasn't going to push him—and she would stay with him regardless. But if it happened, if he could imagine himself as a father, and they had a child together, she'd be ecstatic—which made her all the more sympathetic to Yael. Alex couldn't imagine the pain of having her new baby ripped away from her.

Whatever crazy stuff Yael had gotten herself into, she didn't deserve what had happened. And Alex didn't want to keep running the day's scenes through her head.

The best way to stop the thoughts was to keep busy.

The Uber dropped her at Tenth Avenue in the Thirties. As she'd expected, the office was still occupied. Her friend Noah and two of the solo lawyers who shared the space were in their personal offices, doors closed. The office's receptionist/secretary,

Ruth Issacs, seventy-two years old, wire-rim glasses, and solid black hair that Alex knew couldn't be natural, was packing up a large canvas bag to leave.

Ruth fixed Alex with a knowing look. "Rough day?"

"You could say that. How'd you guess?"

"Been around too many lawyers for too long. Know the look. Child protection cases can take a lot out of you. Besides, Noah got a call from one of the social workers he's friendly with. He wanted to talk to you if you came in." Ruth placed silverware, a plastic container, and a water bottle in her bag, checked for her phone and keys, and then turned back to Alex. "You want me to call him?"

"That's okay. I'll just walk in. You're late getting out."

"Not too late. I'll work the whole night if asked. And paid. I'm a good paralegal as well. Just so you know."

"The whole night? And you're a paralegal? I'm impressed."

"I can't do all-nighters that often, not like I used to. But still, from time to time." She shrugged. "Small office, so I do most everything lawyers don't have time to do. The pay's decent and the attorneys are too. Not like the bigger law firms. I worked for thirty years at one of the biggest firms. Filled with arrogant assholes. Had some twenty-six-year-old *pisher* throw a cell phone at me because I refused to stop work on a brief for another attorney to make calls for him."

Alex laughed. "Young associates are the worst. Except for the older associates. Or the partners. Actually, all lawyers, to be honest, are assholes from time to time. Part of the job description."

"True, but as long as it's directed at the other side and not at me, I don't care." Ruth slung her bag over her shoulder. "You need me, you can always call. You have my number, right?"

Alex did, but she didn't expect to use it.

After Ruth headed out, Alex knocked on Noah's door and

then entered without waiting for him to answer. In a T-shirt and jeans, Noah looked up from his computer as she entered. "Hey." He pointed to the chair. "Sit."

She did. "Casual day?"

"No court, so I dressed for comfort. Especially since I'm planning to be here half the night writing this damn brief. But just in case something comes up..." He nodded at the back of his door. Alex turned. A rumpled blue suit hung from a hook. "I wanted to hear the details of what happened."

"I thought you knew already."

"I heard something. The juicy part anyway." He leaned back in his chair, chuckling. "Always hoped someone someday would punch Barbara O'Brien. Never had a client quite psycho enough to do it."

"Not that O'Brien didn't deserve it, but I doubt it helped my client."

"Nope, and it's making me reconsider whether I want the case."

"Fuck it, Noah," Alex said. "My wedding is in two and a half weeks. I can't stay."

"Wasn't suggesting that you do. But there're lots of lawyers in New York."

"True. But not all of them are any good. I trust you. Besides, what happened wasn't my client's fault. Her husband was the one who flew off the handle."

"I get that, but it doesn't make the case any easier. Want to tell me exactly what happened?"

She gave him a description that was reasonably accurate, including Kolya's coming to the rescue. She excluded any mention of Kolya's maneuver with the phone and gave the sanitized version of the reason for his presence. She'd previously told Noah the cover story—that Kolya worked for the IRS.

"Good thing Kolya was there. I remember he was working

on a black belt in Krav Maga when we were in law school. Does he use it much at the IRS?"

Alex allowed herself a smile. "Some taxpayers can be pretty irate."

"I imagine so."

There was a silence while she wondered whether he suspected Kolya's real profession. If he did, he knew not to say as much. "So, why did you want to see me?"

"To warn you. Barbara O'Brien is not someone to screw with. She's vindictive, and she's got power in this city. She's going to be out for your client's blood. She's fucked over lawyers as well."

"Really? How?"

"She's filed ethical complaints against lawyers. Everything from alleging improper relations between attorneys and clients to conflicts of interest. She even got one guy arrested on charges of molesting a teenager—which was totally fabricated, by the way. Most complaints were ultimately dismissed, but some lawyers involved had real career damage."

"Shit." *No good deed goes unpunished.*

"That's one of the reasons I'm not crazy to take over the case. I don't need that kind of trouble."

"Hasn't anyone done anything about her?"

He shrugged. "Well, your client's husband just punched her. Except for that—no one has managed to do any damage. Of course, maybe no one's really tried."

"Maybe my client's case would offer that chance."

"Maybe. Tell you what, you hang in there for another week, and I'll think about it."

"Another week?" Guests would be calling about hotels and transportation. Issues with the venue or the band or the florist could arise...again. On the other hand, everything for the wedding was currently under control. Unless something unforeseen happened, all she had to do was pick up her dress and show up. Along with Kolya. She could handle any problems online or by phone, couldn't she? "I think I can manage another week." Still, the thought of returning for the wedding, even if she had to put in another week, had lifted her spirits. As did the idea of not leaving Yael unrepresented.

"Great." Noah turned back to his computer. "Changing the subject, did you hear about the explosion in Brooklyn?"

"Explosion?" She hadn't been on any news sites all afternoon.

"Yeah, big one. Took out half a block, from what I read."

The text she'd received earlier came to her mind. *Work emergency.* Was Kolya there? Before or after the explosion? Alex's good mood vanished.

Chapter Twenty-Eight

Kolya emerged from the subway an hour after the bomb exploded. It should have been a quick ride, but after he'd boarded, the train had halted and then idled in the middle of the track, possibly because of some sort of terrorism protocol. He had tried calling Jonathan from the train, but the call went to voicemail. Same with Elizabeth and Teo. He also tapped a message to Alex, letting her know that something had come up and he wouldn't make dinner. Once on the street, he tried the team again. Still nothing. He pocketed his phone and quickened his pace to a limping run, heading towards the lingering clouds of smoke and dust.

Two blocks from the explosion, the police were on the job, blocking access to the scene, waving in police cars, ambulances, and firetrucks, and excluding anyone not there in an official capacity.

Kolya was operating in an official capacity, but not in any way he could explain to the New York City Police Department. He tried calling the team again. Still no answer.

Jonathan, Elizabeth, and Teo were his teammates, but they were more than that. They were his friends.

His hands began to shake, the remnant of his PTSD that still surfaced from time to time when he was under stress. He mentally repeated the mantra he used to ground himself in the present. *This is not Romania. I have control.* The shaking eased.

He weighed trying to push past the police barricade. But the people who tried it were being repelled or arrested, and he didn't see an opening. He tried to calm his concerns, noting the cacophony of noise from the crowd around him, added to the sirens and the cries of the injured. Jonathan and the others would probably be unable to hear their phones.

He tried texting.

Do you need help? I'm here, outside the police barriers.

There was no immediate response. The crowd around him grew in number and in distress. He was shoved from behind into a man in a suit, who turned around, with an angry expression. He regained his footing and apologized. The man in the suit tried to squeeze forward and was pushed backwards. An older woman grabbed Kolya's arm. "I have to get through. I have to."

He gently untangled her grip. "I'm sorry." He wondered why she'd seized on him, but it didn't matter.

More sirens. More people joining the crowd. All ages, all genders, all races—all united in wanting to get through the barricades to check on partners or siblings or children or—like Kolya—friends. People were watching the news on their phones, but there was no news, which added to the general distress. Kolya was shoved again. He shoved back. An elbow in his side. A kick to his leg. Someone shouted, "Fucking let us through."

The call was taken up by the crowd. *Let us through. Let us through. Fucking let us through.*

Police shouted back. Someone on a bullhorn ordered the crowd to stay calm.

There was a surge forward of bodies.

Kolya realized the futility—and danger—of remaining where he was and began to work his way backwards, stepping on feet, pushing his shoulder into small openings, and then following with the rest of his body.

He was kicked, shoved, and cursed, but he continued to press his way backwards.

Then he was free. He took a deep breath and began to retrace his original route, flanked by others who'd also given up on getting through the blue line. He turned on a side street to be out of the stream of humanity headed to the closest subway.

A block farther he felt a vibration, and he checked his phone.

Can't talk now. Can you locate Brody and Forest? Report back but don't approach.

It was from Jonathan. Jonathan at least was alive.

Will try. Where are you?

Brooklyn Hospital.

That they were at a hospital could only mean one thing. He tapped back. *Teo or Elizabeth? Dead or injured? I'm coming.*

Later. Priority is locating Brody and Forest.

He didn't like Jonathan's evasiveness. Someone was hurt or worse. Kolya should be there. He wanted to be there.

But there would be nothing he could do at the hospital. He'd go to offer support, but his presence wouldn't change anything.

On the other hand, finding Brody—and Forest—could stop another attack. That came first. Even though Jonathan, Elizabeth, and Teo were all his friends. Even though they'd saved his life on more than one occasion.

He checked the device that tracked Brody's movements. Brody had crossed the Brooklyn Bridge almost an hour ago, and the tracker hadn't transmitted since. Brody'd been close enough to observe the devastation from the bomb that Forest had planted.

If Brody had been there, wouldn't Forest have been there as well?

He had stopped listening to Brody in real time. But he'd recorded everything. As he walked away from the site of the explosion, he listened to the recording, fast-forwarding past dead air, stopping when he heard voices. The conversation was chilling.

Brody had met Forest, and they'd found the tracker. Kolya had to assume they'd realize when the tracker had been planted —and who had planted it.

It was bad news for the case.

And for Alex's safety.

But the team was at the hospital. Someone was hurt or dead. And, even if Forest and Brody decided to go after Alex instead of going underground, it would take them time to find her. There was a risk but not an imminent risk.

He texted her. *Where are you?*

Office. I heard there was an explosion. Was that your work emergency?

Yes.

You okay?

I'm fine. Does Yael know where we're staying? Her answer was critical. If Yael knew the apartment's address, Yael could tell both her husband and Forest. If she didn't know—it would be safe—at least for a while. It would take time to track it down.

No. Given what you've told me about her husband's activities —didn't seem like a good idea.

Get out of the office NOW. Go back to the apartment. Bolt the door and wait for me. Keep a gun close and don't let anyone in. Text me when you're inside and safe.

???
Will explain when I get there.
K. Don't do anything stupid, Goddamnit.

Chapter Twenty-Nine

Jonathan and Elizabeth, faces streaked with dirt and blood, sat a chair apart in a waiting room at the Brooklyn Hospital. *So, it was Teo.* Kolya crossed the room and dropped into the plastic chair between them.

"How bad?" he asked.

"Pretty bad. Might not make it. He's in surgery," Jonathan said. "Forest? Brody?"

Kolya shook his head. "No idea where they are now, although it seems they watched the scene from the Brooklyn Bridge. They found the tracking device." He felt his phone vibrate and checked. A text from Alex.

Here. Safe.

"Shit," Jonathan said. "That's not good."

Kolya texted back. *Be there soon.* Then he returned his phone to his pocket and his attention to Jonathan. "That's a fucking understatement. Brody's not the brightest light, but even *he* would realize that I'd planted it during our altercation and make the connection to Alex. She's safe for now, but I'm going with her back to DC first thing in the morning."

"Maybe drive her down tonight."

"Don't have a car and couldn't find one to rent tonight."

"Take the van."

"Don't be absurd. You need it."

"Not tonight we don't. But damn. It's still two blocks from Reilly's. We rode here in the ambulance with Teo. I'll give you the keys."

"It's probably inside the police barricades. Unlikely I could even reach it. Amtrak tomorrow morning seems safe enough, given that neither Brody nor his wife know the address of the apartment Alex rented. I'll be back after she's home and safe."

"Stay in DC. You're getting married in two weeks, and we can manage without you. You weren't even supposed to be on the team."

"Yeah," Elizabeth said. "We're doing great here. Haven't you noticed?"

Jonathan looked around the waiting room. It was filling up with the families and friends of those injured in the attack. "Maybe we should move this outside."

He led the way to a small garden with a trellis of roses and a circle of benches and chairs. A small fountain gurgled in the center of the circle. Jonathan and Elizabeth seated themselves awkwardly on one bench. Kolya, on an adjacent wooden chair. Jonathan shifted as if trying to find a comfortable position. Kolya reminded himself that they too had been close to the explosion. "Are you two okay?"

"Fucking wonderful," Elizabeth said. "Ruined a new pair of jeans. My head is killing me. And no idea where the bastard is. Otherwise just great. Ray is very dead, by the way."

"Assumed that. Has a doctor checked you out?"

Jonathan shrugged. "A paramedic gave us the once over and cleaned out the worst cuts. No stitches needed. My ears are still ringing, but not as badly. Elizabeth might have a mild concussion."

"I'm fucking fine," she said. "Besides, there're too many seriously injured in triage right now for anyone to give a shit about us and some minor injuries."

"And Teo?"

"Ray ran out of Reilly's with a duffle bag that held the bomb. Teo ran after Ray, yelling at him to drop the bag." Elizabeth examined her palms. They were clean but covered with small cuts. "He was a lot closer than we were when it went it off."

"Brave," Kolya said softly.

"Yeah, but dumb. Maybe he actually thought he was the boy wonder."

"He hates it when you call him that."

"I know." She brushed the back of her hand against her eyes and then fixed her gaze on Kolya. "I got dirt in my eyes from the explosion."

Kolya didn't buy it, but he didn't press it either. Elizabeth had a well-earned reputation as a hardass, and she wouldn't like him noticing that she'd teared up. She also wouldn't admit to any guilt over her constant teasing of Teo.

He had feelings of guilt himself that he'd also prefer not to disclose—for giving Teo a hard time over the past two years. And, fuck it, even though the kid annoyed him with his eagerness and occasional lapses of tradecraft, Kolya liked Teo. He felt sadness weighing down on him at the thought that Teo might not make it.

But some emotions were more acceptable to display than others for those in the hardass category. Anger for one. "I told you, Jonathan." Elizabeth's voice held pure fury. "We catch up to Forest, and we take the son of a bitch out. And Brody. And anyone else in his fucking group."

"And I told you," Jonathan's voice was weary. "We're not a

wet team. Our assignment is to obtain information on a possible attack. Among other things."

Other things?

"Then we fucking take him and get the information the old-fashioned way." Elizabeth refused to be placated.

"You mean torture?" Kolya had a flash of memory, of hanging in chains from a ceiling in Romania while a man holding a cigar burned his genitals. The flashbacks were less frequent than they had been, but they still happened.

"Whatever works," Elizabeth said.

"Torture doesn't. You're as likely to get misinformation as real information. And even if it did work," Kolya did his best to keep his voice calm and controlled, "it's wrong. I want no part of it, of any person who does it, or of any organization that sanctions it."

Elizabeth met his gaze for a full minute and then looked away.

Jonathan cleared his throat. "I don't sanction torture or targeted killings. Neither does the ECA. You know that, Kolya. Elizabeth is just angry."

"As am I," Kolya said. "It doesn't change what I'm willing to do. But okay. I'm assuming this wasn't the big attack that you think Forest was planning?"

"Unfortunately, not. And also unfortunately, he has a lot more explosives at his disposal."

"Where'd he get them?" Kolya asked.

"That's part of what we need to know."

Kolya narrowed his eyes at Jonathan. He'd known Jonathan a long time, maybe twelve years, and Jonathan was Kolya's closest friend. They knew each other's strengths and weaknesses.

Jonathan was holding something back. *Other things?*

"What aren't you telling us?" Kolya asked.

"What?" Jonathan's expression changed.

Kolya leaned forward. "Don't, Jonathan."

Elizabeth shifted her position on the bench so she could turn towards Jonathan. "Is there something we should know?"

Jonathan looked as uncomfortable as Kolya had ever seen him. "I'm not...I don't..." He paused and gave up. "Fuck it all. Yeah. Okay. I was directed not to say anything, not even to team members."

"What the hell!" Elizabeth, already angry, reacted with fury. "We're out here risking our lives. Teo might die. And you're keeping shit from us?"

"Bradford's orders?" Kolya was also angry, but he kept his tone even. Margaret Bradford, head of the ECA, was ruthless, ambitious, and clever. His capture and subsequent injuries two years earlier had been the product of a misinformation scheme hatched by Bradford.

"Yeah. Margaret. And Smithson." Jonathan named the head of the CIA. "And the President."

Jonathan was possibly the only agent in the ECA to call Bradford by her first name. But then, he'd known her socially growing up, due to his estranged father, a former United States senator,

"The President?" Elizabeth echoed.

"Yeah. They had me in to the White House to explain what Forest was up to and what we needed from him. And that I couldn't disclose what I was looking for, not to anyone. Not even to the team." He took a deep breath. "Fuck it all. Fuck them. I'm sorry; I should have told you anyway."

Jonathan had always had more of a tendency to follow orders than Kolya, who had disagreed with Jonathan's decisions more than once in the past. "And?"

"And here's what I know."

Chapter Thirty

"It goes back to the late 1940s and early 1950s." Jonathan began the story.

"In the period right after World War II, the United States became obsessed with the idea of war with the Russians—sorry, the Soviet Union." He gave a glance to Kolya, who shrugged, not offended, despite his own Russian origins

"Anyway," Jonathan continued, "you know some of this. The race to build more and more nuclear weapons. The fallout shelters. Children in elementary schools being taught to duck and cover in case of an attack, as if a school desk could protect them from an atomic bomb.

"So anyway, when this was going on, there were also people in the government who were worried that the Soviets would win a war and then occupy the United States."

"That seems a bit paranoid," Kolya said.

"Just a bit," Jonathan agreed. "Still, some high-up guy, soon after the CIA was created in 1946 by Truman, came up with an idea. Build secret bunkers around the United States with caches of food and weapons for the American resistance to use should it become necessary."

"High-up guy? Alan Dulles?" Kolya mentioned the name of the man who had been instrumental in the early days in shaping the CIA into the formidable espionage agency that it had become.

"Maybe. I wasn't briefed on that. But back to what I do know. They decided to place the bunkers in existing older structures, hiding them, not only from the Russians but from the curious average citizen. The building began around 1949, pretending to be necessary renovations and repairs. By the mid-'50s, the bunkers were completed. And stocked."

"What kind of weapons?" Elizabeth asked. "Explosives, I assume."

"Also, chemical and biological weapons," Jonathan said. "VX—an American version of Novichok. Vials of anthrax. Everything neatly stored in wood crates and marked for use by American guerrilla fighters if and when it became necessary."

"A lot of Americans would die if rebels used those kind of weapons in this country." Kolya kept his voice controlled.

"Yeah, that was acknowledged. But it was considered a necessary sacrifice to fight an occupation."

"How many bunkers exist?"

"Not absolutely certain, but it's thought that there are around a hundred, mostly in the Northeast, but with a couple in the South and Midwest. Never decommissioned. And it looks like the explosives are still viable. Probably the other stuff is also still deadly."

"So why didn't we close down the sites and get rid of the dangerous shit or render it harmless after the end of the Cold War?" Elizabeth asked.

"We should have, but with the passage of time, the existence of the bunkers was forgotten. And there's a further problem," Jonathan said.

Kolya rolled his eyes. "No one knows where they are."

"Bingo."

"Except for Victor Forest."

Jonathan nodded. "Double bingo."

"But how?" Elizabeth asked.

"Bureaucratic stupidity and amnesia." Jonathan's voice showed disgust. "Information about the bunkers was tucked away in paper files from the 1950s and never put into the computer system. The bunkers were never needed for anything —so no need to keep checking on them. They just sat, waiting for the invasion. The people who'd originated the plan retired and died. After all, we're talking seventy years or so. Then after Craig Rand, aka Victor Forest, was injured and assigned to desk duty at the CIA, he found a reference to secret bunkers, and it sparked his interest. He started researching."

"How do we even know this?" Elizabeth asked.

"Because Rand/Forest alerted his superior that he'd found files on hidden bunkers and what they contained. He was told to locate them. That was before he started believing that the United States had been taken over by lizard people when the gold standard was abolished. So he compiled the list. Then something happened, and he cracked."

"I thought he cracked because he'd been injured," Kolya said.

"It was something more. Something that happened—or something that he learned—when he was on desk duty. Doesn't matter what exactly, just that it happened. Afterwards he destroyed all the original documents, took the list, and disappeared. Victor Forest came into existence and then formed American Gold Posse a few months later."

"That was years ago," Elizabeth said. "Why wait so long to go after him?"

"Couple reasons. First, Forest was good at covering his tracks. The CIA didn't know until last year that Forest was actually Rand. And more than that, Homeland Security thought the sovereign nation groups weren't a real threat and put them on a lower priority. Then the FBI heard from an informer that Forest was planning some sort of massive attack. Someone in the CIA located a memo to the file by Forest's superior mentioning these bunkers and what they contained—and that Forest was the only one who knew where they all were.

"To say that the shit hit the fan is an understatement at best. The CIA had screwed up by letting Forest disappear with the list of the bunker sites and not chasing him down immediately. Homeland Security had fucked up by not realizing the threat. The level of freakout was sky-high so President Lewis decided that fresh eyes needed to be on the job. He gave it to Margaret, who gave it to me. The assignment was not just to uncover the plans for whatever kind of attack Forest may be contemplating but to find the locations of the bunkers. But I was not to tell anyone on the team about the bunkers unless absolutely necessary." He shrugged, clearly embarrassed. "Lewis, Smithson, and Bradford wanted to eliminate even the slightest chance of an accidental leak of the existence of these sites. If the public should ever find out that we have nerve and biological agents hidden all over this country....well, let's just say it wouldn't be good. It's also why I was given a small team for the job."

"And the four of us, sorry, three of us, because Kolya wasn't even officially assigned, were supposed to stop American Gold Posse all by our little selves?" Elizabeth asked.

"No, not all by our little selves. Our task is gathering information on the attack, on the members of American Gold, and on the locations of the sites. Once we know the details, we can pull in the necessary people to finish the job."

"Meantime, we're hanging out here," Elizabeth said. "Getting blown up."

"While you kept us in the dark," Kolya added.

"I didn't make the call, Kolya." Jonathan's tone was both apologetic and slightly defensive.

Kolya felt the anger taking over. "You agreed. You agreed to keeping us in the dark that we were hunting a crazy man with access to these kind of weapons. Because WE might leak information. Jesus fucking Christ, Jonathan."

"I wasn't asked my opinion. It was an order. Which I just disobeyed."

"Well, that makes it all better." Elizabeth sounded as angry as Kolya felt.

"I'm sorry. I'm really sorry. I was going to say something before we had any confrontation with Forest or his people."

"Not counting being blown up this afternoon, you mean?" Elizabeth asked.

"Not counting that. Something more face-to-face."

"*I* had a fucking face-to-face confrontation with one of Forest's people," Kolya said. "Who could now go after Alex."

"Yeah, you did. But would you have done anything differently if you'd known about the secret bunkers?"

"Damn right I would have. I would have told Alex what her friend was involved in, to drop the case, and get out of town."

"And she does what you tell her to do, does she?" Jonathan kept his own voice quiet. "From what I know of her, she makes up her own mind. Anyway, I thought you two respected each other's decisions."

"Of course, Alex makes her own decisions, and yes, I respect them. But if nothing else, she'd have made her decision with full knowledge of the risks."

"You knew that Forest was dangerous. You knew that he and Brody were planning attacks. What difference does it make that you know about the bunkers?"

"The difference is knowing the level of crazy. The difference is knowing that the government for which I work and on whose orders I have repeatedly risked my life, stashed dangerous weapons around the country, even though they could and would kill multitudes of Americans if anyone ever used them. Then after massive negligence, which is what I'd call this, the President sends us out to clean up the mess while ordering you to lie to us. *Yob tvoyu mat.*" Kolya reverted to his favorite Russian curse as he stood up. He turned to Elizabeth. "Please keep me posted on Teo's condition."

He left without waiting for Jonathan's response.

Chapter Thirty-One

The blond guy who had a slight limp and accent—described by Ray—was apparently the same man who showed up with Yael's attorney, claiming to be her fiancé. Who was he really? That was the question Victor wanted answered. Before he made any plans, he wanted information.

Brody didn't want to wait. Brody wanted to go after the guy immediately. But Brody needed to learn patience.

Or had he made a mistake in selecting Brody as his number two.

Not that Victor was worried any longer about Brody's loyalty. The story that Brody had told him along with the fact that he'd surrendered his jacket without a second's hesitation convinced Victor that Brody hadn't turned his back on the cause.

Still his lack of anger control was disturbing.

But Victor decided to let it go. For the moment. Especially since Brody was sitting next to him, penitent, in his office on the second floor of the warehouse he had purchased under another alias—where he met with Brooklyn supporters.

And especially since Brody's anger could be a weapon, if carefully directed.

He glanced around the office. It was sparsely furnished, a desk, a comfortable chair for him behind the desk, half a dozen hard wood chairs in a semicircle in front of the desk. It was a good place to meet with his core supporters. The outer office was supplied with cots, so men could catch some sleep if needed. The downstairs, which still functioned as a warehouse for electronics, was wide open and where he met with the dozens of supporters who would help with his revolution.

A revolution that needed to happen sooner, rather than later, now that they were tracking him. It would need to be something big. Something spectacular. Something like blowing up the bridge where the explosives and other deadly shit were hidden. Also, it meant doing something that would grab the attention of the public—have them glued to their computers while the clock ticked down.

Blowing someone up with the bridge would do it.

He thought of the vice president's visit to New York. Only a day away.

But in order for the revolution to succeed, he had to plan carefully—and that meant knowing just what they knew and who might be on the other side. And it meant arousing the American public. Two tasks.

Which got him back to the point.

Who *was* that guy?

Victor hadn't burned all his bridges with his colleagues in the CIA. Most of them, yeah, but there were a few retired guys who would still talk to him. Who maybe agreed with him about the dangers now posed by the United States government.

One came to mind. Howard Gantz. It was Howard who'd let Victor know what had really happened when he'd been shot. Howard had been angry and disgusted at what had happened to

Victor. Not as angry as Victor, but angry. It had cemented a bond between them.

Howard, though, had lasted a few years longer than Victor at the Company, as the insiders called it. He'd retired two years ago—whereas Victor had left ten years ago. Howard, who knew everyone and everything in the intelligence world, should be able to identify the blond guy.

Victor didn't trust Howard enough to let him know about the revolution in advance. But he hoped that Howard would come into the fold after it started. And Victor knew how to manipulate an asset.

Victor took out his burner phone, but before he dialed, he turned to Brody. "You said the guy's name was Cole?"

"Yeah, something like that. Cole or Cody, I think. Maybe started with a K."

"Karl?" Victor suggested.

"No, not Karl. I could call Yael and ask if she remembers exactly. She probably would. And I should tell her what's going on as well."

"No. Apartment is bugged. You can't call her. Not to ask the guy's name. And NOT to give her any information."

Brody nodded, his expression less than happy.

Victor dialed Howard's number.

Three rings and then Howard picked up. Thankfully. Not everyone answered a call from an unknown number, but spooks —and ex-spooks—knew that spies sometimes used burners to contact their handlers. Spooks would answer unknown numbers. That was what Victor counted on. Once a spook, always a spook.

Howard's voice was cautious. "Who's calling?"

"It's me." Victor wasn't going to give his current name or his former name over a phone, even a burner phone. But he knew that Howard would recognize his voice. And he did.

"Hey, buddy. Long time. How you doing?" Howard's voice changed from cautious to friendly.

"The usual. Some pain. Not too bad. You?"

"Living the good life. Retired. I read, watch television, bicycle. Went fishing once and hated it, but it got me out of the house, which the wife appreciated. Married for forty-three years this August, and we get along great as long as we don't see much of each other."

Victor chuckled. Shelly, Howard's wife, was one of the kindest women Victor had ever met, but Howard liked to complain about her from time to time. "You can always come hang out with me if you want to get away."

"I don't think that's a great idea since I'm not crazy about the weather in Guantanamo and that's where you're likely to wind up. I had a couple people ask me about you, but I told them the truth. Don't know where you are or what you're doing."

It was true. Victor kept it like that. "You being watched?"

"I don't think so, but you know—never sure. You probably shouldn't be calling me, for both our sakes."

"That's why it's been a long time."

"Makes sense. What's up? Has to be a good reason for you to call now."

"One of my people had something of a run in with a guy who I'm pretty sure is in our former business. But I didn't know him. Thought maybe you would. Blond guy. About six feet. Slight limp and accent." Victor turned to Brody. "What kind of accent?"

Brody shrugged. "Wasn't Spanish. That's all I know."

"That's pretty vague," Howard said. "Nothing else?"

"His first name was Cole or Cody. Engaged to a lawyer, although that might just be a cover story. Seems to be a field agent, and he's pretty good in a fight." Victor could see Brody shift uncomfortably. Brody might not want to admit that he'd come off the loser in the altercation, but Victor could put the dots together.

"Not anyone in the Company that I can think of, but I've been gone for two years. Maybe a new guy?"

"Maybe with a different agency?"

"His name was Cole or Cody?"

"Something like that. Something that started with a K sound."

There was silence on the other end as Howard thought. Victor kept silent.

"Blond. Limp. Accent. Around six feet. Cole or Cody." Howard was thinking out loud. "Engaged to a lawyer. There's a guy I know about—never met him—that would fit the description. Could the name have been Kolya?"

Victor turned to Brody again. "Was the name Kolya?"

Brody straightened up. "That was it. Kolya. Weird name."

"It's a Russian name. He's a Russian." Victor was half talking to Brody and half talking to Howard.

"Well, yeah," Howard said. "He's a Russian immigrant. Came over as a kid, I think. I'm pretty sure his name's Kolya. Kolya Petrov."

"Christ." Brody could only hear Victor's part of the conversation. "They're already here and taking over."

Victor agreed, but he wanted more information. He spoke into the phone. "What do you know about this Petrov guy? He's not CIA?"

"Nope. He's with the ECA—you know about them?"

"Yeah. I know about the ECA." The ECA was even more secretive than the CIA. "What else can you tell me?"

"From what I've heard. Good agent. Smart. Capable. Not someone to fuck with. Then there's this story that went around a few years ago, that you might appreciate. His boss at the ECA set him up to be kidnapped and tortured in some kind of misinformation scheme. His fiancée got dragged into it too. They nearly didn't make it. That's why the limp. He was really fucked-up. Worse than you, from what I heard. But this is all top-secret, hush-hush shit, and I'm not supposed to even know about it. But you know, people in the business talk about people in the business."

"No shit. And yet he stayed with the agency after that?"

"He quit for a while, but I think he got bored or something. You know, field agents don't like being behind a desk. And he wasn't just behind a desk, he was a lawyer. Talk about boring. He went back to work for the people who'd stabbed him in the back. Well, not literally stabbed him in the back, but you know what I mean. There might be more to why he went back, but this is what I know."

Victor could feel the ache in his own back as Howard spoke. "And people think I'm crazy."

Chapter Thirty-Two

Alex had the television on, but she wasn't watching it. Instead, she watched the door, keeping the gun that Kolya had bought her years earlier within easy reach on the coffee table in front of her, next to her phone.

After receiving Kolya's text, she'd grabbed a cab on the street —not an Uber, because Uber drivers knew who you were—and had it drop her two blocks from the apartment that they were renting. The short walk back had not seemed so short. She'd ducked into a drugstore and then out again, doubled back, checked windows and car mirrors to see if anyone was following her. Only when she was comfortable that it was safe did she sprint to the building and then climb the stairs to the apartment.

After so many years with Kolya, she knew to take his warnings seriously. And she knew what she should do.

But it would be nice to know exactly what was going on.

It would be nice to know that Kolya was okay.

In the meantime, all she could do was wait and watch the door.

She decided against ordering food for the same reasons she hadn't used an Uber. Anyway, she wasn't hungry. She knew that Kolya was working to prevent a disaster with mass casualties. And the proof that he was doing something essential was the explosion that had just happened in Brooklyn. Last count: fifteen dead.

What he did mattered. To innocent people. It mattered to him. And—to her.

And yet...

It was always the tension: balancing between the importance of what Kolya was doing and the risks his job posed to his life. On occasion, her life.

She had known that his investigation into Yael and her husband carried risks, not just for Kolya, but for Alex as well. Not just physical risks. Her professional reputation. Her integrity.

And now those risks were no longer theoretical.

She heard footsteps outside the door and then the ping of a text. *I'm at the door.* It was from his phone, but she knew better than to let her guard down. Someone could have taken his phone. It had happened before.

She picked up the gun. *Hold it with both hands.* As she approached the door, she held the gun with her finger next to, but not inside, the trigger guard. The position would allow a fraction of a second for her to aim it and fire—if necessary. But it would also prevent her from accidentally shooting Kolya.

She peered through a peephole. Kolya stood there, alone, as far as she could tell. But someone could be out of sight, a gun trained on him—even though she intellectually knew that Kolya would take a bullet before endangering her. Still—he had drilled safety precautions into her.

Still holding the gun, she unbolted the security lock and stepped back. The door swung open, and Kolya entered. Alone. With a sigh of relief, she lowered the gun and stepped into a hug. He held her close for a long minute before releasing her and bolting the door behind him. She crossed to the coffee table and set the gun down.

"You okay?" She saw the tiredness in his face, and something else. Something she couldn't quite interpret.

"I'm fine."

But he wasn't. She could tell just by looking at him. "You said you'd explain what was going on when you got here."

"What's going on is that you're leaving town. I made reservations on Amtrak for both of us tomorrow morning."

She narrowed her eyes. "Like hell I am. You expect me to leave without even giving me an explanation."

"It's too dangerous for you here." He moved towards the kitchen, opened the refrigerator, and peered inside.

"That's not an explanation." She followed him, leaning against the counter while he surveyed the meager contents. "Not really." She knew that there had been an explosion but that alone wasn't enough for Kolya to want her out of town. There had to be more.

He was frowning at the fridge. "Let me find something to make dinner."

"I didn't buy much in the way of groceries." She hated cooking. Back home, he prepared meals. She watched him take out a loaf of bread, a brick of cheddar cheese, a tomato and two cans of lemon seltzer. "And back to the subject you're avoiding—if you think I'm going to just leave town because you say so without anything more, you're sadly fucking mistaken."

"I know." He handed her a can of seltzer. "On both counts. We can talk while we eat. Grilled cheese okay?"

"Drunken noodles would be preferable."

"It would be." He found an iron frying pan in a cabinet.

She watched without further comment as he melted butter in a pan and layered cheese and slices of tomato on top of two slices of bread before topping both sandwiches with a second piece of bread. He found a spatula, flipped the sandwiches, and then flipped again. Then he slid the finished product, bread toasted to a perfect golden brown, onto two plates. He sliced both into quarters and handed her a plate.

It smelled wonderful. As always, even when she was annoyed with him, she appreciated that he not only liked cooking but that he was good at it. And now that he'd arrived safely, she was ravenous. It had been a long day.

She curled up in the chair, her feet tucked under her. She downed her own sandwich and watched him eat half of his before trying a different tack. *Start with what she already knew.* "You were at the explosion in Brooklyn?"

"Not when it went off. After."

"And the team?"

"Not so lucky. They were there when it went off."

"Shit, Kolya. How bad?"

He set the plate down. "Teo might not make it. He's in a hospital in Brooklyn. The others—Jonathan, Elizabeth—minor cuts and bruises."

"Oh fucking damn, Kolya. I like the kid. No wonder you look so grim. You're not waiting with the team at the hospital?"

"I was there. I left." He picked up another quarter of the grilled cheese, took a bite, swallowed, and then sipped the seltzer. "I needed to make sure you were okay. And that you left town. Because Victor Forest and Brody McMillan have figured out what I am. And they know my connection to you. They could and probably will come after you."

She sighed. "I should have realized that had happened. You left some sort of bug on Brody?"

He nodded. "When I helped him to the elevator. I didn't think he'd find it that quickly."

"And you're afraid they'll use me to get to you."

"Not just that. Brody's the kind to hold grudges. He already blames you for not returning his baby, and now in his demented mind, you're part of whatever government conspiracy he thinks he's valiantly fighting. I also suspect he's not too happy that I kicked his ass."

"Probably not. He deserved it, and I appreciate what you did, but you did expose yourself."

Kolya raised eyebrows at her. "He could have hurt or killed you—and maybe Yael—if I hadn't been there."

"I know. Still."

"Still there would have been a lot more dead people if I hadn't heard Forest tell him about the bomb. Which only happened because of my planting a listening device on Brody after I—unwisely—kicked his ass."

"A listening device which he found."

"Forest found it."

"Whatever. They found it. You're blown."

He shrugged. "Yes, but it's irrelevant. I'm leaving town with you. Did you tell anyone where we're staying—Noah—anyone? Because if you did, we need to leave here as soon as we're done eating."

She shook her head. "No. You've trained me too well."

"Good. The train's tomorrow at 4:50 a.m., and we should be okay here until then. I'm going to be taking time off until after the wedding. And maybe I won't go back then either."

She didn't respond immediately, her mind returning to the last time he'd quit. She picked up the seltzer and drank. It was slightly bitter and cold, and the bitterness was what struck her. "You're thinking of quitting again? Because of me?"

"Not just because of you. Because of something I just learned."

"Which is?"

"That government agencies can do things that are careless and stupid. And endanger people's lives."

"You didn't know that?" It was a rhetorical question. Of course, he knew it, and she knew he knew. It was the reason he'd quit the last time. "What underhanded thing did the ECA come up with this time?"

"It wasn't just the ECA. The original scheme was from the CIA in the 1950s." There was a hesitation, as if he was weighing what to say. It had to be a struggle—she knew the rules of the game.

"You don't have to tell me anything you don't want to tell me." *Or can't tell me.*

Then he shrugged. "*Yob tvoyu mat.* I'm not doing to you what they did to me."

She raised eyebrows.

He ignored her questioning look. "The CIA set up secret bunkers, equipped with explosives and nerve agents. A hundred of them. And then fucking idiots that they are, they forgot about them. Buried the records. Lost the locations. Just left all this deadly shit for some nutcase to find. And Forest and Brody did. Forest has a list with the locations of all the bunkers."

Her eyes widened. "The bomb in Brooklyn."

He nodded.

"And what did they do to you that you don't want to do to me?"

"The ECA? Kept me in the dark about what was really going on. What the real danger was from Forest and his playmates."

"The ECA? Or your team?"

"Both. Jonathan was the one concealing the information. On orders from Bradford, of course, but still, he did it." He gave her a small smile. "And, yes, I just violated federal law by disclosing classified information, but I don't give a fuck. You should know just how dangerous the shit is that your friend's involved in. Which is why you have to leave. And why I'm leaving with you."

She was silent for a long moment. "Ironic, isn't it?"

"Yes."

He didn't have to spell it out, and neither did she. Forest was a conspiracy nut who believed aliens controlled the United States. And yet, he had a glimmer of the truth that the secret bunkers represented: that governments and their agents weren't always trustworthy and often exercised power without regard to whom it hurts.

"We've been here before. And then you went back."

"True." He took a long drink of seltzer. "I suppose it was a question of what I perceived to be the greater threat to innocent people."

"Has that changed?"

"Not really."

"So why quit now?"

"Maybe because I keep putting you in harm's way."

"To be precise, this time I'm the one who put myself in harm's way. You warned me that something wasn't kosher about Yael and her husband. I could have backed out. I didn't. *I* asked you to run a background check on them—which alerted you and the ECA to their involvement with a domestic terror group."

"All true. Still, here we are again. You're possibly in danger because dangerous fanatics, planning mass destruction, might use you to get to me after the people I work for exhibited a certain lack of concern for my welfare—or yours. Again. So maybe time for me to quit. I'm still a member of the bar."

Wasn't this what she wanted? Kolya working as a lawyer. It was a lot safer than working in intelligence. But she knew that it was wrong. *Not now. Not like this.* "I don't think it's a great idea."

"What isn't? Quitting or practicing law?"

"Either. The last time you worked in a law firm, you hated every minute of it. You were drinking constantly."

"That was right after Romania."

Romania. Where he'd been held prisoner after being wounded and then tortured for days—burned, beaten, and starved. Where she'd been taken after being kidnapped to pressure him to cooperate—neither of them knowing, at least not initially, that his agency had wanted him captured and wanted him to capitulate in an elaborate scheme. The scheme had worked—preventing the meltdown of multiple nuclear power plants, but at a steep cost to both of them. He still suffered from the psychological and physical injuries inflicted on him. She had been unhurt physically, but the vision of him chained to a wall, barely alive, still haunted her.

"Point. Are you saying you didn't hate being a lawyer?"

"Point." He managed a small smile. "I don't have to be a lawyer. I can find something else to do."

"True, but I don't believe you really want to quit either. Even if the ECA did its usual thing and Jonathan—your closest friend—went along with it. This is who you are, my love. You might be ready at some point to give up the game, but I don't think this is that moment. Not really. You're just worried about me and a little mad."

"More than a little."

"Still."

"Still, it's the logical thing to do. Quit, that is. Given everything."

"Is it?" She suddenly knew the logical thing to do, what she had avoided even thinking about, despite everything over the past few years, because of how much she loved him. But loving him was why she couldn't avoid it any longer. "Or are *we* what's not logical? Your relationship with me makes you vulnerable on this job, and yet if you quit the game before you're ready out of fear for me, sooner or later, you'll resent me." She held up a hand to forestall the protest that she knew would come. "And I know you love me, and you'll never say anything to blame me. But it doesn't mean that the resentment won't be there. Festering."

"Do you really think I'd resent you for my decision? And it is my decision. Don't you know me?"

"Yes. Yes, I do know you." She suddenly felt very tired.

"And I know you." His voice softened. "And, no, you don't put me in danger—at least not in any greater danger than I choose to put myself in. You're what matters most in my life. I'm tired. Can't we just go to bed and catch a few hours sleep since we have to be up early—and maybe put off this conversation until we're back in Washington?"

He did look exhausted. She was as well. There was still time to talk and make a decision. Still time to call off the wedding, although just the thought brought tears to her eyes. Maybe she wasn't thinking straight either. Or maybe she was perceiving reality for the first time.

Although right now, the reality was simple. She just wanted to crawl into bed next to him and have his arms around her. Even for just for a few hours. She picked up her phone and sent a quick text. *Leaving tomorrow morning with Kolya. Please consider taking Yael's case.*

"As you wish," she said.

Chapter Thirty-Three

Victor waited in the living room while Brody woke his wife.

Victor glanced around the room, appreciating the simple decor and the cleanliness. He had been dubious about Brody's choice of a wife—given her Jewish blood—but she'd cut her ties with her family and her tribe, and she seemed to support the cause. He liked her cooking, that she kept the house neat and clean, and that she'd shown herself to be a good mother. But she'd let in the enemy by asking her friend to take on her legal case. Was it just bad judgment? Or something worse?

He heard Brody's angry voice in the bedroom, ordering her to get up and get dressed.

He'd thought of going in with Brody, but Brody was doing the job. And he wanted to be sure of Brody's loyalties. No better way to do that than to let him handle his wife.

Five minutes later, Brody emerged from the bedroom, his hand firmly gripping Yael's arm. She was dressed in jeans and a pink tank top, but her long hair was disheveled and her eyes red.

Weeping. For the baby. Or for something else?

It didn't matter. They couldn't talk in the apartment. Victor could search for the bugs, but he might not find them all. He gestured to Brody towards the door. Nothing was said until the three of them reached the sidewalk outside.

"What's going on?" Her voice was subdued.

Brody glanced at Victor, but Victor gestured back. *Your wife.*

"Where's your lawyer friend staying?" Brody's voice sounded harsh, even to Victor.

"Who? Alex?" She blinked as if trying to clear her mind. "I don't know. I have her number in my phone. I can call her if you want, but it's late."

Brody gave her a slap. It was probably not a very hard slap, since it didn't leave a mark, but it did serve the purpose of getting her to focus. "I didn't ask you to call her. I asked where we could find her."

"I don't know. I think she was at a hotel somewhere—then she rented an apartment."

"You've never been there."

"No. She came to our apartment, or we met at the office. Why? What's going on?"

Brody glanced at Victor, who gave a nod. Yael should know. And then Brody made the pronouncement. "Your friend's fiancé, if he's even that, is a spook."

"He's what?"

"A spook. A spy. A secret agent. Working for the government. Wormed his way into our lives through your friend. Probably they both are—and they're both working with the bitch who took our baby, and it's all a fucking charade."

Yael's eyes widened. "Oh my God."

"Why did you call her?"

"Because she was my best friend in high school. Because I've kept tabs on her, and she's a really good lawyer who I thought would help me get our baby back. And it was your fucking friend's fault that I was even in the situation. Did Ray overdose on purpose to get our baby taken away?"

Was that a little far-fetched? Victor knew that the government was capable of all sorts of tricks, but was Yael going a little too far?

Maybe. Maybe not.

Victor decided to enter the conversation. "Whatever Ray's role, you don't have to worry about him anymore. He won't betray you again."

She nodded. "Good."

She didn't ask for an explanation. He liked that. "You didn't suspect anything about your friend's fiancé?"

Yael shook her head. "Not initially. She talked about her upcoming wedding and showed me his picture. She said he was a lawyer. Jewish."

Victor exchanged glances with Brody. Of course.

"But, fuck, I did start to wonder after he and you," she looked at her husband, "got into that fight. He was a really good fighter for a lawyer. You know, I was kind of surprised at how fast he took you down. I asked Alex about it earlier today, and she gave me some song and dance about him taking martial arts classes to stay in shape."

Victor restrained the impulse to smile. He'd suspected that Petrov had gotten the better of Brody, despite Brody's boasting of his fighting prowess. But no reason to say or show anything that would further humiliate Brody. It would serve no purpose. Nor did Victor feel compelled to disclose his other thought: that Petrov had easily managed to best Brody had increased Victor's interest in trying to recruit him. Even if the man was a Jew. Jews were clever, and if a man like Petrov could be persuaded to turn against the overlords and the Jewish cabal, he could be valuable.

If the man couldn't be recruited, he could still be valuable. His death—and that of his fiancée—could be part of the spectacle that Victor wanted to launch the revolution in less than twenty-four hours. The idea appealed to Victor's sense of the dramatic.

The recruitment would be more useful. Hell, if he could trust Petrov enough, he could send him inside to destroy the very organization he worked for. That would be delicious. Holding Petrov's fiancée—if the engagement was real—would help guarantee his future behavior.

If Petrov could be turned, Victor would find someone else to be the sacrifice. If not—then Petrov and his fiancée would do. And it would be appropriate that the person chosen to die on camera to launch the revolution was not a random bystander, but an agent of the government Victor was going to overthrow.

Either way, by serving American Gold or by dying on camera, Petrov would advance the cause.

Gauging by his bright red face, Brody wouldn't approve of recruiting Petrov, but that was too bad. Victor was in charge. However, if Petrov didn't turn, Brody'd be fine with the plan. Yael's disclosure had clearly embarrassed and angered him. It was probably the reason Brody gave Yael another slap. A little harder, judging by the mark on her cheek. "You should have told me."

"You weren't here. And I ..." Yael's tone changed, hardened, "I was stupid. The bitch. I thought she was my friend, and she was using me."

Brody raised his hand again.

Enough was enough. "Stop hitting her. It's not her fault you both were victims of trained agents," Victor said.

"That's not the point. She's my wife, and she let a spy into our home."

"But she can fix things by helping us find her lawyer friend as well as Petrov. Where's the office?" Victor asked.

"The West Thirties. I can take you, although Alex won't be

there. Not now, not at ten o'clock at night " Yael pulled at her hair, smoothing tangles.

"But now would be a good time to get into the office and search it. See if there might be some clue as to where the two of them are staying. And where your baby is being kept. It's worth a shot."

Chapter Thirty-Four

Noah didn't usually work late at the office. He had a brief due the next day for his least favorite client, a shit who'd absconded from France with ten million euros, half of which belonged to an ex-wife in Paris. The issue involved was *forum non conveniens*, getting a case dismissed because there was a more logical place to bring suit. Getting the case dismissed and sent back to France would be a win-win—as far as Noah was concerned. Noah would earn his fee and get rid of a case for a client he despised at the same time. But first, he had to write the brief.

Forum non conveniens was an interesting legal concept, but he hadn't previously used it for a case, which meant he didn't know the case law, and he needed to research. Normally, he'd prefer to work late at home; however, his wife's sister was visiting from Los Angeles. While his apartment was a decent size for New York City, it wasn't large enough to allow him to work in peace when they had a visitor. So, he stayed at the office, ordering Chinese food and settling in for a long evening.

Despite being the only occupant of the office, he kept his own door closed out of habit —which was why he couldn't really make out the muffled sounds in the outer room. He couldn't hear enough to recognize the voices, but that didn't mean anything. Most likely, some of the attorneys who shared the space had returned, like him, to work. There was nothing of value in the office. Why would anyone break in?

Then his door was kicked in, and he stared at three figures dressed in black, wearing balaclavas. Two of them held guns.

* * *

The lawyer held out until they broke four of his fingers. Victor had to respect him for that. But it didn't really matter, because even once he was willing to tell them whatever they wanted to know, he didn't know much. He didn't know where Alex Feinstein was staying. He didn't know that Kolya Petrov was a spy. Or where he was staying either.

He didn't know their address in Washington. He'd never been there.

What the lawyer did know: that Alex Feinstein was leaving New York and wouldn't be back. And that her fiancé would be leaving with her.

"The bitch was supposed to stay here until my case was done." Yael glared at the lawyer. "Where's my baby?"

"I don't know."

"Break another finger," she told Victor.

Victor raised the paperweight that he'd used to break the lawyer's first four fingers. He didn't really care about finding the baby. The baby was a distraction from what he needed to do. What they all needed to do. From the revolution that he hoped would be starting in less than twenty-four hours. But it was important to Brody, who was important to Victor.

"No, please! Please!" The man quivered. "I'm not sure, but there's someone who might have her. There's this woman who's

Barbara O'Brien's favorite foster mom. And she'd be a likely choice for a baby she'd consider a candidate for adoption."

"My baby is a candidate for adoption?" Brody's voice was even angrier than Yael's. If that was possible.

"O'Brien considers any healthy baby a candidate for adoption. And this foster mom lost out on another baby—so O'Brien would be trying to make up for it. Her name's Kristen. Kristen Temple."

"And how do we find her?" Victor asked.

"Her phone and address are on my phone."

"Which is where?"

The lawyer nodded toward the side of his desk. Victor cautiously moved around the desk and found the iPhone under a pile of papers. He picked it up and looked at the lawyer, and the lawyer recited a six-number code without being asked.

Victor tapped in the code. "Nice phone. Good camera, from what I hear. How much memory?"

The lawyer gritted his teeth. "I got the most available."

Of course, he would. Lawyers had money.

Lawyers were also part of the sickness of modern America. They helped keep the aliens in power. But that was a thought for later. They needed to move this along.

Victor tapped contacts. Kristen Temple's phone number and address were indeed in there. It was odd, though. Why would a defense attorney have the address for a foster mother? He asked the question.

"The baby of one of my clients was the baby that Kristen nearly adopted, but my client got her act together, and the court gave the kid back. After that, Kristen contacted me and asked me if I would let her know how the baby was doing and maybe send some pictures. She was a decent person and took good care of the baby. I sent her some stuff on behalf of my client. Why does it matter?"

"It doesn't. Just curious."

Victor checked the texts as well, to confirm that the lawyer wasn't hiding anything. Texts from clients. From his wife. A bunch of texts from candidates for Congressional seats, for governor. "You get a lot of political texts, don't you?"

"Don't donate money to political candidates. Once you do, they never fucking leave you alone."

"Thanks for the advice. I'll keep it in mind." The idea—of Victor donating to political campaigns—was amusing. He almost laughed, but he didn't.

Victor clicked on a text from Alexandria Feinstein. It confirmed what the lawyer had already told him, that she and her spy fiancé were leaving the next day and asking him to take over Yael's case. Victor could barely contain his excitement. Capture them both. Then turn Petrov or use his death and that of his fiancée to announce the new world order.

Victor sent a text back. *Sure. Want to meet for coffee before you leave, and you can fill me in on anything I might need to know?*

No immediate response. Well, maybe she'd gone to bed. In any case, they needed to move on. It was the middle of the night, but someone else could possibly show up. Some security guard could take an interest.

Lingering any longer could be risky.

Anyway, they had places to go. "Sorry. I have to keep your phone for a little while." Not too long. Phones could be traced. Just long enough to see if Alex Feinstein texted back.

The lawyer perked up slightly at the suggestion that they would leave and leave him alive. "Take it."

"Thanks. That's generous." Then Victor shot him in the head.

Chapter Thirty-Five

Kolya slept peacefully, no sign of the nightmares that still sometimes plagued him. But Alex found herself staring at the ceiling, unable to calm her mind enough to drift off. Having allowed the thought to surface—that maybe they shouldn't be together—she couldn't get rid of it. And yet, there he was lying next to her, his sleeping presence reminding her of how much she loved and wanted him. No wonder she was wide awake. *Think of something calming.* The plot of a Jane Austen novel, maybe. That was how she'd calmed herself enough to sleep years earlier when she and Kolya had been held prisoner in Romania. Then, at Kolya's suggestion, she'd run the plot of *Pride and Prejudice* through her mind to distract herself until she'd fallen asleep.

But Jane Austen novels were essentially romance novels. And Jane Austen heroines eventually wound up with the hero, no matter how improbable the match.

She was contemplating whether to break up with the hero.

So not Jane Austen.

She tried focusing on a recent case she'd tried. But that was no more useful in putting her to sleep than the plot of a Jane

Austen novel. Different reasons. She started thinking of the arguments she'd made, how she could have improved her points, what she would do if it went up on appeal.

Stop.

She turned her mind to music. That was Kolya's trick. After his capture and torture in Romania, when he'd been unable to sleep from pain or fear, he'd run variations of jazz tunes though his mind, mentally improvising on the melodies of "Satin Doll" or "Someday My Prince Will Come." But she wasn't the musician he was. She was an intermediate level pianist, and while she loved music and enjoyed playing, she couldn't remember notes and chord changes enough to improvise without the physical presence of a keyboard.

Anyway, music just reminded her of Kolya.

After an hour, she sighed and gave up.

Slipping from the bed quietly so as not to wake Kolya, she grabbed her phone from the night table and wandered into the apartment's living room.

After settling on the couch, she checked email and texts. A few work emails that she dealt with quickly. She deleted junk emails. Too many of those. Then there were the more difficult emails. One from the florist, confirming the time that she'd be arriving with the arrangements. A message from the venue confirming that they would set up the chuppah at the end of the rose gardens and in front of the two hundred card chairs. One from her brother asking her to confirm that not only would his family's meals be kosher, but that the wedding cake would be as well. She sighed. They weren't planning a wedding cake, but she didn't want to explain that to her brother. One from a cousin who wanted to know if it was too late to accept the wedding invitation.

She clicked out of email. No point in replying to any of them when she wasn't sure there would be a wedding.

But the emails reminded her that if she cancelled the wedding, it would be a major pain in the ass. All the people she'd have to contact. All the arrangements she'd have to undo.

That was apart from breaking Kolya's heart.

And her own.

Was she crazy to even think about breaking it off? Or had she been crazy to think it could work? She mentally listed all the differences that could lead to problems, but beyond such questions as her concern at the danger of his profession or whether they both wanted children or not, was the simple fact that his being with her could endanger him as long as he was an intelligence operative—and he wasn't ready to be anything else.

But they were so good together. They complemented each other. More than that. What was that stupid phrase from the movie: They completed each other.

But could his love for her get him killed?

Stop this. Go to bed. But she was even less likely to go to sleep.

She checked her texts. She had three new. Two were junk. The third was from Noah. His response to her message, asking him to take over Yael's case. *Sure. Want to meet for coffee before you leave and you can fill me in on anything I might need to know?*

Alex tapped a message back, relieved that as much as she opposed what Yael was involved in, Yael would not be left without an attorney. *Would love to but leaving really early. Call me tomorrow night.* She knew not to disclose her location or how she'd be traveling. But what harm could there be in letting Noah know that she was leaving on the early side? At least that was one thing off her mind.

* * *

If they were driving, they would have left already. Or so Victor figured. No reason to wait until morning. So, they had to be taking Amtrak or a plane. If they were taking a plane, the odds were good they would fly out of Newark. The most efficient way to get to the Newark airport from Manhattan was by train.

Either way, Penn Station was a logical place to lay a trap for Kolya Petrov and Alexandria Feinstein.

Sometime early.

What did "really early" really mean?

Victor wasn't sure, but the earliest plane for Washington, DC didn't take off until 6:00 a.m. The earliest Amtrak left after 4:00 a.m.—which made the most sense. If he and some of his people were there by 3:00 a.m., it should be early enough.

It was only around eleven o'clock. Enough time for him to catch a few hours sleep, which he'd need to function at full capacity. He could find a corner somewhere in Penn Station to doze off. Enough time to get half a dozen of his supporters from Brooklyn to Penn Station.

But not enough time to retrieve Brody and Yael's baby.

The text from Alexandria Feinstein had come in while they were in the car, driving towards the East Side of Manhattan and the address of the possible foster mother. Brody drove. Victor was in the front passenger seat. Yael sat behind Brody.

"Turn around," Victor said.

"Why?" Brody asked.

Victor explained. Then he expanded. "The new American revolution is the important thing. We need to know what *they* know—so we can anticipate and counter. Most importantly, we need to know if they've found the locations of the bunkers. That's why Petrov is important. He'll know what *they* know. And if he doesn't cooperate, he'll still serve the cause with his death when we blow up the Brooklyn Bridge."

Having Petrov join, though, would be the most useful

outcome for the struggle ahead. Victor needed information, and having someone inside the intelligence community while the battles raged outside would be critical. Even if he was a Jew.

And he hoped he could turn Petrov. He'd turned others who had less reason than Petrov, who had been betrayed by his own agency, just as Victor had been. Petrov should be willing to join in the movement. Especially with his fiancée as leverage. Assuming the engagement wasn't fake.

And if he couldn't be turned, Petrov would still be important.

"But Lyra needs me," Yael protested. "Brody. Our baby needs us. We have time to get her. Even if we need to be at Penn Station that early."

"Once the bridge blows," Brody said to Victor, "it'll be harder to get Lyra. They might even use her as leverage against us. We have the address of the foster mom. It won't take long."

"We have the address of someone who might be the foster mom. But we don't know for sure. Your baby might not even be there. And every operation comes with risk of exposure. Of capture. We'd have to break into the building and force our way into the apartment. We could be risking the movement for nothing."

"We just risked it going after that lawyer," Yael said.

"Not as big a risk in a commercial building after hours. Especially after eliminating him as a witness. And we needed his information about Petrov. As for the baby, she isn't an essential part of the first attack. Anyway, there isn't time."

"We've got four hours," Brody said.

This was the problem with young people. Always pushing the limits. "I'm going to camp out for a few hours in Penn Station and nap so I can be sharp going after Petrov. He's good, from what Howard said. From what YOU said, Brody. I need you to be your best. We can try to find your baby afterward."

There was a moment of silence.

"You go, then," Yael said. "Drop me off. I'll get Lyra."

"She's my baby too," Brody said. "We'll do it together. Tomorrow."

"Tonight. Getting her tonight. Before anyone finds the lawyer's body."

"They're not going to connect the lawyer's death to you," Victor said.

"Maybe not. But maybe. Alex was working out of his office. What if they move Lyra tomorrow because of what happened? I'm doing it tonight. Besides, in the day, it'd be harder to get in and out without someone seeing us and calling the police."

"That makes sense, Yael. Victor, you've got six other guys coming from Brooklyn," Brody said. "I'll go with Yael. And she's right that it might be easier to get in and out in the middle of the night. We should be able to do this quickly, and I can still get to Penn Station on time."

Victor hesitated. He knew all the things that could go wrong with an attempt to take the baby. He wanted Brody with him and at his best.

And Victor had never seen Petrov. Brody had. Brody could identify him. On the other hand, Petrov had seen Brody. Victor assumed that his own photograph had circulated among those hunting him, but he'd changed his appearance since he'd left the CIA. Given the beard, the glasses, the shaved head, and the lost weight, he was not likely to be recognized. However, Petrov might spot Brody, which would give him a chance to evade capture. So maybe it would be better not to have Brody with him anyway.

Also—he had another thought about the baby. She could also be a useful prop. Maybe letting them collect their child might serve the revolution after all.

One complication. "Do either of you have a picture of Petrov?"

Brody shook his head.

"Not of Petrov, but I have a picture of Alex and me on my phone," Yael said. "It's from years ago, when we were in our early twenties, but she hasn't changed much."

"That'll work. Send it to me. Then drop me off and go. Meet me at the headquarters in Brooklyn."

Chapter Thirty-Six

After his phone woke him, Kolya rolled out of bed, noting Alex's absence with concern. He padded barefoot into the living room, where he saw her form curled on the sofa. *Let her sleep for a few more minutes.* He showered and quickly dressed in jeans and a T-shirt before returning to where Alex was dozing. He said her name and then touched her shoulder. She woke with a start.

"The bed would have been more comfortable." He took her hand and kissed it.

"Couldn't sleep. Or thought I couldn't—but I guess I must have dozed off for a bit." She stood and stretched. "Make the coffee while I grab a shower."

They drank coffee and ate toast, while Alex scrolled on her phone and announced the headlines of the day. Nothing that Kolya considered important to the present situation would be in the paper, although the various posturings of the more extreme political figures running for election in November worried him —if they were voted into office. Especially Lenny Rhodes, the one running for president.

He'd served presidents of both parties and would continue

to do so as long as he remained in his current job, whatever his personal political views might be. But his loyalty was to the principles that underlay the country, not to any individual. And that could be an issue if the wrong person occupied the office of president. Which he could see happening.

He was Russian, after all, and he tended to have a dark view of politics.

Still, he had more immediate worries.

Neither of them spoke a word about the previous night's conversation. No mention of his quitting the ECA. Nor of Alex's concern that maybe they shouldn't be together.

If she wasn't going to bring it up, he wasn't going to either. If they didn't talk about it, maybe she'd just let the thought go.

Although the dark circles under her eyes were clear evidence to the contrary.

So maybe talk about the other stressful matters of the moment.

"You didn't let Yael know that we were leaving, did you?"

"Oh please, Kolya. I'm not an idiot."

"Didn't mean to suggest you were. Sorry."

She gave him a tired smile. "I know. I did tell Noah that we're leaving and ask him to take over her case. Didn't tell him how we're traveling."

Kolya would have preferred that Alex wait until they were back in DC before contacting Noah, but she hadn't communicated anything that was likely to pose a security risk. Knowing that Yael's case would be covered would be important to her. And he didn't want to start a fight. Not now. Not with her wavering on their relationship. "Okay."

"Any word on Teo's condition?"

He shook his head. "Elizabeth did text that he was out of surgery, but that's it."

They finished breakfast, packed toiletries and dirty laundry, and then they were ready to go. He slung his duffle bag and computer bag over his shoulder and then took the handle of her suitcase to wheel it into the hall.

Normally she would have objected to his doing so—insisting that she could wheel her own suitcase. But this time she didn't. She let him. Which he took as a bad sign.

* * *

Penn Station at 4:20 a.m. was not as deserted as Kolya would have expected. There were the homeless, of course, and a few police officers. Most of the shops were closed. A donut shop was open, and they stopped to pick up two coffees. Alex, who normally avoided sweets, selected a cream donut for a snack later. He chose a simple glazed. Then they headed for the Amtrak waiting area where a heavyset woman glanced at their tickets before waving them into the cordoned off enclosure—where maybe fifty passengers were passing the time until boarding began for the 4:50 a.m. train.

The station had changed in the almost two years since the October when he'd narrowly managed to avoid an ambush at Penn Station—only to walk into one a few hours later in lower Manhattan.

Because his boss had leaked where he was going to a mole. Because his boss had wanted him to be captured so he would feed false information to a Romanian far-right terrorist.

He pushed the thought away.

They found two seats near a corner of the area. Alex pulled out her phone, tired as she was, and started to read a brief that one of her partners had sent her. While she read, Kolya scanned the people in the enclosure.

Many, like Alex, were on their phones. One older woman read a paperback. Several people slept, sprawled back in their chairs. One middle-aged man snored loudly. But there were a few men, maybe six, who were neither reading nor sleeping.

They were, like Kolya, evaluating the other passengers in the waiting enclosure, but unlike Kolya, were trying not to be obvious, their gazes moving from person to person, then down again at their phones, almost as if they were comparing the image of individual live people to a photograph.

None of them were familiar, but Victor Forest had a lot of followers.

"*Yob tvoyu mat.*" Kolya spoke the curse words softly. He had another vision of Penn Station almost two years earlier, of men following him. He took a deep breath, let it out, counting to ten, then he was back. Good. Not the time for a flashback.

Alex looked up from her own phone at his words. As she did, one of the men scanning the room fixated on her.

"What is it?" she asked.

"We need to get out of here."

She nodded. "Suitcase?"

"Leave it."

She stood, tucked the phone into her jeans, swung her purse over her shoulder, and still carrying the large coffee, strode towards the exit. He left his computer, any attempt to access it would wipe it, and then caught up to her.

Seven men followed.

Chapter Thirty-Seven

It was a large apartment building in the East Twenties. An older building. Yael figured it was from sometime in the last century. No doorman, which meant that people either used a code to get in or they were buzzed in by a resident. And that made it easier. The thing about large apartment buildings in New York City was that no matter the hour, someone in some apartment would always be getting takeout delivered from somewhere.

Yael knew that all they had to do was wait, lurking in the shadows across the street. And it didn't take long. Twenty minutes after they arrived, a man pedaled a bicycle to the door, locked it to a rail, and took a brown paper bag from a basket in front of the handlebars.

Yael and Brody crossed the street as the cyclist texted someone upstairs to open the door, then they rushed forward as the door opened. The delivery guy—short, dark-haired, dark-skinned, maybe Hispanic, maybe from some Arab country—didn't seem bothered as they pushed through after him, but then it was New York. People did stuff like this.

They didn't bother him as he pushed the button for the

elevator, but they took the stairs. He wouldn't remember them. And they only had to climb two flights to the third floor.

Of greater concern were the cameras—scanning the lobby and the outside of the building. But that's why they had worn hoodies, Yankee baseball caps, and medical masks—as if they were worried about some phantom virus—concealing most of their faces. Not enough visible to identify them—if it would even matter after the revolution began.

Yael believed in the revolution, believed that the government had taken too much power and that the people had to take it back. The government, after all, had taken her baby. But once she had Lyra again, she would be okay with letting Victor and Brody fight. She just wanted to get her baby and go hide somewhere while the men fought it out.

Losing Lyra had almost destroyed her. She was a mother and that was more important than anything else.

When they reached the door marked as "3C"—the apartment number that had been in the lawyer's phone—the image of Noah when Victor shot him rose in her mind, and she felt a surge of nausea. Noah had offered to help her. She didn't like what Victor did, not the torture, not the killing. But it wasn't her place to say anything. She wasn't in charge. Whatever Brody and Victor thought was necessary, she'd have to accept.

Anyway, getting her baby was what mattered.

She quickly stripped off the hoodie, cap, and the mask. Brody stepped to the side of the door so that only she would be visible through the peephole.

The hoodie gone, Yael wore a nice T-shirt and a pair of dress jeans. For an extra touch, she put on a pair of glasses. Clear glass, but glasses made one look intellectual. Trustworthy.

Steady. You can do this.

She pounded on the door and shouted. "Fire. You have to get out."

There was no response.

She pounded again. "Fire."

She heard it then, the sound of someone on the other side of the door. Someone looking through the peephole. A hesitant voice. "Who are you?"

"Maria Locke." Yael used a name she'd seen on the mailbox of an apartment on the seventh floor, counting on the fact that New Yorkers didn't know their neighbors.

"I've seen your name." The voice was still hesitant. "I don't smell smoke."

"It's not smoky here because it started on the fifth floor. Everyone else on this floor already got out." Yael tried to make her voice both soothing and urgent. "You need to get out too. Quickly."

"The fire department?"

How thick could the woman be? "You're Kristen, right? Kristen Temple?"

"Yes. That's me."

"The fire department is on its way. One of your neighbors told me that you were home, and you have a baby. You can't afford to wait, Kristen. The elevator's not working. For the baby's sake."

"Okay. Okay. I hear you." The sound of bolts unlocking. "Can you help me? I'm here alone."

"Of course."

"Thank you, Maria. You're a good person. Thank you."

Another sound, the faint wail of a baby.

I'm coming sweetheart.

The door opened, revealing a middle-aged woman in a red bathrobe, with frightened eyes. Yael stepped inside. And Brody followed behind her.

Chapter Thirty-Eight

Seven men. He'd only spotted six in the waiting room. So was the seventh man the leader, Victor Forest? Kolya discarded the thought—because it didn't matter. What mattered was evading them—and protecting Alex. Which might be contradictory goals.

They were in the large rotunda of Penn Station, the majority of the shops—newsstands, fast food offerings—still closed, with only the donut shop offering a haven for the hungry and caffeine-deprived. It was still early, maybe twenty to five. A few more people were headed towards the waiting areas. But not many. Not yet. In an hour, commuters would begin to trail in. For now, it felt as if they were alone in the space—he and Alex and the seven men maybe twenty feet behind and closing.

He caught sight of a police officer, lingering near the one open shop—a cup of coffee in one hand, a donut in the other. But one coffee-drinking officer would be a liability rather than a help against seven armed men. By the time he radioed for backup, the cop would be dead. It would be another life that Kolya would have to try to protect. Victor Forest would be more than happy to kill a police officer whom he would regard as a representative of the illegal government he opposed.

Do not approach the officer.

He felt the weight of the gun that he wore on his hip, under the loose T-shirt, his HK .40, loaded with thirteen rounds, with three extra magazines secured on the holster and in his pockets—the small plastic gun he'd carried into the parental visitation strapped to his ankle was only good for close personal defense. But being armed was small comfort. He couldn't engage in a gunfight here, in this public space. There was no cover for him or for Alex. And innocent people could wind up dead.

The unwanted mental image of the gunfight that had proceeded his capture and kidnapping nearly two years earlier intruded. With an effort, he pushed the image away.

Alex matched hm, stride for stride. "What now?" she asked.

"Faster, but don't run. Yet."

They picked up the pace, still walking. The men behind them also increased their speed. Far ahead of them were the exits to Eighth Avenue. Easier to lose the pursuers once Kolya and Alex got to the street.

Not if more men were waiting outside.

Anyway, the men were too close, and the exit just a little too far.

Closer than the exits—an escalator funneled passengers to the lower level of Penn Station to catch trains to New Jersey or Long Island. From the lower level, passengers would take another set of stairs to reach the trains. And with that thought, he had a plan. It wasn't much, but it was something.

"Down the escalator. Ahead of me. Fast as you can," he told Alex. "At the bottom run. Go down one of the staircases to a boarding platform. There are other stairs that lead back up to the main floor. Get out of Penn Station. I'll slow them down."

"Like hell. I'm not leaving you." Her voice was calm but determined.

"If this works, I'll be behind you."

"And if it doesn't?"

"It doesn't. But you getting away improves my odds of doing so as well." It was her argument to explain why they shouldn't be together. He hated using it, not wanting to give her more grounds to justify a breakup—but he hated more that she could be in danger because of him. "When you're clear, get rid of your phone. Sometimes they can be tracked even if off. If I'm not with you, I'll find you."

"How?"

"Through Noah's office. Leave a message for me with the receptionist."

"Fine. I know the drill." Her voice didn't sound quite as annoyed as he knew she was.

"Good." They reached the top of the escalator. "I love you. Now go."

"I love you, too. Don't do anything stupid, goddamn it."

"You either."

The men were approaching fast. Alex flipped the lid off the coffee that she still held, turned, and threw it. The hot liquid splashed in the face of the closest man, an older man who bore a resemblance to photos of Victor Forest. His hands flew to his face.

And Alex was off. She took the steps two at a time, and Kolya followed on her heels, ignoring the protests from his bad leg. Behind him, he heard a voice shouting orders to catch them. Then the scrambling of men on the escalator.

But they'd have to descend single file—or at most two abreast.

Alex reached the bottom of the escalator, and with a quick glance over her shoulder at Kolya, sped out of sight down the corridor past the still-closed food stands, towards the multiple staircases that led to Amtrak or New Jersey Transit train platforms.

He jumped the last three steps, landing with the bulk of his weight on his good leg, pulling his HK from his holster at the same time. He swung around, gun leveled. Seven men raced down towards him, crowding the escalator, the man who might be Forest, at the rear, face red from the hot coffee.

Kolya fired at the man in front, hitting him center mass. Then he shifted his aim and fired three more times at the men immediately behind the first man.

The first man, tall, a circle of dark hair surrounding a bald spot, fell backwards. But no blood so he was probably wearing a vest. Still the impact of a .40 caliber bullet on his chest would hurt—maybe break some ribs. The men immediately behind had frozen with the first shot, crouching down, and pulling out their own weapons, even as the escalator continued to carry them downward.

But Kolya was already running, pushing his injured leg.

That the man he'd shot had survived was not a big concern. The point hadn't been to kill him or all of them. It was unlikely Kolya'd be able to do so without being shot himself. Anyway, the last thing he wanted was a prolonged gunfight. The point had been to buy Alex and himself a few extra seconds, which he hoped would be enough time to escape.

He ran in the opposite direction from where Alex had headed, towards the subway lines. With luck, they'd all follow him, which would allow Alex to reach safety.

Five did.

Chapter Thirty-Nine

Alex hurtled down the stairs of platform four towards the track where an Amtrak train would be pulling in any moment. Once down, she stopped to catch her breath and glance around. No one on the platform yet. No pursuers. Hopefully, Kolya's delaying tactic had prevented them from seeing which stairwell she'd descended.

No sign of Kolya either.

Despite his saying he'd be behind her, he must have run in a different direction. Of course. She should have expected that he'd try to lead the threat away from her. *Son of a bitch. He was doing it again. Being the protector. Putting himself at greater risk.* All because of her. Again. It was happening again. But the anger wasn't really aimed at him. It was aimed at herself—for not acting on what she knew—what she should have always known—about being with Kolya.

Not now.

She had a momentary respite, but she wasn't out of danger yet. Even if none of the men had followed her to the platform, they could still find her when she tried to leave the station. And she had to get out. She needed to get to safety and then contact Kolya. Whether their relationship had a future or not was not the issue. Getting them both out of this situation and out of New York was.

She walked down the platform, toward a staircase exit maybe five hundred feet away that would put her close to Seventh Avenue. She was still a little winded from the sprint to the train platform, and the slower pace allowed her to catch her breath. Just in case she needed speed to escape when she climbed back up to the main level. She knew, even if she'd evaded them so far, the men who'd chased her and Kolya could be up there, watching and waiting. *Reserve strength for an all-out sprint through the station and up the escalator to the street.* Once outside, she could lose herself in the maze of Manhattan.

For now, they weren't following her. It was a comforting thought.

The comfort was brief, lasting only until she heard footsteps behind her.

Heavy footsteps.

Not running, just as she wasn't running. Maybe he wasn't following her, but there had been no one on the platform when she'd descended. Who was it?

She resisted the urge to look.

Instead, she increased her speed. The footsteps behind did as well. One set or two sets of footsteps? She wasn't sure.

If the person or persons behind weren't following her, why increase speed?

Whoever it might be, he—or they—was gaining on her. She again pushed down the temptation to glance backward. It would slow her down. But she didn't need to look to know that one or two of the men who'd followed her and Kolya had to be behind her.

She could do this. She just needed to stay calm.

She broke into a run. Whoever was behind did so as well.

The thudding of heavy footsteps against the cement of the platform.

She felt the rumble of the ground and the sound of metal wheels on metal tracks announcing the imminent arrival of an Amtrak train, maybe the one that she and Kolya had planned to take back to Washington. Could she somehow maneuver to get on the train and hide?

No. There would be no hiding on the train.

Her best bet was still to get out of Penn Station. To get to the street. To do that, she needed to reach the staircase and climb, and it was still too far away. Maybe two hundred feet. Maybe less. And climbing would slow her down.

She pushed herself to run faster. One leg. Other leg. *Think of nothing but running.* But she wasn't a runner, and she wasn't certain she could keep up the pace until she reached the stairs.

One thing was certain—whoever was behind her was catching up.

She couldn't outrun them, but maybe—she could outmaneuver them.

She shot a quick glance backward then, not at whoever was chasing her, but at the bright light on the front of the oncoming locomotive.

It was also closing in. But it was still far back enough. Maybe.

Maybe not.

But it was the only idea that came to her.

She jumped down onto the train tracks. The landing jarred every muscle and joint, but she stayed on her feet. She took a second to collect herself, and then she ran again, still on the tracks.

She heard a thud behind her as a man jumped down. The conductor of the train saw them now, and the blast of the train's warning horn shook her.

She ran faster, still on the tracks.

Chapter Forty

Kolya's delay tactic at the escalator worked initially. The men took a few minutes to regroup, and even though they were still following, he had a head start, enough so that two years earlier, that would have been the end of the game. But that was before his right leg had been shattered under torture. Now, while he still could run, his bad leg slowed him down.

He pushed it anyway, knowing he was undoing months of physical therapy. Pain shot up his right leg with every stride.

If he could just make the entrance to the subway for the C line—if there were maybe a train...

If. If.

Kolya checked the reflection behind him in the glass of a closed kiosk. The five men were behind, but they were gaining, even if the fifth man lagged behind the other four. That there were only five was also disturbing. Had he put two men out of commission? Or were one or two of them after Alex?

She was fine. She had to be. He forced the thought of Alex out of his mind and concentrated on running.

Deep breaths. Ignore the pain.

The lower corridor was not completely deserted. Huddled against the walls, surrounded by shopping bags, a few homeless people slept or watched the show. Maybe half a dozen people in twenty-foot intervals.

They knew to stay out of the way, which minimized the risk of any innocents getting hurt—if it came to a shoot-out.

Kolya also wondered whether the cop with the coffee and the donut had heard the shots at the elevator and had called for backup. If so, help would be arriving soon.

Maybe not soon enough.

The fucking leg was threatening to collapse. The men behind him were closing in. He wasn't getting away from them, and if he couldn't outrun them, he'd have to confront them. Five against one were not good odds. Still, he was not going to be taken prisoner by far-right fanatics. Not after Romania.

Better to go down fighting.

He hoped that Alex at least had managed to reach safety.

As he ran, he pulled his gun for a second time from his holster and then abruptly stopped and swung around, holding the gun level with two hands. With luck, he'd take a couple of them with him.

But he didn't shoot.

The men following him had skidded to a stop, their own guns pointed at him. Four of them anyway. The fifth, the man who'd been splashed with the coffee and who'd trailed behind, also had a gun but was pointing it, not at Kolya, but at the head of one of the homeless who had lined the halls, an older woman wearing two sweaters and a scarf. She turned terrified eyes towards Kolya.

"If you shoot," the man said. "I will too. Drop your gun."

"No thanks."

"Then I'll shoot her."

"And I'll shoot as well."

"There're more of us. You'll be dead."

"Probably. But I might take one or two of your thugs with me, Forest. Maybe even you. This time, I'll go for head shots."

A gleam of teeth on the coffee-burned face. "You know who I am, then."

"I do now."

"I don't want you dead, Petrov. If you drop your weapon, you won't be hurt." The man held the old woman firmly by the collar of one of her sweaters. "And I'll let her go. It's a fair offer."

"Counteroffer. How about we all just wait for the police? They'll be here soon."

His words brought a short bark of laughter. "You got balls, Petrov, I gotta give you that. But here's the thing: You may not care if I shoot the hag here, so time to up the stakes." The old woman muttered something in protest. Forest ignored it and continued. "I bet you'll care if a lot of people die from a nerve poison. I assume you know that VX was stored in those bunkers your alien government hid, and that I found those bunkers. I have a bottle of it on me. And how many commuters will be surging through here in another hour, do you think?"

Kolya felt a chill. "You're bluffing. You wouldn't be carrying something that deadly."

"You're willing to risk killing hundreds or thousands of people? And, yes, I would carry it. Because I'm a little crazy, as I'm sure your superiors have told you." Forest showed teeth again. Releasing his grip, he shoved the old woman against the wall. She slumped to the ground. Then, still holding the gun with his right hand, he jabbed his left hand into his jacket pocket and removed a small glass jar. "Want to find out? Go ahead and shoot me. It's glass. I drop it, it'll break."

The bottle looked old. Still, the odds were good it was a bluff. Would Forest have been chasing Kolya with a bottle of

VX in his pocket? Wouldn't he have used that card immediately when Kolya confronted him?

Probably. But still there was a chance it wasn't a bluff. Because Forest was a fanatic and as he stated, a little crazy. And, as the explosion in Brooklyn had demonstrated, Forest had access to the contents of the secret bunkers, which included VX, and he didn't give a shit about killing innocent people.

VX was deadly stuff. Breathing it in, just touching it, could be fatal. And while Penn Station was relatively deserted now, time was ticking. People would soon be racing through the corridors on their way to jobs, to trains. Shopkeepers would be opening their doors to customers. Soon there could be thousands of people traversing this corridor.

Was there a chance that Alex would come through this corridor, looking for him?

He had to assume it wasn't a bluff.

"Stalemate then. You leave, and I won't shoot."

Forest shook his head. "Not a stalemate. Checkmate. You surrender or I'll drop it. If the police arrive, I'll drop it."

"If it's VX and the glass breaks, you'll die first. And your men."

"We'll be dead, but the revolution will go on. And the complacent sheep who'll be killed with us—well, they should have rebelled against the overlords. You have ten seconds to drop your gun."

It was a high stakes game of chicken. Whether the bottle contained VX or not, Kolya would be dead either way. If he surrendered, he would be killed, probably slowly and painfully. If he didn't surrender, he'd still die. If it wasn't VX, he'd be shot by Forest or his men. If it was VX, Kolya would die, but a lot of other people would die as well.

Including maybe Alex.

Was an easier death for him worth the risk to others? Kolya lowered the gun and let it drop.

Chapter Forty-One

The rumble of the approaching train, the squeal of the brakes on steel combined with the blast of the warning horn. The cacophony was so loud that Alex couldn't hear the man or men running behind her on the tracks. She knew he or they were there, just as she knew the train was gaining on her and wouldn't stop in time.

She glanced over her shoulder as she ran.

There was one man on the track behind her. The train had almost reached him, but he wasn't looking behind him, intent on catching her.

The train let out another blast of its horn.

She jumped again, this time onto the tracks running parallel to the track where the train had been bearing down on her, turning as she did so. The man behind her tried to follow, but his timing was off. He leapt, and the train caught him in midair. She heard the scream as the train hit him, and then he disappeared under it.

She turned again, and resumed her run, this time racing the train, seeing the shocked faces of passengers staring out the window at her. There was an acrid smell that resembled smoke but wasn't. More screeching of the wheels as the train slowed further. Then she was faster than the train, outpacing it, but not by much, using the train for cover, not wanting to be seen by anyone still on the platform.

She assumed that there had been a second man, someone who'd stayed on the platform when she and her pursuer had leaped onto the tracks. If so, he could still come after her. *Stay out of the line of sight for as long as possible.*

She also knew that police would be swarming down the stairs any minute.

She had to get out of Penn Station to find Kolya—to know whether he was okay—or in trouble. If he'd been taken, she was the only one who'd know—the only one who could get him help.

The train finally shuddered to a halt. She continued to run.

She crossed the tracks again, this time in front of the now motionless train, as voices shouted at her to stop. She ignored the calls. No one chased her. No one was close enough to intercept her.

Then she was at the stairs, and she sprinted up two levels to the hall that she and Kolya had entered less than an hour earlier.

After reaching the main hall, she slowed to a walk, to be less conspicuous and to catch her breath. A quick smooth of her hair, which she wore long and loose. A glance down at her clothes, grateful that she'd decided to travel in comfort, in running shoes, jeans and a dark T-shirt. The light blue cardigan she was wearing, though, was a little more distinctive and might identify her. She dropped it in a garbage can.

Minutes later, police rushed past her, responding to the emergency of a person run over by a train. While their presence might ensure her safety, she needed to avoid being detained. Finding Kolya was the first priority. Then there was the problem of the questioning that would inevitably follow detention—questions that, given Kolya's profession, would be awkward to say the least. She, like Kolya, was bound to the secrecy that his job demanded—which meant that she couldn't identify the dead man as a member of a sovereign nation group that was planning an attack. She could make up some fiction, but lying to the police was an offense in itself. Once she knew he was safe, the two of them could deal with any necessary complications with the New York authorities.

She ignored the police and was relieved that none of them gave her a second glance. They headed towards Track Four. She headed towards the exit.

She reached the escalator to Seventh Avenue. A quick glance around assured her that she was not being followed. Minutes later she was out of the station and onto the street. As she crossed against the light, dodging traffic, hearing the blare of horns from impatient drivers and the squeal of car brakes, she remembered Kolya's warning: *Get rid of your phone.* Just before she reached the east side of Seventh Avenue, she tossed her iPhone under the wheels of a *New York Times* truck.

* * *

A small store on Thirty-Second Street just off Seventh offered hot coffee, packaged pastries, magazines, newspapers, and burner phones. It also offered a refuge from the too-empty streets, where she felt dangerously conspicuous. Alex bought a cup of coffee to replace the one she'd tossed on her pursuers and a sad-looking lemon Danish. The rush of adrenaline had subsided, and she felt the exhaustion from the letdown, her poor night's sleep, and her desperate dash to escape. Three stools and a counter in the back of the store provided a haven of sorts, and she perched on a stool as she downed the luke-warm coffee and the Danish, which tasted even worse than it looked. She bought a second cup of coffee and two newspapers, and returned to her stool, thumbing through the pages while letting the caffeine and sugar do the job of reviving her. The longer she lingered, the more pedestrians would be on the street. The more people on the sidewalks, the safer she would be.

At 6:30 a.m., with the increased bustle of pedestrians on the street, she was ready to leave. She purchased a burner flip phone and left the store.

She'd try to contact Kolya through Noah's office, as Kolya had suggested, and if he hadn't reached out to Noah yet, she'd call Jonathan or Elizabeth. But without her iPhone, she didn't have their numbers. She was untethered to the electronics that had taken over life in America.

But her data was backed up in the cloud. All she needed was access to a computer. Of course, gaining access to a phone or computer was a challenge in itself. Internet cafes were a thing of the past. And she couldn't just borrow a stranger's device.

Stupid. She didn't need an internet cafe. The simple solution was to walk to Noah's office, only a few blocks away.

Going there might be a risk—Yael knew the address—but Alex didn't have any other ideas.

And maybe—just maybe—Kolya would have already contacted the receptionist—or even would be waiting for her. If not, Noah had a laptop, and the receptionist had a desktop. She could use one of them.

She walked two blocks down Sixth Avenue to Thirtieth Street and then turned right. She periodically glanced over her shoulder. No sign of any of the men who'd been following her and Kolya.

No sign of Kolya either.

Foot traffic had picked up enough that she blended in. She increased her speed, propelled by worry for Kolya and fear for her own safety. She had spotted no one trailing her, but then she'd thought she'd gotten away earlier when she'd descended to the train platform, and she'd been wrong.

A small voice in her head suggested that if she had already broken up with Kolya, she wouldn't be in this situation. A louder voice retorted that Kolya was the one in greatest danger. Because of her.

She told both voices to shut up.

On Tenth Avenue, she turned right, and her pace slowed. There were four police cars in front of the entrance to Noah's office. Her heart rate increased, and she hesitated.

But it was unlikely that police had identified her as the woman who'd been running on the train tracks. And even if they had, how could they possibly have known that she'd show up here? No, there had to be some other reason for the police presence.

And in any event, if Victor Forest or his thugs showed up now, the police would be on her side.

She strode forward.

Chapter Forty-Two

Lyra had lost weight but not as much as Yael had feared. Her cheeks weren't quite as plump as they'd been before Barbara O'Brien—that terrible woman—had snatched her baby away. Yael had also worried that if Lyra had started on a bottle, she might reject the breast. But Lyra latched onto the nipple like a champ, as if she'd never been separated from her mother. Her little hand entwined around Yael's finger as she nursed, the two of them cuddling together on one of the many cots in a room that had once been offices.

"She knows me." Yael smiled down at her baby.

"Of course, she does." Brody paused his pacing. He was unable to sit still, even though they were safe in the Brooklyn warehouse that served as American Gold Posse's New York headquarters. About a dozen armed men were in various positions around the warehouse, upstairs and down, awaiting Victor's return and his new orders.

The revolution was about to begin.

The men were on edge. So was Yael—because when Victor returned, he'd be bringing Alex, who had once been her best friend, along with Alex's fiancé. Yael told herself that she didn't feel bad about what might happen to either of them. After all, she'd asked Alex to help her, and Alex had betrayed her trust by bringing in her fiancé, who just wanted to trap Brody and Victor. If anything bad happened to Alex, it was on Alex.

Yael had nothing to feel guilty about.

Nothing.

She just didn't want to have to speak to Alex. Or see her. Even if Alex had tried to get Yael's baby back and not charged her anything to do so. Yael also didn't want to speak to or see the fiancé—what was his name—Kolya—even if he'd stopped Brody from hurting her.

Brody wouldn't have hurt her. He'd been angry and maybe a little out of control, but he wouldn't have hurt her. Or Lyra.

She didn't think he would have.

She hoped he wouldn't have.

And anyway, Alex hadn't succeeded in getting the court to send Lyra home.

So neither Alex nor Kolya had really done anything for her or for her baby. What happened to them was not her business.

Even if it was her husband doing bad things.

Yael's main concern was whether she had enough baby supplies. They'd bought some diapers and wipes, grabbed a few more diapers and some clothes when they took Lyra from Kristen's apartment, but more baby items would be needed. Soon, if not immediately.

"Do you think Lyra saw what happened to Kristen?" she asked Brody on his next pause to touch the baby's head.

"She's only four months. She wouldn't understand even if she did see it."

She hesitated before saying what she thought, but Brody wouldn't turn on her, even if she disapproved of his actions. "You shouldn't have shot Kristen."

"I did what needed to be done."

Yael wondered—how much did a four-month-old baby actually understand? Brody'd used a silencer, so the gunshot hadn't been loud, but Lyra had still cried.

Maybe because Lyra could sense that Yael had been upset over the second person she'd seen die in the past day.

"Still. Kristen did take care of Lyra for almost a week." Good care, too, from what Yael could see. Except for the loss of weight, which was understandable for a baby who'd had to learn to take a bottle. Lyra's room had been beautifully furnished, her clothes immaculate, clean baby bottles standing on a table, ready to be used. "I feel," she hesitated again but plunged on, "a little bad about her."

"No reason to feel bad. She was part of the false government that stole our child. She would have told them that we took Lyra —and they'd be hunting for us."

"I thought—with the revolution starting—they'd have other things to worry about."

"This was safer, and she deserved it for trying to steal our child. And you need to stop questioning me. Your job is to support me and my decisions."

"Yes, of course. I was out of line. Sorry."

But there was still that image in Yael's mind. And the concern that Lyra also had the same image. But she couldn't do anything about either, so she curled on her side, holding Lyra close, and drifted off to sleep.

Chapter Forty-Three

To mentally survive while being held captive required detaching from the reality of what was presently happening and the fear of what would happen. There were two ways to do it. First technique: Concentrate on something that engaged the mind but not the emotions. Some might play mental chess. Others might solve math problems. Kolya's preference was to picture his hands on piano keys playing variations of jazz tunes. But from unpleasant experience, he knew that method worked best when captors left him alone. Then there was the other option. Detach oneself by focusing on sight, sound, and smell. It was similar to the grounding method of dealing with PTSD to which he still occasionally resorted. In the two years since Romania, Kolya had become very good at it.

Even if he hated that it was necessary.

Both methods required that he banish any thought of Alex.

In the moments immediately after his surrender at Penn Station, he turned to grounding.

He began the process as four men surrounded him, focusing on the two men holding his arms as they hustled him towards the Eighth Avenue exit. The one holding his right arm had drooping eyes as if he hadn't slept well, and several cuts on his chin from careless shaving. The one on his left smelled of garlic and had a smudge that looked like spaghetti sauce on his shirt. The man in front of Kolya had a left leg longer than his right. The man behind him clicked his teeth.

And off to the side, Victor Forest prominently displayed the jar that might or might not contain VX.

Kolya obeyed the hissed orders from Forest, remaining silent, as the five of them climbed up the stairs to reach the sidewalk. A few early commuters passed—going down as the six of them ascended—none of the commuters even glancing in Kolya's direction. It was New York. Everyone minded their own business.

He noted the appearance of the people passing and guessed at their occupations: Maybe a lawyer; maybe a nurse; maybe a construction worker, maybe a salesclerk. And maybe not.

They passed him and Victor Forest without the slightest idea of the threat that was so close. Which was as it should be. Whether the VX threat was real or not, anyone noticing Kolya or his captors would be in danger.

Outside, the sky had lightened ahead of the sunrise that was still maybe half an hour away. A white Ford Transit with the insignia "White's Plumbing" pulled up to the curb. Forest pulled open a side door, and Kolya was pushed inside.

Victor Forest was the last to enter the van, still clutching the jar that might contain a deadly nerve poison.

The back of the cargo van was fitted with three long benches, one on each side, and one running down the middle. The benches were equipped with old-style seat belts, and each bench held four seat belts. Kolya sat against the van wall, the man with garlic breath on one side, the man who'd clicked his teeth on the other. Victor and two others sat opposite him on the middle bench.

Kolya's wrists were zip-tied behind his back, tight enough that he couldn't squeeze his hands through, but not enough to constrict circulation.

The restraints triggered a flashback of Romania, of being cuffed and then tortured, and the panic began to rise. He fought it down with the techniques he knew too well. *Focus on details. The feel of the van wall against his hands. The smell of the men around him. The sound of car horns and the rush of tires outside.* He took a deep breath and let it out, counting to ten.

Then again. And again.

The panic receded.

Garlic Breath patted him down and removed the small plastic gun on Kolya's ankle. A seat belt was snapped around his waist.

"Seat belts? You obey seat belt laws issued by the illegitimate government?" Kolya leaned back against the wall of the van, resting on his shoulders and arms. It was mildly uncomfortable.

Victor fastened his own belt after setting the jar down on the bench. "I'm not obeying anything. New York traffic is crazy. Don't want anyone in here breaking something because the van has to make a sudden stop."

"Considerate."

Forest picked up on the sarcasm in Kolya's voice. "Speaking of which—let me know if the zip tie hurts. I can't leave your hands free, but there's no need to make you too uncomfortable. After all, we have a lot in common, me and you." Forest's tone was friendly, warm.

"Not really. I'm not crazy."

"Really? I think you are, and you just don't realize it."

Whether he was completely sane was a question that occurred to Kolya from time to time, given his decision to stay in the game, even after what had happened to him. It was not something he cared to discuss with Victor Forest. "Did you kidnap me to discuss my mental health?"

"Among other things. But later. When you and I can have some time alone." Forest had left the jar that maybe contained VX on the bench, between himself and the man with the longer left leg.

Garlic Breath to Kolya's right shifted uncomfortably. "That thing could fall from there and break."

"We're not moving yet," Forest said.

"Still. What if some taxi rams us?"

"Or you knock into it accidentally." Drooping Eye Guy with the shaving cuts also weighed in. "Or one of us does."

"I suppose you're right. I'll put it away." Forest slid it back into his jacket pocket.

So, judging by the nervousness of Forest's thugs, the jar did contain VX.

Somehow that made Kolya feel—not relief—but at least justified in his decision to surrender. There was some tiny bit of comfort in knowing that whatever he might have to face—he'd spared others a horrific death.

For now.

Unless Forest had lied to his own people, which was also possible.

The other comfort—that Alex had escaped—was muted by uncertainty. He had to believe that she was safe—that she'd gotten out of Penn Station, contacted Noah and then Jonathan, and that she was on her way back to Washington. But he didn't know for sure, and the odds were good that he never would.

"Maybe somewhere more secure than your pocket?" Garlic Breath asked.

"I have to keep it on me. Otherwise, Mr. Petrov here might get ideas." He glanced at Kolya.

"He can't do anything. He's handcuffed and strapped in."

Forest rolled his eyes. "Yeah. So? There was this guy who was being transported to a gulag in Siberia. In chains. In a secure prison van. Managed to get loose and kill all his guards."

"Damn," Drooping Eye Guy said. "He got away?"

"No, he died. But he killed eight armed men first. And that's exactly the kind of thing someone like Petrov would do." He turned his gaze on Kolya. "And I know what you're thinking. That if you free yourself and attack me and the bottle breaks in here, the damage will be contained. You'll die, along with all of us, but like I said, you're probably willing to do it. But will it just be us? VX doesn't evaporate. Sooner or later, someone will open the van door. A cop. Some kid. A middle-aged taxi driver. And once the door opens, VX fumes and even the liquid could pour out onto the street. How many people might be affected? So think hard before trying anything heroic or stupid."

Kolya had already considered the possibility—and discarded it. Even if he could have freed his hands. For the very reasons Forest outlined.

There was a long silence. Forest checked his phone. The other men alternated watching Forest and watching Kolya.

He decided to switch detachment techniques. He mentally retrieved an Ellis Marsalis tune that he'd recently learned. "Twelve's It." Key of A minor. He heard the opening notes on the piano, pictured how he'd place his hands on the keys.

The driver glanced over his shoulder. "I can stay here for a while, but not forever. How long?"

"Ten—fifteen minutes." Forest tapped something on his phone. "Leave no one behind. That's the rule. Unless they're dead."

The music faded.

They were waiting for the last two men in Forest's posse— the two men who had followed Alex.

Kolya could hear a new sound, the wail of sirens approaching. Multiple sirens. Police? He took a deep breath and let it out slowly, counting. It wasn't working any more than focusing on jazz had worked, but it was all he had. Another deep breath. More counting.

"We need to get out of here," Garlic Breath said.

Forest's phone buzzed. He read it out loud. "Two minutes."

Two minutes later the man whom Kolya had shot at the escalator entered the van. He looked in pain, pressing a hand against his chest. "Shit. I think I got half a dozen broken ribs." He glared at Kolya with hatred. "You motherfucker."

"You'll live, Tom. Stop whining. Carter? Alex Feinstein?" Forest demanded.

"Dead." Tom sat down heavily on the middle bench. "At least Carter for sure. Feinstein, probably. Crazy bitch jumped on the tracks. Carter went down after her—I was too far behind, and the train was coming. I saw the train hit him. Her too, I saw her disappear when the train pulled in. Crazy fucking bitch."

Chapter Forty-Four

Jonathan and Elizabeth had slept maybe five hours on hospital chairs. Jonathan had had worse nights: Years earlier he and Kolya had smuggled an informant out of Afghanistan, and neither of them had slept more than three hours a night for four days, but then he'd also been a few years younger, and while the middle thirties wasn't officially middle age, the lack of sleep was more troublesome than it had been in his late twenties.

But the least Jonathan could do for Teo was to be there. At least until they knew if he'd survived surgery.

Anyway, there wasn't anything much they could do at the moment to track Victor Forest and his American Gold Posse. The technical section of the ECA had been checking various video feeds online around the site of the bombing—so far nothing. The video feed of Yael and Brody's apartment was being monitored, but no one had come home since the previous evening. Which, given everything, was to be expected.

Jonathan had no clue as to where Forest might be or what he might be up to. But given the seriousness of the bombing in

Brooklyn, he'd put in a call to Margaret Bradford for more ECA agents.

They would be arriving sometime in the morning.

"You should call Kolya." Elizabeth hadn't spoken this many words since Kolya had stormed out the previous night.

Jonathan suspected that she shared Kolya's anger at being kept in the dark about the danger that Victor Forest posed—and the existence of the secret bunkers. But that was something to be discussed later. The immediate issue: Deal with the suggestion to call his friend. "Not now."

"Why not? Because you'd have to admit that you're an asshole?"

Jonathan contemplated whether the silent treatment was preferable to open hostilities. "Is that what *you* think? That I'm an asshole?"

"Yeah. I do. Even if I didn't walk out like Petrov."

At six in the morning, the waiting room still had a few people waiting, like Jonathan and Elizabeth, for word on someone's condition. No one was close enough to hear a conversation in normal tones—and, even if she was angry, Elizabeth was professional enough to keep her voice down.

And Jonathan could as well. "You're the one who always insists on following orders and protocol."

"Not always. I've broken the rules for a team member. On occasion. As you damn well know, because you were there breaking them with me. As you do all the time. But not this time. Kolya, Teo, and I are your colleagues and your friends, and that's not even counting whatever else the fuck you and I are— and you left us all in the dark."

Jonathan found himself getting irritated. "In our business, we only know what we need to know. You know the game. Okay, so I didn't tell you everything. That's not the reason Teo got hurt. What's the big fucking deal?"

Elizabeth slouched down in her chair. "I know how the game's played. Sometimes information is withheld that could harm an asset or an operation if we should be taken or compromised. But letting us know what was really at stake would have put no one and nothing at risk. It would have alerted us to just how dangerous the situation is. Maybe Teo wouldn't have chased Ray down and been that close to the explosion if he'd known what Forest was up to."

"Kolya called to warn us that Forest had planted a bomb. I didn't keep that from Teo."

"Still."

"Still. He knew that Ray's bag possibly contained a bomb, and Teo chased him anyway. Nothing I said or omitted saying made him do that."

"Yeah, I guess. The boy wonder can be impulsive."

"Teo hates it when you call him that."

"I know." Elizabeth's voice softened. "And if he survives and emerges reasonably intact, I'll stop teasing him."

"Don't do that. You stop being a jerk to him, and he'll think he's dying."

Elizabeth smiled. "Okay. Happy to be a jerk."

"Now that's settled—still think I'm an asshole?"

"Of course—because you are. Just as I'm a jerk to Teo. Kolya, at least, should have known what he and Alex were up against."

"Yeah, and I know that as well."

"After what the two of them have been through, he has a right to be angry about being lied to."

"It wasn't really a lie...I didn't..." Jonathan stopped himself. He didn't like the description of what he'd done—it was an omission of facts, rather than a lie—but legalistic. Elizabeth was on target. Omitting essential facts can be as much of a deception as an outright lie. "Okay. Fine. I'm an asshole. But I did fill both of you in and apologize to Kolya before he left."

"Maybe you need to do it again. Maybe even a little groveling."

"Kolya wouldn't require me to grovel."

"You sure?"

"Not completely. Pretty sure. But I'll say whatever I need to. Not just to keep him in the agency but we've been friends for a long time. Besides, I have my best man speech all prepared. I'd hate to waste it."

"So, we agree—a little groveling at the least is in order. And once you're done, you can ask if he or Alex have any ideas about how to find Forest and his merry band of morons. Which means you should call sooner rather than later."

Jonathan checked his watch unnecessarily since it had only been five minutes since the last time he'd looked. "It's unlikely they've reached DC yet, even if they took an early morning train. Once Kolya gets Alex safely home, he'll be more willing to hear me out. And he's not going to keep back any information that could help the operation. He is a pro. I don't believe he's really resigning."

"He's getting married. He might be tired of all the shit that comes with this job. God knows I am."

"You thinking of quitting?"

"No." Elizabeth shrugged. "Nothing else I'd prefer to do."

"It's the same with Kolya. He's drawn to this work. Like you. Like me. For whatever psychological twisted reason all of us do this." Jonathan saw the doctor who'd been operating on Teo enter the waiting room and head in their direction. He touched Elizabeth's arm, and they rose to meet him.

Chapter Forty-Five

Alex stepped into the entrance hall of the building. No police on the ground floor. The law offices shared by Noah and the other solos were on the second floor. She had just buzzed for the elevator when the door opened, and Ruth Issacs exited. Her eyes were red. Ruth caught sight of Alex, grabbed hold of her arm to pull her out of the building and onto the sidewalk.

"Don't go up there. Horrible. Never thought something like this...Never in all my years of working." Ruth searched in a battered black handbag and came up with a slightly used tissue to wipe her face and blow her nose.

"What's happened?" Alex asked.

"Noah's dead. Murdered." The tears were flowing again. "I got to the office at six-thirty to get some work done, and I found him. Someone broke his fingers and then shot him."

Alex felt her legs grow weak. She put out a hand to brace herself against a wall. "Noah's dead. No. No. No." She'd just seen him the previous night. He'd joked about Kolya's job and warned her about Barbara O'Brien. They'd been friends since law school. "I think I'm going to be sick."

"I already was."

"Has anyone called Iris?" Noah's wife was also a friend. Noah and Iris were supposed to be coming to Alex's wedding.

"The police are notifying her."

Alex glanced at the four police cars in front of the building. She'd wondered what they were doing. Now she knew.

"The office is closed for right now. There's police and forensics." Ruth had tears in her eyes. "I still can't believe it."

"I left here yesterday around seven."

"Noah was the last one in the office. They think he was killed around ten o'clock."

"Who killed him? A client?"

Ruth shook her head. "There are always some clients who aren't happy with the results of their court cases, but no serious threats as far as I know. I don't think it was related to his work."

No, not to *his* work. To Kolya's work.

It was too much of a coincidence that Noah would have been killed a few hours before she and Kolya had been targeted at Penn Station. Was that why Noah's fingers had been broken?

Alex suddenly remembered the midnight text she'd received from Noah's phone asking her to meet for coffee. Noah was already dead when she received the text. The killer must have sent it—to lure her and Kolya into a trap. What had she replied? That she was leaving early. Would that have been enough information to track the two of them down?

Apparently so.

This was all her fault. She should never have taken Yael to Noah's office. She hadn't appreciated just how murderous Yael and her husband might be. And now, Noah was dead.

And Kolya—where was he? Her carelessness had put him in danger as well.

Why the fuck had she come to New York?

But she'd deal with the guilt later. Her first priority was to locate Kolya. "Did my fiancé leave a message for me this morning? Or come to the office looking for me? Tall, blond, good-looking guy."

"I checked the messages on the office phone for the cops. Nothing for you. No one came by either. I called all the attorneys to tell them the office was closed and that the police wanted to talk to everyone who works there." Ruth fixed her gaze on Alex. "That probably includes you, even though you don't work here on a regular basis."

"Yeah, probably does. And I will contact them. After I find my fiancé. He was supposed to meet me here. Or leave a message for me." But since he hadn't, Kolya could be dead or a prisoner. The thought startled her. Was it possible he was dead? No, he couldn't be. He couldn't. She would have felt something, wouldn't she, if he no longer existed? But it was possible. More probable that he was a prisoner. *Get in touch with Jonathan.* He and the ECA were the only ones who would have the resources to rescue Kolya if he were in trouble. "Can I borrow your phone? Or a laptop? I lost my phone, and I need try to get in touch with someone?"

Ruth studied her a moment. "You lost your phone? AND your fiancé in the same morning?"

"I hadn't thought of it quite that way, but yes."

"The morning after Noah was tortured and killed."

"Also true."

Ruth glanced to the right and left. "I think you should come with me to my apartment. It's walking distance. You can use my computer, and I'll make you some coffee."

"That's very kind, but not necessary. I just need..."

"What you need is to get the hell off the street where you can make calls in private." Ruth placed the used Kleenex in her black purse and zipped it shut. "Because I don't know exactly what's going on, but I do know that you're in trouble."

Chapter Forty-Six

y the time they reached wherever they were going, Kolya's arms had gone numb. He could only guess at the destination—the back of the van had no windows, and from where he was seated, he had no view through the front windshield. But it didn't matter. All that mattered was that he kill Forest and as many of his followers as possible before he died.

Hopefully it would be enough to stop Forest's revolution.

Anything else would be up to Jonathan, Elizabeth, and whomever else the ECA sent in.

He hadn't spoken since hearing that Alex was dead, and his silence apparently annoyed Victor Forest. It was a small victory, but not something he found comforting.

He knew that there was a possibility that Alex was still alive. He knew that using lies about a loved one to break an opponent's resistance was standard procedure. Maybe there was a chance she was still alive.

But the strong possibility was that she was not.

Kolya could focus on nothing—the techniques he'd used so many times no longer worked. Breathing techniques didn't help.

In fact, breathing hurt—there was a sharpness in his chest with every inhale. The thought that he was, even if only for a short time, still breathing while Alex was not, was close to unbearable.

The physical reaction to being restrained had activated the PTSD symptoms that never completely disappeared. He felt the trembling of his body, a combined rage and fear. But the images that flashed through his mind were worse than the physical reaction.

Some of the images were from his captivity in Romania. The moment when he, half-dead from torture and starvation, opened his eyes to Alex bending over him. The realization that they'd kidnapped her to force his cooperation. The moment when, after freeing his hands and killing his guards, he'd tried to persuade Alex to escape without him. That she'd have a better chance without him, given that he couldn't put any weight on his leg. He could see her face as she stretched out a hand to him. "We escape together, or we die together."

Other images were just as painful. Maybe more painful. Her lying in bed next to him, her face soft with passion and love. The touch of her body.

She had been right. They should not have been together, not if he was going to be in such a risky career. She should have left him. Or he should have never gone back to intelligence work.

He had no way to know if she was really dead. He'd never know either, because he wasn't coming out of this alive. And that was fine with him.

The van pulled inside a building that looked like an abandoned warehouse. Given the accents of the men surrounding him, he assumed they were either in Queens or Brooklyn. Garlic Breath unsnapped his seat belt and took hold of Kolya's right arm. Drooping Eye Guy took the other, and together they pulled him out of the van.

"Home sweet home. For now." Forest exited the van behind Kolya. "Ready for that talk I mentioned earlier?"

Kolya didn't respond.

"I'll talk then. You can listen." Forest shrugged and then spoke to his men. "Take him upstairs."

Moving from the van into the new environment brought him into the present and out of his memories. Which was good. He needed to be present and aware in order to act. And that meant that he had to push thoughts of Alex into the back of his mind. For now.

Focus.

The downstairs was cavernous. Two other vans were parked inside. The ceiling was possibly thirty feet above them. Metal shelving and bins lined the walls. Clearly, a warehouse of some kind, but it was no longer being used to store goods for sale. There were a few men in the warehouse, carrying AR-15s. One man had an AR-15 and a grenade launcher.

But it was a closed space—filled with members of the American Gold Posse, who were plotting to attack and kill Americans. This would be a good place to break that jar in Forest's pocket and find out if it did contain VX.

But he needed an opportunity. He just had to watch for the chance.

They marched him up a set of steel stairs leading to a landing that had been the warehouse's offices, or so Kolya assumed. On that second level was a large room filled with cots.

To Kolya's surprise, one of the cots was occupied by Yael and her baby. She was nursing her child, her chest covered by a baby blanket, an expression of bliss on her face. When she saw him, her expression changed to something harder to read.

Her presence and especially that of an infant didn't change his mind about what he needed to do. He still was the only person who could stop Forest from going through with whatever he had planned. But beyond that, Alex deserved justice. The men responsible for her death deserved to die.

But did the baby deserve to die?

He tried to ignore the voice in his head.

If he managed to get to Forest and break the bottle of VX, Kolya would very likely kill every person in the warehouse, including Yael and her baby.

The baby was innocent, even if Yael wasn't.

He knew what Alex would say. Or do. But she was gone. Probably gone—he amended. And he was about to do something to honor her that she would hate.

Maybe there was another way. Maybe just kill Forest with a more conventional method. Gun. Knife. Hands. If he could. Then kill as many members of Forest's gang as he could before they killed him.

Stupid thought. He felt the pressure of the zip tie on his wrist, and the grip of two men on his arms. He knew how to break a zip tie, but the odds of his being able to do so with his arms held were slim. Even slimmer—the odds of breaking the zip tie and then killing Forest.

Still, he had to do it.

Forest's office looked as if he hadn't replaced the furniture from when the space had been used as a warehouse. Metal desk from the 1950s. Three metal chairs in front of the desk, a high-back battered leather executive chair behind the desk. Four-drawer metal filing cabinet. Black and white linoleum floor.

Garlic Breath and Drooping Eye Guy pushed Kolya into one of the metal chairs, ran a rope through the restraints on his wrists, and tied him to the chair.

So much for breaking the zip tie. He needed to be able to raise his arms behind him as high as he could and then slam them down against his body. He couldn't do that with the addition of the rope. Or with guards watching him.

Victor Forest seated himself in the executive chair, pulled his gun from his waist, set it on the desk, placed the bottle of VX on the desk as well, and then nodded at Garlic Breath and Drooping Eye Guy. "Dex, you stay to watch him. Roger, you can go get coffee and come back."

Garlic Breath —Roger—left, closing the door behind. Dex—aka Drooping Eye Guy—leaned against the wall behind Kolya.

A gun and VX, tantalizingly close but not close enough, not with his hands bound behind him.

Forest turned to Kolya. "I understand why you're not speaking. You weren't playing a role with Miss Feinstein—she really was your fiancée. The news of her death must be deeply upsetting. I'm sorry. I didn't intend for her to die."

Kolya said nothing. He used his fingers to test the flexibility of the zip tie and the rope holding him.

Forest spread out his hands in what he apparently intended to be a sympathetic gesture. "But you need to understand the truth. Her death is on the organization that sent you out to spy on me and on the unlawful government that pays you. Not on me."

"No one from my agency chased Alex onto train tracks." When he twisted his wrists, the zip tie gave slightly but not enough. Enough twisting, and the tie might break.

It would take too long.

Maybe shift tactics, pretend to listen. Maybe Forest would lower his guard.

Forest beamed, as if he'd won a victory with Kolya finally speaking. "But she wouldn't have been chased at all if the ECA and the so-called government weren't trying to hide the truth—if they weren't trying to hold power illegitimately and suppress the American people. Which is what you were helping to do."

There was nothing worth responding to, so Kolya didn't.

Roger returned and switched off with Dex, who agreed to return in twenty minutes.

Forest continued, "I told you we had a lot in common. That's why I wanted to talk to you and not just kill you. You're a capable and intelligent man who could be an asset in the revolution, if you can put aside your anger and listen to me. We both chose to work for the overlords, thinking we were being patriots, and we were both betrayed by them. I know what they did to you. Setting you up to be kidnapped and tortured. Leaving you to die." Forest leaned forward, his hands clasped together in a show of sincerity. "And yet you went back to work for them."

If Kolya could have moved, he would have shrugged. "I didn't like being a lawyer."

"I think it was more than that. I think you're a patriot who wants to do right by this country. But you haven't seen the truth. I have. After they did to me what they did to you."

"What did they do to you?"

"You know that I was in the CIA and was shot in the back when I was in the field?"

"Yes, I do know that."

"Of course, you must have read my file. What you don't know—and what I didn't know at first—was the truth behind what happened. The CIA sent me to Prague to meet with an agent who had penetrated a terrorist group. What my superiors didn't tell me was that the group had begun to suspect our agent's loyalty, and the CIA decided to sacrifice one of its own—me—to keep our asset from being uncovered and killed. I was outed and shot by our own asset to burnish his credentials with the terrorist group.

"I woke up in a hospital in France in terrible pain and was flown home to the US where my injuries were treated, and I was called a hero. For a little while, that's what I thought I was.

Then I was assigned to desk duty and research, because of the ongoing pain from being shot. Sound familiar?"

"A little." Despite his grief and his anger, Kolya was struck by the similarity of what had happened to the two of them.

"More than a little. We were both set up by our agencies that we were devoted to in disinformation schemes that caused permanent injuries and could have killed us. Our lives counted for nothing."

"I assume you discovered what had really happened while you were on desk duty."

Victor nodded, his eyes gleaming with something close to madness. "I discovered all sorts of interesting things. The fact that I had been set up. I wasn't a hero; I was a sucker. Then I found the list of the bunkers. That's when I started reading. I read everything that had been written about the history of the United States for the past one hundred years and realized what was being hidden, even from people like me who worked for the CIA. The government had been taken over—back in 1933— when it went off the gold standard, and all us fools were just cogs in a plot to subjugate the people of the United States. That's why the bunkers with poison and explosives were created —to be used if the people found out the truth and rebelled against the aliens."

"Aliens? You mean non-Americans?"

"Some non-Americans. And Jews. Jews were involved. After all, Jews influenced the Roosevelt administration and were the reason the US got into the war in Europe. But I also mean aliens. From other planets. All those sightings of UFOs— those were in the CIA files too. And I put it all together. Many of our leaders and the leaders around the world weren't human, and they were taking over. Worse, they've embedded in the bureaucracy, making rules and laws that will keep them in power. Taking us off the gold standard was just the first step.

Then there are the Jews who are in league with them—forcing us all into a one world order where the aliens will rule. That's who's in charge of the United States government now. The aliens."

"I'm Jewish," Kolya said. "I don't know anyone from another planet."

Forest gave a short bark of laughter. "Not all Jews are in on it, of course. There are some that are loyal to the real United States. Not a lot but a few. Which is what I think you might be —given what I know of you. Because of what they did to you. They wouldn't do it to someone in on the plot. So, I figured you didn't know about the aliens any more than you knew about being set up. But because you're Jewish as well as an ECA agent, if you agree to join me, you have knowledge and contacts that will prove useful in fighting against them."

Kolya had spent years of his career battling against far-right extremists of one kind or another who believed antisemitic conspiracy theories. But he'd never encountered this combination of antisemitic conspiracy theories and batshit crazy. Jonathan had said something about Forest believing in aliens from other planets taking over the world, but Kolya hadn't fully processed what that meant. A mentally unstable man with dozens of followers and access to one hundred secret bunkers filled with explosives, biological weapons, and nerve poison could kill a lot of people.

He'd already known that Forest was dangerous. But this took it to a new level.

"Tell me more," Kolya said.

Chapter Forty-Seven

Ruth Issacs's apartment was small and neat, the living room furnished with a heavy oak dining table, a leather reclining chair, and a yellow, white, and black plaid couch. The kitchen was just large enough for a small round table with two chairs. The walls were decorated with framed black-and-white photographs—one of a protest march for abortion rights, several of an attractive young woman with long hair posing with various people from the 1960s and 1970s. Ruth poured water and measured coffee. Alex looked at the photos. "Is that Peter, Paul, and Mary?"

"Yes."

"And...is that you, Ruth?"

"Yup. That was from the antiwar march on Washington in 1971. I worked with the organizers. I was something of a firebrand back then."

"My mother was at that march. And my father. It's where they met. Shame the world didn't turn out as they'd hoped."

"The moral arc of history is long, and it zig zags. I'm not sure if we're in a zig or a zag right now."

"Sadly true. You said I could use your computer?"

Ruth flipped the switch on the coffee machine. "Follow me."

Ruth's bedroom held a small pine desk with a laptop. Ruth seated herself, tapped her password on the keyboard, and then ceded the chair to Alex before returning to the kitchen.

It took Alex less than five minutes to locate Jonathan's phone number, which she tapped into the burner phone.

His voice, when he picked up the call, was cautious. Of course, he wouldn't recognize the number of her burner phone. "Yeah?"

"It's Alex, Jonathan. Have you heard from Kolya?"

His voice changed to concerned. "No. Haven't talked to him since last night. What's up?"

Her heart sank. She'd held out hope that Kolya was safe, but if he was, he'd have tried to contact her, either through Noah's office or through Jonathan. She took a deep breath and then began.

"I think he's in trouble." She described the events at Penn Station in a few terse sentences. "We were supposed to reconnect through my friend Noah, but Noah was murdered last night, probably by my former friend, her husband, and Victor Forest. The paralegal at the firm said there's been no word from Kolya. If he didn't contact you either, then I'm really, really scared."

"Fuck. Yeah, worrisome. The team's here with me. We're on it. We'll find him. Where are you? Are you safe?"

"Yes. I'm at the apartment of a friend."

"Anyone that Yael or her husband might know?"

Alex hesitated on that question. "Yael might have seen her in passing, but I don't think Yael would know her name. Or where she lived."

"You know that if Victor Forest has Kolya, you're a target."

"I'm well aware." She'd been a target several times because of Kolya's work.

"I can move you to a safe house."

But if Kolya wasn't a prisoner or if he did get away, sooner or later he might try for Noah's office. She didn't want the ECA to control her movements or her communications. More than that —she wanted the ability to act on her own if necessary. "No thanks. I'm okay where I am."

"You sure?"

"Very sure."

"Okay, but don't let anyone else know where you are. Not your family. Not the wedding planner. No one. No phone calls. No emails. No texts."

"Got it." Alex knew what she was supposed to do. She'd failed to follow the rules the previous night, which was probably why Kolya was missing. Not something she wanted to share with Jonathan—not until Kolya was safe. "You'll let me know if you hear anything?"

"Of course."

"Right away? Not in a week?"

"I'll let you know as soon as we find him—unless telling you could endanger him. Or the operation."

Which was what she'd expected. But not what she wanted. There was a letdown that was physical as she hung up the phone. Yes, Jonathan would throw whatever resources he could muster into the hunt, but there was no guarantee that he'd find Kolya. Or find him alive. And even Jonathan might not put Kolya's life above the ECA's objective of stopping Victor Forest.

She couldn't completely blame him. One man's life against the lives of thousands of people.

But it was Kolya's life.

She didn't want others sacrificed, but Kolya's life mattered.

She'd do whatever she could to find him, with or without Jonathan.

She returned to the kitchen and seated herself at the small kitchen table, where Ruth was eating a lemon cookie and drinking coffee. Ruth jumped up to pour a cup of coffee for Alex and shove the plate of cookies in front of her before returning to her chair.

Jewish mother to the core.

"Any luck?" Ruth asked.

Alex shook her head and sipped her coffee, trying to keep herself calm. He had to be alive. He had to be. She returned to her earlier thought. Wouldn't she have felt it in her heart if he were dead? "Our wedding is set for two weeks from now." She felt the stupidity of the comment. At that moment, she didn't care about the wedding. Not about the years of waiting, the months of planning, or the family that would be gathering. None of that mattered. All that mattered was that Kolya was alive and well. That was why she had considered cancelling the wedding—not because she didn't love him, which she did, with every ounce of her being—but to keep him safe. And yet she was the one who'd given Forest enough information to find the two of them at Penn Station. "The wedding's not what matters."

Ruth nodded sympathetically. "I know that it's not your prime concern, but weddings are important. I love weddings. They're so full of love and....hope. Most of the time. Sometimes they're just full of shit and shitty people, but I don't think that would be true of yours."

"No, I don't think ours would be full of shit or shitty people. Assuming it happens."

"It's going to happen, honey. Kolya is going to turn up. He'll be fine, and you're going to have that big day. And I want an invite. Noah said he expected great food and music. He told me that Kolya is a great jazz musician." She leaned forward. "He told me something else, by the way. He said that your fiancé claimed to work at the IRS, but Noah didn't believe it. He thought Kolya was a secret agent for the CIA or something. That's why I knew you needed to get off the street and somewhere safe when you told me that he was missing."

Alex didn't want to lie to Ruth, but she couldn't confirm Kolya's profession either. She worded her answer carefully. "He's not in the CIA."

"That was a lawyer's answer." Ruth picked up her coffee.

"Which is what I am."

"So, he's a secret agent, but not for the CIA."

"I didn't say anything of the sort, Ruth."

"Course you didn't." Ruth finished her coffee, stood, and carried her cup over to the sink to rinse it out. "Have one of those cookies. They're from an Italian bakery on Seventh Avenue. Or I could toast a bagel for you. You should eat something."

Alex shook her head again. "I ate earlier. Do you think the police are done with whatever they need to do at the office?"

"I'd give it another hour or so. Why?"

"Because it's where Kolya might look for me—if he can." If he was alive. "Maybe we can head back over. Just in case."

"Tell me this: Don't you think there might be people looking for you as well as for Kolya?"

Alex hesitated. "Maybe."

"I thought so. You stay here. Use my computer. Watch TV. There are lemon cookies. Bagels. Cream cheese. Coffee. Help yourself to whatever. I'll head back to the office and watch the phones. If Kolya shows up, I'll call you. If anyone else shows up..." Ruth opened a drawer under the coffee maker, pulled out a compact 9mm pistol, and stuffed it into her purse. "I'm just a harmless old lady who doesn't know nothing."

Chapter Forty-Eight

They gathered at the ECA apartment in the West Village. Four new agents had flown in at Jonathan's request: Tehila Melaku, a former Mossad agent of mixed Ethiopian and Ashkenazi Jewish ethnicity; Marty Davis, a seasoned agent who had come to the ECA from the CIA; Frick, who only had one name and who had once been with FBI; and Jay Lee, a Korean American with a special forces background.

They sat on card chairs around a rickety secondhand table in the apartment that—as Kolya had once noted—smelled of something that might have been cat urine. Jonathan explained the task: to find and stop Victor Forest's revolution. He included the details about the bunkers, the omission of which had so angered Kolya.

"How's the kid?" Frick asked.

"Teo made it through surgery and it's still pretty iffy, but the doctors are hopeful," Jonathan said.

"Here's hoping on my part too," Tehila said.

"Agreed," said Elizabeth. "Hate to lose the boy wonder." She looked over at Jonathan. "I mean it."

She did. Under the teasing and surface hardness, Elizabeth was good people.

"And Petrov?" Frick asked. "I understood he volunteered to join the team."

Elizabeth glanced over at Jonathan, her expression challenging him to tell the truth about Kolya walking out. Jonathan threaded his fingers together, took a breath, and began. "Kolya decided to return to Washington."

Then his phone rang. He checked the number, no one he knew, and cautiously answered. "Yeah?" When he heard Alex's voice, he held up a hand for silence and put the call on speaker.

* * *

"Christ," Marty said after Jonathan hung up the call. "Petrov was supposed to be on light duty in preparation for his wedding. How's the fuck does he always wind up in the shit?"

"Just a lucky guy, I guess," Frick said.

"He gets in trouble because he takes risks to get the job done." Tehila was friends with both Alex and Kolya. "Which I assume he did here as well, didn't he?"

"Yeah," Jonathan agreed. "To get us information, he put himself in a position where he could be identified by the bad guys."

"Are we diverting from the mission to find him?" Jay, the newest member of the team, didn't know Kolya well.

"Fucking A," Frick said.

"Not a diversion," Elizabeth said.

"Correct. If we find Kolya, we'll find Forest. And probably a bunch of American Gold assholes," Jonathan said. "So, finding him advances the operation."

"Unless Kolya's already dead," Marty said. "Hate to be a downer, but it's a possibility."

"Yeah, there's that," Jonathan agreed. "But let's operate on the principle that he's still alive. The fact that Kolya was attacked in Penn Station —which has cameras everywhere— gives us something to start with."

"Can we hack into Penn Station's cameras to see the feed remotely or do we need to go in person?" Tehila asked.

"I'll contact Mark Leslie in technical, but it wouldn't hurt to go to the scene and get physical access. Also talk to people. There're people and shops and kiosks all around. Lots of homeless living in the tunnels. Maybe someone saw something."

"What's our cover?" Marty asked. "We're not getting access to official videos by pretending to be with the IRS."

"Fuck that," Frick said. "One of our own is missing. Not the time to be playing games. We tell them national security matter. Maybe we can get Bradford to call. Jonathan, ask her."

Jonathan was on first-name basis with Margaret Bradford, head of the ECA. "Won't do any good. Margaret won't break protocol and identify the ECA. She'll just tell me to figure something out."

"Fine. I'll fucking use my FBI ID."

"You didn't turn it in when you switched agencies?" Elizabeth asked.

Frick shrugged. "No one asked for it. They were all too worried about getting caught up in the Carl Ford scandal to see to little details like me handing over my identification. And I figured it might come in handy sometime."

"Okay then." Technically, it was illegal for Frick to use FBI credentials if he were no longer in the FBI, but Jonathan didn't mind breaking a few laws here and there for the greater good. "Frick, Marty, Tehila, and I will cover Penn Station. I know some people in the New York City police department so we can get a look at the feed from traffic cameras around the outside of Penn Station. Jay and Elizabeth—that'll be your job."

Chapter Forty-Nine

Never agree too quickly. Kolya knew the basic maxim for allowing the appearance of being recruited. He had to appear interested but questioning. Not eager. Not siding too quickly with those he had been opposing. If he appeared too eager to join up with Victor Forest, he wouldn't be trusted. Not that he needed the full range of trust. Just enough trust to allow him to get his hands on a gun.

So, after Forest had explained more of his theory about aliens and the gold standard and how Jews fit into it all, Kolya put on an interested but doubtful expression.

"You're correct that I've been angry about what happened to me. And I do see the parallels between what happened to me and what happened to you. We were both fucked over. Still, being fucked over and believing that aliens are running the country are a little different. Do you have hard evidence?"

Victor waved a hand casually. "I have testimonies. Videos." He opened the laptop and tapped on some keys. Then he turned it so that Kolya could see the screen. "These are two of them. I have dozens."

A young woman on the screen, shoulder-length blonde hair,

wearing a flowery long-sleeved dress and high heels, spoke of being an intern in the White House and seeing President Thomas Lewis change from human into lizard shape. Another video had a clean-cut young man in a blue suit stating something similar about the Speaker of the House.

If Kolya hadn't been fighting down his grief and anger over the possibility of Alex's death, he would have had a hard time keeping himself from laughing. But between his emotional state and his years of undercover work, he managed. "Okay, interesting."

"But not enough?"

"Not quite."

"What else do you need?"

"Maybe the history books that you mentioned? The ones you read through before deciding to leave the CIA."

Forest shook his head. "Don't have everything here. But maybe I can get my hands on one or two. So, I'll see what I can find, and meanwhile, I have some things to do. People to contact. The revolution is going forward, and it will be streamed."

* * *

He was allowed to use the bathroom and then his hands were zip-tied in front instead of in back. Roger and Dex secured him, a second zip-tie passing through the restrains on his wrists and then around the rail of one of the cots in the large room outside Forest's office.

He had considered trying to free his hands to attack the guards, but that would defeat the goal: to kill Forest. Avenging Alex mattered personally, but beyond that, he had to kill Forest before the man could follow his craziness to its illogical end. After that, Kolya'd happily kill as many of the others as he could manage before they killed him, but without Forest, the revolution against the imaginary aliens would be over.

Kolya had to wait for the right moment, which meant convincing Forest that he believed in aliens and was willing to join up with the other lunatics.

Focusing on what he needed to do helped control the pain over Alex. While the pain was a constant ache, like the injury to his leg that had never completely healed, it eased somewhat when he focused on the task.

Kolya sat on the cot and watched, evaluating which of the men might successfully defend Forest. Roger and Dex, guarding him, didn't worry him. Neither seemed trained or even particularly alert. Other men, heavily armed, gathered in small groups, were harder to gauge, but the numbers were concerning. He counted maybe ten in the upstairs space where he was tied to a cot. When they'd arrived, he'd seen maybe twenty-five downstairs. Some were doing what men did in preparation for an action: cleaning weapons, checking ammunition. Others played cards, ate, and smoked. Surprisingly—or maybe not surprisingly—no one was scrolling on a phone, maybe because they only had burner flip phones, which would be harder to trace.

He couldn't kill all of them, not without the VX.

Brody, nearby, pacing, wasn't high on Kolya's list of concerns.

Yael, seated on a nearby cot, patted her sleeping baby. He didn't look in her direction, not wanting to let his hatred show. She was the reason Alex had rushed to New York. If not for Yael, Alex would still be in Washington, making last-minute decisions about appetizers and the music selection.

He had never seen Alex in the wedding dress that she'd chosen. He'd been out of town on assignment when she bought it, and afterwards she refused to show it to him. She was supposed to have a final fitting two days before the wedding, but she'd told him he couldn't come with her. "I want it to be a surprise when I walk down the aisle. Don't worry. You'll like it. It's very sexy." She'd laughed.

His throat tightened.

Brody approached the cot where Kolya was tied. Before either of the guards could react, Brody slammed a fist into the side of Kolya's face.

"That's for hitting me when I wasn't looking."

Pain spread out from the point of impact. Kolya welcomed it. It diverted his mind from his psychological agony.

He shook his head to clear it and spat out the blood from where his teeth had cut his cheek.

Brody drew back his arm for another blow. To Kolya's surprise, Yael stood up and faced Brody. "Does it make you feel all tough to beat up a man who can't fight back? And you lost the fight to him because you weren't as good as he is. Not because he hit you when you weren't looking."

Red-faced, Brody swung towards her, his fist landing on her face instead of Kolya's, knocking her back down onto the cot. "Shut up." He shouted the words. "Who the fuck do you think you are?"

Her hand on her cheek, Yael muttered, "I'm your wife."

"Yes. MY wife. Which means you OBEY me. You do not disrespect me. You don't side with some fucking spy who took advantage of me." His eyes were bulging with fury. "Are you working with him? Or is it that he's a Jew, and you fucking Jews all stick together?"

"I'm sorry." Yael mumbled. "I wasn't siding...I didn't mean..."

"Shut up. I don't want to hear it." He turned back towards Kolya, but by then, Forest had arrived—and he stepped in front of Brody.

"I'm trying to persuade Petrov to join us. Beating him up

isn't an effective recruiting strategy." Forest's voice was quiet but steely.

"He disrespected me," Brody growled. "So did my wife."

"I'm making the decisions about Petrov, not you. How you handle your wife is your business. She does need to know her place. Speaking of a woman's place," he turned to her, "Yael, you should make lunch for us all. The kitchen is through the doors to the right of my office. I'd like something hot. A burger maybe."

Obediently, she stood up. "But the baby? I can't cook and hold Lyra. Brody? Will you watch her?"

"Not my job," Brody said. "Not the job of any of the men here. We've got men's work to do. She's sleeping. She'll be fine." He sounded calmer, but there was still anger in his voice.

"If she's not watched, she could roll off the bed. This is the age that babies start rolling."

"Fine." Brody scooped the baby up and then set her on the cot next to Kolya. "Petrov can keep the baby from rolling. That fit in with recruiting him?" Brody glanced at Forest.

"You mind, Petrov?" Forest actually looked amused.

Kolya motioned with his tied hands. "Hard to grab a rolling baby when I'm attached to a rail."

"Just yell if she starts rolling. Someone will grab her," Forest said. "Meantime," he placed a thick book on Kolya's lap. "Some light reading. You should be able to turn the pages, even with the restraints. This will tell you everything you need to know to come on board."

* * *

The baby on the cot continued to sleep, as Kolya flipped the pages of the book. It was a surreal experience. Reading a book by someone just as crazy as Forest while tied to a cot and watching a baby.

The baby twitched in her sleep and made soft cooing sounds. Kolya wondered: What did babies dream? Of milk and their mother's breasts? Or, as Freud thought, of floating in the womb? Or do images from prior lives drift through their minds, until they grow old enough to be solidly rooted in the present?

Kolya didn't believe in reincarnation, or in any sort of afterlife existence, although he'd read a *New York Times* article about researchers at a medical school who had compiled lists of children who seemed to remember past lives. It had been an interesting article and an interesting thought. Interesting, but not comforting, even if he believed it, which he didn't. The idea that Alex might be reincarnated as someone else he'd never know did not lessen any of the pain of her loss. The end of life was the end of existence.

Still, wondering what might be in a baby's mind was more engaging than the book that Forest had plopped on his lap.

He turned pages, skimming descriptions of UFOs, of people with multicolored eyes who were pretending to be human. He read with some curiosity the diatribe against the change from the gold standard in the 1930s. He skipped the chapter that "proved" Hitler was not the villain of World War II.

Periodically, he glanced at the baby lying next to him. Lyra still slept, tiny hands in fists. Once, she opened blue eyes to smile at him and then returned to her nap.

He discarded the idea of breaking the bottle of VX.

* * *

The baby woke again, this time crying, probably because she needed a diaper change, judging from the smell. Roger, the guard closest to him, simply shrugged when Kolya pointed it out. Brody was too busy pacing and brooding to attend to his daughter.

Yael reappeared, bearing a platter filled with hamburgers and homemade French fries. She handed filled paper plates out to the men as they lined up, eager for their food. She didn't turn her head as the baby continued to cry or when Kolya called to her that the baby needed to be changed.

After serving the members of American Gold Posse, Yael carried a hamburger on a paper towel over to Kolya and set it on top of the book.

"Thank you." Despite everything, Kolya was hungry. He'd last eaten before leaving for Penn Station.

"You can thank Victor for allowing you to eat." The words were hostile, but her tone was not. She collected her baby and retreated to her cot to change the diaper.

Hunching over, Kolya managed to eat, grease and red liquid from the medium-rare burger squirting onto the pages of the book on his lap—an appropriate metaphor.

Forest reappeared after Kolya had finished and had wiped his hands on the paper towel. "What do you think?"

Kolya knew he was asking about the book, not the food. "Persuasive."

"Yes." Forest nodded. "It helped convince me."

Kolya paused. "Me too." He closed the book.

"So, you're on board?"

Kolya nodded. "I joined the ECA because I was idealistic, believing in the promise of America. I was betrayed. In more ways than one. I've decided. I'm not going to be their puppet anymore."

"Very good." Forest's tone was solemn. "I'm pleased you've seen the light. You'll be helpful. Next: All members of American Gold Posse swear an oath of allegiance—to me and to the real United States. Are you willing?"

"I am."

"Then raise your right hand and repeat after me: I, Kolya Petrov, renounce all ties and allegiances to the aliens who have taken over the United States and the world. I renounce the worldwide coalition of Jews who are supporting them."

Kolya raised his right hand as far as the zip tie allowed and repeated the words. Kolya would do or say whatever he had to—even if he found it personally repugnant—to convince Forest that he was sincere. He had no problem renouncing the worldwide coalition of Jews supporting aliens—since it didn't exist.

Forest continued. "I swear absolute allegiance to the leader of American Gold Posse and to the restoration of the real America. I will obey every order. If I fail to do so, I willingly submit myself to the just punishment of American Gold Posse."

Kolya spoke the words.

"Okay then." Forest smiled.

"What do you want me to do?" He thought that the deception was working, but Forest was making no move to release Kolya's hands.

"First, tell me who's hunting me. How close they are. Because it'll help us plan when to strike."

Kolya shifted his position to take the strain off his shoulders. "There are three agents in New York from the ECA—Jonathan Egan, Elizabeth Owen, and Teo Lorenzo." Kolya, like any seasoned intelligence operative, knew what to do when in hostile hands. *Tell as much of the truth as possible as long as it does no harm.* Giving Forest the names of the team would not hurt any of them, especially since there was a chance Forest already knew their identities, and doing so might buy Kolya the trust he needed. "Lorenzo was injured in the explosion in Brooklyn. They know that you have access to explosives, but they think that the bombing was personal—because of Ray—and not the start of a revolution." A lie, but nothing that Forest could check.

"Where are they located?"

The team's location, on the other hand, was not something he could disclose. Kolya gave the address of the safehouse where Bob had held Ray. It was blown anyway. None of the team would have returned.

Upon request, he also identified the head of the ECA—which would have been known in CIA circles—but gave a false address for her. Just in case Forest had any of his followers in DC who might try to attack her.

"This is all good stuff," Forest said. "Helpful. But I have to be sure of your loyalty. That you'll obey me absolutely. I'm going to release you, but you're going to have to perform one task."

"Fine." Kolya had expected this, but he'd agree to anything that would give him the possibility of killing Forest. "Whatever you want me to do."

Roger cut the zip tie from Kolya's wrists and then stepped back out of reach, too quickly for Kolya to react and grab for the gun on the man's hip.

He'd have one chance, and he couldn't fuck it up. Kolya flexed muscles to restore feeling.

Forest removed a Glock from a holster at the small of his back. He removed the magazine and clicked out all the rounds, except one. Then he snapped the magazine back in place and held it out. "Take it. You have one shot. To prove your loyalty, you need to kill Yael's baby."

Chapter Fifty

Frick's credentials worked, and the team had no problem getting access to the video footage from the early morning. Police had already been there investigating a death on the train tracks. The cameras had caught the whole thing—from the men following Kolya and Alex, to the maneuver on the stairs, to Alex's escape, and Kolya's capture. Jonathan knew what had happened but not why.

Kolya was a close friend. From what Kolya had said since his experience in Romania, Jonathan assumed that Kolya'd rather die than be taken prisoner. The video didn't have sound, so Jonathan couldn't hear what Victor Forest aka Craig Rand said to Kolya to make him drop his gun.

Forest was holding a small bottle. Whatever it was, Forest must have used it to pressure Kolya. Jonathan could guess what was in it, but he'd rather know for certain.

"The homeless woman that Forest held at gunpoint," Tehila said. "She'd know what Forest said."

"If she can speak a coherent sentence," Frick said.

"Won't know unless we ask, will we?" Marty said.

"Fan out and look for her," Jonathan said.

Marty volunteered to check the subway stations. Frick, the streets around Penn Station. Tehila took the main floor. Jonathan, the corridors underneath.

The homeless people who'd lined the walls early in the morning had relocated since the encounter with Forest. The corridor where Kolya had been taken was empty of the unhoused. Jonathan checked the other hallways in the underbelly of Penn Station. He paid to enter the closest subway entrance and found half a dozen homeless people, none of whom showed any recognition of a photo of Kolya or the blurry shot of the woman.

Jonathan's phone buzzed.

"Traffic images from outside Penn Station show Kolya being forced into a white Ford Transit with the logo "White's Plumbing" on the side." Elizabeth's voice was brisk. "We've also got a plate number. Jay and your cop friend are reviewing other traffic videos to see if we can trace their route. Patrol cars have been alerted to be on the lookout but not to approach."

"They been told why?"

"Of course not, Jonathan. I'm not an amateur. They do know that there's national security implications and that the people inside are very dangerous. That's what I told your friend, and he didn't ask anything else."

"Good. And tell Paul thanks from me." Jonathan knew the police captain from his time in the FBI in New York—when he and Kolya had cemented their friendship as partners taking down the Russian mafia.

"Will do. And on your end?"

"We found a video of Kolya surrendering. Looking for a homeless woman who might know what persuaded him to do that."

"What're you thinking?"

"Forest threatened Kolya with something to get him to

surrender. Something he was holding in a small jar. I can guess what it was—but we need to know for certain."

"Fuck."

"Yeah. Fucking shit."

"I'll be in touch." Elizabeth clicked off.

* * *

Tehila had found the homeless woman in a bathroom on the main floor and texted the rest of the team to meet them at a table just outside a donut shop. The woman was drinking a cup of coffee and eating what looked like a cream-filled donut when Jonathan pulled out a chair and seated himself. She wore a purple sweater over a white sweater over a green buttoned shirt, a red tattered scarf wound around disheveled gray hair.

Marty was already seated with a coffee. Frick showed up after Jonathan, carrying two chocolate glazed donuts.

"Marilyn, these are the friends I mentioned. Jonathan." Tehila nodded in Jonathan's direction, "Marty. And Frick."

"Frick? What kinda name is that?" Marilyn took another bite of the donut.

"As in Frick and Frack," Frick said.

"First or last name?" Marilyn asked.

"Both," Frick said. "It's kind of a joke."

Tehila shot him a look, and Frick retreated to eating his donut.

"Funny." Marilyn finished the donut and picked up the coffee. "Really appreciate the donut and the coffee." She took a long slurp, spilling some on the purple sweater. "Damn." She picked up a napkin and patted the spot.

Jonathan started to speak, but Tehila signaled him not to. "Marilyn was just about to tell me what happened this morning. It was pretty scary, wasn't it?"

"You bet," Marilyn said. "That man woulda killed me. I tried telling the cops. They didn't wanna listen. They were all upset about some guy who got himself run over by a train. Didn't wanna talk to some crazy old homeless woman about some man threatening to kill her."

Tehila put a sympathetic hand on Marilyn's arm. "I'm listening."

"We all are." Jonathan made his voice as soothing as possible.

"Nice to be listened to. Hey—you're a good-looking guy." Marilyn turned her eyes towards Jonathan. "Nice sweater. Cashmere, isn't it? I like it when men dress nice." She looked down at her coffee-stained purple sweater. "I used to dress nice. I used to be pretty, too. Before I got old. Before I lost my mind. Did I tell you I used to be a buyer in a department store?"

"You did." Tehila's voice was warm. "Then you were laid off and stopped taking your meds."

"Couldn't afford them." Marilyn lapsed into silence for a moment. "Didn't like them either. I used to do a lot with purple. Purple shirts. Sweaters. Like this one. Damn." She tried to blot the coffee stain again.

"How about you tell us the story of this morning?" Tehila said. "And after you're done, we'll go shopping. I'll buy you a new sweater."

"Purple?"

"Whatever color you want."

"I like purple."

"Purple it is," Tehila said.

"Okay then. I was sitting with my morning coffee. There's this guy who gives me coffee every morning. Not the best coffee, but it's free. Anyway, I sat down with my coffee in my usual morning spot, and this guy runs by me. Another nice-looking guy. Not as nice a dresser as you." She smiled at Jonathan. Two teeth were missing. "Blond, though, and I used to be partial to blonds. Had kind of a limp. It was early. Really early. Anyway, I thought it was funny that someone'd be running like that. Sometimes commuters run, but not like that. Then I realized. These five other guys were chasing him. The blond guy stopped and turned around with a gun in his hand, and one of the guys chasing him grabbed me. Here." She pointed to her collar and then pulled it down and showed a bruise. "Said he'd shoot me. I almost peed in my pants, I was so scared. Then he shoved me aside, pulled out a bottle, and said he'd drop it."

"What kind of bottle?" Tehila asked.

"No label. Just glass. Little bottle."

"Did he say what was in it?" Tehila's hand patted Marilyn's sleeve.

"V something. He said it would kill all of them and anyone coming through Penn Station. What was it? Two letters. First letter was V. Don't remember the second. G? B?"

"X?" Jonathan asked. "VX?"

"Yeah, yeah, that's it. VX. Do you know what it is?"

"I know what it is." And it changed everything.

Chapter Fifty-One

For a second, Kolya wasn't sure he'd heard correctly. Not even a second. Because the brief pause that had followed Forest's command was broken by a piercing scream from Yael.

"Nooooo!"

Kolya glanced over at her. Yael had Lyra clutched to her breast, both arms wrapped protectively around the baby. He turned his eyes back towards Forest.

"Are you kidding me?"

Forest shook his head. "No. Not kidding." He held the gun out again, offering it to Kolya. One round in the chamber.

But was it a live round?

If Kolya were sure that the round was live and not a blank, he'd accept the gun, and use it to shoot Forest in the head. He'd be killed immediately of course, but he'd already accepted the fact of his own death.

More likely, the round wasn't live. After all, it was a test. Was Forest really crazy enough to hand a loaded gun to a man who had reason to want him dead? Forest believed in crazy shit, but he was not stupid. If Kolya took the gun and fired it at the infant, he'd have shown his loyalty—whether or not he killed the child. But if he tried what he planned to do—to use the gun to kill Forest—and the round was a blank, then Kolya'd die immediately, leaving Forest alive.

But there was a chance that the round was live.

And, if that were the case, Kolya would murder a baby. He had a sudden vision of the child lying on the cot, opening her eyes, and smiling at him.

"I don't shoot children." There was little chance that Kolya could talk his way out of the situation, but he decided to give it a shot.

"We're warriors. A baby doesn't belong here. And you just swore to obey my orders."

"I did. But I don't understand why this is necessary."

"You don't have to understand. You have to obey. There will be terrible and sad things that we have to do, and I have to know I can count on you."

The safest thing would be for Kolya to follow Forest's order. Hopefully, the bullet was a blank, and the baby would be fine. He'd have proven himself, and he'd be free. He'd just have to wait for the opportunity to kill Forest, which would happen sooner or later. But if it wasn't a blank?

He stood and took the gun from Forest's hand. Forest smiled at him.

Brody rushed towards Kolya. Four men blocked him.

"You'll have to shoot me too." Yael still clutched Lyra to her chest. "Victor, please."

Kolya checked with Forest. Forest shrugged, a so-what-if-you-shoot-her-too gesture.

Was the round live? Or was it a blank?

He felt the weight of the gun in his hand. A Glock 22; .40-caliber rounds. Glocks weren't his favorite—he preferred his HK .40—but this was a good weapon. Accurate. Powerful.

There'd be little left of the child if he fired a live round into her head.

He began to walk towards Yael.

Tears streamed down her face as she watched his approach. Brody was being held by the four men, but he was strangely silent. Did that signal anything?

Nothing that Kolya could count on.

Yael's lips moved, but he could barely hear her voice. "Please."

"She won't suffer," he said softly. "It'll just be a flash of light."

"And me?"

"Same. If you hold her in that position, over your heart, it'll be instantaneous. But you don't have to die. You can put her down on the cot."

"No." Yael whispered the words. "No. I'm not putting her down. She's my baby. Where she goes I go." She was shaking. The baby, wrapped in a blue blanket, slept peacefully.

Was the round live or a blank? It had to be a blank. But he wasn't sure.

Roger was shadowing him on the left. Victor was two steps behind. Victor was between Kolya and his other men. If any of the men behind him tried to shoot Kolya, they could hit Forest.

Kolya was maybe three feet from Yael. Her terrified gaze never left his face. Roger was maybe two feet to Kolya's left. Kolya halted, took a deep breath, and he raised his right arm, pointing the gun at the child's head on her chest.

Then he swirled, to his left, dropping the Glock and snatching the gun from the holster on Roger's hip, knocking him to the ground in the same motion. He continued to turn, Roger's gun lowered and ready to fire.

But Forest had already rushed him, grabbing hold of Kolya's right hand with both hands, and they struggled for control of the gun. Kolya aimed his left elbow at Forest's face, but Forest ducked his head just in time. He aimed a kick at Kolya's bad leg, but they were so close together that the kick had little force.

Kolya slammed his left forearm onto Forest's wrists. He didn't need complete control of the gun, just enough to aim it at a vital organ. But Forest clung on to the gun, keeping it pointing away from them.

Had it been just the two of them, Kolya would have prevailed. Forest had had martial arts training, and he was good, but he was twenty years older than Kolya. Youth did have an advantage.

But it wasn't just the two of them.

The men who'd been holding back Brody, and even Brody, rushed to Forest's defense. Together, they wrestled Kolya to the ground. Brody stepped on Kolya's arm to hold it down as Forest bent over and removed the gun.

"I told you not to trust him," Brody said.

"So you did." Forest picked up the second gun, the gun that he'd handed to Kolya to shoot the baby. He pointed it at Kolya's chest and pulled the trigger. An explosion of sound, but nothing else. "A blank. But you guessed that, didn't you? That's why you went for Roger's gun?"

Kolya didn't respond. He'd failed. He felt the weight of the failure as much as he felt the weight of the men pinning him to the floor. He would die without avenging Alex or stopping Forest's planned attacks.

"But if you thought the gun was loaded with a blank, why didn't you go ahead and pull the trigger? The baby would have been fine, and you'd have proven yourself."

The answer was obvious, so Kolya didn't bother giving it. Forest could figure it out for himself—or not.

From his position on the floor, Kolya could see little, but he did see Yael approaching.

"It was all fake? The baby wasn't going to be shot. I wasn't going to be shot." Yael's voice was quiet, even calm. "Brody, you knew?"

Brody was somewhere over Kolya. His voice was loud, proud of his own role in the deception. "We needed Petrov to think it was real, and you're not much of an actress, Yael. So, we let you think it was real as well. You're fine. The baby's fine."

"Yes." Yael's voice was distant. "Lyra's fine."

Kolya noted the words and the tone and wondered if Brody was astute enough to understand what he'd done to his wife and that she knew what he'd done to her. Probably not. But it didn't matter. Yael would continue to be the submissive wife. Brody would continue to be an asshole.

And Forest would continue to be a dangerous lunatic who'd killed Alex and would kill a lot more people.

Kolya could do nothing about any of it. He waited for the bullet.

But he wasn't shot. Instead, Kolya was pulled to his feet, and his arms were tied behind him at his elbows and at his wrists, no pretense of concern over the discomfort.

Forest was grimacing as he straightened his back. He leaned backwards, stretching, and then forward. Then he turned his gaze on Kolya as he was pushed back onto the cot where his ankles were bound as well.

"I thought maybe—because of what happened to you—you were one of the good ones. I made a mistake. You made a mistake as well, swearing loyalty and then betraying your oath. You'll pay the price." He then patted Brody on the shoulder. "I can use him for something spectacular to signal the start of the revolution. As we discussed—if he failed the test. Also, as we discussed, Tom and a few of the guys are taking a run out to near Montauk to pick up some weapons that came in by boat. We'll need more than just what's in the bunkers. In the meanwhile, do whatever you want as long as you don't kill him."

"Will do," Brody said.

"Good. Oh, and remember, he's going to be the star of a show. Make sure he's presentable." Forest turned and walked away.

Kolya could feel his body shaking, the PTSD making itself known. But his voice was steady as Brody drew back his arm. "Fuck your mother." He repeated it in Russian. "*Yob tvoyu mat.*" Then he gritted his teeth, not wanting to give Brody the satisfaction of hearing him cry out as the beating began.

Chapter Fifty-Two

Yael changed Lyra's last diaper and dressed her in her last remaining outfit. Babies went through so many diapers, so many clothes. She focused on Lyra's face, the blue eyes open and watching her, while she tried to ignore the sounds behind her, the pounding of fists on a human being, the grunting of the men doing the beating. Kolya was mostly silent.

She turned around, Lyra in her arms, as Brody landed a hard blow with the butt of a rifle on Kolya's right leg and Kolya screamed. She felt a chill go through her. *Don't let it get to you. He's the enemy, he's the enemy. What happens to him isn't your concern.*

She approached. "Brody. I have a problem."

She didn't want to look at Kolya, but she couldn't help it. He was barely recognizable, the blood coating his face, one eye blackened and swollen shut. *He's the enemy. He's the enemy.* But that thought competed with another. *He could have pulled the trigger and risked killing her and Lyra, and he would have been safe. He didn't. Why? There could only be one reason—he hadn't been sure it was a blank.*

Brody struck Kolya's leg again, soliciting another cry of pain. "I'm busy, Yael." He turned to her, grinning. "Finally got the bastard to scream."

The sheer enjoyment of cruelty in Brody's face made her take a step back. *Who was this man?* She'd thought that Brody was a freedom fighter, not a sadist. But this wasn't fighting for freedom. This was torturing a helpless man for the fun of it.

She couldn't criticize Brody, not after what had happened earlier. Not openly, anyway. She couldn't risk him turning on her or the baby. Still... She wanted Brody to stop. She thought of a comment that might work.

"I'm proud of you for protecting the real America. But be careful. Victor wants him alive for now, and if you accidentally kill him, Victor will not be happy."

"You're right." Brody glanced at Kolya. "Didn't want him to be too comfortable while he's waiting to die. I can stop now that he's learned who's in charge. The real Americans. Not some fucking aliens. Or their Jew allies." He turned back to her, his expression slightly apologetic. "I didn't mean you, Yael. You've renounced them. I don't think of you as a Jew."

Even though he'd screamed at her for being a Jew earlier.

"I don't think of myself as a Jew anymore either." Yael looked down at her baby. "Isn't she beautiful?"

Brody's face softened, and he reached out a blood-soaked hand. Then he drew it back without touching Lyra. "Don't want to get blood on her or her clothes."

"Good. 'Cause this is her last clean outfit." She glanced over at Kolya. *He could have pulled the trigger. He would have saved himself if he'd risked killing Lyra. And her. He didn't.* "What happens next?"

"We take Petrov to the room I told you about. We're going to put him in it, wait until the vice president is scheduled to speak," he prodded Kolya's leg again with his foot, eliciting a moan, "and then blow up the bridge. Stream the whole thing."

Kolya may or may not have heard his fate described. He lay on his tied arms, eyes closed, taking deep breaths.

"You think he's conscious?"

"Hard to say." Brody shrugged. "Let's make sure he is. He should be awake to enjoy what time he has left."

Yael cocked her head to the side. "He looks pretty bad. Is that what Victor wants for a visual?"

Brody hesitated, looked down at his handiwork. "Shit," he muttered. "Probably not. I guess I got carried away. Should have stuck to areas that wouldn't be visible. Go get something to wash him off."

She carried Lyra into the kitchen where she found a mixing bowl that she filled with water and then pulled a dish towel out of a cabinet. She carried the towel, the bowl, and the baby back to the cot where Kolya was tied. Setting Lyra next to Kolya, she steeled herself to wash off the blood, dunking the towel into the cool water.

Before she began, she saw him lick dry lips. She cast a glance over her shoulder. Brody was talking to one of the men, not looking in her direction. "Thirsty?" She didn't wait for an answer, using the towel to squeeze some water into his mouth. He swallowed greedily. She dunked the towel into the bowl again, sopping up more water so he could drink again, placing the end of the cloth in his mouth so he could suck out the moisture. His uninjured right eye fluttered open, and he looked in her face. "Thanks." The word was spoken so quietly she barely heard it. She dunked the towel in the water again. He closed the uninjured eye as she began washing blood from his forehead, cheeks, jaw, and around his right eye. She tried to be gentle, but he still grimaced in pain as she worked.

The caked mats in the blond hair were especially tough to get out.

He could have pulled the trigger. Now he's going to die.

When she finished, she dropped the towel into the bowl of now red water, which she carried with her baby to the kitchen. She rinsed out the bowl and left the towel soaking in the sink. Then she returned to where Brody stood. The man Brody had been talking to moved off. "That's as good as I can do." She waved vaguely in Kolya's direction. The bruises and cuts, the blackened eye, still evidenced that Kolya'd been beaten, but his face was cleaner. "He still looks pretty shitty."

"Yeah, he does. Well, fuck. Victor'll just have to explain it." Then he turned his attention to Yael. "Anyway, you said you have a problem."

"I just told you. This is Lyra's last outfit. Her last diaper."

"Oh shit." Brody shifted back into the concerned father mode. "We should have stopped at a drug store or something last night."

"Drug stores don't have baby clothes. We need clothes and baby wipes as well as diapers. Can you send someone out?"

"No can do. Got a few guys running errands and the rest are busy doing stuff for the revolution. After all, it begins tonight. And anyway, men don't go shopping for baby diapers and clothes. That's woman's work."

But there were no other women in the warehouse.

"Then I'll go." She saw Brody's expression and decided to push a little more. "I have to. Lyra stays in a dirty diaper, she'll get a rash. She'll start crying. You don't want that. Nobody wants that. And clothes. She can't stay in a pee-soaked sleeper. All the other clothes are dirty too, and even if I hand-wash stuff, it'll take a day to dry."

Brody hesitated and then he nodded. "Okay—you go. Get

enough supplies to last four or five days. After tonight, no one's going out. Take Lyra with you. No one here has time to watch her."

She nodded and retrieved a purse and a backpack from the cot where she'd been nursing Lyra. She put on the hoody and baseball cap she'd worn to enter Kristin's apartment building. She slung the backpack into place on her shoulders and returned to Brody, who took the purse from her. He rooted through it.

"No keys." He pulled her keys out and dropped them on the floor. "You won't be needing these. They'll be looking for our car, and they're watching the apartment. No phone. No credit cards. There could be an alert for our credit cards. They'll be watching for your cell as well." He removed her phone from a front purse pocket and her credit cards from her wallet. They also went onto the floor. "Cash only. You have?"

"Couple hundred. Should be enough. It may take a little while to find a store with baby clothes. And I'd like to get a baby pouch too, so I can carry her and have my arms free." She also had a subway pass with twenty dollars on it.

"I want you back by early afternoon. We're going to start getting things ready, and I want to be sure the two of you are safe."

Brody had been fine with terrifying her, to test whether Kolya would follow an order to kill their baby. Brody hadn't told her or asked her. *And Kolya could have pulled the trigger, but he didn't.* And now Brody and Victor were going to blow him up with a bomb.

Not just Kolya. They were going to kill other people. A lot of other people.

But Brody claimed he wanted her and Lyra to be safe.

Maybe he did. He did love them—in his way—but that

didn't excuse what he'd done. It didn't change her revulsion at the sheer sadism Brody had just displayed.

She involuntarily glanced at the cot, where the bound man lay unmoving, eyes still closed. Then she smiled at Brody, her submissive and loving smile. "Be as fast as I can."

Chapter Fifty-Three

The threat of VX meant that any attempt to rescue Kolya had to be weighed against the risk of releasing a deadly nerve poison in a very crowded city.

Jonathan knew it. The team knew it. That accounted for the glum faces as they sat in the safe house, waiting for word on the white van. Or it could just have been the lack of anything they could do.

In this line of work, risk was a given. Risk created bonds between the agents who shared it. They had each other's backs. And sometimes...they didn't.

Kolya wasn't just a colleague. He was Jonathan's closest friend. He'd been Jonathan's best man at his wedding, and Jonathan was supposed to return the favor at Kolya's wedding in two weeks.

Elizabeth, Frick, Marty, and Tehila were also Kolya's friends, even if not quite as close as Jonathan. Elizabeth, Frick, and Marty, along with Jonathan, had risked their lives and careers to save Kolya in Romania. Elizabeth and Kolya had dated for a brief time before Alex had arrived in Washington. Kolya and Tehila shared the bond of being two of the three Jews in the agency. Tehila and her wife occasionally had Shabbat dinner with Kolya and Alex.

The chances of locating the van, and doing so before Kolya was killed, were small. Even if they found the van—a long shot —their options were limited by the VX. They couldn't shoot at the van. They couldn't rush it. They couldn't even approach.

Even if it cost Kolya his life.

Jonathan did not call Alex. There was nothing he could tell her. There was nothing he wanted to tell her. In fact, just of the thought of having to tell her the situation made him sick. She was also a friend.

Anyway, she knew enough. She knew Kolya was in trouble.

She didn't need to know that the people holding him had threatened to use a deadly nerve poison and preventing the release of that poison was more important than saving Kolya.

The team drank coffee, checked for posts on social media from known members of American Gold Posse, and mostly avoided talking. Nothing to talk about.

It was around two in the afternoon when something finally broke. The white van had been spotted. The call from Paul in the New York City Police Department was to the point. "State police spotted the van on Long Island. Montauk. Loading boxes from a private house. Sending the address."

"We're on our way. Tell the state police not to approach, but not to let them leave. And we'll need a hazmat team on site."

"Got it."

Jonathan signaled the other agents to get ready. The computers were locked down. Phones pocketed. Weapons checked. Jackets donned. But there was a restlessness in the team. Jonathan could feel it. It was Tehila who put it into words. "Are you going to call Alex?"

Jonathan hesitated. "And tell her what?"

"That we have a lead on the van that was used to kidnap Kolya."

"And that we might not be able to save him because there could be a nerve poison in the van? That's what I should tell her?" Jonathan shook his head. "Anyway, the whole operation is classified, and we shouldn't be alerting any non-ECA personnel to what's happening."

"We wouldn't even know about the van if it wasn't for Alex," Tehila said. "Quite apart from the fact that she's not going to call *The New York Times*, she's a former ECA attorney. She's lived with Kolya for years, and she knows the game. She deserves to know what's happening."

"We don't know what's happening to Kolya. If we had something definite, that would be one thing, even if it were bad news." Jonathan was waiting at the door for the rest of the team. "It'll just upset her without giving her anything more."

"At least she'd know he was taken alive. And do you think she'd be any more upset than she already is—imagining the worst?"

"Agree with Tehila," Frick said. "She should be in the loop, to the extent possible."

Marty nodded.

"Okay. Fine. " Jonathan said. "You're right. But we need to get on the road. Now. Whoever's not driving can call."

* * *

Barbara O'Brien had learned of Kristen's murder and the disappearance of the baby in her custody soon after she'd arrived in the office. The police claimed that they didn't have any suspects, that the videos of the perpetrators had not shown any faces. Barbara didn't need to see faces.

It had to be the parents. The bitch of a mother and the son of a bitch who'd broken her nose.

She spent a few hours that morning checking up on different cases, and then she turned her attention to the missing baby.

No one had ever snatched a baby out of her care. No one had ever harmed a foster mother.

No one had ever hit her, either.

She was going to get that baby back, and the parents would never see the child again. They'd be in prison for the rest of their miserable lives. As for the lawyer who'd represented Yael McMillan, she was on Barbara's hit list as well.

Barbara didn't care whether Alex Feinstein had been involved in the murder and kidnapping or not. Barbara would see that the damn lawyer lost her license. Maybe even went to prison as well.

First things first: Find the baby.

At two o'clock, she sent out an email that she would spend the afternoon making home visits. Before she left her office, she opened a safe that she kept under her desk, removed a Smith & Wesson revolver, and loaded it with six bullets. If she found the criminals, she'd be ready.

Her first stop was Brody and Yael's apartment. She rang the bell, hammered on the door, but no one answered. An elderly woman in a pink-and-white housecoat poked a head out of the neighboring apartment and said sourly that she hadn't seen anyone go in or out for at least a day.

Barbara waited until the woman closed her door before breaking the locks and entering the apartment.

No one was home.

Barbara walked through the apartment. It was as neat as she remembered it, and she could have searched for drugs or other illegal substances, but she didn't care if there were drugs or not.

She wanted to find the McMillans and the baby they'd stolen.

She checked the hall before she left the apartment, not wanting a run-in with the neighbor and not wanting the neighbor to call the police. She walked down the stairs and then onto the street, deciding on her next step.

The paperwork she'd filled out for Yael had not listed any family in the vicinity, which meant that Barbara didn't really have any good ideas where Brody and Yael might be staying, if they were even still in the city.

But Yael's lawyer might know.

Chapter Fifty-Four

Alex had spent the morning at Ruth's apartment on the computer, searching for any information on American Gold Posse. She'd found little more than she already knew. Nothing to indicate where the group might be located in New York.

Periodically, she texted Ruth and got the same answer back. *Nothing to report.*

She ate one of Ruth's bagels for lunch, not because she was hungry, but because she needed to keep her strength up.

Was it only last night that she'd contemplated breaking up with Kolya to keep him safe? Was it less than a week ago that she'd teased him about the music selections for the wedding?

She couldn't sit still. She closed Ruth's computer and paced through the apartment, trying to find something to distract herself. But she couldn't focus enough to read, and the television held no appeal.

She texted Ruth again.

Nothing.

She wanted to call Jonathan, but she hesitated. If he had

anything to tell her, wouldn't he call? And she never initiated calls with Kolya when he was in the field.

So, she paced, pulling up her memories of the years that she'd known him. Kolya sitting next to her in law school. She'd been attracted to him, but they were initially just friends. At the time, she'd been engaged to another man, even though she knew that Kolya had deeper feelings for her.

She remembered their first meeting at the ECA, years later. The night they moved from "friends" to lovers.

The morning he'd proposed.

The magical trip to Paris after his assignment in Berlin.

But the image of Romania also intruded. Romania—where she'd seen him chained to a wall after he'd been beaten and tortured. She remembered when Max, the sadist guard, had offered Kolya the choice of watching him rape Alex or having him break Kolya's uninjured leg—and Kolya hadn't hesitated for a second, offering to sacrifice himself to protect her.

Then her phone rang.

Twenty minutes later, she was back at Noah's law office. Ruth, seated at her desk, was the sole occupant, the attorneys who used the space opting to work at home. Alex cast a glance at the closed door to Noah's office and averted her eyes.

"I told you to stay at my apartment." Ruth held up a hand as a call came in. She fielded it smoothly. Then she turned back to Alex. "You're safer there."

"Fuck being safe. Do you have a car I can borrow?"

"I have a car. It's parked in a garage on Tenth Avenue. Why?"

She explained what she knew. Kolya had been caught on video being forced into a white van, and the van had been spotted near the eastern end of Long Island. A team of agents was headed to the area as were the state police.

"Well, that's good, isn't it?" Ruth said. "You just have to sit tight and wait."

Alex hesitated. Jonathan had disclosed the possibility that a nerve poison might be in the van. She liked Ruth. But how much information did Ruth need to have? She answered slowly. "For reasons I can't really explain, I think that saving Kolya might not be the top priority. I should be there—if nothing else—so someone is putting his life first."

"Do you know where this van might be?"

Alex shook her head. "I figured that I'd head in that direction and then try calling Jonathan again when I hit South Hampton." It wasn't much of a plan, but it was better than just sitting and waiting.

"Oh honey." Ruth reached out to pat Alex on the arm. "That's just stupid. Long Island's too big to just start driving without knowing where you're going."

"I know. I don't care. Will you loan me your car?"

"I have a better idea. The lawyers here use an investigator for some of their cases, and he has contacts in the state police. I'll give him a call. See if he can find out where this van is. And I'll come with you." She pointed to a chair opposite her desk. "Sit. It may take a little time, but better to know where we're going before we start."

Chapter Fifty-Five

Kolya managed to roll partly onto his left side to take some of the strain off his arms and shoulders without putting pressure onto his bad right leg. Brody and the other men nearby checked on him periodically, but the beatings didn't resume.

He estimated that it had been a couple of hours since Forest handed him the gun with the instruction to shoot Yael's baby, although he had no way to judge. He'd heard Brody describe how they planned to kill him. The rope around his elbows and the zip tie on his wrists were tight, but he tried to feel for weaknesses in the restraints.

He felt terrible, from the strain of being held immobile to the aches and pains from the beating. The water that Yael had given him had helped a little with his thirst, but it hadn't been enough. Worse, his present situation periodically blended with memories of Romania, giving him an almost out-of-body sense of unreality. But the flashbacks from PTSD were preferable to thoughts of Alex. She was probably dead. Forest did use deception to manipulate, and he had tried to induct Kolya into the group. However, convincing Kolya that Alex was dead would not be an effective recruitment tool. Forest would have tried to use Alex's safety as incentive for Kolya to join up—so it would have been in his interest to mislead Kolya into believing Alex was alive.

He was tempted to let go and embrace his upcoming death. He was exhausted, mentally, emotionally, and physically. If what Brody had said was true, at least he'd die quickly. Death by explosion was messy but instantaneous. There was something to be said for a fast death.

Just let it happen.

He might not have any choice in the matter, anyway.

He had a little time to live. Nothing would happen until they moved him.

Still, he couldn't just let go. Maybe there would be a chance to do something. He had to try, because he wouldn't be the only person dying in what would be Forest's opening salvo for his revolution.

Kolya rested, using his breathing techniques, and ran variations of jazz standards though his mind. He pictured his hands on piano keys and heard the melodies—"Satin Doll," "Moonlight in Vermont"—and then visualized improvisations. Both techniques helped him fight down the PTSD and avoid thoughts of Alex.

Despite the discomfort, he drifted off once or twice, waking when Brody, Dex, and Roger approached the cot where he was lying.

He tensed, feeling the fear flood his body.

"We have to carry him?" Roger asked. "Awkward, and it's a lot of stairs."

"We could just push him down the stairs," Dex said.

"No. Victor wants him alive until the explosion. Untie his legs," Brody said. "He can walk."

Kolya kept his eyes closed while he was rolled onto his back and his legs were freed. He opened the one eye that wasn't swollen shut after he was pulled into a sitting position.

"Stand up," Brody ordered.

Kolya swung his legs over the side of the cot and felt the tingling of circulation returning, but the muscles were still cramped from being tied for so long. While his right leg was not broken, it was hurting badly with the change of position and pressure. He glanced down at the floor and saw a small metal ring that held two keys, and then he turned his eyes on Brody, whose hostile gaze had remained fixed on Kolya.

Brody had forgotten about the keys.

It wasn't much. But it was something. A metal key could cut through a zip tie. It would take time, but if they didn't kill him immediately, Kolya might be able to free himself.

The trick would be getting hold of the keys without being noticed. A second trick would be keeping the keys hidden until he could use them.

At least the three men were focused on him, not on anything around them—or on the floor.

"I said—stand up," Brody repeated, his tone harsher, promising punishment if Kolya didn't obey.

Kolya bent forward at the waist and pushed up with his quads and calves, rising to his feet. He swayed, and then his legs gave out. He fell, twisting to land on his bound arms and his back.

As he hit the floor, he felt for the metallic shape.

He had managed to land so that the keys were hidden under his body. But the keys were in the wrong spot—under his shoulder. Not close enough for him to grasp, not with his arms and hands bound.

"Goddamn bastard," Brody growled and turned to the other two. "Pick him up."

Kolya scooted backwards on the floor, as if he were trying to escape the men reaching for him, shifting his body to position his hands closer to the keys. The maneuver moved the keys closer—against his forearm instead of his shoulder. Better, but not quite close enough. The keys were still just out of reach.

Roger and Dex grabbed his arms. The motion, dragging him on the floor before pulling him to his feet, did what he hadn't been able to do by himself. His left hand touched the ring of the keys, and he grabbed it, closing his fingers tightly around the metal as he was yanked upright.

The two men held his arms, but he staggered, his right leg giving out again.

Brody was in front of him, not in back. "Walk, you fuck."

"I'm trying." Kolya kept his voice defeated, the tone of someone resigned to his fate. He didn't want to risk another beating—or worse— a close examination that would reveal the keys. He stiffened his right leg to allow him to put weight on it, enough so that he could limp forward while being supported. Awkwardly and painfully, he was half-helped, half-dragged across the floor to the stairs and then down the twenty steps.

The main floor was busier than it had been earlier. More men. More weapons. There was an electric feel of excitement. A few heads turned to watch his limping progress across the floor, but most of the men ignored the parade. They were gearing up for battle.

The white van that had transported Kolya earlier was gone. Instead, he was shoved into the back of a blue-and-white van, painted with the name and insignia of Brooklyn's power company. Inside, wires and pipes were stacked on the floor. Bits of equipment hung from hooks. To the side were white-and-orange cones, screens to shield workmen, and a black-and-white sign, "DANGER ELECTRICAL WORK." Roger and Dex positioned him against a wall and pulled on white jumpsuits. Brody also donned a white jumpsuit and a cap and then plopped into the driver's seat in the front of the truck. He turned on the engine.

A row of pipes underneath his ass, Kolya slumped against the wall of the van, resting on his arms and hands, the two guards uncomfortably close on either side. He scanned the area near him. Nothing that he could use. The keys hidden in his hand were his only small glimmer of hope.

"Victor's not coming?" Roger called up to Brody.

"He's there already. Getting things ready." Brody started the engine and then turned to glance back. "Watch him at all times."

"Yeah, yeah," Roger muttered. "He's not going anywhere."

"You sure of that? Check that he hasn't loosened any of the restraints. Remember, he's very dangerous."

"Yeah, okay." Roger grabbed Kolya's shoulders and pulled him forward. "Dex, check the zip tie and the ropes."

Dex tightened the rope around Kolya's elbows and inspected the plastic zip tie on his wrists. "Let me see your hands," he ordered.

He forced Kolya's fingers open.

Chapter Fifty-Six

Yael stopped at a drugstore first. She bought small packages of diapers and wipes, so they could fit into her backpack. When she returned to the warehouse, she'd need a crate of each. But she couldn't carry that many diapers on the subway.

Surprisingly, the drugstore had a baby sling for carrying an infant. She bought it along with the diapers and wipes, entered a bathroom, and changed Lyra. "You need a new outfit, baby girl." But there were no nearby baby stores for clothes.

She positioned Lyra in the baby pouch.

After leaving the drugstore, she walked five blocks to a subway entrance. She changed the subway lines three times, finally boarding a number one train and exiting at Thirty-Fourth Street in Manhattan.

She checked her watch. She'd been gone for more than an hour. Brody had told her to be back early. But she had to buy some outfits for Lyra, and she didn't know any places in Brooklyn. She knew that Macy's on Thirty-Fourth Street had baby clothes, and she was doing exactly what she'd told Brody she would do.

He couldn't be angry.

But he could—if she took too long.

Her memory flooded with images: Kolya approaching to shoot her and the baby—or so she'd thought—until he'd grabbed Roger's gun to try to shoot Victor instead; Brody's smug assertion that he'd known that the gun held a blank; Brody's pleased face after he'd beaten Kolya bloody.

The foster mother that Brody had shot.

He's still my husband.

She didn't immediately head for the baby department. Instead, she roamed the main floor, checking out makeup and accessories. A white silk scarf decorated with roses caught her eye, and she tried it on her hair. Pretty. When had she last bought something for herself? The scarf was on sale for thirty-five dollars, and she peeled off two twenty-dollar bills to buy it. The middle-aged salesclerk cut off the tags and helped Yael wind it around her neck.

She moved to the makeup counter and checked out different shades of lipstick. When had she last worn makeup? Brody didn't like her to wear makeup. He thought women should look natural. She found a subdued red lipstick that the woman behind the counter assured her complimented her complexion and her hair color.

She bought that as well.

Next, she rode the elevator up to the sixth floor and began hunting for baby outfits. She picked out a white sleeper with pink bunnies, two sleepers with dinosaurs, another three with butterflies, and two in pink with small, embroidered hearts. They were six-month outfits, a little big, but Lyra would grow into them.

And they were on half-price sale. A good bargain.

The salesclerk, a young man in a white shirt and dark pants, smiled at her and Lyra when Yael took the clothes to the register. "How old?"

"Four months."

"She's beautiful."

"Thank you." Yael paid in cash and stuffed the bag of new outfits into her backpack. She'd change Lyra later.

She left the store but couldn't bring herself to get back onto the subway to return to the warehouse and to Brody. *Maybe a snack and something to drink first.*

She found a coffee shop two blocks from Macy's and ordered a blended strawberry lemonade and a chocolate chip scone. She ducked into the bathroom to change Lyra's diaper and switch her into one of the new outfits, the sleeper with pink bunnies. Then she picked up her order and seated herself at a table for two, arranging Lyra in the baby sling so she could nurse unobtrusively.

While the baby drank breast milk, Yael drank her lemonade. It was perfect, cold and sweet. She was thirstier than she'd realized. She drained half the glass, but her enjoyment of the drink brought a twinge of guilt. More than a twinge. Drinking the lemonade brought back what she had done—and what she hadn't done.

Kolya could have pulled the trigger. He didn't. Then, when he was tied up and beaten, she did nothing to help him. Squeezed a few drops of moisture into his mouth before cleaning his face for the sadistic display that Victor and Brody had planned. She was sitting in a coffee shop, enjoying a cold drink, and all she'd done for a man who'd risked his own life rather than take the chance of killing her and her baby, was offer him a few sips of warm liquid. She hadn't tried to stop the beating. She hadn't tried to talk Brody out of killing him.

She could have at least offered Kolya a glass of cold water.

Maybe something to eat. Instead, she'd walked out and left him to Brody's tender mercies.

He could have pulled the trigger.

She knew what they were going to do to Kolya.

She knew what they were going to do to New York.

She looked down at the baby on her breast. At least she had Lyra back. Lyra, the most important thing in her life. If she took Lyra back to the warehouse, she could be putting her at risk. She no longer trusted that Brody would put Lyra—or her—first.

Don't go back.

She could just get on a train and disappear. Brody hadn't taken all of her credit cards—she'd hidden one inside a pocket in her purse. She could call her parents in Maryland, as Alex had suggested, and ask if she could come home. Even if they had been hurt that she'd excluded them, her parents would welcome her. They were loving parents who hadn't deserved being shut out of her life and who deserved to meet their granddaughter.

But anyone looking for her would check with her parents. The police. Brody.

She wished she could talk to Alex who would know where Yael could hide out. Even if Alex had told Kolya about Brody and Victor, she had still tried to get Lyra back. Brody had said that Alex was dead. But Yael no longer trusted anything that Brody told her. Maybe she wasn't dead. If Yael could only find her.

And what to tell her in turn? That Yael hadn't helped Alex's fiancé—that he was a prisoner and had been beaten senseless while Yael had done nothing? That he was going to be brutally murdered?

It wasn't too late—at least not too late to save Kolya's life.

Not too late to save the other people who'd die if the bridge blew.

They weren't going to set off the explosion until nine o'clock, in approximately three hours.

She nibbled on the scone and checked her watch again. Almost four hours since she'd left the warehouse. They'd be moving him soon.

She looked down at Lyra, who'd finished nursing and fallen asleep again. *He could have pulled the trigger.*

And she made her decision.

If Alex was still alive, and Yael could contact her, maybe the two of them could do something to help Kolya.

She could call the police, of course, but she feared that the police would fuck it up. They'd send a SWAT team in, guns blazing, and Kolya would still wind up dead—either shot by the police or from Victor setting off the explosion early. And the police would take Lyra from her again.

To save Kolya required something more subtle. Sneakily intelligent. Between Yael and Alex, they could come up with a plan. If Yael could contact her. But she didn't have a phone, and without a phone, she wouldn't be able to reach Alex.

Except—she suddenly thought of a possibility. The law office where Alex had taken her after court.

The law office where Victor had tortured and shot Noah.

Someone there would know how to reach Alex. It wasn't far away, either. Just a few blocks. Yael could walk there in fifteen minutes. Maybe this was why she'd chosen to shop for baby clothes at the Macy's in Herald Square instead of anywhere else in Brooklyn or Manhattan. Because her subconscious mind had made the decision before her conscious mind caught up.

If Alex were alive.

If Yael could steel herself to go back.

Chapter Fifty-Seven

lex paced in front of Ruth's desk, unable to sit still. "When is your investigator going to call back?" The door to Noah's office was shut, the room not yet cleaned of the evidence of murder, and Alex was just as happy not to see where Noah had died. The rest of the office was eerily empty, given that it was midafternoon, but the attorneys who normally worked there were either in court or working from home. It was only Alex and Ruth.

"When he has something." Ruth paused from typing a document request. "His contact in the state police has to get back to him. Maybe you could sit down. Read a book. Play a game on your phone."

Alex gave a short bark of laughter.

"Okay, stupid suggestion. But you need to calm down. We'll leave as soon as we know something."

"It's rush hour now. It'll take us five hours to get to the end of Long Island. Maybe more, depending on traffic."

"And if it turns out the information is wrong, and that the people holding Kolya are not in Montauk but here or in New

Jersey or upstate, we'll be five hours out. Did you try calling *your* contact?"

"He's not picking up." Alex had called him five times. She knew that Jonathan would not contact her again unless he had news. He'd already broken laws to tell her as much as he had.

"Okay, then, we wait. And while we're waiting, I want to finish these. They're due in two days, and I'd rather not stay up all night tomorrow." Ruth pointed towards the room that Alex had occupied at Noah's invitation. "Find some way to keep yourself occupied until we get some news. You're driving me crazy."

Alex could acknowledge the fairness of Ruth's complaint. She borrowed a laptop from Ruth and retreated to her temporary office. She decided against contacting anyone in her law office just in case someone was tracking her business, and instead, she skimmed recent court decisions that interested her. Moving to political news, she read articles on the presidential election campaign. She didn't like President Lewis —he'd set Kolya up in Romania and would have allowed him to be killed, but that far-right Christian Nationalists supported Lenny Rhodes, the man running against Lewis, scared her. Still, she couldn't imagine that he'd win. She had faith in people. Faith in the country.

Anyway, she had enough real worries for the moment.

Then she heard Ruth's voice. "Can I help you?" Her voice was sharp and not particularly friendly.

Alex didn't hear the response, but Ruth's tone was a signal. She closed the laptop, and cautiously cracked the door of the office to see who had entered. Then she yanked the door open and strode out. "Yael?"

Yael, her head covered in a white scarf with red roses, turned to Alex. "Alex. I'm so glad..." The first words came out in a rush. "Brody said you were dead, but I thought maybe...maybe he was wrong...Anyway, so I thought if I came here, maybe someone would know...Anyway, here you are."

Yael had never stammered before, to Alex's knowledge, not during their years of friendship, not during any of their conversations about getting Lyra back. She was stammering now. Fear? Embarrassment? Or something else?

Guilt?

"Yes. I'm here. And you have your baby." Alex smiled at the sleeping child. Adorable. But that wasn't the point. "And you got Lyra back...how?"

"I...Brody and I...I didn't..." Yael flushed. "Can we not do this right now?"

"And you didn't have anything to do with killing Noah?" Ruth asked.

"I didn't want anyone hurt. I just wanted my baby."

The statement was almost a confession. Alex felt her anger rising. Yael had to have told Victor and Brody the law office's location. Whatever she had wanted didn't matter. Noah was still dead, and Alex doubted that Yael had tried to stop the murder. Yael bore responsibility not just for Noah's death but for Kolya's kidnapping. "And you came here—why? To find me? To finish off what your husband started?"

"No. No. He doesn't know where I am. Alex, you have to believe me." Yael leaned forward to grab Alex's arm. Alex tried to pull her arm away, but Yael held on. "I'm here because...because he didn't pull the trigger... he could have protected himself, but he didn't. He protected me. He didn't know whether the bullet was real. He's a good person. And now they're going to kill him."

"He?" Alex pulled Yael's hand from her arm and held on to it. "Are you talking about Kolya?"

"Yes. Of course. Didn't I just say so?"

"You said everything but his name. He's alive?"

"He was when I left. He should still be alive. That's why I wanted to find you. Brody would kill me too if he knew." Yael swayed as if dizzy.

"Go sit down, honey. I'll get you something to drink from the kitchen." Ruth jumped from her chair and headed towards the back.

Yael sank into a chair in Alex's office, arranging the baby on her lap. Alex seated herself behind the desk and took a deep breath. Kolya was alive, but he was going to be killed if nothing was done.

She restrained the impulse to shake Yael. Despite her own impatience, Alex knew that Yael was defying her husband and the cult to help Kolya. As an experienced attorney, she also knew that the best way to induce an emotional witness to talk was to be kind. And patient. Even if it was hard. Even if someone you loved was in danger.

Alex spoke calmly. "Start from the beginning."

* * *

The state police had surrounded the van with a ring of flashing lights. Officers, stationed behind their cars, held guns and rifles, but as Jonathan had hoped, none of them had approached the van, which was parked in front of a yellow ranch house that needed a coat of paint and a new roof. A state police car blocked the driveway.

"There're at least three guys in the van," the officer in charge informed Jonathan. The officer didn't know exactly who Jonathan was or what agency he worked for, but his boss had received a call from the White House indicating that the state police were to follow Jonathan's lead. "There may be more inside the house. I have men stationed around the back. I can get a SWAT team to rush the house?"

"Not yet." Jonathan shook his head. He didn't know if VX was in the van or in the house, but he had to assume it was. "Hazmat team on the way?"

"Yeah."

"For now, we hold position. No one in or out until they get here." Jonathan glanced at his team. They were fanning out, to help cover any possible exits from the van. He saw the grim expressions, and the looks from Elizabeth and Tehila. None of them liked the situation.

His phone buzzed, and he took it out to check the number. Alex. He clicked the phone off without answering. No reason to take the call. There was nothing he could tell her.

Chapter Fifty-Eight

The fake power company van lurched to a stop. No one had spoken for the duration of the trip; Roger and Dex didn't seem any more interested in talking to each other than to Kolya. That had been fine with Kolya. He didn't want to hear anything from any of them, let alone engage with them.

Once the van halted, there was a bustle of activity. Brody jumped out and opened the back. Roger and Dex handed out the screens, the orange-and-white cones, and the sign proclaiming "DANGER ELECTRICAL WORK"—but both men stayed in the van, close to Kolya.

Still, with their attention elsewhere, Kolya stretched his hands and fingers to feel between two of the pipes under him. Within a few seconds, he located the keys that he'd hidden just in time—just before his guards had checked the restraints and forced his hands open.

He hooked a finger around the key ring and pulled it up and into his palm. For better safekeeping, he slid the keys into his back pocket. If anyone patted his ass, they'd feel the metal, but the pocket was probably safer than his hands.

Brody slid the side of the van open. "No one's around. Get him."

They were under the Brooklyn Bridge, or so Kolya assumed from what he'd overheard earlier. They hustled him from the van to the back of a set of stone stairs and through a door marked "Electrical Equipment" and then through a second door, concealed behind a wood panel. A stone staircase wound downward.

His bad leg hurt with every step. The bruises throbbed, and he thought he might have a broken rib or two. He could barely see through his left eye. He nearly fell down the stairs, but the men gripping his arms held him up.

At the bottom, Victor Forest, dressed in green fatigues, was busy setting four floodlights to illuminate a large room, where wooden crates were stacked against the walls. He glanced over at Kolya and the three men.

"There." Forest pointed to a metal pole in the middle of the room.

They dumped Kolya on the floor. Brody tied him to the pole with two ropes, one around his chest and one around his waist, his arms and wrists still bound behind his back. Between the ropes and the possible broken ribs, Kolya could only take shallow breaths. The deep breathing technique he used to calm himself was impossible.

Kolya closed his good eye against the brightness of the lights trained on him. He'd found one of the secret bunkers, for all the good the knowledge would do him. He still had the keys, but the odds of freeing himself were slim.

He'd try anyway.

He maneuvered the keys out of his back pocket and into his hand. He positioned the sharp side of one key against the plastic zip tie binding his wrists and began a rubbing motion.

"His face is really fucked up, Brody." Forest's voice was annoyed. "What were you thinking?"

"What does it matter? Who's gonna care that a bad guy got beat up?"

"That's the point," Forest said. "He's the bad guy. We're the good guys. We talked about this. Don't want people to think that we'd beat up a man who couldn't fight back."

Brody shrugged. "Okay. But you can just explain that it happened when he tried to kill you."

"I know, but still—it's not a great visual," Forest said. "But whatever. I'll work with what we've got."

Kolya cracked his good eye open to see what was happening. Forest was setting a cell phone on a tripod about three feet from his right side.

Forest noticed that Kolya was watching and gave him a brief wave. "I hope you appreciate that your death is going to help usher in the real America. And millions will watch it happen. After all, who can resist a real-life television drama: the suspense, the tension of a man waiting to die. You'll have a moment of fame. Some people would be willing to die for that."

Kolya mentally paraphrased a saying attributed to Lincoln about a man being tarred and feathered. *If it wasn't for the honor of the thing, he'd just as soon skip it.* Then he rolled his head against the post to look at the crates that lined the walls around the room. "Plastic explosives?"

"Yes. They're old, but they work. As already demonstrated. And that's VX in those two far crates. Some biological weapons, but I'm not sure just what. Also canned peaches, pears, and plums. I'd offer you some, but they're a little old."

The explosion would scatter the nerve poison and biological weapons and kill more people than the initial blast. Thousands more at least. It would be a painful way to die.

"What do you think killing thousands of innocent people

will accomplish?" Kolya's voice sounded cracked and dry, even to him.

Forest frowned at him. "The people of this country need to wake up. I want them to see what their alien government has done—stockpiled weapons to be used against them. And I'll give the aliens a chance to surrender the government before anyone gets hurt. You're one of their agents, and they might want to save you. I don't think they will, but if they surrender, your life will be spared. And if they don't, they'll get to see you blown up, as well as Brooklyn Heights and lower Manhattan. Then we repeat this in every bunker around the country, until they surrender, or the people rise up and we prevail."

It was a terrifying and crazy plan, designed to maximize chaos and death.

"I know we're under the Brooklyn Bridge." Kolya coughed, his throat dry. "Where are the other bunkers?" Little chance that he'd be able to do anything with the information, just as there was little chance he'd saw through his restraints in time, but he still wanted to know on the slight possibility that he'd manage to escape. The information would be critical to stopping Forest's revolution. He continued to gently rub the key against the zip tie. There was a slight dent in the plastic but nothing more.

"Around." Forest tapped a pocket. "Nothing for you to worry about. You just worry about putting on a good show."

Brody had begun running wires between the various crates. He stopped and straightened. "They won't see him blown up. They'll just see a blur of fire when the whole place goes up."

Forest nodded. "True. Just seeing one large explosion isn't quite as gripping as watching a man blown apart. We'll set a separate device and timer for two minutes before the big explosion."

Brody finished running the wires from the crates to a timer.

He opened one of the crates and removed what looked like a brick of C-4. He motioned to Forest, who shook his head.

"Too much. Too big an explosion, and we're back to the audience just seeing a fireball." Forest pulled off a small handful of the putty-like material, molding it into a ball. Then he carried the ball over to where Kolya was tied, molded it into the rope across Kolya's stomach, and attached a detonator. He smiled down at Kolya. "With the blast at your waist, it'll blow off your head and your limbs. I thought about killing you slower and more painfully, but the public has to be served. Don't worry. It'll be messy, but instantaneous. Not prolonged suffering."

"Considerate." Kolya couldn't help himself.

"And you'll be reunited with your fiancée. Isn't that what you want?"

In a way, but not if it meant other people dying. Alex would not have approved his giving up. But he had to keep any thoughts of Alex at a distance to focus on whatever small chance he had of freeing himself. Kolya leaned his head against the pole behind him and didn't answer.

"I suppose I should have offered you a last meal," Forest said. "But that's just sentimental. I never understood the pretend courtesy before an execution. Remember to struggle for the camera."

Then he ran a wire from the detonator to a timer, set it, and strolled back to the tripod to survey the room. He ran a quick test video and showed it to Brody.

"It looks good," Brody said. "Everything in the room's visible."

"And me?" Forest ran a hand through his hair and straightened the collar on the fatigues. "How do I look?"

"You look like a war leader. Ready for the intro?"

"I am. But he's not." Forest nodded towards Kolya. "I'll turn the sound off after I speak, but I don't want him shouting anything. Or mouthing words that someone who could lipread would understand."

"Right." Brody ripped a piece of duct tape from a roll and approached Kolya. "Any last words, Petrov?"

Kolya looked up with his good eye and quietly spoke his favorite Russian curse. "*Yob tvoyu mat.*" Then he translated and elaborated. "I just told you to fuck your mother, but then, you already have, haven't you, you demented lunatic?"

Brody drew back a fist.

"Don't," Forest said. "I don't want to have to clean up blood. And I want him conscious for the duration. Increases the drama."

"Fine." Brody slapped the tape across Kolya's mouth.

Chapter Fifty-Nine

The door of the law office was unlocked, but then it should be, in the middle of the day. Barbara O'Brien touched the gun in her pocket for reassurance. Then she placed her hand on the doorknob and turned it, slowly creaking the door open.

The reception desk was empty. Most of the offices looked dark. She didn't understand why in the middle of a workday the office would be so empty.

Where was everyone?

But it wasn't completely empty. She heard voices and saw lights under one door.

Gripping the gun in the pocket of her jacket, she approached slowly. She wouldn't bring the gun out unless she had to. She knew that the offices were shared by attorneys who had no involvement with her cases, but if Barbara could locate Alexandria Feinstein, she'd have a way to find the bitch who'd killed Kristen and stolen a baby.

She listened just outside the door but couldn't make out the words. But she was pretty sure she recognized the voices.

Alex Feinstein wouldn't know what hit her. Barbara was not going to be stopped.

She pushed the door open and marched inside. Alex Feinstein was seated at a desk, and across from her, Yael McMillan held the baby she'd stolen. Barbara had been right all along—not only was Yael a murderer, Alex Feinstein was an accomplice.

Barbara pulled the gun out of her pocket and loudly announced, "Don't move, either of you. You're under arrest."

Yael gasped and clutched the baby to her chest. But Alex Feinstein just glared at her with dark eyes. "You're not a cop. Put the fucking gun away before someone gets hurt."

Barbara was furious. How dare that lawyer not only help a killer, but act as if she, Barbara, were nothing more than an annoyance. She raised her voice. "Yael McMillan, you're a killer and a kidnapper. Alex Feinstein, you're an accomplice. And I will shoot both of you if you don't obey."

"You're going to shoot two unarmed people and then do what? Call the police and tell them that you killed two people who were not a threat to you?" Alex Feinstein tilted her head to the side. "Is that what you're planning? Because it doesn't seem really well thought out, if you ask me."

Barbara opened and shut her mouth twice while she thought of a response. "I'll tell them...that you threatened me, and I feared for my life."

"Threatened you? With what?" Alex's tone remained calm. "A subpoena? A dirty diaper? Because you're threatening a lawyer and a nursing mother, and those are our weapons. Or did you bring a drop gun? Because that's what you'll need if you're going to shoot someone in cold blood and claim self-defense. But if you only have one gun, you've got a problem."

Barbara felt her face going red. No, she hadn't thought it out, had she? She'd counted on her ability to intimidate. She'd counted on Alex Feinstein and Yael McMillan simply and meekly obeying at the sight of her gun. That they weren't obeying was infuriating. That Alex Feinstein didn't even seem concerned was humiliating.

Then something hard and metallic was shoved against her back.

"Sweetie..." It was an unknown voice. Female. "I have a 9mm pistol lined up with what passes as your heart, and I don't particularly care what happens with the police. Now *you* drop your weapon and put your hands up or I will do the children of New York a big favor."

* * *

Barbara O'Brien was the last person Alex had expected to see. Dealing with Barbara was the last thing she needed. But Barbara was just a distraction. Kolya. What was happening to him? Was he still alive?

She was grateful that Ruth had gone out to the kitchen to make tea—that Ruth carried a gun and that she had realized what was happening and acted.

Ruth directed Barbara to sit in a chair, which she did. Alex retrieved Barbara's revolver. Only six shots, but it was something. The more guns the better.

"What do we do with her?" Yael asked.

"Duct tape," Ruth said. "My desk. Top drawer."

Yael went for the duct tape. Barbara glowered at Alex and Ruth. "Let me go or you're going to prison. All of you."

"Should we tell her what's going on?" Ruth asked.

"Do you think it would make any difference?" Alex responded.

"No."

"Then don't."

Yael returned and handed Alex the duct tape.

"I'll have your law license, you fucking bitch. I'll see you disbarred." Barbara's face had turned bright red.

"Shut up." Alex wound the tape around Barbara's wrists and arms, taping her to the chair. Barbara began to shout curses.

Ruth patted her on the shoulder. "You'll feel a lot better if you calm down. Take deep breaths." She turned to Alex and Yael. "The other room. I don't think we need Barbara to be in on our conversation."

* * *

They sat side by side in front of Ruth's desk. The baby had woken up crying. Yael changed a diaper and offered a breast. Alex tried to call Jonathan again. Still no response. She sent a text asking him to call her—that it was urgent. But she'd learned her lesson with the text that she'd thought was going to Noah. No way would she put in a text what she knew or how she knew it.

She turned to Yael. "You said that they're planning to kill Kolya tonight? How?" She kept her voice calm. Years of legal training helped her maintain a calm facade when she wanted to scream.

But she couldn't lose it. She had to be able to function.

"It'd be easier to show you on a computer or smart phone." She glanced at her watch. "It should be about to begin now." The baby had fallen asleep, and Yael tucked her back into the sling.

"Use mine." Ruth scooted over and Yael and Alex crowded next to her.

Yael tapped on keys and pulled up a streaming platform on the dark web with the image of a man, in green fatigues, standing in a cavernous room. "What I thought. It's starting. That's Victor."

"Turn the sound up." Alex felt her arms trembling.

On the screen, Victor Forest stood in a military pose, arms by his side. "People of the United States," he intoned. "You have been lied to and deceived."

He began to rant about aliens in charge of the country. He referenced the 1930s, the end of the Gold Standard, that Hitler was fighting aliens and the United States had joined on the wrong side.

"Do we have to listen to this Nazi shit?" Ruth asked.

"Shhh. Wait," Yael said.

They waited. After another few minutes, he got to the point. "I'm standing in a secret bunker, one of many created by the false government in towns and cities around the country. All of them contain terrible weapons of destruction. Explosives. Nerve poison. Diseases. To be used against you, the citizens of the United States, if you ever learned the truth, by the aliens who are ruling you."

"Kolya told me the bunkers existed, but not to be used against Americans," Alex murmured. She also remembered with a pang how angry he'd been at being kept in the dark about the bunkers—and how it had led to the conversation about breaking up.

She'd considered leaving him to protect him. Ironic.

"Shhh." Yael motioned for silence. "It's coming now."

"Much as I deplore the loss of innocent life, I have decided that we have no choice but to declare war against this illegitimate government, like our forefathers did in the Revolution. Unfortunately, innocent lives will be lost...unless the government surrenders. In," he consulted his watch, "exactly two hours, we will blow up this bunker to signal the start of the new American Revolution, to be followed by an explosion in a different location of the country every day until the people rebel and the tyranny ends."

Then he stepped to the side so the camera could show the cavernous room—and in the middle of the room, a man sat on the ground, tied to a pole, tape across his mouth and lower face, head bowed. From what was visible of his face, the upper part of was bruised, one eye swollen shut, to the point that he was almost unrecognizable.

Almost.

"Oh my God. Kolya." Her heart felt like it was going to burst from her chest.

"Jesus fucking Christ," Ruth said.

"Shhh," Yael repeated.

Alex wanted to throw the laptop on the floor or pound the wall. She wanted to do something violent. But that wouldn't help Kolya. Instead, she dug fingernails into her palms.

"This man," Forest pointed to Kolya, "is a secret agent working for the aliens who are subjugating you and all the people of this country. He's a killer who got those bruises when he tried to kill me. Still, we offered him the choice to join us, but he chose the aliens and tyranny. So, unless my terms are met in time, this man will be blown up along with the contents of this room. He'll be blown up before the rest of the room, so his masters can watch him die." He indicated the explosives on the rope that bound Kolya. "I will wait for the aliens' answer."

Then Forest walked out of the camera view. Kolya was the only person visible. He was alive—she could see his chest move, but she didn't know if he was conscious.

Alex placed a hand against his image on the computer screen, as if she could reach through it to touch him.

"Victor wanted a big audience, and he figured that since people like to look at car wrecks, the sight of a man waiting to be blown up would be irresistible. Anyway, that's what Brody said." Yael shifted the baby's weight.

"You know where he is?" Alex asked.

Yael nodded. "It's a secret room. In Brooklyn."

Alex noticed that Yael didn't give the exact location. She took a deep breath and controlled the impulse to shake Yael. "Where exactly?"

"I'll take you there."

That would do.

"Why nine o'clock?" Ruth asked.

"There's some sort of big fundraiser dinner in lower Manhattan for President Lewis. Lots of people with money. The vice president is supposed to speak," Yael said. "The explosion might not carry far enough, but the nerve poison and the biological weapons might."

"We should call the police," Ruth said. "I mean they're leaving him alone. It wouldn't be hard to rescue him and stop the explosion."

"No. No police." Yael shook her head. "If Victor realizes that a rescue is underway, he can explode the bombs remotely. And I don't trust the police to do this right. They'll put on sirens and rush in. It needs to be done quietly and carefully if you want to save his life." She gave Alex a sideways glance. "That's apart from the fact that I'm not too eager to talk to the police right now. Also, I'm sure Victor's left some guys there, to make sure that nothing goes wrong."

"They know they're going to be blown up?"

"They know it's a chance. They'll leave maybe twenty minutes before the explosion, but Victor told them that if they die, they'll be heroes of the revolution. Someone needs to deal with them and turn off the video stream—quietly—and then disarm the bombs."

"I don't know how to disarm a bomb." Ruth turned to Alex. "Do you?"

Jonathan and an ECA team could do it. They could get in quietly, kill any guards, free Kolya, and disarm the bomb. But no, they were at the end of Long Island. At least three hours away. No point in calling Jonathan again. Even if he wanted to, he wouldn't make it in time. "I don't. But Kolya probably does. If he's conscious."

If he was conscious, even if badly hurt, he could tell her what to do. If he was still alive. But he was alive. He had to be. They just had to get there in time.

"I guess we're it," Ruth said. "I'll go get my car."

Barbara O'Brien issued a long string of curses and threats. It was somewhat muffled by the closed door.

"Do we just leave her?" Yael sounded dubious.

"Could anyone else come in?" Alex asked. "Even if the office is officially closed? Can't risk police putting a BOLO out on us."

"Don't worry. No one will come in for the next few hours, anyway." Ruth returned to her computer and sent out emails and texts, announcing that environmental toxins had been found on site and would have to be cleaned up. "We may all go to prison if we survive the night, but we should be clear for the next few hours."

Chapter Sixty

Kolya had managed to cut the plastic zip tie almost halfway through. But then what? He was in full view of the camera; Forest had left Roger and Dex, who lurked near the stairs. Forest had wanted him to struggle for the camera. If he freed his hands, he could put on the show that Forest wanted and while doing so, he might be able to slide or loosen the rope around his elbows without either the guards or the camera picking up on it. But then there were the ropes tying him to the pole. Freeing himself of those wouldn't exactly be inconspicuous.

He put those thoughts aside and concentrated on the keys and the zip tie. *Free his wrists and then worry about the next step.*

Each stroke was awkward, given the position of his hands, and he had to be careful not to move. Not to change expressions. And, above all, not to drop the keys.

He mostly kept his head down, so that anyone watching him on the stream would see as little as possible of his face. Not that his face would be all that recognizable, given the bruises, the swelling, and the duct tape across his mouth. Whether he could be recognized would matter if he survived to return to work and needed to go undercover.

If he survived, his work was what would keep him sane.

But he didn't expect to survive.

He ached from the beatings, and his bad leg hurt as it hadn't for over a year. His arms and shoulders were cramped from being tied behind his back; his throat was so dry from thirst he could barely swallow. The PTSD was in full bloom.

When a flashback took over, his hands shook, and he had to stop and concentrate on keeping his grip on the keys.

He could only take shallow breaths, which made him light-headed and did nothing to banish the shadows of the past. The mantra that he used to calm himself—*it's not Romania, I'm in control*—didn't help either. He wasn't in control, and it didn't matter that it wasn't Romania.

In some ways, it was worse than Romania. The physical pain of Romania had been worse—as bad as the beating from Brody had been, as uncomfortable as he was now while waiting to be blown up, it didn't compare to the days of torture he'd endured in Romania.

But in Romania, he didn't have the burden of knowing that if he failed to free himself, his death would also mean the death of thousands of other people.

In Romania, he didn't have the pain of Alex's death. The physical pain and the flashbacks were preferable to the thought that Alex was dead.

If she were dead.

Maybe she wasn't. But that was wishful thinking.

Concentrate. Don't think of Alex. He didn't have that much time.

Small movements. Gentle strokes.

"Maybe we could leave now." Dex's voice echoed off the walls.

The sudden sound brought Kolya's head up. He squinted across the room. Dex and Roger were difficult to see, with the floodlights between him and the two of them. He just saw the shape of two figures. Then he let his head droop again.

"Quiet," Roger muttered. "This is live."

"Victor turned off the sound on the iPhone before he left. No one can hear us."

Kolya could, although neither of his guards would care.

"If we leave now," Dex said, "we might have a chance to get far away enough before the explosion. Why do we have to stay?"

"To make sure nothing goes wrong."

"What could go wrong?" Dex asked. "He's not getting loose. The bombs are set."

"We leave twenty minutes before the bombs go off."

"That's not enough time."

"It's what we agreed. It's what Victor told us to do. He's our leader. And if we die, we'll be remembered as heroes."

"Forty minutes. We can check that he's secure, that nothing's loose, and leave. An extra twenty minutes."

"I'll text Victor. If he agrees."

Kolya doubted Victor Forest would agree. Forest was the type to like sacrifices, as long as he wasn't making them. But the thought gave him a flicker of hope. If his hands and arms were free when the two men checked him, maybe...maybe he could do something.

The image of a guard approaching him when he was chained to the floor in Romania flashed through his mind.

His hands shook. He paused again, gripping the keys. *Think of something else.* The opening notes of "Take Five." Key of E-flat minor. 5/4 time.

The trembling passed. He turned the keys in his hand and continued to work.

Chapter Sixty-One

Ruth's car was a light blue 1968 Cadillac Coup de Ville in perfect condition. Under other circumstances, Alex would have been thrilled to ride in such a classic car. But not now, not with the image of Kolya tied to a pole, waiting to die, burned into her brain. Now she only had one thing on her mind.

"Faster!" Alex checked her watch again. Did they have enough time? They'd been in the car at least half an hour.

"Doing my best. It won't help your fiancé if we're stopped by the cops. We'll get there." Ruth changed lanes and cut off a taxi. The driver honked at her. She stuck a fist with her middle finger extended out the window. Then she changed lanes again, swerving in front of a FedEx truck.

Alex rode shotgun. Yael sat in back with Lyra in a baby car seat next to her. Ruth had dug the car seat out of a storage area in the office—explaining that Noah had kept it on hand for the rare occasion when a client needed a ride.

Of the four of them, the baby was the only one who was calm.

Alex couldn't believe that just a few hours ago her biggest worry had been whether her relationship with Kolya put him at greater risk. Her biggest worry now was whether the three of them would get there in time to save him.

All she wanted was to hold him in her arms. And she might never do so again.

Stop it.

"We have a plan?" Ruth asked.

Alex pulled her thoughts back to practicalities. "Yael and you stay in the car with Lyra. I'll go in. If Yael's right and there are men guarding Kolya, they won't be expecting someone to come in behind them. I'll shoot them, turn the feed off on the camera, free Kolya, and either he can defuse the bombs or tell me how to do it. Also, we just hope to hell that Victor Forest will think that the iPhone or the internet fucked up so he doesn't remotely trigger the explosives."

"I'm coming too," Ruth said. "The more guns, the better."

"We can't let them see us coming."

"Honey, I'm a seventy-two-year-old woman. I'm invisible. No one will see me."

"Alternative idea," Yael said. "Ruth stays with Lyra. I go in first. All the men know me. I'll tell them that Victor and Brody want them to leave."

"You don't think that they'd have cell phones and be able to check?" Alex asked.

"Maybe," Yael said. "But it's a better chance than the two of you sneaking in."

"You're a mother. Your child needs you," Ruth said. "I'm going with Alex. Don't argue."

"But..." Yael started.

"I'm better with a gun than I am with a baby," Ruth said.

"Ruth, you know how to shoot?" Alex asked.

"Damn right. And I can hit a target. If I'm close enough. You?"

Alex, at Kolya's insistence, was reasonably competent with a gun, but with Kolya's life in the balance, she knew her nerves might cause her to miss. Unlike Kolya, she wasn't a professional. But she'd do whatever she had to. "About the same."

Alex's phone chimed the tune that indicated a call.

* * *

Jonathan had checked his phone and seen not only that Alex Feinstein had called multiple times, but that she'd texted him, telling him it was urgent. But they were in a standoff at the end of Long Island. The men in the van weren't giving up. The police weren't moving in, not with the possibility of VX in the van. Jonathan had nothing to tell Alex—which was why he didn't check his phone when it buzzed with a new incoming message.

Then Elizabeth tapped him on the shoulder.

"You need to see this. Mark Leslie sent me a link. He sent it to you, too, but you're not checking your phone." She handed him her phone. He stared at the image of Kolya tied to a pole in front of stacked crates. "The crates contain explosives. They're going to blow him up and probably part of New York City. In less than an hour."

"Where is he?"

"Mark hasn't been able to triangulate the signal. It's being passed through servers in six different countries."

"Fuck. This is a fucking sideshow." Jonathan grabbed his phone dand dialed Alex. She answered on the first ring. He didn't bother asking if she'd seen the video. "Do you know where?"

"Yes." Alex's voice was calm. "Under the Brooklyn Bridge. We're headed there now. We decided not to call in the police because Victor Forest can remotely detonate the explosives if a SWAT team rushes in. Stealth has the better chance."

We?

"Alex, who are you with?"

"Why?"

"Because having people who know what they're doing increases the odds."

"Then we've got slim odds. But we're Kolya's best chance. You can't get to him in time. Even if you took a helicopter. By the time you land somewhere in the city and then get to the bridge, it'll be too late. If we free him, hopefully Kolya can defuse the explosives so that Brooklyn and lower Manhattan don't blow."

"If the bomb doesn't go off, Forest could be back with a lot of armed men."

"I know. It's a risk that we have to take."

"We'll get there as quickly as we can. You'll need to get in and out fast. Once you're out, contact me. We'll send in police to secure the site."

"Copy that." Alex's phone clicked off.

Jonathan made two calls and then looked at the team. "We're going to leave this to the state police. The real show is in Brooklyn. A helicopter will be picking us up in twenty minutes."

"Before we go," Frick said, "given that neither Kolya nor Forest is in that van, what do you think the odds are that those assholes would drive from Manhattan to Montauk with a loose bottle of VX?"

"Pretty slim," Jonathan said.

"Agreed." Tehila picked up an assault rifle and opened the

door of the van they were in. "Give me two minutes. At most." Elizabeth and Frick did the same and followed her.

Jonathan sighed and motioned to the two remaining team members, Marty and Jay, who also picked up weapons and exited.

Chapter Sixty-Two

Victor's heart raced, his hands shook. Something could still go wrong, but he was close. So close to the goal. The revolution he planned was finally about to start. No wonder every part of his body was on edge.

The first strike of the revolution would be the destruction of the Brooklyn Bridge, along with the traitor who'd sworn an oath of loyalty but had immediately betrayed that oath. The explosion, which would also take out the vice president and a horde of aliens supporting him, would signal the uprising to happen around the country.

Victor and Brody were holed up in an apartment owned by a member of American Gold Posse half a mile from the bunker under the Brooklyn Bridge, far enough away that the initial explosion wouldn't reach them—although the nerve poison might—if they stayed in place. Victor had decided that he needed to be close enough to deal with any issues with the iPhone camera or even with the C-4.

If the iPhone stopped transmitting.

If the wires on the explosives came loose.

The two men he'd left guarding the scene were good, loyal

soldiers, but they weren't technically skilled. Hell, to be honest, they were fucking stupid. So, he needed to be close. Not too close. Close enough to go back to fix things if necessary—but not so close that he'd be unable to get out of range.

He and Brody would leave the apartment at the twenty-minute countdown—which should give them enough time to get a few more miles between them and the bridge. The two men he'd left to guard Petrov had been told to leave at the same time. Sadly, they would probably not get clear of the VX. He regretted it, but in the grand scheme of the revolution, a few sacrifices had to be made.

And he did have a remote connection, both to the iPhone and to the timers. He could pause either if necessary. Or, conversely, he could trigger the explosives early if there was reason to do so.

Not that he anticipated it being necessary.

A theatrical spectacle needed to build up to the grand climax.

And that climax would happen in less than an hour.

He sat at a metal desk in front of a window overlooking the street. Outside the window, two floors below, New Yorkers walked their dogs, carried groceries, strolled the streets, unaware. Some of them might survive. Many wouldn't. They were as unconscious of their danger as they were of the true nature of the government. He almost wanted to open the window and shout at them. *Wake up! Time to rebel!* But he didn't. It wouldn't do anything, and they'd just dismiss him as crazy.

Anyway, he couldn't pull his gaze away from the laptop screen and the vision of Petrov waiting to be blown up. He fixated not just on the image, but on the number of views. It was even better than he'd hoped.

Thousands of views. Tens of thousands of views. By the time Petrov died, he could have an audience of millions.

Too bad that Petrov wouldn't know—or appreciate—his fame.

He felt the excitement building—just as it had before a dangerous assignment—back when he'd stupidly risked his life for the CIA. He felt it in his stomach, rising through his whole body.

Irritatingly, though, Brody, his hand-chosen second-in-command, wasn't feeling the same. He should be celebrating their success. Cheering at the success of their planning. But he wasn't. Instead, he was pacing, barely glancing at the laptop. Worried about the fucking wife and the baby.

The wife who'd taken the baby shopping and so far as either Brody or Victor knew hadn't returned.

"Did you call the warehouse?" Victor didn't take his eyes off the screen.

"Five times."

"Did you call her?"

"I destroyed her phone. I was worried that she could be tracked."

"Well, then, she'd have no way to get in touch if she was delayed. Don't worry so much." Victor finally turned away from the computer.

"I shouldn't have hit her." Brody paused in his pacing. "I need to watch my temper. She just made me mad when she spoke disrespectfully."

"You didn't hit her that hard, and she knows that real men have to assert authority over their women. She loves you." Victor kept his tone soothing, despite his annoyance at Brody for interrupting the Petrov show. "She'll come back. Remember that women love shopping. She's enjoying herself buying things for your baby."

"But she could get caught in the blast. I should go look for them."

"She knows when and where it's going off. She'll be careful. She knows to avoid lower Manhattan and Brooklyn Heights."

Victor did have a few doubts about whether Yael would come back. It wasn't the slap that worried him. His order to Petrov to shoot Yael's baby without letting her know that the bullet was a blank might have been a mistake. He'd thought it was a brilliant idea at the time, and he and Brody had agreed that Yael's reaction would be more genuine if she didn't know what was happening. Maybe she'd been more upset than they'd realized.

Would she go to the police?

But he shook off the thought. Above all else, Yael loved her baby—and the police would take the baby away. She wouldn't risk that.

Beyond that—Yael was a good soldier's wife, believing in the cause, doing everything to help American Gold and Brody. She'd had a scare, but neither she nor the baby had been hurt. She'd return in her own time.

Meantime, this was distracting from his enjoyment of the moment. And Brody needed to focus, not wander the streets in search of his wife. "We've got less than an hour to go. This is what we've been working towards for years. We'll find her afterwards."

"I guess." But Brody resumed his pacing.

It was getting on Victor's nerves.

"Stop that. Come watch the feed. We're getting hundreds of comments." Victor tapped on the computer keyboard to bring up the image again. Petrov sitting with head bowed, accepting his fate.

Then he started to read the comments.

Is he already dead? He's not moving.

He moved once in fifteen minutes. He's not dead yet, but he's not struggling.

This is boring.

Let's see him react. I wouldn't just be sitting there if I were going to be blown up.

Is he drugged?

What's his face look like? Why is he keeping his head down?

There were dozens of comments in the same vein. *Boring? Boring???* Blood rushed to his head.

He'd created a spectacle to transfix and transform the country.

People were finding it boring!!

Fucking Petrov, just sitting there, not moving. He'd told Petrov to put on a good show. He should have expected that Petrov wouldn't obey orders. Fucking bastard!!

And the idiots he'd left guarding Petrov—they should know to motivate Petrov without his having to micromanage.

But apparently, they didn't.

He picked up his phone and paused the feed. Then he dialed.

* * *

Kolya finally cut all the way through the zip tie that held his wrists. The release was a physical relief, and he gently rubbed sore spots to stimulate circulation, even though his arms were still bound at the elbows. But to keep the guards or the camera from realizing he'd freed his hands, he kept any motion minimal. He remained with his head lowered.

One obstacle down.

Then Dex's phone chimed.

Kolya could hear only Dex's side of the conversation, but he got the gist. Forest was annoyed that Kolya wasn't putting on a better show.

Viewers were complaining.

It would have been amusing, except for how bad he felt, both physically and emotionally, and except for the fact that he was still likely to die.

Dex clicked off his phone. "Hey you. Petrov. Lift your head up. Look at the camera."

Kolya didn't. His head continued to droop while he carefully, slowly, crossed his wrists behind his back and hunched his shoulders together. The maneuver moved his elbows closer and loosened the rope that was tied around them.

He was close to freeing his arms. Frustratingly close.

To get the rope completely off his upper arms more quickly would require more movement than he could do unobserved. Then he'd still have to deal with the rope around his chest and the rope around his stomach under the gaze of the camera and the two men guarding him.

He'd have to do this very slowly. If he had time. The clock was ticking down towards the explosion.

He pushed that thought out of his mind. *Focus on freeing your arms. Don't think about anything else.*

Not about his likely death. Or, worse, about Alex.

Sweat trickled down his back. His hands shook. The PTSD whispered to him. He needed to shut it down.

He couldn't take deep breaths because of the tightness of the rope around his chest and the pain in his ribs. But he could still use some of the techniques. Instead of deep breaths, he counted each intake and outtake of air.

He calmed.

But the situation was about to change.

"You were told to lift your fucking head."

This time Kolya did lift his head, his good eye squinting as he turned his gaze towards the two guards, who were grinning as they closed in on him. They paused by the iPhone, and Dex turned off the camera.

"Victor told you you'd have an audience." Dex's voice dripped with malice. "He's not happy with your performance."

"You looking down and not moving is boring. The people want to see struggle. They want to see distress." Roger kicked Kolya's injured right leg.

A white flash of pain racked his leg, and he arched backwards. The tape across his mouth kept him from crying out. A fist to his cheek started the flow of blood down his face.

A blow against his ribs took away his breath.

He couldn't fight back, but he could struggle against the ropes holding him, which seemed to be what they wanted. Ironically, his struggling against the ropes binding him to the pole and the blows raining down on him allowed him to push down on the rope tied around his elbows. The rope slipped from his elbows to his wrists and then to the floor.

He kept his arms in the same position to conceal what had happened. His arms were free, even if he was still tied to the pole.

Not that it would do much good if he was beaten to death.

But after the first blows, Roger and Dex stepped back.

"Keep your head up and keep the viewers happy. Or we'll hurt you even worse instead of letting you die in peace," Roger said, as the two of them retreated to their previous positions behind the camera.

They turned the iPhone camera on again.

Head up, Kolya did as instructed, pushing his chest and upper body against the ropes that bound him to the pole, despite the discomfort. The knots were tight and well-tied, and there was almost no give.

Almost.

Chapter Sixty-Three

Victor was once again glued to the laptop screen, glowing with satisfaction at the show he'd orchestrated. His guys had done the job. Petrov's head was up—bloodied but up—and he was writhing against the ropes.

"Could he get loose?" Brody—finally—had paused his pacing and was engaged in watching Petrov's struggles. Back to being Victor's second-in-command.

About time.

"Don't think so. The ropes might loosen slightly, but not enough for him to get free, not with his wrists and arms tied."

"Hard to read his expression with the tape and the blood and all."

"Not really necessary," Victor said. "He has to be afraid. He knows he's going to die." Victor glanced at the top of the screen. "In less than half an hour."

He did wish he could hear what Petrov had to say, hear Petrov beg for his life, but the gag was necessary. Petrov otherwise could have announced his location, which would have warned the public—including the vice president—to get out of the vicinity.

With Petrov showing signs of agitation, the audience had become more engaged. There had been some comments asking what had happened while the feed was off; a few noted that Petrov's face had become bloodied and speculated that he'd been beaten. But that didn't worry Victor. So what if they knew that Petrov had been hurt? The audience had been told that Petrov deserved what was happening to him, and they also needed to know the consequences of opposing the new American revolution.

Real Americans didn't have sympathy for those who worked for aliens.

That not everyone appreciated what was about to happen wasn't the point. The point was the attention. And he was getting even more views. He savored the upticking of the audience like a fine wine. And with the increased views, more comments. He read some of them out loud.

Does he look scared?

Hard to make out what he's thinking. Face is too fucked up.

Too bad he's gagged.

Trying to get free. Don't think he'll make it.

Think we'll see his head blow off?

He glanced over at Brody to check whether Brody was also enjoying himself. He seemed to be—but then he pointed out that some of the comments were empathetic. Victor thought of tracking these commenters down. Empathy with the enemy was betrayal of the cause.

Is this real? If so, this is terrible.

Someone needs to stop it.

A few doubted the reality of what they were seeing. Victor couldn't completely blame them. Americans had been fooled so often by the media and the government.

Fake. Fake.

This is a Hollywood production.

But a thrill went through him every time he saw a comment that understood and applauded.

Time for revolution.

Our turn.

Down with tyranny.

From the last group, there were thumbs up, thumbs down, hearts.

The comments reinforced what Victor believed. They could win this fight. Thousands—tens of thousands—would flock to the cause.

Chapter Sixty-Four

The shaking was worse, through his whole body. So was the dizziness. Pushing against the ropes compressed his cracked ribs. His leg throbbed. Kolya tried to open his left eye, but the eyelid was too swollen. His own body was working against him.

But he could feel the ropes giving, not a lot, just enough so that he could take slightly deeper breaths.

Maybe enough that he could squeeze his arms under the ropes.

Maybe.

Maybe not.

But if the ropes were too loose, someone might notice. The two guards. Forest watching the live stream. Some random person posting a comment. And then it would be over. Forest would call Roger and tell him to tighten the ropes. If they inspected him, the guards could realize that Kolya's arms were free and bind them again. Or they could just shoot him.

But if he could take out the guards, the live stream wouldn't matter.

If.

Possible but not likely.

So, keep going or stop and take his chances?

Kolya took as deep a breath as the cracked ribs and slightly loosened ropes would allow and let it out slowly. The breathing helped with the PTSD but not so much with the pain or the lack of food. Or with the knowledge that he had less than half an hour left to live.

Wait for the guards to leave and then try to free himself? That was cutting it too close. He needed time to disarm the explosives. Besides, were the guards even going to leave? Were they willing to let themselves be blown up for the sake of their cause?

Kolya let his head drop again and stopped struggling, sagging forward against the ropes. He heard an exasperated exclamation of *fucking bastard* from Dex and ignored it.

"Head up, Petrov. Move." It was Dex.

Kolya didn't.

"You want us coming over again?"

He did.

Roger sounded scared. "Half an hour left. We should get out now. We might be able to get away."

"We have a duty. We swore to stay here as long as Victor wanted us to." Dex pronounced the words solemnly. "His orders were that we keep Petrov alert and moving. And what's Petrov doing? He's playing dead again." He raised his voice in anger. "We can hurt you bad. That what you want? Look alive for the camera."

Kolya didn't move.

Roger made a noise of exasperation. "Okay, so let's kick the shit out of him. Turn off the camera. We don't wanna be filmed."

* * *

The doorway was, as Yael had learned from her husband and passed on to Alex, behind the electric panel. Alex descended the stone stairs slowly and deliberately. She held her gun with both hands. Behind her, Ruth just as quietly followed, carrying her own gun.

There was enough light from the room below that Alex could see the stairs, but because of the bend in the staircase, she couldn't see the room below. She placed one foot at a time, shifting her weight so each footstep was silent. She placed a hand against the damp wall once to steady herself.

She had a fleeting thought of Yael and Lyra.

Another step. Something rolled under her forefoot. A stone, maybe. Maybe a nail. She ignored it.

Kolya was still alive, but he wouldn't be for long unless she could get unnoticed to the bottom of the stairs. Nor would she, for that matter. If the bomb went off, she and Ruth and Yael and Lyra and thousands more would be dead.

Don't think about any of that right now. She had to concentrate on her own movements—on what she had to do.

She was going down the stairs. One step at a time. Then, she'd shoot anyone between her and Kolya.

Another step.

She knew Ruth was behind her, and that was weirdly comforting.

When Alex was three-quarters of the way down, the stairs took a ninety-degree turn, and she had a view of the entire room. She could see the pole that she knew Kolya had been tied to, but she couldn't see him. Instead, she had a view of two men approaching the pole, their backs obscuring any view of Kolya.

Were they going to kill him now? Hurt him more?

Anger flared, but she took a deep breath and let it out. *Focus.* Then she continued, placing each foot carefully.

She had to be closer before she could shoot.

* * *

Time to go if he wanted to avoid getting caught in the blast. Victor took a last look at the image on the screen and realized that Petrov was no longer fighting his restraints. With half an hour to live, instead of fighting with all his might, Petrov had once again assumed a lifeless posture, head down, not moving.

This was the countdown to the big moment, and Victor didn't want to risk losing the audience now. The audience that had found Kolya's lack of movement—boring.

He was more than irritated. He was angry. This was screwing up his show. Would anyone keep watching? The explosion would still be impressive. It would still hopefully take out the vice president. But what was keeping the audience was the thrill of waiting for a man to die—and then watching it happen.

Petrov was again not doing his part.

Then the screen went black.

"Fucking shit." Victor was breathing hard. *Don't panic.* It might just be a technical glitch on his end. He restarted the computer and signed on again, but the screen was still black.

Had the internet gone out? He clicked on another site, and it came up. He returned to what should be the live stream. Still nothing.

"I got nothing on my phone," Brody said.

That was worse than Petrov's not moving.

The explosion would happen regardless of whether the camera caught it or not. But this was not what he'd planned.

Victor didn't just want the explosion to happen. He needed it to inspire and terrify—what were the words—shock and awe.

"Fucking shit." He took out his cell phone and called Dex. No answer. He tried Roger. Also, no answer. "Damn." Had the men already fled? They were supposed to be there for another ten minutes. But if they didn't answer, there was only one thing to do.

"We have to go check what's happening," he told Brody. "Get the stream back online."

"There's not time. We'll be killed. It'll take us fifteen minutes to get there, and everything's blowing in twenty-five minutes. Even if we can get in and out in time, we won't be able to get far enough away to be safe."

Victor took out his phone. A few clicks and he nodded. "I just pushed the time back forty minutes." That would give them time to get in, find out what was going on, fix it, and get far enough away.

* * *

When Forest had bound Kolya to the pole, he hadn't tied Kolya's legs. That had been a mistake. Kolya's right leg was injured, but he could still use it for what he needed to do, even if doing so would hurt.

Kolya kept his head down, his good eye open a slit. He shifted his arms behind his back at a pace that was painfully slow but that hopefully would not be noticed.

If he survived, he could do a stint as a living statue.

Dex and Roger halted briefly by the iPhone to turn off the video stream.

Kolya watched the two men approach. Roger was about three feet ahead of Dex. Kolya knew that they intended to use their fists and their feet on him. That meant that they had to be close. Close enough that he just might have a chance.

A very slight chance.

"Let's do this fast." Roger was the more nervous of the two.

"We will. Come on, Petrov. Move it. Your performance is falling down."

Kolya shifted his arms again behind his back. Neither of the two idiots noticed. He flexed his fingers and felt the tingling in his arms as the blood circulated.

He planned out each step and mentally recited them. One. Two. Three. He doubted he'd get to three, but he was ready.

The PTSD was mercifully quiet for the moment, respecting his need for concentration.

Roger was approaching Kolya on his right side. Which meant the right leg. It would hurt, and the right leg wasn't as strong as the left, but hitting the exact spot was more critical than the leg strength. Or the pain.

Dex followed close behind Roger. Which was exactly what he shouldn't do. If they'd spread out, approaching Kolya from both sides, even his small chance would be gone. But he couldn't have asked for better positioning.

He took another calming breath, let it out slowly, and watched for the right moment. Timing would be everything.

Roger reached Kolya's foot and took another step. Kolya snapped his right leg upwards and sideways, into Roger's kneecap, dislocating it. Roger screamed and fell backwards, stumbling into Dex. Roger fell, grabbing Dex's shirt and pulling him down as well.

The kick had hurt Kolya's bad leg, but he ignored the pain. He pulled his arms all the way around his body, positioning his hands under the two ropes that held him against the pole and that his struggling act had managed to loosen. He then slid down on the floor, wiggling the ropes up his torso and over his head.

It took only seconds to free himself, but it was still too long.

While Roger was on the ground, groaning and holding his knee, Dex recovered his balance. He stood and pulled a Glock from the small of his back.

He aimed at Kolya's left leg. The clear intent—incapacitate, not kill, so the entertainment of having the world watch Kolya being blown up could proceed. Kolya desperately rolled to the side.

Two shots rang out.

Dex's eye disappeared as the bullet exited his brain. The gun dropped from his hand as he slumped onto the floor. Kolya snatched it up.

From his place on the floor, Roger pulled out his own gun. He leaned up on an elbow to aim. Kolya fired first, hitting him in the chest. Roger fell backwards. He took one gasping breath, and then he lay still.

Kolya ripped the tape off his mouth and narrowed his good eye against the brightness of the floodlights to try to identify the person running towards him.

It couldn't be, could it?

But it could. *Alex was alive and here.* He blinked back tears even as she reached him and knelt in front of him.

He managed to choke out her name.

"You look terrible, love." She placed cool hands against the bruises on his face.

He pulled her to him and kissed her, which hurt his ribs and his face, but he didn't care. The physical pain, the PTSD, everything that had happened to him over the past day didn't matter. Alex wasn't dead. She was in his arms.

How had she survived? How had she known where to find him? None of it was immediately important. He'd find out later.

"I'm fine." His voice shook.

"Sure you are." It was a familiar phrase from her but spoken lovingly.

Not something to argue. She was alive, and nothing else mattered.

He closed his eyes, wanting to hold on to her and the

moment. Then he roused himself. The danger to them, to others, wasn't over. "The explosives. I have to stop this."

She nodded, her expression grim. "I know. Jonathan's on his way, but he won't be here in time. Can you manage?"

"Pretty sure I can. You don't happen to have a wire cutter or a knife on you, do you?"

"I have a knife." That came from a small-framed older woman holding a compact pistol. She'd followed Alex, but he'd barely noticed her in the joy of seeing Alex alive. The woman plunged a hand into the pocket of her oversized gray sweater and came out with an impressively large pocketknife. "I'm Ruth."

"Thanks, Ruth." He accepted the knife and opened it. He'd find out more about her when it was safe.

Forest may have known how to construct an elaborate bomb that would be triggered by anyone trying to disarm it, but he hadn't bothered. Kolya had watched him and Brody set the detonators and timers. Kolya's job would be easy.

He hoped.

He dealt first with the C-4 that was attached to the rope that had been across his body. And even though that would be a small blast that would not bring down the bridge, he couldn't risk any chance that it might trigger the stacked crates of C-4.

Kolya carefully detached the detonator from the ball of C-4 and cut the wire to the timer for good measure. He slid the detonator towards the far wall, away from any of the explosives. Then he picked up both men's guns, tucked one into the side of his jeans, the other at the back, and struggled to his feet, wincing from the pain. A wave of dizziness hit him, and he grabbed onto Alex to keep himself from falling.

She held him tightly. "You're hurt. I can disarm the bombs. Tell me what to do."

A calming breath. Another. The dizziness lessened. "Just help me walk."

Chapter Sixty-Five

Lyra woke five minutes after Alex and Ruth left the car. Yael took her out of the car seat, changed her diaper, and picked her up to let her nurse, all the time watching out the window.

The car was parked on Brooklyn Bridge Boulevard, directly across from the entrance to the underground room. Ruth had left the keys so that Yael could drive off if she didn't hear from them when there were ten minutes left before the planned blast —which would mean that the two of them had failed in their rescue attempt.

She didn't like the idea, but she would do what she needed to.

She had to protect Lyra.

Still, if she'd just wanted to protect her baby, she wouldn't be in this car right now. She had decided to save Kolya and all the innocent people who'd be killed because she'd finally realized the truth about Brody. And about Victor.

She'd gotten sucked into the American Gold Posse not just because of Brody but because she believed in doing the right thing, even if it was illegal. Even if it was dangerous. She'd wanted a better life for everyone in the United States, and she'd thought Brody wanted that too. His idealism had been one of the things that had attracted her.

She'd had questions, but she'd pushed her doubts down, especially after Lyra had been born. But the chain of events—from the murders the previous night to the scare about shooting her baby to Brody's enjoyment at hurting a man who'd protected her and her baby—had opened her eyes.

She'd seen who Brody really was—a sadistic control freak. And Victor was nuts. All this shit about aliens taking over the government. And the craziness of blowing up the Brooklyn Bridge and sending a nerve poison into the air. How had she not realized this before?

Some part of her must have known. She'd just buried her doubts and her questions, and she had helped Brody. A good little mindless wife.

She didn't create the situation. She didn't set the bombs or kill anyone. But she bore some responsibility for the murders and for the planned attack. Because she'd known...and done nothing.

Which meant that she had to help stop what Brody and Victor had planned. And which was why she found it difficult to just wait in the car while Alex and Ruth took risks to stop what she had helped put into motion.

Lyra finished nursing, and Yael cradled her against her chest as she watched the foot traffic around the bridge. Late afternoon, and people were hurrying home from work. She spotted a woman shepherding three little girls. An elderly man walking a dog.

A middle-aged man with a briefcase stopped briefly to admire the Cadillac. She was thankful that the car had tinted glass, so he couldn't see inside.

The man temporarily blocked her view of the sidewalk. She

strained to see past him. Then he moved off, and she saw them, a block away, striding purposefully towards the bridge, Brody and Victor, both carrying duffle bags—probably containing guns.

Despite the tinted glass, she slid down in the seat to make herself as small as possible, but neither man gave the car a second glance. She fumbled in the diaper bag for the burner phone that Alex had loaned her.

Yael dialed Ruth's number. The call went to voicemail. She tried again with the same result. She watched with dismay as Brody and Victor neared the entrance to the bunker. She knew what would happen once they got inside.

Maybe this was the time to drive off to protect her baby. But that would mean abandoning Alex, Ruth, and Kolya. If Alex and Kolya didn't know that Victor and Brody were coming, they might be surprised. They might be disarming the bombs and not watching. Which would give Victor and Brody the advantage.

Alex, Ruth, and Kolya would be killed. Thousands would be killed. The little girls she'd spotted. The old man with his dog. She'd made a mistake in following Victor and in trusting Brody, but she still believed in the basic principles that had led her to make that mistake.

People mattered. Their lives mattered.

She pulled on the baby sling and settled Lyra inside. She hid the gun that they'd taken from Barbara O'Brien inside the sling. Then she opened the back door of the car and stepped out.

Chapter Sixty-Six

Close up, Kolya'd looked much worse than he'd appeared on the screen. Alex could tell how much pain he was in by the trembling of his body as she helped him stand. When he almost fell, she wanted to weep. She knew not just how hurt he was but that the PTSD that he'd almost conquered would be back in full force. But he kept his focus on the destination and the goal of defusing the explosives because he wanted to keep innocents from dying—even though she knew he was suffering.

She loved him for it.

There were maybe a dozen crates with wires running to each of them. She helped him to the first crate and steadied him as he detached a detonator, and then cut the wire leading to it. It took him only a few minutes, but the time was ticking down. He carefully set the detonator on the ground and shoved it across the room with his foot.

"Just fucking cut the wires. I'll carry them across the room," Ruth said.

Alex had almost forgotten Ruth's presence.

"That works," Kolya said.

Then Alex helped him move to the next crate.

"Why not just cut the wires? Wouldn't that be faster?" She held him around the waist to steady him.

"It might. But I don't know if that could create a spark through the wire that would trigger a denotator."

"You don't know?"

"Explosives are not my area of expertise. I know that removing the detonator will work. Beyond that, not so sure." He pulled out the next detonator from a C-4 brick.

"There's ten more crates. I can help." She shuddered internally at the idea, but they were running out of time.

"The detonators can go off even if not attached to the C-4. It won't kill, but it'll cause some damage. I don't want you hurt."

"I'll be hurt a lot worse if they go off while still attached."

There was a moment of silence as he finished. Then he slowly nodded. "Point. Okay. Fine. Gently pull the detonators from center of a C-4 brick and set them on the floor. Make sure there's no C-4 left on the detonator. I'll cut the wires after. Just be very careful."

"I will be." Alex glanced around the room for Ruth and saw that she had moved away and was examining the other crates in the cavernous room—the crates that were not wired to explode.

"What's in these?" Ruth asked.

"Don't touch," Kolya said. "Some of them have canned food. Some have VX. There might or might not be biological weapons. I don't know which are which." With Alex's help, Kolya moved on to the next crate.

Alex took the crate next to him. She checked on Ruth, who was ignoring Kolya's warning.

"You think that the crate that says peaches isn't peaches?"

"Don't." Kolya's voice was alarmed.

"Too late." Ruth opened the lid and peered inside. "Looks like canned peaches." She closed the lid and dragged the crate across the floor towards the stairs. She was strong for a small woman of her age. Alex reminded herself not to be surprised at anything Ruth did.

"What are you doing?" Alex asked.

"Blocking the stairs. In case that crazy motherfucker comes back. It won't stop him, but it'll slow him down."

"Good idea." Kolya turned his attention back to the explosives. "Keep checking the stairs."

Alex touched the C-4. It felt like Play-Doh. Soft. Malleable. She gingerly pulled the metal detonator out from the center, making sure that no explosive material remained, and set it on the floor. Kolya finished the job by cutting the wire. Ruth picked up each detonator to join the others against the wall, far from the explosives.

They worked in silence. Alex checked on Kolya and saw him place a hand against the wall to steady himself. She stopped to move to his side, but he shook his head at her. "I'm okay. We need to get this done."

They moved from crate to crate. Three left. Two. Then one. Alex periodically glanced towards the stairs, as did Kolya. Ruth checked as well.

But it only took a few seconds to descend the stairs.

Ruth, carrying two detonators, stopped halfway across the room. "Shit."

Alex turned to see Ruth hit the floor as a burst of gunfire racked the room.

Chapter Sixty-Seven

Kolya pushed Alex down as he pulled the gun from his waistband and dropped next to her. He raised the gun and fired in the direction of the stairs, blinking his good eye against the glare of the floodlights. He could only make out shadows on the other side of the lights. From the muzzle flashes, he knew that two people were firing from the stairs. The crate blocking the stairs had prevented them from getting closer without being detected—but not from shooting.

Another burst of gunfire clipped the floor near him.

From her position on the floor, Alex fired her gun. Across the room, Ruth also fired.

"Ruth, okay?" Alex called.

"Peachy." Ruth's voice sounded strained.

The floodlights gave Forest or whoever it was the advantage. That was something Kolya could change. He aimed and pulled the trigger. An explosion of glass and electric sparks. He shot three more times, taking out the rest of the lights.

The room plunged into darkness.

Kolya's hands shook. He took a breath and let it out slowly, counting, and his hands steadied.

A familiar voice called his name. "Petrov. You won't get out of here alive, but maybe the women can."

Victor Forest. The second shooter was probably Brody. Kolya raised his gun and fired, guessing the location from Forest's voice. But the dark protected both sides.

"That was rude considering I'm making you an offer here, Petrov." Forest again. A cell phone flashlight lit up, but Kolya, Alex, and Ruth were at least thirty-five feet away, out of range to be seen. But the cell light gave Kolya a target. He aimed and shot. He didn't hit either man, but the phone turned off.

"*Yob tvoyu mat*," he muttered.

Alex touched his arm, and then she whispered in his ear. "Still one crate with a detonator."

If Forest triggered the C-4, he'd be killed too. With a sane person, that would be some guarantee of safety. But Forest wasn't sane. He was perfectly capable of sacrificing himself in service of his crazy revolution.

Jonathan and the team were on the way. But the team was at least fifteen minutes out. They had to survive until then.

"I know. I'll go for it. Stay down."

"You can barely move. Don't be fucking absurd."

"You can't pull the detonator out while lying on the floor. You'll have to raise up enough to reach it, which means you could be hit."

"They can't see me. And anyway, you're better with a gun than I am, and you can cover me."

What she said made sense, but he had just found her again. He didn't want her at risk. "No, Alex." He muttered and tried crawling back but his injured right leg spasmed, and he collapsed.

"Stop being an idiot. And you know I hate it when you get all male protective." Alex spoke in his ear, and he surrendered.

"Okay. I'll start shooting when you're in position."

"Fine. On three."

There was another burst of gunfire from across the room. He wasn't sure, but he thought he heard something heavy scraping the floor. The crate, of course. It had slowed them momentarily, but it wasn't much of a barrier.

Kolya pulled the second gun from the back of his jeans and placed it on the ground near his right hand. He held his fire as Alex scooted backwards.

A whisper. "One. Two. Three."

He opened fire, aiming for where he'd last seen the spurts of flame. There was no return fire. He pulled the trigger until the gun clicked empty.

He dropped the first gun and picked up the second.

Then he dropped and flattened as the AR-15s returned fire. But the muzzle flashes were no longer on the stairs. They were on the same level as Kolya.

The two of them were still at the far end of the room. That was something.

He hissed Alex's name and then listened. No response, but he heard the soft sound of someone inching forward on the floor. Then she was next to him.

"It's done." Her voice was barely audible.

"Are you okay?"

"Fine." But she sounded breathy.

He couldn't see to know whether she was telling the truth. He felt a cold wave of fear.

The gunfire ended, and Forest tried again. "I'm willing to die. I assume you are, too, Petrov. Are you willing for your fiancée to die as well? Just after you found her again? Along with her friend? But if you surrender, I'll let the women go."

"Such a deal." It was Ruth's voice. "Who could resist?"

Another burst of fire aimed at Ruth. Kolya shot again. The gun was a standard Glock with seventeen rounds. The standard AR-15 held thirty. He didn't have additional magazines. He assumed that both Brody and Forest did. Alex had a 9mm HK with a thirteen-round capacity. He had no idea what Ruth was using, but it wasn't an AR-15. Which meant that the three of them would run out of ammo before Brody and Forest did.

If that happened, it was over.

Kolya or Alex or Ruth needed a lucky shot. Two lucky shots.

Or they needed to stall long enough for Jonathan and the team to come to the rescue.

"How do I know you'll let the women go?" Kolya called.

"You have my word."

"Sorry, not good enough."

"I have always told you the truth."

"Not really. Not if you define truth as having a relationship to reality." Kolya raised his voice. "But I'm willing to deal—if I have assurances that they're safe. Once they're out of here and confirm by phone that they're out of range of any explosion, I'll surrender."

"NO!" Alex didn't bother to whisper. "I'm NOT leaving you. Not ever."

Not ever? He wished he could see her. But he whispered what was necessary. "Playing for time."

"You're going to die for people who betrayed you, and you think *I'm* the one not in touch with reality?" Forest returned. "No deal. If I let them leave, what's your incentive to surrender? And they could call in the troops if they're out. You want to save them? Surrender first."

"Isn't that a perfume?" Ruth's voice.

"What?" There was genuine confusion in Forest's voice.

"Surrender First. Isn't that a perfume?" Ruth again.

Despite the desperate situation, Kolya almost laughed.

Another burst of gunfire. Kolya aimed for the spot where he'd seen one muzzle flash and pulled the trigger. Once.

How many rounds left? He wasn't sure. But he had to continue to at least fire periodically, to keep them at a distance.

How long since the gunfight had started? Only minutes, but in the midst of an emergency, time seemed to stand still.

The unwanted memory of another gunfight surfaced—the gunfight that had ended with his being taken prisoner and flown to Romania. Sweat ran down the back of his shirt.

He reached out to Alex, trying to ground himself in the present. He touched her shoulder and felt dampness. Sticky dampness. It had to be blood. She must have been hit when she went for the last detonator. Terrified, he pulled her to him, trying to find the source.

"Calm down, Kolya. I'm okay."

"Sure you are." He ran hands over her, finding dampness on her upper arm. But he couldn't see how bad it was. Even if a major organ wasn't involved, she could bleed out if she didn't get help.

For the first time, he seriously considered surrendering. He'd give his life for her—if he could trust Forest's word. But he knew better. Forest was an unreliable lunatic. Sacrificing himself wouldn't save her. Forest would just kill all of them, either by shooting them or by blowing them up.

Her best chance of survival was for him—for all of them—to hold out. Until help could arrive.

"Just don't fucking die." He spoke words to Alex that she'd said to him so many times. But his voice shook.

"You neither."

Chapter Sixty-Eight

Yael entered the small room that had been marked "Electrical Equipment," and creaked the outside door shut. Then she removed the sling holding Lyra and placed it and her baby in a corner of the room. Lyra was asleep so she was blessedly silent.

The door to the bunker was where Brody had said it would be: behind an electrical panel. The door pushed inward, and Yael slid inside soundlessly. The stairs were totally dark, but she heard gunshots.

She placed her left hand on the cement wall as she descended. She smelled gunpowder and mold. Descending slowly, she felt for each step with her foot. The stairs took a ninety-degree turn, which explained why no one had noticed the light when she slid through the door.

She heard voices below her, and she froze, trying to let her vision adjust to the lack of light. It didn't. She was blind.

So were Victor and Brody.

She crept down another few steps.

She was close enough to hear their words.

"We need to end this." Brody's voice was low and quiet.

A jolt went through her. She wasn't sure if it was fear or anger...or something else. He was the father of her child. She'd thought she loved him for so long, but she'd loved who she thought he was, not who he really was.

He'd shown himself when he used her and her baby as a test for Kolya. When he'd beaten a helpless man. When he'd planned with Victor to murder not just Kolya but possibly thousands of people.

She'd been an idiot.

"I know. I just tried to trigger the explosives, but nothing happened." Forest confirmed what Yael now knew—that he was crazy.

"You were going to kill us—and you didn't say anything?" Brody sounded both angry and scared.

"Our deaths would inspire thousands. You knew what you signed up for."

"I signed up to fight a revolution. Not to become a suicide bomber. I thought we were going to lead American Gold Posse into a new era."

"We will, alive or dead. But I also prefer that we survive to lead the revolution."

"So—maybe we should leave. We're shooting in the dark, and so are they. It's a fucking stalemate. There's other bunkers."

"We already announced Petrov's execution. We streamed the buildup to the explosion. We let him go, and we look weak to the hundreds of thousands of people who were watching. We've got the door covered, and we've got more ammunition. All we need to do is wait until they run out of bullets. OR we might get lucky and shoot them. Then we stream blowing up the bridge and Petrov—alive or dead."

Just below where she was on the stairs, flame from gunfire lit the room. Yael retreated to the bend in the stairs.

This was stupid. She needed to leave. She'd left Lyra alone, and she shouldn't leave her for more than a few minutes. *Get her and run.*

But that would mean leaving Alex, Ruth, and Kolya to die.

Could she sneak close enough to Brody and Victor to shoot them?

She doubted it.

The dark was a disadvantage to both sides but probably helped Brody and Victor more. Because they had the firepower to wait. And she couldn't see where she was going or what she was shooting.

Light would help. Lighting up Brody and Victor—but not the others. From what Yael knew of Kolya, he was good at his job. He could probably shoot Victor if he could see him.

Light would change the odds.

And that gave her an idea.

She carefully retraced her steps up the staircase and squeezed through the door to the electrical room. After a gentle kiss on Lyra's forehead, she pulled her phone from her pocket and downloaded an app that offered a timer. *Two minutes should do it.* She'd need the time to make her way back up the stairs in the dark. Then she picked up a loose brick from the floor and again descended, a little quicker, but still careful how she placed each foot.

She reached the fifth step from the bottom and placed the phone behind the brick so that only the bulb that was the flashlight would be exposed. Then she retreated up to the bend in the stairs. She positioned herself so that the wall would protect her, but she could still shoot around the corner.

She waited for the minutes to tick down.

Chapter Sixty-Nine

Kolya thought that it was a wound in Alex's upper arm. Not the shoulder. Not the torso. If so, she would survive intact—if Forest didn't kill them—if she could get medical help—if she didn't bleed out. A lot of ifs. He ripped off part of his shirt and pressed it against the wound.

She'd wanted to break up to protect him, and she was the one bleeding.

This was his fault. She was right—they shouldn't be together.

Not now.

"I can hold this. You need to keep them off." She pushed his arm away.

As long as he could. He ejected the magazine of his gun and checked by feel how many rounds were left. Only five, including the one in the chamber.

Then Forest and Brody both fired their weapons. He fired twice, once in the direction of each muzzle flash.

Three rounds left.

Alex pressed her gun into his hand.

"How many are left?" he whispered.

"No idea."

He checked Alex's gun. Two rounds.

"*Yob tvoyu mat.*" He assumed that Ruth's gun also was low if not out. If they ran out of ammunition, they would die. Or he could hold his fire and wait for Brody and Forest to approach—and then shoot. That would give him a better chance of killing them.

And it would give Forest and Victor a better chance as well.

Illustrating the problem, both men opened fire again. Kolya fired Alex's gun twice, aiming where he'd seen the muzzle fire.

Alex's gun was now empty. He again picked up one of the guns that he'd taken from his guards. It still had three rounds.

"Petrov." Forest's voice sounded across the expanse of the room. "I thought you loved your fiancée. You were devastated when you thought she was dead. And you're willing to sacrifice her? You're kind of a jerk, aren't you?"

He'd had that thought.

It didn't change anything.

But the odds suddenly changed. A light clicked on, behind Forest and Brody, illuminating their side of the room but not reaching Kolya, Alex, or Ruth. He could see from the shadows that the men were crouched behind the crate of peaches that Ruth had pushed across the room.

Who had provided the light? It couldn't be Jonathan. The team would come in with assault rifles and flash bangs. Who was this?

Alex supplied the answer. "It has to be Yael. She's how we found you."

"Yael?" He remembered her initial hostility towards him. He also remembered her terror when she thought that he was going to kill her child, and her giving him water after Brody had beaten him. Maybe it wasn't crazy that she'd changed sides. "And the baby?"

"We'd left them both in the car. I don't know."

If Yael was here, trying to help them, the baby was close by. Two more lives at risk. He needed to take out the danger.

The light helped, but the crate that Ruth had shoved against the stairs offered his opponents some protection.

If he had enough ammunition or a more powerful weapon, Kolya would fire until the crate disintegrated. A wooden crate didn't offer much protection. But he didn't have that kind of firepower. He had to incapacitate or kill both men. It would be hard enough to do so with only three rounds if he could see them. Impossible if he couldn't.

A shot rang out from the top of the stairs.

It missed both men, hitting the crate and shattering jars inside. Another two shots followed.

Yael? Most likely.

Kolya raised himself on his elbows, holding the gun in both hands, and waited.

"Fuck!" Forest must have swung around to fire up the stairs, although Kolya couldn't see him. Yael had retreated up the stairs, and Forest's return fire missed its target. "Brody. You're at the better angle. Shoot."

In his rage, Forest raised above the crate, exposing his head.

Brody didn't shoot. But Kolya did, missing when Forest ducked down again. He mentally cursed the injured eye. Shooting with only his nondominant eye working had thrown off his aim. Not a lot. Just enough.

Two rounds left.

If he could get maybe ten or fifteen feet closer, he'd still be out of the range of the small flashlight, but it would be an easier shot.

"Stay down," he whispered to Alex. "I'm going to get closer."

She reached over to grasp his arm, and then she let go. "Be careful."

He inched forward on his stomach, using his arms and his good leg to propel himself. He moved slowly, not wanting any sound to alert Forest. He hoped Forest's attention would remain focused on Yael and the light beaming out.

"Goddamn it." Forest fired towards the stairs. He remained concealed behind the crate. "Brody! Shoot the light. Then shoot whoever is up there."

Both men shot. The bullets ricocheted off the concrete stairs towards them. The light wasn't hit.

Kolya crawled closer.

"FUCK!" Forest was screaming. "You need to take out the flashlight and then get the shooter on the stairs."

"If you come up the stairs, Brody, I'll shoot," Yael called.

"Yael?" Brody's voice held both surprise and something else. Anger? Hurt? Kolya didn't know, and he didn't care. "You'd kill me? I'm your husband. Lyra's father."

"I don't want to, but I will. Don't come up and I won't."

"You want Petrov to kill me? And what're you going to tell our daughter about what you did?"

"I'll tell her that you planned to murder a lot of people, and I did what I needed to. Or you could walk away."

"You're blocking the way out."

"I guess I am. You drop the gun, and I'll let you pass."

Forest tried. "Yael, you know why we're fighting. Why this has to happen. You're a warrior for the truth."

"And you're batshit crazy, Victor. Took me too long to realize."

Forest fired at her.

"Don't, Victor," Brody said. "Even if she's betraying the cause, she's my wife. And she could have my baby with her."

"I don't care about your fucking baby or your fucking wife. She's a traitor, and she's on their side. We're in a fight here for our revolution."

"Fuck you, Victor. I'm fighting this war for my family, and you want me to kill them? Fuck you."

"We're in the middle of a gunfight for the new world, and you're turning traitor?"

There was a moment's pause. Then Brody responded, his voice quieter. "Petrov hasn't shot at us the last few minutes. If he's out of ammo, it's over. We go over, finish the job, hook up the explosives, and get out of here. No need to kill Yael. I'll discipline my wife after this."

"She's on the stairs with a gun, shooting at us. She's sided with the aliens, and she poses a threat. This is not negotiable. Are you a soldier or not? And if Petrov is out of ammunition, we'll deal with him after we deal with her."

"And if he isn't, he'll shoot me if I go up the stairs."

"I'll cover you."

Brody shouted. "Yael. Where's Lyra?"

"Fuck you, Brody." Yael shot again.

"Go up the stairs and shoot her." Forest's voice was harsher. "She needs to be killed."

"No."

"I've given you an order."

"And I fucking said no. Didn't you hear me?"

"Yeah, I fucking heard you." Forest shot him. He turned to fire up the stairs at Yael, and then he darted toward the stairs, lit by the flashlight.

Kolya rose on his elbows, grasping the gun with both hands. *Two rounds left.* He took a breath, held it, aimed, and pulled the trigger. Twice. He couldn't afford to miss.

And he didn't.

Chapter Seventy

Kolya couldn't remember just how he'd gotten back to Alex—whether he'd crawled or whether Ruth had helped him limp across the room, but he remembered being on the floor, cradling Alex in his arms. The area lit by Ruth's cell phone allowed him to see that Alex was still bleeding from her upper arm. Not a serious wound if she got to a hospital, but her eyes were closed.

Then again, even with a minor wound, bleeding out was possible.

He pressed a hand on her upper arm.

"I already called for an ambulance." Ruth hovered nearby. "Actually, I said we needed more than one."

Yael and her baby, both unhurt, appeared at the edge of his vision. Yael appeared to be crying.

"Not necessary for me." His body was shaking, his right eye was throbbing, and pain wracked him every time he took a breath, but it didn't matter. Only Alex mattered.

"Don't do the macho thing. Nobody likes it. Especially not her." Ruth laid a gentle hand on his shoulder that she probably meant to be comforting but wasn't. "She's going to be okay."

He nodded and then turned his attention back to Alex, not knowing if she could even hear him. "This is my fault. I'm so sorry. You were right. We shouldn't be together."

Alex opened her eyes at his words. She spoke slowly but distinctly. "I was wrong. Sometimes you need me to save you, and sometimes I need you to save me. I knew that, but I'd forgotten. And anyway, I'm not fucking returning my wedding dress."

"If you weren't with me, you wouldn't need to be saved."

"Unless I was walking across the Brooklyn Bridge when it blew up. Which it didn't. Because we stopped it. You. And me."

"And me," Ruth said.

"What about me?" Yael's voice trembled.

"Yes, you too," Ruth said. "But then we were only here because of Alex. And if you dump her, Kolya, I'll hunt you down."

"I'm not dumping her..." Kolya trailed off.

"Damn right you're not." Alex's voice was loud and strong.

"Fine. You win." Kolya didn't have the energy to argue any more. Or the incentive.

"Good. Now shut up. I need to rest." She closed her eyes again and leaned against him.

"Me too." Still holding her, he stretched out on the concrete and closed his eyes.

Their rest was brief. A few minutes later, the room was flooded with lights and people. Jonathan, the team, EMTs, and a host of police had come to the rescue.

Chapter Seventy-One

The bunkers were secured, the explosives and VX to be decommissioned, and almost three hundred members of American Gold Posse were taken into custody and charged within twenty-four hours. Jonathan and the team took the lead in Brooklyn but brought in additional personnel from other federal agencies to round up the conspirators around the country.

Two days later, Jonathan reported all of this to Kolya, who was lying on a leather couch, leg propped up on pillows, in the living room of the Georgetown townhouse he shared with Alex. A jazz tune that Jonathan recognized as Ellington's "Satin Doll" played on a speaker connected to Kolya's phone. Jonathan was not a jazz fan, but still, this wasn't bad.

A set of crutches leaned against the coffee table within Kolya's reach, but he did look better than Jonathan had expected. "The eye patch is a nice touch. Makes you look sinister. You managing okay?"

"It's a little awkward, between the crutches and only having one working eye. Especially when cooking."

Jonathan knew what the response would be, but he mentioned it anyway. "You could let Alex cook."

"No thanks. I like food that isn't burned. Apart from the fact that she's away for the next two days. The eyepatch and crutches are temporary, anyway. Should be able to get rid of both within the week."

"Just in time for your bachelor party."

"No fucking way are you getting me to a bachelor party." Kolya added a few phrases in Russian and then switched back to English. "Remember I can shoot perfectly well even with one eye."

"Fine. Whatever. After all the work I've put into finding ways to humiliate you."

"I'm sure you'll think of something for the wedding that will be embarrassing."

"Do my best. Anything I can do for you in the meantime?"

"Did you get Alex what she needed?"

"Of course."

* * *

The courtroom was empty of spectators, except for Yael's parents, who sat near the back of the room, after a tearful reunion with their daughter. The same judge who'd held the initial hearing in the CPS case against Yael presided, but her demeanor was definitely warmer than the last time Alex had appeared before her.

It was four days after the events at the Brooklyn Bridge. Alex, her right arm in a sling, would have preferred to be at home, resting in bed next to Kolya. Still, the question of custody for Lyra had to be resolved, and the judge had granted an emergency hearing. This was Alex's case. She was damn well going to finish it, hurting or not.

Yael, holding her baby, sat next to Alex, having learned her lesson about keeping quiet unless addressed by the judge.

It was a lesson that Barbara O'Brien should also have learned. But Barbara O'Brien stood up at the counsel table, despite the very young CPS attorney's attempt to restrain her, and jabbed an angry finger at Yael and Alex.

"That woman is a criminal who should be in prison for murder. Along with her attorney and everyone else in their criminal gang," Barbara shouted.

Alex felt a guilty pleasure at watching Barbara make a fool of herself.

The judge's reaction came quickly. "Sit down. One more outburst and you'll be removed from the court and charged with contempt."

Barbara sat.

The attorney for CPS stood nervously. "I apologize, Your Honor. Ms. O'Brien is rightfully upset that the foster mother of this baby was murdered. There is credible evidence that the respondent was involved in the murder. And then the respondent and Ms. Feinstein unlawfully restrained Ms. O'Brien when she tried to confront them about it."

Alex leaned back and consulted with Ruth, seated directly behind her, and then rose in her turn. "My paralegal just confirmed that counsel received the sworn statements yesterday from the New York City police and the federal officials that I've also provided to the court." She then returned to her seat. Opposing counsel did not.

The judge looked over her glasses at the CPS attorney. "That is correct, isn't it, counsel? You received the documents?"

He looked down and shuffled a pile of papers. "I do have them, Your Honor." He looked even younger and less experienced than the last time they'd been in court.

"Then sit down." The judge cleared her throat. "According

to these statements, the respondent was not only the victim of her abusive husband but risked her life to stop him and his terrorist gang from blowing up the Brooklyn Bridge. Do you contest these facts, counsel?"

The attorney rose. "No. But the actions against Ms. O'Brien..."

"I'm not finished. Sit down."

He sat.

Alex felt a touch on her elbow. Yael leaned in and whispered, "Brody wasn't always abusive. He did care about us, in his way. Which he showed at the end."

Alex reached over to grasp Yael's hand. "I know," she whispered back. "Now hush."

Love was complicated, wasn't it?

Alex turned her attention back to the judge, who'd taken no notice of the whispered exchange.

The judge looked down at the papers in front of her. "Furthermore, Ms. O'Brien has admitted that she aimed a loaded gun at a four-month-old baby. Her actions could not only have resulted in harm to the child, but Ms. O'Brien could have prevented Ms. Miller and Ms. Feinstein from stopping the planned explosion."

The attorney rose again. "Ms. O'Brien only had the gun because..."

The judge pointed at him. "If you interrupt me again, I'm citing you for contempt."

The attorney plopped into his seat with a defeated expression.

The judge continued. "Ms. O'Brien recklessly endangered the life of a child by threatening to shoot her mother while holding the baby. By doing so, she also committed an assault on Ms. Miller and Ms. Feinstein. This is not a criminal court, but I have passed on the information to the appropriate authorities with the recommendation that charges be brought. Further, counsel, I am astonished that your office did not move the court to dismiss this case as soon as you received the documents that are now in front of me. Since you didn't see fit to do the right thing, I will do so now. Case dismissed. The custody of the minor child, Lyra McMillan, is returned to her mother." Then the judge beamed at Yael.

Yael turned to Alex and embraced her. Ruth hugged both of them.

Chapter Seventy-Two

The roses were in full bloom in shades of pink, white, yellow, and red, intermingled in beds that surrounded the two hundred chairs set on the lawn. Earlier, dark clouds had threatened rain, but by four-thirty, the clouds parted, and sunlight illuminated the scene, which was a relief to Kolya. He liked the outdoor setting.

Kolya was not religious. He was generally averse to formal ceremonies, to crowds, and to public displays, but he made an exception for his own wedding.

It was important to Alex, which made it important to him.

Unlike orthodox Jewish weddings, reform Jewish weddings do not segregate guests by gender. Nor were guests separated by their relationship to the bride or groom, since one side would have been crammed with Alex's great aunts, great uncles, aunts, uncles, first cousins, second cousins, cousins once removed, along with dozens of friends and work associates, all together totaling one hundred seventy-five guests, while the other side would have been comparatively empty, with maybe fifteen guests, mostly but not exclusively, work colleagues.

Not that the imbalance bothered Kolya. It was being the focal point of attention that he found uncomfortable. He liked being in the shadows, going unnoticed, both by nature and by necessity for his profession. But as the groom, he could hardly fade into the background—and the still-visible bruises on his face and around his eye made him feel more conspicuous.

At least he could open the injured eye, and he hadn't lost any vision.

Jonathan, standing next to Kolya under the chuppah, a silk sheet decorated with flowers and held up by four poles, offered reassurance. "Relax. No one will even notice the bruises. Or you for that matter. You're not the star attraction here."

"I know. I'm waiting for the star." He watched the door from the mansion that opened into the garden, as did all the guests.

"As are we all," Jonathan said.

And then she appeared.

The band played a jazz rendition of "Love is Here to Stay." Alex smiled at him as she walked down the aisle, flanked by her parents. The dress was everything she'd promised it would be, a strapless silk gown that tightly embraced her upper body, and then flowed out from the waist, showing off her figure. Her long dark hair curled down her back, and instead of a veil, she wore a crown of pearls and small white flowers. She had a small white bandage wrapped around her upper arm, but with decorative lace on top so that it appeared to be a fashion statement.

To Kolya, she had never looked more beautiful.

In a reform variation of the Ashkenazi orthodox wedding tradition, Alex circled him four times, and he limped around her three times. The rabbi waxed poetic on love and the strength of their relationship. They drank wine together, and Kolya pronounced unfamiliar Hebrew words that made the marriage official in Judaism.

As he slid the gold band onto her finger, next to the sapphire engagement ring, he spoke one word. "Always."

"And forever." She slid the matching gold band onto his finger.

Kolya kissed her as the rabbi pronounced them husband and wife.

Then finally two wine glasses wrapped in white cloth were placed on the ground. Kolya and Alex stomped on the glasses in unison—and cries of mazel tov broke out.

They were married.

The dinner, salmon in a cream sauce, was reasonably good for wedding food. Dessert was a table of assorted sweets: brownies, macaroons, cupcakes, cookies, without the wedding cake and its sometimes dubious traditions. Jonathan, as best man, gave a speech that praised Alex, made fun of Kolya, and lied about how Kolya's bruises came from his job at the IRS.

"Dangerous job, the IRS," Jonathan said. "Irate taxpayers can be damn scary."

Alex's family laughed at the jokes. Those in the know also laughed at Jonathan's description of the dangers of the IRS.

The music alternated between jazz and klezmer. Kolya and Alex managed a slow first dance together as a married couple, despite the brace on his leg, and the ribs that still ached, to an Etta James tune, "At Last."

"This isn't so bad, is it?" she asked him.

"It is, but it's worth it to see you in that dress." Then, as she rested her head on his chest while they swayed to the music, he amended his statement. "Actually, not bad at all."

In fact, it was almost perfect.

After their dance, they circled the room to greet friends and family. Alex's brother Aaron managed to wish them mazel tov without any sarcastic undertones. Alex's Aunt Shelly, eighty-seven years old and still going strong, who knew Kolya's real profession, gave him a wink and a kiss.

At the table with Kolya's work colleagues, Elizabeth, wearing diamond earrings that flashed in the light, offered the observation, "Nice wedding even if marriage sucks."

"Stop being a jerk." Tehila smacked Elizabeth's arm and then spoke words in Hebrew that were probably a blessing, although Kolya wasn't sure. Frick simply saluted with a glass of Scotch.

Teo, in a wheelchair, raised a glass of wine. "Great wedding. *L'chaim.*"

Teo's injuries had been severe, but he was young, and the doctors thought he'd make a full recovery. He'd be back in the office on limited duty before Kolya and Alex returned from their honeymoon.

Teo blushed when Alex kissed him on the cheek.

Yael and her baby, at a table with three lawyers from Alex's law firm, and Ruth, who had moved to DC to join that firm, rose to embrace them both. "I'm staying with my parents for now. Come see me when you're back in town." Yael looked teary. Kolya felt for her. Given what had happened with Yael's marriage, celebrating a wedding must be difficult. But she'd wanted to come.

Ruth gave a smile and a thumbs-up.

Also at the table was a blonde woman with striking green eyes, whom Kolya stopped to greet. "Glad you could make it, Lisette—sorry, it's Lizzie now, isn't it? Everything good in Texas?"

"It is. And thanks for the help with that...matter last month."

"What help?" he asked, innocently. At Lizzie's request, Kolya had manipulated some data to allow two orphaned children to be adopted by the woman who'd been their housekeeper. Not completely kosher, but not something anyone would check. He caught Alex's glance. He'd explain later.

Murphy, a tall, attractive woman, whom Lizzie introduced as her friend and partner-to-be, offered congratulations before turning to Lizzie. "Okay, honey. I do get it. But time to move on."

Lisette—no Lizzie—had helped Kolya stop an attempted coup in Germany by a neo-Nazi gang. There had been a spark of attraction between them, and had Kolya not been in love with Alex, he might have explored possibilities with Lizzie. But he was, so he didn't, letting Lizzie know that he was unavailable.

He hoped she'd take Murphy's advice. Lizzie deserved to be happy.

By the time they finished their circle of the room, Kolya's leg was protesting. He sat on a chair on the edge of the dance floor. Alex sat next to him, and he took her hand. "Can we go home now?"

They'd spend the night at their townhouse in Georgetown and then take a morning flight to Paris for the honeymoon.

"Not just yet." Alex glanced towards the band and waved. The band broke into "Hava Nagila," and the entire room spilled onto the dance floor. "And, yes, I know I said we wouldn't do this. But that was before I got shot saving you. Now you owe me."

"Oh fuck." Kolya knew what was coming. This was one Jewish wedding tradition that he'd hoped to avoid. But it was a mild protest. She was right. He owed her.

Friends and family surrounded Alex and Kolya, lifting their chairs into the air as a circle formed around them.

Alex held on to one end of a white scarf and tossed him the other end. He grabbed it. The chairs tipped precariously. Alex and Kolya remained connected by the white scarf as the two of them were swirled in the air by friends and family holding the chairs aloft. The dancers circled the elevated chairs, stomped, and wove in the traditional steps of the hora.

Alex's face glowed, and she laughed in pure joy. Forgetting his dignity, Kolya laughed with her.

"Don't let go," she called to him over the blaring of the strings and horns.

"Never."

Epilogue

Kolya, on his laptop, didn't look up when Jonathan strolled into his office and seated himself in the extra chair. President Rhodes' chief of staff had sent a memo out demanding that all government employees submit an email describing what they had done to advance the interests of the United States in the past year. Don Harding, the new head of the ECA, ordered agents to comply but not to disclose anything that was classified. Kolya had had his issues with Margaret Bradford, the former head of the ECA, but those seemed trivial now. Bradford had always put the country first, even if it had cost Kolya personally. Putting the country first was not something Kolya assumed about the new director.

Or the new president.

Kolya returned to typing.

"I just wrote classified. Several times." Jonathan stretched back in his chair. "What're you doing?"

"Same." Kolya finished and hit send. "I was tempted to add some colorful language and list some of the far-right nutcases I'd eliminated in the past year, but I restrained myself."

"Probably a good idea. Unless you're planning on accepting the buyout."

"No. Don't need the money. I have a rich wife. Anyway, I took this job to protect the country, which seems to need protection more than ever. You?"

"Not planning on it either. I had a rich grandfather. They want to get rid of me, they'll have to fire me."

"Which they probably will," Kolya said. "Both of us. And the rest of our team as well. Given that all of us worked on taking down American Gold Posse, and charges against the members have been downgraded or dismissed."

"President Rhodes blames anything illegal on Victor Forest, who is conveniently dead. He views the other members as patriots, misled by a charismatic leader."

"Clearly. And he thinks they'll support him. He'll probably offer them jobs in fucking Homeland Security."

"All true. Still." Jonathan leaned forward with a serious expression. "You need to be careful, Kolya."

Kolya shrugged. "Don't we all?"

"You more than most. You're a naturalized citizen. You could be targeted if you piss off the wrong person."

Kolya already knew. But he'd sworn an oath to protect his country and its Constitution from all enemies, domestic or foreign, and he intended to keep doing just that. But he also knew better than to say that out loud inside the office. Anyone could be listening.

"I'm always careful."

Jonathan rolled his eyes. "And yet you always wind up injured."

"There's risks to the job. I'm careful about how I take those risks, but sometimes it's not enough."

Jonathan grinned. "That's one way to put it. Hey, changing the subject—the gang's meeting up for lunch. Frick, Elizabeth,

Teo, Tehila, and Marty. Usual place." Jonathan's tone had changed, but he affected a nonchalance. He stretched and then stood. "You interested?"

Kolya understood. The meeting was for more than lunch. Going to it would be the opposite of being careful. Ironic that Jonathan invited him right after issuing a warning of the personal danger to Kolya from pissing off the new administration.

Then again, maybe it wasn't ironic.

"I'm interested." Kolya grabbed his jacket and followed.

Acknowledgments

Thanks to my critique group, Cari Davis, Steven Laine, Keenan Powell, Efrem Seegar, Susan Wolfe, and Debbie Burke, who read various chapters of Imminent Risk as it was being written and provided invaluable feedback. A special thanks to Steven Laine and Debbie Burke who took the time to read and comment on the entire novel.

Thanks to my husband, the award-winning author, J.B. Manning, for his patience, his sage advice, and his meticulous editing. Without his support and encouragement, I would not be the writer that I am today.

About the Author

S. Lee Manning is a writer living in Vermont. Her Kolya Petrov thrillers - *Trojan Horse, Nerve Attack, and Bloody Soil* - have been finalists for Silver Falchions, and *Bloody Soil* won best genre novel of 2023 from Independent Publishers of New England. *Deadly Choice*, a stand alone domestic thriller was an Eric Hoffer finalist and a Top Pick from Killer Nashville. Before turning to writing full time, she was an attorney whose legal career spanned from the firm of Cravath, Swaine & Moore to the New Jersey Division of Law to solo practice. Manning lives with her writer husband, J.B. Manning, and their two cats, Xiao and Dmitri.

For updates, check out her website: https://www.sleeman ning.com/

Also by S. Lee Manning

TROJAN HORSE

NERVE ATTACK

BLOODY SOIL

DEADLY CHOICE

www.ingramcontent.com/pod-product-compliance
Lightning Source LLC
Chambersburg PA
CBHW030915300726
48970CB00001B/164